a brand new ending

a novel by S.A. ROLLS

First Print Edition

Published by S.A. Rolls

Copyright © 2013 S.A. Rolls
Cover Art Copyright © 2013 L.J. Anderson
Cover & Print Formatting by Mayhem Cover Creations

ISBN: 978-1482052244

For Jenice,
Without your enthusiasm, this story might still be unfinished.
You are the wind beneath my wings.

a brand new ending

A NOVEL BY
S.A. ROLLS

ACKNOWLEDGMENTS

I would like to thank:

All the people who have supported me in this journey. Without it, this story would not have been written. You know who you are.

Alex, who has been an incredible confidant since I wrote the very first sentence. I can't thank you enough.

Dan, who took the time to meticulously go through every single word and make this story readable.

Natalie, who volunteered to be my awesome tester. Your words and thoughts mean a lot to me.

Kate, who at the beginning of this adventure let me pick apart her brain and momentarily live the insane life of a psychiatric hospital aide.

And the biggest thank you goes to my readers. You all took a chance on me and my novel. I will be forever grateful.

"Though no one can go back and make a brand new start, anyone can start from now and make a brand new ending."

—Carl Sandburg

Phoenix

I dig my fingernails into the cold, steel beam, my eyes watching the masses of people and cars rushing behind me. It's Tuesday night. Just another ordinary day. Everybody busy worrying about what they are going to make for dinner, or if they'll make it to their daughter's dance recital on time. But for me, it's another day of pain. Another day filled with crippling fear.

I bet none of them have even noticed me standing here, my hood pulled tightly over my head as I stare down at the frigid, dark abyss that lies beneath me. The cold wind whips through the steel cables, the ominous sound making my heart race even faster. It's almost as though the devil is laughing at me, waiting for me to do the deed. In my hands I clench tightly to a piece of folded paper. It contains my goodbyes. Not to anyone in particular, but to the world.

I jump at the sound of a ringtone and, startled, it

made me loosen my grip on the paper. I watched it float down to the sidewalk at a pace that made it impossible for me to grab in time. Pulling out my phone from my jacket pocket, I realize it's not my phone that is ringing. *Who would even be calling me? I have no one.* I go to put it back in my pocket, but instead hold it out in front of me. I stick my hand out over the railing as far as it will go, clenching it tight. My knuckles turn white. Then I release it.

The phone falls so fast my eyes can barely stay focused on the outline of the metal. Within seconds, I make out a small, white ripple in the water, the phone swallowed up by the blackness below. Instantly, a feeling of nausea overtakes my stomach. *I have to do this. I have nothing to live for. It's not like anyone will care...or notice.*

Pulling up the sleeve of my jacket, I run my fingers along the bruises and scars that adorn my arms. I think back to all the times I've shown Elaina, only to hear her blame them on my clumsiness. She knew the truth. I could feel it. The look in her eyes always told me she did.

It was always too convenient that she worked late nights. I tried to never be home when he was, but somehow he would always make it into the house without a sound. Escaping was impossible. As much as I wanted to leave them both, I couldn't. I had nowhere else to go and no money or resources to start a new life. There is no other option but one. I want the pain to stop. I want the fear to end.

Shifting my eyes around again, I notice there is a break in the crowd, no one on the bridge's walkway in sight. I slip my feet between the slits in the railing, lifting my body off the ground a few inches. The wind blows harder at this height. My hood flies off and my hair starts whipping in the wind so fast that it stings my face.

Swinging my right leg over the railing, I straddle it, my hands visibly shaking as I clutch onto it. After a few seconds, I notice there are people approaching not far off, as I quickly pulled my other leg over the railing. If I was going to do this, it would have to be now. My body is now facing out over the ocean again, my hands holding onto the railing behind me. Staring out before me, I take in the slowly-dropping sun. The lower half of the sky now a vibrant orange. My mind and body are eerily peaceful, ready to leave this painful life behind. I look up at the sky again, with tears fogging my eyesight.

"I'm sorry, dad," I whisper through a choked throat, before unlatching both my hands from the railing.

Braeden

Pulling myself away from the shower wall I finish rinsing the soap out of my hair and shut the warm water off. Stepping out, I realize how freezing my apartment is, already missing the warm spray of the shower against my body. Grabbing my towel off the hanger, I run it through my hair before wrapping it tightly around my waist. I look at myself in the mirror, stroking my chin, feeling the scruffiness. *It's going to have to wait.*

Putting on my glasses, I can clearly see how worn-down I look, a result of too much overtime. I pick up my phone off the counter, hitting the home screen to check the time. It's just after five thirty.

I yawn loudly, my body wanting nothing more than to head back to bed. It's Tuesday night, my seventh straight day of working the night shift. I'm exhausted, to say the least. I quickly put on deodorant and a few sprays of cologne before turning off the light and heading to my bedroom. I open up my closet, pulling out my uniform. Pale green scrubs.

Pulling them on, I run my fingers through my hair, trying - yet failing - to tame the longer locks on top. Grabbing my messenger bag from the floor, I swing it around my chest and head out to the living room. I go over to the fridge and pull it open to grab a bottle of water and an apple, tossing both into my bag. I picked up the milk carton and noticed that it's incredibly light. It was full this morning.

Moments later I hear the front door swing open. Peeking around the fridge door, I stare at the figure coming through the entry.

"Hey," I say, turning my attention back to the nonexistent food in the fridge.

"What's up?" he says, dropping his belongings in the middle of the walk way.

I shut the fridge.

"Can you not leave your shit in the middle of the hallway? Other people do live here besides you," I explain slightly irritated.

"Whatever, man," he says, plopping down on the couch.

I toss the carton into the sink.

"By the way, I need your half of the rent. It was due

five days ago," I mutter.

He says nothing in return, his attention preoccupied with something on his phone, the light from it illuminating his face. A sly grin is plastered on his face.

"Bret!" I yell.

"Jesus Christ, man, when did you turn into my fucking mother?" he says back.

I stare at him in silence, now thoroughly pissed off.

"Rent, got it," he says, his attention back on the phone.

"I'll be back in the morning," I say as I pull open the front door, not waiting to hear a response.

When I reach the outside of my apartment building, the cold air instantly hits me, making me realize that I forgotten to grab my coat. Most days are cold in San Francisco, but winters are the worst. Tonight is especially chilly and the heavy fog was starting to roll in. My walk to work is long, but having a car in the city doesn't work out so well and you'd have to sell one of your kidneys to pay for a parking spot. Some days I ride my bike, but I don't feel like fighting with the idiotic drivers in this city today.

After walking a few blocks, I come upon my favorite coffee shop and step inside. Pulling my bag off, I set it in the chair I always sit in. *My routine.* I walk up to the counter, all the girls smiling and giggling.

"Evening, Braeden," the tall blonde at the cash register says, her chest pointed out.

I can't seem to hold back my smirk.

"Evening, Lacey," I say, pulling out my wallet.

"Large coffee?" the brunette barista asks over the coffee machine.

"Yeah, can you add a shot to it?" I ask.

"Rough night?" Lacey asks.

I look back over at her.

"My night hasn't even begun," I mutter.

I give her some cash, hoping that finishing up this transaction will end this awkward conversation. When she hands me my change, I give her a polite smile before walking back over to the chair. Reaching into my backpack, I pull out a book, opening it to where I bookmarked it last.

After a few minutes of reading, I am pulled out of my concentration when I hear the commotion coming from behind the counter. I glance up from behind the pages, both girls arguing over who is going to bring me my drink.

I shake my head slightly, trying to divert my attention back to my book. To be honest, I have no interest in any of them. Moments later, I feel a presence before me. Looking up again, I see Lacey standing in front of me, my drink held outward.

"Thank you," I say, taking the glass from her.

I take a sip, the hot coffee filtering through my cold body.

"Do you want any crème or sugar?" she asks.

"No thanks, I like it black."

"Ok."

Things fall silent again and I resume reading my book. After a chapter or so, I can see that she is still hanging around, pretending to wipe tables but her eyes are still clearly on me.

"So what book are you reading?" she asks, now looking over my shoulder.

I put my finger into the book to act as a bookmark before showing her the cover.

"Oh, what's it about?" she asks, her voice elevated.

"It's about neuroplasticity," I tell her.

Her face instantly tightens, a confused look appearing. *How the hell am I going to explain this?*

"It's just boring medical stuff," I quickly say, hoping she will leave me alone.

"Oh ok." She smiles.

Her eyes start to shift from me to the counter. I turn around in my chair, seeing now that there is a semi-long line of people.

"Do you need to go?" I ask, praying she will say yes.

"I guess," she sighs. "It was nice talking to you, Braeden."

"You too," I say, giving her a quick nod.

She walks back behind the counter and I breathe a sigh relief. Finally getting back into my book, I sip my coffee, which is now lukewarm from the stellar conversation I just had. Pulling out my phone I check the time. Six Forty.

I bring the glass up to my lips, drinking the rest of my coffee in one gulp. Putting the book back in my bag, I stand up and throw my bag back across my chest. Walking towards the door quickly, I slip out, hoping to leave unnoticed. The walk to work is just a few blocks from the coffee shop and before I know it, I reach the front steps of the hospital.

Walking around the back, I go in through the employee entrance, immediately entering the staff room. I'm happy to see that it's empty. Getting over to my locker, I unlatch it, throwing my backpack in. I hear the click of the door open behind me. Shutting my locker, I turn around to see Donovan walking over to me, rubbing his arm.

"Rough night?" I ask, already knowing the answer. I can see it in his face.

"She bit me," he responds, a light laughter accompanying his tone.

"Did she break the skin?"

"Yeah, but luckily I'm not a pussy like you."

I roll my eyes. "Sorry I don't spend my entire time at the gym," I retort. "Was it Celia?"

"Yeah, she is strong for such a small woman," he says, rubbing it some more.

He walks over to his locker which happens to be next to mine.

"Hey, you know you're wearing your glasses right?"

I turn around to look at myself in the sink mirrors.

"Shit," I utter. "I forgot to put my contacts in."

"You should probably take them off," he suggests.

"Yeah, that will make my night a whole hell of a lot better," I say rolling my eyes. Being blind won't help my workday.

Shrugging, I look at the clock on the wall.

"All right, my shift started, I'll catch you later."

"Sounds good. Hey, bar tomorrow night. You're off, right?"

"Yup, see ya then," I say as I enter the main hallway.

Working at a psychiatric hospital definitely has its moments. I work in the North hall, which is exclusively for younger patients but the hospital has been full for so long that it has turned into a mixture of all ages. The hospital is quiet at the moment, something that is very rare. Night times are always rough for patients and their conditions.

Passing by the nurses' desk, I say hello. The rest of my night I am in auto mode. When I reach my station, I pull out the charts and read the reports from the day. I make my way to each room, checking on who is asleep and who is not. *Another routine.* Before I know it, it's eleven o'clock and time for my lunch break. Walking back to the staff room, I pull open my locker and grab the apple and water out of my bag. I also decide to get my book, hoping to get some more reading done since I didn't get very far at the coffee shop.

Setting myself down in the chair, I put the book in my lap, opening it up to where I last left off, while taking a bite of my apple. A few minutes in, I hear the click of the door and I curse under my breath. I continue to stare down at my book, trying everything in my power to not see her. I can feel her presence in front of me, her shoes in my line of sight. Shutting my book a little more abruptly than I should have, I look up, seeing her standing in front of me.

"Hi, Braeden," she says, trying to give me her most seductive voice.

"Hello, Lucy," I respond.

She sits down in the chair next to me, her upper body leaning in towards me.

"Something I can help you with?" I ask, getting annoyed.

"Actually there is," she says, winking.

"No," I respond.

She huffs.

"Come on, Braeden," she pleads. "It's not like it would be the first time."

I sigh.

"You know that was a one-time thing, Lucy," I explain. "And this is a place of business."

She crosses her arms, pouting like a small child. Not wanting to deal with this at the moment, I get up, needing to get away from her. Lucy and I did sleep together once, but it was quite some time ago and let's say I wasn't in the right state of mind when I made that decision. I regret it every time I see her and, much to my dismay, she constantly reminds me of it. Heading into the linen closet, I check to make sure everything is stocked. When I go to make my rounds on the patients again, I notice that one of my favorite patients is awake.

"Hey, Liam," I say.

"Braeden," he says smiling.

"What are you doing awake? It's two in the morning."

"Couldn't sleep..." he states.

"Voices?" I ask.

"Yeah..." he says, a nervous look on his face.

I look at him, my heart in agony. Liam was admitted to the hospital after a nervous breakdown that led him to claim someone or something was trying to kill him. His parents never come to visit and no other family members seemed willing to care for him. He could get violent at times, identifying some of the other aides or doctors as demons that are here to hurt him, but for some reason he was always good for me.

"I'll be right back," I say, leaving his bedroom.

Making my way to the kitchen, I grab a small carton of milk and a chocolate chip cookie. Walking back quickly, the sounds of shouting and screaming reach my ears. Pushing the door open, the other patient who rooms with Liam has him pinned to his bed, both of them screaming in each other's faces.

"I need backup!" I shout out into the hallway.

Setting the cookie and milk on top of the counter, I rush over and get my arms around the patient on top. He's strong - easily three times the size of Liam. As soon as I touch him, he turns around and tries to punch me in the face. I duck at his every swing and we finally get them apart. Liam is breathing heavily, tears running down his face, his pajama top ripped. Sometimes I forget that he is still a child. The other patient continues to scream at the top of his lungs, another aide has a firm grasp on him.

"He stole it from me!" the man yells, his finger pointed out at Liam.

"What did he steal from you?" the other aide asks.

"My M16!" he yells. "I need it..."

"Why do you need it?" I ask.

"To kill those motherfucking ragheads!" he continues to screams.

"But you're not in Iraq right now," the other aide explains.

"The hell I'm not! I have direct orders from my sergeant to clear out all suspicious buildings," he shouts, his voice a mixture of pure terror and agony.

He continues to try and squirm out of the aides hold.

"Why don't you take him to the day area, he probably just needs a moment to calm down. If he gets worse, restrain him," I order.

Shifting my attention back to Liam, I walk over,

grabbing the cookie and milk off the table. I hold it out to him. A large smile comes across his face. I know that our cookies are his favorite.

"Thank you, Braeden," he says, taking it lightly after wiping the tears on his pajamas.

Sitting down at the foot of his bed, I watch him eat it. After a few nibbles, he speaks.

"You know I didn't take his gun right?" he asks concerned.

I laugh lightly.

"I know, Liam," I respond.

"So, what's wrong with him?"

I look over at the empty bed. "He was in the military. He suffers from PTSD."

"What's that?" he asks.

"Post Traumatic Stress Disorder," I explain.

He looks at me confused.

"Well, let's just say he hears voices like you too."

"Oh."

Liam finishes up the cookie and milk, wiping the tears from his face.

"Finished?" I ask.

He nods. Holding out my hand, I take the milk carton from him.

"Do you want to try to go back to sleep?"

"Yeah," he says yawning.

I walk over to the bedside, tucking the sheets in around him.

"If he gives you any more trouble, I want you to tell me…OK?"

To be honest, he should be moved but the reality of it was we didn't have to space. He nods again.

"Good night, Braeden," he says softly.

"Good night, Liam," I respond.

Slipping out of the room, I throw away the carton and head into the day area.

"Is he alright?" I ask the other aide.

"Yeah, got him to calm down, but I had to give him an injection," he says.

"Great," I say. "I think the situation has subsided, he can go back to his bed now but we'll monitor them closely."

When I walk back past the nurse's station again, one of them stops me.

"Are all of your beds full?" she asks me.

I stop to think for a minute, knowing that the hospital has been at max occupancy for quite some time.

"I might I have one spot open, in Rain's room. Is it a female?"

"Yes," she says, looking at a piece of paper. "She'll be coming in soon from the general hospital. Suicide attempt."

I become instantly nauseous, memories flooding my mind.

"How?" I ask, while swallowing the lump in my

throat.

"Jumper, from the Golden Gate."

My eyes widen. We've never had a jumper before. *How did she even survive?*

"How old is she?" I ask.

"Nineteen," she says, continuing to read from her paper.

"Your father was her attending physician in the emergency room."

A strange chill runs down the length of my body, the sensation scaring me a little. The nurse notices.

"Are you all right?" she asks me.

I nod, saying nothing.

"Well, she should be here around four," she says.

"Ok," I say, heading to get the bedroom ready.

Phoenix

I feel nothing. The pain is gone from my body. My anger with the world and those that caused me that pain is no longer there. Nothing but peace. And then, instantly, the most excruciating pain I have ever felt in my life. Needles. Thousands of them hitting all over my body, my heavy, wet jacket pulling me further underneath the cold blackness.

Every time I gasp, my lungs fill with water instead of air they so painfully need. That's when the panic sinks in. I try to cry, my body not able to ignore the pain. I thrash around, trying everything I can to reach the surface but it feels miles away. I don't know how long it has been since I jumped. Each second seems like an eternity. As I struggle to keep myself upright, I start to feel something swirl around my feet. *I didn't die from the fall but now I am going to be eaten by sharks.*

I then realize that whatever is swimming in circles around my feet is not harming me, but helping me stay afloat. However, the frigid water is making me become numb, my arms and legs not wanting to move anymore. Soon the darkness overtakes me, my mind numb.

~

Light. Lots of light.

My eyelids are being pried open, the light waving in front of me. I can make out an outline of a figure leaning over me but no sharp details come through. Their mouth is moving, but I can't make out any of the words. After an unknown amount of time I begin to pick up on things. I can hear a constant beep and the sound of a siren and then a faint male voice.

"Can you hear me?" the figure standing above me asks.

I swallow, trying to talk but I can't. Instead, I just nod. Looking down at me, I notice I am strapped to a gurney, with oxygen tubes stuck in my nose. My chest begins to tighten and tears want to fall. *I have failed.*

"Do you know where you are?" he asks me.

I nod again.

"Can you tell me your name?"

I swallow hard.

"Phoenix," I choke out.

"Last name..." he says, as he continues to write down stuff on a piece of paper.

"Harper," I continue.

He doesn't ask any more questions. I try to sit up but I notice that I am tightly bound, and I can feel my clothes no longer on.

"Where am I going?" I ask nervously.

"The hospital," he says dryly.

My heart quickens as my infinite fear of hospitals rises up. I can only imagine how they'll treat suicide victims. *They'll call my family. She'll be there. He'll be there.* As my heart begins to race, the beeping of the monitor increases. I try to get out of the restraints and the guy in the back of the ambulance notices.

"Phoenix, just calm down," he tells me, as he holds onto either side of my shoulders.

I start to cry again but I don't stop thrashing my body around. I hate the fear that he has created inside me and the inevitable pain that always followed. I have no way out. What I thought was my only option has failed miserably. Life now clings to me like a disease.

The EMT rummages in a drawer beside him, pulling out a syringe. My heart races even more as I watch him place it into my IV drip and, within seconds, I am lost in the darkness. The darkness is what I'm beginning to crave more and more.

Braeden

I spend the next hour setting up the room for the new patient, trying to keep the noise down while Rain was sleeping. As I lay out the sheets, I feel a rustle behind me and I quickly turn around. Rain is now standing directly behind me. I jump, clutching my chest.

"You should be asleep," I say, throwing the sheet on the bed.

She just smiles at me. I look around the room, the situation creeping me out a bit.

"Each of us is an angel with only one wing and we can only fly by embracing one another."

I look at her confused, as a long shiver runs down the length of my spine.

"What?" I ask.

I look into her eyes and they seem glazed over, like a dark cloud has eclipsed them. Seconds later, she shakes her head, as if pulling herself out of whatever trance she was in.

"Oh, hello, Braeden," she says, the same smile on her face, but her expression seems confused. "That's funny. I don't remember getting out of bed."

"I, uh, think you were perhaps sleepwalking," I state.

"Oh," she giggles.

She looks down at the bed that I had just prepared, a new gown folded on top. Her smile widens.

"I can't wait to meet Phoenix."

Phoenix

I open my eyes slowly, realizing that I am no longer in the back of the ambulance, but in a hospital room. I also know that I am not alone. Though a small crack in the sheet that divides the room, I can see a mass in the opposite bed.

I shift a little, every bone and muscle in my body screaming with pain. Rubbing up and down my arms, I can feel the IV that is attached to me. I continue along my chest, feeling the heart rate pads that are glued to my body.

Extending my neck backwards, I look at all the machines, the constant buzzing and beeping still apparent. I watch the heart rate line jump up and down and it saddens me. I silently curse at it. As I watch, a familiar sense overwhelms me - Fear.

I start to panic. Reaching down, I feverishly rip all tubes and pads from my body. A long constant beep fills the room. I have to get out of here fast!

Peeking around the curtain divider, I notice that the person in the bed is asleep, their body facing away from me. I also see something of theirs that will come in handy. Tip toeing over to their bedside chair, I pull off the long coat that is hanging behind it. Sliding it on over my hospital gown, I cinch it tight to cover any of the exposed fabric. Looking down, I notice my feet are covered in nothing but socks. *Maybe they won't notice.* I take a few steps away from the chair and head directly to the door. My heart is racing so fast I swear it is going to explode, but I know I can't stay here. He'll find me, like he always does.

Just as I reach the doorway, I just barely notice the door handle moves downward. I freeze. The door pushes open abruptly, whizzing past my face and missing me by mere inches. In front of me stands a tall man in a bright white doctor's coat, a smile a mile wide on his face. He turns around to tell someone something.

"It's OK, Barbara, I don't need your assistance after all."

The man turns his attention back to me. *Maybe he will think I am a visitor.* I divert my eyes away from him and try to take a step around him, but he matches.

"Gonna be a little cold out there without any shoes on," he says, looking down at my feet, his face turning from a smile to a grin. I look up at him again, an intense blue looking back at me.

"I can't let you leave here, Phoenix," he says, a look of compassion on his face.

I now notice how he is towering over me and flashbacks instantly take over my mind. My palms begin to get sweaty and my heart rate flies at an all-time high.

His face.

His hands on me.

His fingertips clutching onto my arm.

His hand hitting my face.

I begin to feel extremely light headed and the doctor notices immediately, the grin from his face falling.

"Phoenix, I need to take you back to your...."

His voice trails off and my vision becomes blurred again. My body feels weak and moments later, I feel myself being lifted into the air then being gently set back down on the bed. And as much as I try, I can't seem to stay awake.

Braeden

The last few hours of my shift drags on, my body fighting to stay awake. Once I finish setting up the new patient's bed, I get Rain to go back to hers. I stand in the hallway, my back against the wall, replaying what she had said over and over in my head. No one knows about the new patient but me and the nurse. I look down. The hairs on my arm are standing upright. Something about this new girl has got me in a trance.

I saunter through the halls again, wishing I was home in my bed. Walking into the laundry room, I transfer the things from the washer to the dryer. With nothing else to do I walk back into the staff room, grabbing my book. Maybe I'll actually have some time to read now. Opening it up, I pick up where I left off, but the minutes pass by slowly. I begin to yawn frequently. After some time, I glance up at the wall. Four thirty in the morning. Two and a half more hours. I see the door being pushed open, Lucy entering.

"New patient is here."

Phoenix

I swear that my life is becoming the same scene over and over. I wake up in a hospital bed again, all the tubes and pads reattached. I still feel pretty drowsy, and I notice that my arms are restrained against the bed. I look to my left, noticing the same doctor next to me. He is writing inside a chart, and notices that I am awake.

"Hello, again," he says with a smile.

I don't respond, my nerves still on edge.

"I didn't get a chance to introduce myself earlier, I am Dr. Harris."

He holds his hand out and I look at him confused. He laughs lightly, almost like he is nervous.

"Sorry," he states. "The arm restraints are just protocol."

He reaches over, letting me loose.

"I can trust you, right?" he asks.

I nod my head as I look up at him shyly. When he reaches over me, I tense up. I don't think I'll ever get use to being in a room alone with a man. When he stands back up I'm able to relax a little. He opens up what I presume is my file and furrows his brow while he reads it. I swallow the growing lump in my throat.

"There is something I want to talk to you about," he starts. "We both know why you are here, Phoenix, and I just want to ask you a few questions."

"OK," I say softly.

"When you came to us, you had a mild case of hypothermia from the cold water, but once we got you out of your wet clothes and some fluids in you, you vastly improved."

My heart beats faster.

"However, when a female nurse examined your body for other injuries, we noticed multiple scars and bruises along your body."

I can feel my throat starting to close, the anxiety growing. I'm pretty sure that he can gauge my reaction because moments later, he pulls up a chair and sits down next to me.

"I want you to know that anything you tell me will stay between us. Doctor-patient confidentiality."

I remain silent. Looking down at my arms, I remember every scar and how I obtained them. I open my mouth, only to close it abruptly. *He probably thinks they are self inflicted.*

I look over at him, wanting to tell him, wanting someone else to know what that asshole has done to me. Just as I go to speak, the door opens slowly. We both turn our heads and what I see shoots a wave of fear through me. Elaina and Carl squeeze through the door, her face lighting up when she sees me. But I can't take my eyes off of him. I shift in my bed, a pool of tears forming in my eyes, my vision blurred because of it.

"Excuse me," Dr. Harris says, standing up from his chair. "Can I help you?"

"No," I hear Carl says harshly.

"We're here to see our daughter," I hear Elaina state. *Our daughter.*

"Oh, well, welcome," Dr. Harris says, holding out his hand.

When Carl reaches out, my stomach wrenches.

"Oh, sweetie," Elaina says as she sits down on the bed, reaches out, and starts playing with my hair. "You gave us quite a fright."

Liar. I know that this is all a show for the doctor, Elaina has never cared about me before, so why would she start now? I look over at Dr. Harris and he is directly staring back at me, a worried expression on his face.

"Listen, man, can we get some privacy?" Carl tells Dr. Harris.

I cringe at his words. I continue to look up at Dr. Harris, silently begging him to stay.

"I'll just give you guys a few minutes," he says, sliding past Carl.

Alone. With the people that caused me to be here. As soon as Dr. Harris leaves the room, Elaina sits upright, removing her hand from my hair.

"What the hell were you thinking?" she says in a harsh tone. "How dare you put this on Carl and me?"

"On *you*?" I shout.

"We have been worried sick about you," Carl says in a raised voice.

His voice makes me nauseous. Tears instantly start to fall and I can't seem to hold them back. I want them to leave; I never want to see their faces again, but I have now realized there is no escaping. I notice a small women coming through the door and Elaina instantly puts back on her mother act.

"Shhh...there, there..." she coos, while rubbing her hands on my shoulder.

I begin to feel nauseous. Minutes later, I see Dr. Harris come back in the room, my nerves calming a little. He can't hurt me with all these people here. Dr. Harris and the women who entered earlier are now standing at the foot of my bed.

"She is just having a hard time," Elaina says, turning

around to face Dr. Harris.

Carl steps closer to me, reaching out to put his hand on my shoulder in a fake attempt at consoling me. Instinctively, I jolt my upper body sideways, everyone clearly noticing my reaction. Everything falls silent except for those god damn machines. For once I welcome the noise.

"Phoenix," Dr. Harris says after a long pause. "This is Dr. Young, she would like to speak with you."

I swallow as I try to wipe the tears from face. I keep my eyes on the doctors, not wanting to look at Elaina or Carl.

"I'm sorry, but we need to take Phoenix into another room so I am afraid that you will have to leave this room while she is away," Dr. Harris says to them.

I hold back a smile. It's the best news I have heard all day.

"And may I ask what you are going to be asking my daughter, as her mother I have the right to know," Elaina says harshly.

"I am afraid I can't divulge that, we have a strict doctor-patient confidentiality agreement."

"That's fucking bullshit," I hear Carl say, his voice sounding agitated.

Elaina puts her hand on his forearm as if to comfort him. She turns her attention back to me.

"We'll be back later sweetie," she says, giving me a kiss on the cheek before getting up from the bedside. As

I watch them walk closer and closer towards the door, I feel I can breathe again.

"Phoenix," Dr. Young says. "If you wouldn't mind..."

I pull the sheets off myself, pivoting my feet around so that they touch the floor. Dr. Harris helps me, my body still extremely tired from the medication they gave me earlier. I don't retract from his touch this time. When we leave the room, I glance out at the rest of the hospital, a million things going on around me. I look down the hallway, a pair of dark eyes glaring back at me.

Carl is standing at the end of it and he is staring straight back at me. A chill runs down the length of my spine, my knees becoming wobbly. It's like he is in my head because I know exactly what that stare means. *I'm dead if I tell.*

He slips on his jacket before exiting out the front of the hospital. I shift my attention back to the doctors.

"Were going to be in here," Dr. Young says, holding a door open for me. "This is my office."

I walk over slowly and enter the room. Inside is a nicely-furnished office and I instantly know what I am doing here. She's a psychologist and I tried to commit suicide. The next hour goes by slowly, my heavy eyelids drooping from time to time. So many questions about how I feel and why I felt like I had no way out. I give short answers, just wanting to get through this as fast as possible. That is until she asks me about my scars and bruises. All I see is his eyes, the hair on my arms standing up. I wrap my arms around myself.

"These are not self inflicted," she says, gently putting her hand on mine.

I jump back a little.

"You can tell me," she declares.

Easier said than done. I can feel my body starting to shake but I remain silent. She sits back in her chair, clearly disappointed.

"Well, as your assigned therapist, I think it would be good for you to spend some time at a specialized hospital."

I snap my head up.

"The fucking insane asylum?" My mouth blurts out.

"It's a psychiatric hospital and I think that will be best for you," she states.

"Do I have a choice?" I ask, already knowing the answer.

"I think this is what is best for you and your family," she repeats.

I roll my eyes.

"Whatever," I say, crossing my arms.

As long as I don't have to go home.

~

When I leave her office I begin to panic. *What was I going to do now?* The idea of the psychiatric hospital was making me nauseas. Fear of the unknown. When I get back to my room things move fast. Once Dr. Harris releases me I am asked to get dressed.

"I will be your attending physician over there as well, and I will be tracking your progress."

"OK," I say, feeling slightly more relaxed.

"Take care of yourself, Phoenix," he says.

"Thanks, Dr. Harris."

"Please, call me Neil," he says with a smile. *What's with the special treatment?*

I can't help but return one.

"I'll be seeing you soon, Phoenix," he says, before leaving the room.

When I get outside, I am ushered into the back of an ambulance, my heart is racing. I've only ever seen psychiatric hospitals in movies before and they often looked more like haunted houses than actual hospitals. The ride over is short and before I know it, I am being taken in through the patient entrance.

I look around and become dazed. The hospital is quiet and it's still dark out even though it is early morning. The person from the ambulance leaves me, a nurse from behind the counter greeting me.

"You must be Phoenix Harper?" she asks, sounding like she actually cares.

I nod, while swallowing the lump in my throat. I can feel my body shaking ever so slightly. Once I get signed in, I am ushered into a different room.

"Here we are," a new lady says to me, handing me

folded clothes. "This is what you are allowed to wear here. You can have some of your own clothing as long as they contain no strings."

I almost ask her why but I catch myself. *Strangulation.* I stand in the middle of the room, realizing she isn't going to leave. As I slowly start to undress, I begin to feel like a prisoner. *I am not to be trusted.* Once I'm changed, I'm moved into yet another room. I feel like my heart is going to jump out of my chest any moment. After a few minutes, the woman leaves and in walks a man. The first thing I notice is his eyes. Even though they are hiding behind a pair of square framed glasses, I can see the electrifying green from behind them. And his smile...there are no words to describe how it makes me feel. A sensation I have never felt before now. My nerves instantly settle, the feeling unfamiliar to me. His demeanor has the same effect on me as Dr. Harris'. I stand there in my clothes, feeling extremely exposed due to their paper-like state.

"Good morning, Phoenix," he says, setting the box down on the counter. He shifts on his feet. "I am just going to go through your belongings, to make sure everything is here for when you leave."

I fold my arms around my torso, as though I am trying to comfort myself. He starts to pull out everything, his hands all over my stuff. I can feel my cheeks becoming warm, but then he picks up a certain item. The only thing that is mine. Something that hasn't been tainted by anyone else. I reach up and touch my throat, not even realizing that they had taken it off at the hospital. A flash of my childhood comes across my mind.

~

The glow of the candles lights up the kitchen with a soft light. I can hear the rain bouncing off the roof and the tree tops swaying in the wind. Looking down at the cake in front of me, I can't help but smile. It's barely standing because the layers of the cake have started to slide apart. He spent all day in the kitchen making this for me, refusing to let me help at all. There was really only one problem.

"Dad, I'm turning 15, not 11," I say, pointing to the number of candles on top of the cake.

He looks down at it.

"I know, I just didn't get to store to buy more," he says, with disappointment is his voice. I laugh.

"It's ok, dad."

"Are you sure you don't want to invite anyone over? Pretty boring here with your old dad," he says, elbowing me.

"No, I'm kinda enjoying it just being you and I..."

After I blow out the candles we both spend the next hour in the kitchen, eating cake and just talking. My father and I were always close. When we finish, I stand up and start stacking up the dishes. He reaches out, putting his hand on my forearm.

"We can do those later," he says. "I want to give you your present, sweetie."

"OK."

We both get up from the table and head into the living room. On the coffee table is a small box, horribly wrapped I might add, with a bright pink bow on top. I walk over, sitting down on the couch waiting for my father to come. A few minutes later, he appears, a coffee mug in hand.

"Go ahead, sweetie," he says, gesturing toward the package.

I lean over, grabbing it off the table. Sliding my fingers between the paper, I rip it open, the bow falling to the floor. Inside is a small jewelry box. I can tell it's old by the yellow-tinted coloring of the box. Opening up the top I see a small golden chain. Lifting it up out the box, I now see the small heart pendant attached to it. Nelson walks over to me, sitting down beside me on the couch, gently taking it from me.

"It was my mother's," he starts.

Leaning his arms over my head, he puts it on me, clasping it in the back.

"I promised her when I had a daughter I would pass it on, but only when she responsible enough to take care of it."

I could feel myself wanting to cry. Once it was on, I shifted back around to face him and we both remain silent for a second. He clears his throat.

"Well, I just wanted to tell you I am very proud of you, Phoenix, and what a wonderful woman you have become."

"Come on, dad, you don't have to be so...serious," I say nudging him.

He sits upright, trying to regain his composure.

"I'm going to go get a refill, you want some?" he asks.

"I don't think you are supposed to offer your 15 year old daughter coffee. Especially at nine o'clock at night." I laugh.

"Oh, right," he says, looking down at the cup.

I just stare at him for a few seconds.

"I love you, dad," I say.

"Love you too, kiddo," he says, a smile on his face.

~

I pull myself out of my memories, watching this boy clutch onto the thing most dear to me in his hands. I hold back the tears, turning my head to the side, hoping to hide my emotions from this stranger. He continues to pull out my items although there are very few since I wasn't planning on living. He writes everything down on a piece of paper and then hands the clipboard to me.

"Please sign here."

Reaching out, I take the clipboard from him, my fingertips brushing across his briefly. It's now that I can really see his face. His dark brown hair and his strong jaw line. His beautiful lips. I read over what he has written and my heart instantly races. I look up at him, thoroughly upset.

"I can't keep any of this with me?" I say loudly.

A look of guilt comes on his face.

"I'm afraid not," he says.

"Why, because I'm gonna use it to fucking kill myself?" I cry out, grabbing the necklace off the table.

"It's for your own safety," he says softly.

Reaching out, he puts his hand on mine, trying to pry it gently from my fingertips. At our first full contact the hair on my arm stands up, goose bumps following shortly. A single tear starts to fall and all I feel is my body fall, my vision gone.

Braeden

When I grabbed her hand, the feeling I felt was indescribable. I felt every emotion imaginable. Fear. Pain. Happiness. Sadness.

It was almost as though her emotions were flowing from her to me. There's something different about this girl. Something that just draws you in.

When she fainted I caught her in my grasp, making sure that her delicate body didn't hit the floor. Scooping her up in my arms I could tell that she was incredibly light, even for how small she is. As I walked down the hall with her in my arms I moved at a slow pace, almost as thought I was afraid I would wake her. She looked so peaceful. When I set her atop her bed I pull the covers up and over her.

"Sleep tight, Phoenix," I whisper.

After I made my last rounds before my shift was over, I found myself at Rain and Phoenix's room. Standing outside the door, I push it open slowly. Rain's bed is empty, not something out of the ordinary. Looking to the bed on the left, I see a mass, her entire body covered by the blankets. My feet move me forward and I am now standing over her, watching her back rise and fall. *Great, now I'm a fucking stalker?*

After a few minutes, I lean even more over her, noticing that tears are falling from her eyes even though they are closed. I hear her mutter something a couple times and then her eyes snap open.

"What do you want? Do you have my necklace?" she asks harshly.

"I can't give it to you, you know that," I respond softly.

I actually feel guilty telling her no. In a flash, she reaches up, grabbing my glasses off my face, throwing them hard into the opposite wall. I hear them crack. She rolls back over, pulling the covers back over herself.

"Leave me alone," she says, her voice muffled by the blanket.

Stepping away from her bed, I walk over, picking up what is left of my glasses. I look back at her once more before leaving the room.

~

Rubbing my eyes, I glance up at the clock, thankful to see it has finally reached seven. Running my hands through my hair, I put my foot on the step of the trash can, dumping the shards of my glasses in and quickly release my foot to let the trash can lid slam shut. I stand there, just staring at it.

A push on my shoulder snaps me out of my trance. I look over, seeing someone standing next to me, the person holding out something to me.

"Thank you," I say, opening the envelope, making sure all the cash was there.

"Yup," Bret responds.

"Did you buy milk?" I ask him.

He just looks at me, a dumbfounded expression on his face. I roll my eyes.

"I'll pick some up on the way home," I mutter.

I look up at the clock again.

"Who are you covering for?" I ask, knowing this is not his usual shift.

"Daniel needed to go to some family bullshit," he says, rolling his eyes.

"Oh," I say.

"Did we get any new basket cases in last night?" he asks.

A wave of anger flows through my veins. A man like him shouldn't be working here.

"Yeah, we got a new girl, room eight," I say softly.

He perks his eyebrow up, his mood changing.

"Well, I'm off...guess I'll see you at home," I say before leaving to head to the staff room. Pulling open my locker, I hang up my ID tag and pull my book down from the shelf, stuffing it into my bag. Throwing the bag over my chest, I head out the back door into the open air. The wind has picked up, making it even colder. I start to make my way home. The early-morning streets are busy with people getting to work, everyone coming and going in all directions. I contemplate taking the bus but I know it will just be more crowded.

I continue to walk, happy when I round Market Street because that meant home was not far off. While waiting for the crosswalk to change, I look over at a small café with a young brunette sitting outside reading a book. My mind instantly turns to Phoenix. Her face when I refused to give back her necklace. The feeling when her fingers delicately grazed my hand. I can't explain this feeling.

The sound of beeping reaches my ear and I look up, the crosswalk sign blinking orange. I go to jump off the curb when a piece of paper being blows across the street wraps around my ankle. I kick my leg out as I run across the crosswalk trying to shake it loose but can't seem to make it budge.

When I get to the other side of the street, I reach down and peel off the paper. I stride over to the nearest trashcan, planning to toss it instead of letting it clutter the streets, but I stop. I take time to really look at the folded piece of paper, noticing the drawing on the front. It's a hand-sketched heart, cracking down the middle. There are nails stuck in it and the cracks are repaired by stitches, but there were more cracks opening in another spot. Something about the drawing moves me and I continue to stare at it. I can feel the pain behind the drawing. Looking around me, I slide the paper in my pocket, heading into the small corner store near the apartment.

Walking into the back, I pull open the door, grabbing a gallon of milk and head up to the register, but not before stopping off in the cookie and cracker aisle. With my head still facing forward, I grab the colorful rectangular box, a sly smile on my face in the process. *Definitely need these today.* I make it to the cash register and put my things up on the counter.

"Morning." The cashier smiles and starts to ring up my purchases. "There's going to be a shortage of these if you keep eating them like you do."

I just smile, shaking my head lightly. I pull out some cash, handing it to him.

"Hey, how is your daughter's strep throat?" I ask him.

"Much better. Please tell your father thank you for getting her an appointment so quick," he says.

"Will do." I smile. "Well. I'll be seeing you around."

I wave back to him.

Pushing the store door open I step back into the cold, sliding the milk carton into my bag. I hold the other box in my hand by its string, feeling like a child again.

When I reach our apartment building, I opt to take the elevator instead of the stairs, my body beyond exhausted from the long shift. Sliding my keys into the front door, I open it, shut and lock it behind me. I turn around, sighing immediately. Our apartment looks like a tornado went through it, shit everywhere.

"Fucking Bret," I mutter under my breath.

Walking over to the fridge, I put the milk in it, immediately turning around and head to my room. Sliding my backpack off, I place it on the back of my desk chair and plop my body down on my bed, not bothering to change out of my scrubs. Reaching over, I grab the box of crackers from my bedside, sliding my fingers underneath the tab, opening it slowly. I grab a cracker, checking to see what animal it is. Giraffe.

I bite the head off first, something I've done with every cracker since as far back as I can remember. I always use to say it was so they couldn't feel the pain. I laugh at the notion. I eat a few more crackers before closing the box. Setting it on my nightstand, I continue to lie on the bed, staring at the ceiling. After only a few minutes I find myself having a hard time keeping my eyes open. I fall into a deep sleep, my body trying to make up the deficit that I have accumulated over the week of working double shifts. My body may be asleep, but my mind, however, is not.

~

"MOM!" I shout when I enter the house, clutching onto a piece of paper in my hands.

I pull my backpack off, hanging it on the hook by the front door. Looking around the house, I see no sign of her. Turning around I look up at my dad who is just walking in the front door.

"I'm sure she is just somewhere where she can't hear us," he assures, ushering me to head upstairs.

"You go check up there and I will check the backyard. I know she wanted to pick some of the vegetables from the garden."

"OK!" I say, fleeing up the stairs as though this is a game of hide and seek.

I head immediately into their bedroom.

"Moooommmm!" I shout again, waiting for her to pop around the corner at any moment. "I got an A on my spelling test!" I say, waving the piece of paper in the air.

But there is nothing but silence. Shrugging, I head back downstairs, pulling open the slider to the backyard. Hopping down the granite steps, I make my way around the pool side, trying to see my dad down in the garden. I can see the white of his doctor's coat, the sun shining off his dirty blond hair. I stand up on my tippy toes to see if she is with him. She isn't. When he

*reaches me, he gives me a soft smile, but I can tell
something is not right.*

*"Why don't you go inside and start your homework,
I'm sure she just went out for fresh air," he says,
squeezing my shoulder.*

*"OK," I respond, turning around to head back into
the house.*

*Walking over to the fridge, I put my test in a clip on
the fridge. I grab my backpack, set it down on the
kitchen table, and pull out my workbook. When I get
halfway through the first page, something pops in my
head. The shed.*

*I fly up out of my chair, still in hide-and-seek mode. I
run back outside and across the yard, reaching the shed
in record time. Grabbing the door handle, I pull open
the door. The inside is dark due to the lack of windows.
Fumbling around on the wall, I find the light switch.
After the lights flicker on there is no sound, except for
the shrill of my screams. It's her. Her delicate body
gently swaying, her feet not touching the ground.*

~

My body jolts, waking me up instantly. There are
beads of moisture on my brow, my scrubs damp from
night sweats. I rub my eyes, not affected by my dream,
it's one that I have constantly. I guess it's more of a
memory than a dream. Shifting over, I look at the clock.
Four o'clock in the afternoon.

I groan, grabbing my phone out of my bag. I dial

Donovan's number to see what the plan is for tonight. It rings a few times, eventually leading to his voicemail. I decide to not leave a message. Setting the phone back down, I pull my body off the bed and head to the shower.

I look at myself in the mirror, yawning loudly. Pulling my shirt off I throw it in the corner of the room. I go to do the same to my pants, but my finger comes across something in the pocket. Reaching in, I pull out the paper I had forgotten about. I stare down at the drawing again, still taken aback as much as I was the first time I saw it. I let the shower run and let the room fill with steam. Sliding my fingers between the folds, I open the paper, noticing there are words handwritten on the back.

Life is a notion that now sickens me. If I had wings, I would fly free. But since I don't, I guess I will choose to jump instead of float.

The note has no signature or indication that it was meant to be delivered to anyone in particular and I find myself wondering how it came to be on the streets of the city. The words are heavy in my heart, the drawing leaving me speechless. The feelings of when my mother took her own life haunt me every day. Suicide doesn't just affect those that decide to remove themselves from this world, but each and every person who loved them.

Folding up the note again, I leave the bathroom and head back into my bedroom. I walk over to a corkboard on my wall and pull out an unoccupied push pin. Reaching up, I put the folded note up on the board, sticking the pin back in the top, making sure to not pierce any of the drawing. Something about that drawing pulls me in, the words swirling around in my head over and over. It's as though I can feel what they felt. I stare at it for another second before turning around and heading back to the shower.

Phoenix

I feel myself being blinded, opening my eyes slowly. I notice that there is a harsh stream of sunlight coming through the window, hitting right on my pillow. I grumble, pulling the sheets over my head and I inhale an unfamiliar scent. I open my eyes again and slowly remember everything.

Pain. Cold. Daggers. Green. Fear. I peer out from under my covers slowly, only to have a pair of eyes staring back at me.

"Morning!" a small girl says standing over me.

Her eyes are large, a vibrant brown. Her hair is as dark as night and travels down the length of her back in a loose braid. I slide out from under my sheets but keep them close against my chest.

"Don't be afraid, Phoenix." She smiles.

Goosebumps break out all over my body when I realize no one knows my name here besides the nurses and *him*. I think she noticed my uneasiness.

"Don't worry, I tend to have psychic abilities," she says, holding out her hand. "I'm Rain."

Lifting my hand out from under the covers slowly, I shake hers. We both fall silent.

"Do you want to have breakfast with me?" she asks.

"Uh sure," I answer. "I need to use the bathroom first though."

"Sure, it's just through there," she says, pointing to the closed door.

Pulling my covers off, I swing my feet out, the tile cold on my toes. I use the bathroom quickly, washing my hand and then head back into the bedroom. Rain is holding out a different pair of clothes for me.

"They don't have any strings so they should be OK," she says, the smile now gone, a worried one replacing it.

"Thanks," I say softly, pulling them on.

Once I am dressed, we exit the bedroom, the hallway a lot busier than the previous night. My heart begins to race, realizing that this is all real. This isn't a dream. *It's more like a nightmare.*

As we make our way to what I assume is where we are eating, I take in my surroundings. There are people everywhere, a mixture of aides and patients. Their faces look tired, as if the life has been drained from them. I can see the pain and the hurt, a sight I am all too familiar with. I feel someone's arm slide into mine. I look over to see Rain standing next to me, our elbows locked together. We don't say anything, she just smiles.

"Sit," she says bubbly, while holding out a chair for me.

I slide into the seat, now alone at a table. Playing with my fingernails, I find myself thinking about him and the feeling that flowed through me before I passed out. Betrayed by my own body.

I can feel my cheeks burning and my heart starting to race. I look up from the table, shifting my eyes around the room. There are mostly female aides in here, except for one unfamiliar guy, who is looking back at me. I quickly look away and back down at my hands.

"He's not here," I hear a voice say, looking up to see Rain sliding into the chair next to me.

"Who?" I ask, trying to pretend like I don't know who she is talking about.

She just laughs.

"There isn't much you can keep from me, Phoenix," she says.

I smile shyly.

"Just in case you were wondering, he works nights and gets off at seven."

She shimmies in her chair, handing me a fork and

knife.

"We're allowed to have these?" I ask.

"Yeah, they count them when we leave though," she says, taking a bite of food.

I do the same, the food feeling incredible, fulfilling the nutrition deficit my body has been collecting. We both eat in silence until a figure comes up to our table. It's the male aide that was staring at me, or at least I think he was. *Maybe I'm just paranoid.*

"Girls," I hear him say.

My heart is racing so fast I can hear the boom in my ears. I don't look up from my plate of food.

"I don't think we've met," I hear him say. "You must be Phoenix."

My eyes widen, knowing I have to look up at him. Shifting my eyes upward, I look into his eyes, nodding slightly. I quickly look back down. I can still feel him hovering, his body leaning in closer to my back. I begin to feel nauseous, my vision blurry. After a few seconds, he leaves. When I know it's clear, I sit straight in my chair, looking over my shoulder slowly, relieved that he is no longer in the room.

"He is the devil," I hear Rain say and I whip my head around to look at her.

She doesn't say more than that, but I tend to agree. We both resume eating. When we both finish, I pick up my tray and utensils, handing it to the aide. She looks over the tray, making sure all the utensils are there.

Rain and I leave the kitchen, her arm in mine again.
Being so close to someone would usually scare me, but
Rain is just...comforting.

"Do you want to go for a walk? I can show you the
rest of the hospital..."

"Sure," I whisper.

She grabs my arm and we make a quick right out
through a pair of doors, into a small courtyard. It's cold
and the wind is harsh but it feels indescribable, like I
can finally breathe. I unhook my arm from Rain's,
stepping towards the surrounding gates. I feel free for
the first time in so long. I feel like no one can touch me
here. I feel safe. Tears start to fall, my emotions
overtaking my mind. To be so close, yet so far away.

Rain comes up next to me, as though she can feel
what I'm feeling. She puts her arm around me, her
touch soothing. And then she says something to me, her
eyes staring out in the same direction of mine.

"Life isn't about waiting for the storm to pass
Phoenix...it's about learning to dance in the rain."

I look over at her, her face expressionless, as though
she is somewhere else. She's starting to freak me out a
little bit.

Braeden

Reaching into my closet, I pull out my favorite pair of jeans and my blue and black plaid flannel shirt. Swiping my hands through my hair, I go to grab my shoes out of my closet, a small part of me not surprised that they are nowhere to be found. *Bret.* Grabbing a pair of socks, I leave my bedroom heading immediately for his room. His door is closed but I push it open anyways, the mixture of cigarette ash and alcohol seeping from the carpet. Pulling my shirt up over my nose, I start to kick the mounds of clothing laid upon the floor. *Looks like we're not getting our deposit back.*

In the far right corner of the room, I see them, my

black high top lace ups. I grab them and make my way back to the hallway, the bong and used condoms on the nightstand don't go unnoticed. Sitting down on the couch, I begin to lace up my shoes when I hear my phone ringing.

I groan while leaning back into the couch, pulling out my phone out of my pocket. Putting it up to my ear, I hold it with my shoulder while I continue to lace up my shoes.

"Yea," I say into the phone.

"Dude, are you coming or what? We're already fucking way ahead of you..."

"Yeah, I'm just about to head out the door," I explain.

"Alright, hurry up!" he shouts.

I hang up the phone without a response and slide the phone back into my pocket. Grabbing my keys and wallet off the counter I head out the building. It's only a walk of a few blocks from my place to the bar. Once I reach the front, I can see it's packed with patrons spilling out the front door. Maneuvering through the crowd, I spot the bouncer, giving him a pat on the shoulder.

"How are you doing tonight?" I shout over the music.

"Great! It's a full house!" he yells back. "Make sure you keep that friend of yours in line this time, he's already hit on all the bartenders."

I smile crookedly.

"I will, thanks, man," I respond before stepping into the main room.

Light sounds of jazz hits my ears, instantly calming me. I spot Donovan easily, as he is always the tallest guy in the room. Once he spots me, he lifts his hands in the air, waving me over.

"Where you been, my man?" he asks, leaning down to wrap his arms around me.

"I clearly do have some catching up to do," I mumble, smelling the alcohol on his breath.

Wrangling myself out from under him, I grab the nearest chair at our table and slide into it. I nod at our other guests, most of them from Donovan's soccer team. A few seconds later, a tumbler glass is set in front of me and I already know what it holds.

Looking up, I am greeted by one of bartenders, a red-headed woman with tattoos covering every inch of the exposed skin on her arms.

"Thanks," I say, giving her a small smile.

"You look like shit, Braeden," she says, pushing on my shoulder.

"Thanks," I say sarcastically, grabbing the glass and taking a sip. "Jesus Christ! How much rum did you put in this thing?"

"Don't be such a pussy." She laughs. "No woman is ever going to want to sleep with you if you act like that," she says, smacking the side of my head.

"I'm pretty sure men don't want to sleep with an

abusive bitch, either," I shoot back.

She just winks at me before leaving our table and heading back behind the bar to tend to the rest of the customers. I continue to sip on my rum and coke, watching the people around me, but remain silent. I turn my attention to the band that's on stage. They are frequent players at the bar. I tap the rim of my glass, my body responding to the music, knowing every note of the guitar solo. I laugh to myself, remembering the guitar lessons I took as a kid. I thought I was going to be the next Jimi Hendrix. The last thing I wanted to do was follow in my father's footsteps, but after my mother's death, I wanted nothing more than to help people - to give people the help that they deserved. It's amazing how unpredictable life can be. I feel a push on my shoulder again, my empty glass replaced with a new one.

"Thanks," I respond, giving the red head a crooked smile. I then feel a flick on my opposite shoulder.

"Hey, man, come have a smoke with me," Donovan says.

I grunt, pushing my chair out from the table, grabbing my glass, the condensation from it dripping against my skin. We make our way out the back door, into a small alley behind the bar. I lean up against the brick wall, listening to Donovan mumble on about how he scored the winning goal of tonight's match and how he is going to get so much ass from his new found celebrity status.

I start to tune him out, my eyes fixated on the end of the alley way, watching the masses of people walking by. After some time, I bring my attention back to him.

"I gotta go take a piss." he says, whacking me on my chest.

"Jesus Christ, man, quit fucking hitting me," I say, rubbing my chest.

"Such a pussy!" he says shaking his head. I roll my eyes at him. "You know you still owe me for that," he adds.

"For what?" I ask, confused.

"For saving your ass in third grade. If I didn't hit that asshole first, that face of yours wouldn't be so pretty." He laughs.

"I could have handled it myself," I defend. He just laughs, pulling open the back door.

"You coming?" he asks.

"Nah, I'm gonna stay here, fresh air feels good."

"Whatever, man, make sure your weak ass doesn't catch a cold," he jokes.

"You do know that you can't actually get a cold from being cold right?" I tell him.

"There you go with that medical bullshit again." He laughs. "See you inside," he says before heading back in.

Lifting my body off the wall, I walk the length of the alley way, breathing in the fumes from the Chinese restaurant next door. When I get to the end, I continue to watch the crowds go by. The stream of solid red lights, the sound of blaring horns fills the night air. Everyone in such a hurry, too busy to enjoy life. *Guess I'm guilty of that.* Just as I am about to turn around to head back to the bar, a figure across the street catches my eye. Dark brown flowing hair, bright beautiful eyes.

I take a step forward, the hair on my arms standing upright. I squint into the darkness and see that the figure still standing there, smiling back at me. I take one more step towards it. Then another.

There is silence for a moment, like nothing else exists on the planet. Until I hear the sound of tires screeching on wet pavement, instantly snapping me out of whatever world I was currently in. Looking to my left, I am blinded by two headlights coming straight at me. The bumper of a cab grazed my kneecaps, making my knees buckle and I fall to the ground, the glass in my hand shattering against the asphalt. I feel a sharp pain in my right hand and see a rusty red mixing with the water and oil on the ground.

"What the fuck do you think you are doing?" the cab driver screams to me as he gets out of his car. "You fucking kids, can't keep a hold of your god damn liquor."

I whip my head from his direction to the sidewalk behind me, the figure now gone, as though it simply vanished into thin air. I feel arms wrap around mine, my body being lifted off the ground.

"You alright, man?" I hear Donovan say behind me, his hands brushing debris off of my clothes.

"Yeah," I say, now looking down at my hand.

"Holy fuck, dude," Donovan shouts, putting his nose inside his elbow. I look down at my hand, and then back up at him.

"Are you scared of blood?" I say laughing.

I hold my hand up to his face and Donovan takes a step back. I take another one toward him, both of us repeating our steps. Donovan breaks into a sprint back to the bar and I follow, laughing the entire way.

"Who's the pussy now?" I shout.

When we get back into the bar, I am immediately met by the red-headed bartender. She grabs my arm.

"I have a first aid kit in the office," she says, nodding her head in the direction of a hallway.

I follow her, my hand now fucking stinging. When we make it to a closed door, she pulls a pair of keys from her pocket, causing the hem of her shirt to ride up. It's now that I notice her arms are not the only places she has tattoos. When she gets the door open, she ushers me in.

"Sit," she instructs, pointing to the office chair up against the desk.

I do as I'm told. She walks over to a file cabinet, coming back with a small cloth pouch.

"I can do it myself..." I tell her, reaching out to take

it from her. She smacks my hand away.

"Sometimes it's nice to be taken care of," she says, her face deadpanned.

Grabbing a stool, she sits down and slides towards me. She doesn't stop until I have to open my legs, her body sliding between them. Reaching down, she grabs my hand again and puts it in her lap.

"Now, hold still."

I can feel myself becoming anxious. Something about her touch is rough yet gentle. She takes the antiseptic wipe packet in her hand and rips it open in one swoop. She wipes it across my palm, the once-white cloth now a murky brown. When she finishes, she grabs the roll of gauze and wraps what seems like a thousand layers around my hand, clearly having no clue what she is doing. She binds it with a few pieces of tape. She stops her work, looking down at it and then back up at me.

"Fuck, it will have to do," she says, examining it once more.

"Thanks," I say, pulling my arm into me.

When I look back up at her, she has a vicious smile across her lips. Her hand comes up around my neck and pulls her stool even closer to mine. I can now feel her legs touching the inside of mine. In one swift motion, she hops from her stool onto my lap, her legs wrapping around my waist, and I pulse with desire. Reaching up with my good arm, I weave my fingers through her hair, pulling her face to mine. Her kiss is harsh and it makes me more frenzied. My other hand finds the lower part of her back, making her bottom half grind into me, until a sharp pain ruptures through my hand. *There must be glass in there.*

Moments later, she lets go of my hair to pull her tank top off, exposing more of her tattoos. The artwork is breathtaking and I find myself transfixed.

"Hey, Harris, you gonna fuck me or stare at my tits all day?" she announces.

I smile crookedly, lifting her off me harshly and slam her body down onto the desk, causing papers to fly off in every direction. Reaching up, she grabs at the hem of my shirt, a silent signal for me to remove it. I do so in one swift motion and throw it on the floor behind me. Her hands find the button of my pants, her fingers working fast to remove them, while her teeth gently gnawing on my bottom lip. They eventually fall off my hips, gathering down at my ankles. I quickly reach down as well, grabbing the front of her jeans, pulling on them hard. I hear the button pop, which then bounces across the floor.

"Easy boy," I hear her breathe into my mouth.

Looking down, I catch a sight of her perfectly manicured regions, underwear obviously not a concern for her. Pushing my fingers between her lips, she moans with pleasure.

"You like that?" I call out to her.

"Don't give me that shit," she says, rolling her eyes. In one motion, I push two fingers inside of her forcefully, making her gasp.

"Fuck!" she screams out.

I smile widely, she rolls her eyes again in response. Her wetness and warmth encase my fingers as I slowly pump them in and out of her. Her hips are now bucking, her hands grabbing at the few things still on the desk.

"Fuck me," I hear her beg.

"I thought women didn't like to fuck pussies?" I tease, knowing it will piss her off.

"Oh, fuck off..." She laughs and I pull my fingers out from inside her, now leaning over her body now so that our faces are parallel.

"You know you want it," I say just above a whisper.

She gets a pouty look on her face and starts shaking her head. I take myself in my hand and push the tip between her lips, moving it back and forth on top of it.

"How about now?" I ask coyly.

She bites her bottom lip but doesn't respond. I take my cock again and push just the tip inside her, her wetness more apparent. I don't say anything, just cock an eyebrow.

"Fine!" she finally screams. I just smile, waiting for her to say it. She rolls her eyes once again. "I want you to fuck me!" she screams at the top of her lungs, everyone in the bar probably hearing it.

As soon as those words leave her lips, I push inside

of her. Her arms come up around my neck and interlock behind me. Using my hand to hold onto her, I thrust, both of us moaning in unison. She feels incredible, the sensation almost too much to handle. We both fall silent, only the sounds of whimpers coming from her. As I continue to move, I reach down, hooking her around her back with my bad arm, lifting her midair, her legs now hooked around me again.

We remain upright somehow, while she now bobs up and down on me. It feels beyond fucking incredible. It's apparent that she knows what she is doing, which turns me on in a weird way. Her moves are fast and I know that my release is not far off. Setting her back down on the desk, I thrust with all my might, our kisses becoming more animalistic, both of us at our breaking points. Just after a few more seconds, she cries out, her body rigid, her hips lifting off the surface of the desk.

I hold onto her hip bones, fighting back my urge until she is finished. Once she falls silent again, I thrust one more time before quickly removing myself from inside her and release into my hand. I bend over until I finish and the room falls silent. She shimmies off the desk and picks her top and pants off the floor.

"There's a janitor sink over there," she says, pointing into the corner.

Picking up my jeans from around my ankles with my wounded hand, I shuffle over to the sink to clean up. When I finish, I walk back to her.

"Shit," she says, looking down at the missing button on her jeans and proceeds to look for it on the floor. I just smile. Leaning over, I grab a safety pin from the floor, fish the fabric through of her jeans, and fasten it shut.

"What are you? Fucking MacGyver?"

I lean in to kiss her but she stops me by putting her hand on my chest.

"I'll call you, alright?" she says, before slipping out from under me, heading straight for the door, slamming it shut behind her.

Sighing, I button up my jeans and grab my shirt and overcoat from the floor. Leaving the office, I take a gaze down the hallway - no one in sight. Slipping out the back door, I make it out of the alleyway and onto Market Street. My hand is now burning. There's one more stop I need to make for the night.

Shutting the door to the taxi, I arrive at the hospital. Walking through the automatic doors, the hospital is frenzied, typical for a Friday night. My hand is now aching like a son of a bitch and blood is seeping through the gauze. Hitting the button for the elevator with my elbow, I wait for it to recall back to the lobby floor. When I hear the doors open, I step inside, hitting the second floor button. When I reach the floor, things seem to be a little more relaxed than the previous. As I walk past the nurses' station, a curly-haired women points to a door.

"Thanks, Sue," I whisper before heading in that direction.

Using my hip, I push open the door, seeing a hunched over mass behind the desk. He picks his head up, pushing the sliding glasses up onto his nose.

"Evening, son," he says, a smile on his face as he pulls himself away from his desk.

"Don't get up," I say, ushering him to remain sitting.

"Nonsense." He waves, getting up anyways. He walks over to give me a hug.

"Good to see you," he says, releasing his arms from me, putting his hands on either side of my shoulders.

"I just saw you two days ago."

He pats my shoulder before letting go.

"So what can I do for you? You don't come down to my office too much," he states. I hold my gauzed hand up, giving him a small grin. He gets a concerned look on his face.

"Are you alright?" he asks, taking my hand in his.

"It burns like a motherfucker but yeah. I think there might be a piece of glass in there still." I say. Walking over to a counter, he puts on a pair of rubber gloves.

"Don't use that language, Braeden," he says softly before starting to unravel the gauze. "I thought someone who is in the medical field would wrap a wound better than this."

I laugh. "Let's just say it wasn't me."

When he gets all the gauze off, he tosses it in the

trash.

"Yeah, there are a few shards in there." he says as he pokes around the open wound. "Sit," he says pointing to the empty chair.

I do so, sliding into one. He grabs a pair of forceps and begins picking out the pieces of glass, slowly. When he finishes it, he re-wraps it with fresh gauze.

"Do I even want to ask how you got glass in your hand?" he asks.

"Probably not," I admit.

He puts his tools away and walks back over to me, leaning against the edge of his desk. I look up at him.

"So, how's work been?" I ask him.

"Extremely busy," he sighs. "Something about winter time...."

We both fall silent for a second. I get a chill, like the temperature in the room suddenly dropped.

"I heard you were the attending physician for one of our new patients," I say, trying to be nonchalant about bringing her up.

His face gets serious. "Phoenix...yes."

My heart skips a beat, the feeling making me nervous. Just hearing her name affects me.

"How is she doing?" he asks.

I shrug.

"She only came in a few hours before my shift ended and, let's just say, it was less than pleasant."

"That's only natural."

"I know," I say, holding back what I really want to ask. We both fall silent again. My insides turning, wanting to know everything about her.

"There is just something about her..." I say just above a whisper, so low that I hope my father doesn't hear.

"Braeden," he says, making me snap my head up. "I know that she is just another patient but I must ask something of you."

I stare at him confused.

"I fear that she is not the only one harming herself," he says heartbreakingly.

"Why makes you think that?" I ask, starved for information.

"When she was admitted to this hospital, her mother and stepfather came to visit. Luckily, I happened to be in the room at the time. I observed them."

He pauses. I almost scream out for him to continue.

"Phoenix was extremely distraught after the incident, like any human being would, but something about her changed rapidly when they walked in her room. She became rigid and the look on her face... I've seen it before. On victims of abuse. She was terrified," he resumes.

A wave of anger comes over me.

"What can I do?" I ask.

"I have a feeling that they may show up at the hospital, please just keep a watchful eye," he answers.

He looks at the clock on the wall.

"Well, I need to get back to work," he says, leaning his body off of the desk. He gives me another hug.

"Love you, son," he says.

"Love you too, Dad," I say as he pulls away.

I walk out from around the chair, heading towards the door until I hear my father speak again.

"Braeden?" he calls out.

I turn around to face him again, my back to the office door.

"Tread lightly with Phoenix, son," he says. "Some people don't want to be saved."

I don't respond, but nod my head slightly before pushing the door open, heading back through the hospital and into the cold morning light.

Phoenix

Forty eight hours. It seems like an eternity. I lay in my bed, the room completely black. Rain is snoring lightly, the sound somewhat of a comfort to me. *To know that I am, for once, not alone.*

Knowing that I won't be getting any actual sleep for some time, I get up out of my bed, put on a pair of slippers and pull open our bedroom door, the soft glow from the hallway light illuminating my face.

"Be safe." I hear Rain say. I just smile, knowing better than to think I could get out of here undetected.

"I'm just going for a walk, be back soon," I whisper back.

Shutting the door slowly behind me, I look in both directions, a pair of unfamiliar eyes looking back at me.

An older woman with grey hair gives me a small smile from behind the nurse's counter, clearly my disturbance deterring her from her work. I give one in return and head toward the day room. I finally have time to observe my surroundings for the first time since I've been here by myself.

As I saunter down the hallway, I keep close to the wall, my right shoulder scraping across it as though it is there to support me. There are security cameras everywhere, observing every angle of the floor. I'm shocked I hadn't noticed them before. A feeling of panic sets in. I wouldn't be able to hide even if I wanted to.

I walk faster down the hallway when a door to my right flies open, my body slamming into something hard. I fall backwards, my butt hitting the cold tile floor. Looking up, I see a figure standing over me. Something makes me shift my eyes from the figure above and into the room it just exited. It's dark, but some light is shining into it, my eyes meeting the face of another young women wrapped up in a blanket on her bed. The look on her face is something I am familiar with. Fear. Terror. Just as I get a good look at her, the door slams shut. My eyes shift from the room back up to him. Rain's words enter my mind. *The Devil.*

I go to scramble to my feet, a feeling in my gut telling me to get away from him but I am frozen in place. He just continues to stare down at me, his eyes following down the length of my body. Before I can scramble to my feet, I feel a pair of hands helping me up. I get up on my feet, my eyes boring into him. Once I am vertical again, he quickly steps out and around us. As he walks away, he pulls his ID tag on over his head, running his fingers through his hair as he rounds the corner and out of sight. I look over to see who it was that helped me up and I am met with a pair of soft eyes. Standing beside me is a young boy, who I am guessing is around sixteen years old. He gives me a soft smile and I notice that he is still holding onto my arm, making me feel slightly panicked.

"Are you OK?" he asks softly.

I nod, swallowing the lump in my throat. I instinctively pull my arm away from him, even though his touch is nothing but gentle.

"I'm Liam," he says, still continuing to smile.

"Phoenix," I say, giving him a small awkward wave.

Neither of us speaks for a second.

"Thanks for helping me up," I say, realizing how rude I am being.

"You're very welcome," he says as he folds his arms behind his back.

I gnaw on my bottom lip while we stand in the hallway together, not knowing what to say next. I'm not used to these social situations.

"I was just about to go get myself a cookie, would you like to join me?" he asks softly.

"Sure," I squeak out.

He starts to walk down the hallway again and I follow behind him quietly. When we reach the patients' kitchen, Liam reaches in, grabbing a container. He pulls out two cookies, putting each of them on a small napkin. Turning around, he hands one to me and then heads out. He walks into the day area and sits down on one of the couches. I follow, setting myself on the one directly across from him. I can feel myself becoming fidgety, my elbows resting on my knees. I hesitantly look at my cookie. Liam is already almost done with his. He looks up, realizing I am staring at him. He laughs lightly.

"These are my favorite. Just about the best thing in this place." He smiles. "Braeden always makes sure we have plenty of them on hand."

I widen my eyes, my heart races just hearing his name. I look down at my cookie, my fingers picking at the corner of the napkin.

"So, you know Braeden?" I ask, trying to not sound over eager.

"Yeah, he has been really good to me since I've been here. Kinda think of him as a big brother," he says, smiling. I gnaw on my lip some.

"If you don't mind me asking, how long has that been?"

"Three years."

I just look at him, his face blank.

"Isn't that hard? Don't you miss your family?" I ask.

He shakes his head.

"Being in here is better than being out there," he says, looking out the closest window. "It's obvious that my family doesn't care about me. It's been about two and a half years since they last visited me."

My heart aches for this boy. He is younger than me by a few years but he seems so much older. More mature.

"So, what are you in here for?" he asks, eating the last part of his cookie.

A cold sweat breaks out through my body. I hesitate to answer.

"Don't worry, Phoenix, I've heard it all. And I promise you that there are crazier people in here than you."

I chew on the inside of my lip.

"I tried to kill myself," I admit, an odd sensation of relief coming over me.

He doesn't ask any more questions about it. I slowly nibble on my cookie, the taste somewhat comforting. Something normal in this crazy place. Liam perks up, looking at something behind me. My heart begins to race as I slowly turn in my seat, my eyes finding an unfamiliar massive figure towering over me.

"Hey, you two, did you save one for me?" his voice booms, the white of his teeth bright because he is smiling so hard.

The figure moves out from behind me, walking

around and takes a seat on the couch beside me. He looks at me, the smile still on his face.

"You must be Phoenix." He waves, almost like a small child would. "I'm Donovan."

I smile back at him.

"Nice to meet you," I say quietly.

We all fall silent and I just keep my eyes on my cookie, pulling the chocolate chips off and eating them one by one. Donovan and Liam talk, and I sort of phase in and out, my stomach feeling like it's been turned inside out. Then, suddenly, Donovan moves, his arms flailing up in the air in what I assume is part of the telling of an embellished story. My body reacts and I flinch, a whimper leaving my throat. I just look down at the floor, feeling the burn in my cheeks, completely embarrassed.

"I'm so sorry, Phoenix," he says, the tone of his voice apologetic. "I should know better than that."

"It's OK," I mutter.

I keep staring at the ground, contemplating just getting up and heading back to my room.

"Well, I gotta go finish my rounds. Your man Braeden decided to call in sick," he says to what I am assuming is Liam.

I snap my head up.

"Is he OK?" the words flowing out of me before I can stop them.

I look out from under my hair; Donovan looks back

over at me, the smile back on his face.

"Yeah, he was just a little under the weather."

"Oh," I respond.

"Nice to meet you." He nods, and goes to get up slowly from the couch. "Goodnight, Phoenix."

"Night," I whisper.

It's just Liam and I again and I can hear the rain hitting the roof top, the melody it creates is quite calming. I hear Liam yawn, looking at the clock on the wall. He stands up from the couch, stretching out his body.

"I am going to try to go back to bed," he says. "I think the voices have all gone to sleep."

"OK." I respond.

"Do you want me to walk you back to your room?" he offers. I smile.

"No thank you, I think I am going to stay out here a little longer."

"OK, night," he says.

"Good night, Liam, and thank you."

"Anytime," he says before walking out.

I am alone again. Usually this would scare me, never knowing what may lie ahead of me or what mood my stepfather would be in. It was always a convenient time for him, my mom was never home when he usually came home from the bar. But tonight is different and that makes me smile. In a place where I truly know no one, I feel the most at home.

Braeden

I lay awake in bed, it now obvious that I'm not going to get any sleep. I sincerely regret calling in sick, knowing that I will do nothing but stir all night. My body begs for sleep but it never comes. I turn to my side, watching the clock on the wall tick away.

Sighing loudly, I throw the covers off of me and get up. Grabbing my uniform, I throw it on and head into the bathroom. I splash cold water on my face with my good hand, my other one still wrapped tight. I open my medicine cabinet, intending to grab my glasses, but then remember their fate. Phoenix. *Like I could have even forgotten about her.* Slamming the cabinet door shut, I grip the sides of the sink, anger and fury filling my body. She's just a girl for Christ's sake. *How can everything remind you of her?* I look up again at myself in the mirror, remembering what my father said. *Some people don't want to be saved.*

Grabbing my contact containers from the edge of the sink, I put them in and spray myself with a squirt of cologne before flicking off the light. Taking my jacket off the hook along with my bike, I leave the apartment in a hurry. When I get to the top of the staircase, I lean my bike against the wall to zip up my jacket, knowing it's going to be beyond cold outside. I hurry down the stairs, the weight of the bike burning my bad hand. When I get outside, I realize it's raining, but jump on my bike anyways. By the time I reach the hospital, my body is trembling from the cold. I lock up my bike and head up the back stairs and into the employee area. The feeling of anxiousness starts to creep up, an involuntary action. Taking a deep breath, I leave the staff room, the hospital is eerily quiet. As I round the corner, I spot Donovan leaned over the nurse's station, his laughter echoing around me. He instantly notices me, a confused look on his face. Walking over to him, I set my elbows on the counter top.

"I thought you were under the weather?" he says, wiggling his eyebrows. I just sigh.

"Couldn't sleep and, strangely, I decided to come here of all places," I mutter.

Donovan leans back, looking at me strangely.

"What?" I ask.

"Dude, you are, like, dripping all over the floor, were you out frolicking in the fucking rain?"

"I rode my bike here." I say.

He shakes his head.

"You are just asking to get a fucking..."

"If you say a 'cold' I'm gonna fucking slap you," I say emotionless.

"For someone who got a hot piece of ass the other day, you are one emo motherfucker." He laughs while smacking me on the back. I don't respond. My eyes look to the side, finding her door immediately.

"She's on the couch in the day room," I hear Donovan say, my head snapping back to face him.

"Who?" I ask.

"Phoenix," he says nonchalantly.

"You know her?" I say a little louder than expected.

"I do work here, asshole," he states. "We hung out. I think I scared the shit out of her though."

I stand upright.

"What?" I ask sternly.

"Yeah, I moved a little too fast and she freaked," he explains. My heart rate spikes.

"What was she doing?" I ask, clearly confused.

"She was eating cookies with Liam," he states.

I can't hold a smile back, Donovan noticing it immediately. I leave him and walk down the hallway, my steps getting shorter and lighter, as I know that I am getting close to the day area. When I get to the opening of it, I am confused because not a single light is on in the room. *How can she be in here?*

I go to turn around until I see a soft shimmer coming over the back of one of the couches, the moonlight coming out from behind the clouds. I take a few more steps, rounding the corner, a beautiful sight before me. Phoenix is sitting on the couch, but her upper half has fallen over, a light snoring sound coming from her nose. I can't stop staring at her. *What does this beautiful creature hold over me?*

I take another step towards her, her long, flowing hair thrown across the armrest. I go to reach out to touch her, immediately remembering what Donovan said. I can't seem to get my father's voice out of my head. *I've seen it in abuse patients.*

Instead of moving her, I back away slowly from the couch, walking over to the linen closet, pulling out the warmest blanket we have. Going back over to her, I almost expect her to be gone, as though she is a figment of my imagination. *Like she is too beautiful to be real.* I smile when I see her still on the couch, except she has now shifted her body down so she is now vertical. Opening up the blanket, I lay it over her body gently, knowing this is all I can do for her.

Phoenix

I hear voices stirring in my head, and then a sharp pain shooting up my back. Opening my eyes slowly I upright myself, realizing I'm still in the day area. I never made it back to my room last night.

Grabbing the blanket, I pull it up to my chest, getting up from the couch slowly. The room is now full of other patients, making me semi-uncomfortable. I start to make my way back down the hallway, the hospital quite different then it was last night. It's hurried and busy, and I can feel my anxiety kicking in. I start to make my way around the corner faster, my nose picking up a familiar scent, but I can't pinpoint where I know it from. I soon realize it's coming from the blanket wrapped around me. Pulling it up over my nose I inhale, the smell intoxicating. It smells like home after the first rain.

I feel someone watching me, making me look upwards. All I see is him, and no one else. The room around me becomes foggy and everyone else becomes a blur in my vision. It's now that I realize he has been watching me smell this blanket. Now he really knows I'm fucking insane.

My knees start to become weak, feeling completely embarrassed. Before he has time to see my crimson cheeks, I bolt down the hallway in the opposite direction, opening my door quickly, and then slamming it behind me. Leaning up against it I breathe in and out, heavily. Rain comes out from the bathroom, a smile on her face.

"Are you hiding from someone?" she asks giggling.

I slouch, letting the blanket falling to the floor. I breathe out one last loud sigh.

"What the hell is wrong with me?" I ask. For the first time I'm starting to think I belong here.

She comes over to my bed, sitting down and patting besides her. I shimmy my way over and plop myself down.

"I can't..." I mutter. "There's no way..."

Rain lifts her hand up and she rubs the back of my hair, stroking it softly. I close my eyes and instantly flash back to when I was little and my mother used to brush my hair. It is my favorite memory of her.

Although, there aren't many to chose from. I open my eyes again and turn my head to Rain, an apologetic look on her face. I know I don't have to speak for her to understand me. She continues to rub my hair, calming me greatly.

"What do you have to lose when you have nothing left?" she says.

~

Getting out of the shower, I wrap my body in a towel and brush my hair, staring at myself in the mirror. My face is extremely pale with dark circles under my eyes. I touch them with my fingertips, small patches of puffy skin adorning them. Pulling my towel off I go over every scar, for once my arms and legs are not decorated with new bruises. Each scar brings back a certain memory. He will always have a hold on me. These scars will never go away.

Looking back up at the mirror, the sound of cracking glass reaches my ears, but I know it's just a memory. It's as though I can still feel the warm blood oozing down the back of my arm.

~

"Phoenix!" I can hear her scream from the bottom of the stairs.

I lay curled up in my bed, wishing and hoping that I can somehow disappear from the Earth this instant. I have no desire to live. I can hear feet stomping up the stairs, not knowing if it is her or him. Maybe he has

*come to finally put me out of my misery. The door slams
open. I don't turn around to see who it is.*

*"Phoenix Grace," she says, throwing the covers off
of me. The cold air hits my wound, it making me wince.*

*"I have told you to come down..." she begins to say,
pausing mid sentence. She grabs onto my arm so hard
that it makes me flip over.*

"Mom," I scream out. "You're hurting me."

*"What the hell happened to you?" she asks. "I told
you to stay out of trouble."*

*I don't say anything, knowing she won't really listen
to me. I just stare at her, my eyes burning from crying.
She just stares back at me and then puts my arm down
slowly. She turns around and leaves, shutting my door
behind her without saying another word.*

~

I pull my hands off the sink and head back into the
bedroom. I grab a new outfit, sliding it on. Putting my
hair up into a high ponytail, I sigh, not really knowing
what to do next. That's one thing I have learned in here,
days go a lot slower when you have nothing but time.
As Rain and I leave the room, she gives me a reassuring
pat on the back.

"Sometimes the right path isn't the easiest." She
smiles.

We walk back down the hallway, my eyes scanning
and my heart racing. Moments later, we are approached
by tall slender women with a clipboard.

"Phoenix Harper?" she asks, looking at me. I nod.

"I'm Doctor Conrad, if you could please follow me," she says, ushering me in the opposite direction. I look over at Rain.

"It's going to be OK," she assures me.

I bite my lip, nodding slowly. I follow behind the doctor quietly, until we reach a door, her name across it. She opens the door, telling me to enter. When I get inside I know exactly what this is. Another psychological evaluation. Time to find out how crazy I really am.

Braeden

I finish up my duties and it's close to seven in the morning, technically when my shift ends. As I walk past the nurses' station, many of the aides are gathered around. I walk over, wondering what's going on. I immediately spot Donovan.

"What's happening?" I ask, knowing something is wrong.

"Code blue man," he says. *Death of a patient.*

My heart rate spikes and I find myself gripping the counter top.

"It's not her," he says silently and calmly. I let out a big sigh, Donovan turning to me.

"I knew it," he says, his tone of voice still quiet.

We break off from the rest of the group and go down the hallway a little bit.

"I can't explain it," is all I can mutter. "Something about her…."

He puts his hand on my shoulder.

"You always do this." He sighs.

"Do what?" I ask.

"It's because of your mom, right?"

A twinge of anger runs through me, him knowing full well I don't like talking about it.

"I don't know what the hell you are talking about," I spit.

"Braeden, I know we all get attached to patients after a while, Liam looks up to you like a brother. But any time we have a suicidal patient come through here you look like someone ran over your cat."

"I've never had a cat," I respond. Donovan just chuckles.

"Just be careful, is all I'm saying," he shrugs. "She is a human being with feelings, not a figment of your imagination." *It was almost as though he could hear my thoughts.*

The rest of the day goes in a flash, putting my mind on my work. But no matter how hard I try to shut her out, I can't. When I reach her and Rain's bedroom door, I pause, my heart racing. Pushing it open slowly, a part of me is disappointed when the room is empty. I go inside, quickly making work of changing the bed sheets, her scent flowing around me. The blanket I put on her this morning is balled up in the corner.

When I finish up their room, I turn around to exit when I see her frozen in the doorway. Her hair is up and brushed away from her face, giving me a clear view of all her features. She is more breathtaking then I remember. Her eyes shift from me to the surrounding room. She won't keep eye contact with me. I shimmy on my feet a little. *It's now or never.*

"Hello," I say. She seems hesitant to respond.

"Hi," she responds softly, her voice like soft music.

We both quickly fall silent again. I can almost feel the sensation in my fingertips, remembering our first encounter. She smiles and I am memorized.

"You look different without your glasses."She laughs.

I smile. "Is that a good thing or a bad thing?"

She shrugs. I hear a loud noise coming down the hallway, snapping me out of this state of nirvana. Donovan's massive figure passes by the doorway, a huge box in his hands. I sigh when he passes, hoping he didn't notice us until I see his figure again coming at us backwards. He just smiles. *Asshole.*

"Braeden, I need your help," he states.

I curse at him under my breath, not knowing when I will get to speak to her again like this. I take a step towards her, her taking one to the side.

"Have a good day, Phoenix," I say as I walk past her.

I get out into the hallway, shooting Donovan daggered looks. He shoves the cardboard box at me, it makes a clinking sound.

"You're in charge of decorating," he states. I open the boxes slightly, seeing masses of lights and ornaments.

"Why the hell am I in charge of this?" I whine.

"I don't know, because you have an eye for that shit."

"What does that suppose to mean?"

I look around Donovan; Phoenix is watching us in the hallway. He turns around slowly, seeing her as well.

"Phoenix can help you," he states.

She stands upright, almost as though she didn't know we noticed her.

"No, its ok," I say, not wanting her to feel pressured.

"I'll help," she says quietly.

Donovan just winks at me, and then walks around me and out of sight.

"Are you sure?" I ask again. "Don't feel like you have to. It's not something a patient is responsible for."

"What else am I going to do? Rain went outside to paint," she says. Her face falls into a serious expression. "Unless you don't want me to, or I'm not allowed to."

I smile.

"Some help would be great, since other people around here are clearly incompetent," I say, nodding in the direction Donovan wandered off.

I turn around, heading down the hall. I can hear her shuffling behind me. When we reach the day area, I notice there are more boxes and a tree stand sitting in the corner by the TV. I set the box, along with the others, on the couch. I open my mouth to speak to her until I see a massive tree coming through the room. Donovan pops his head up over the top of it.

"Where do you want it, boss?" he asks.

"I assume where the tree stand is," Phoenix says sarcastically.

We both turn to her, her hands immediately flying up in front of her mouth.

"Girl's got some fire in her," Donovan says shocked. "I like it."

"I'm so sorry," she says, her voice shaking.

"Don't apologize," I say. "You're allowed to say whatever you want here."

She slowly pulls her hands down, while Donovan slides the tree into the stand.

"Well, I'll leave you two at it," he says before turning around and heading back out. Looking down at the boxes, I start to go through them, finding the one full of plush ornaments. There are no glass balls or anything sharp for obvious reasons.

"What can I do?" she asks, her face hiding behind her hair.

"Do you want to do the tree first?" I ask.

"Sure," she responds.

I hand her the box. "I'll do lights, you can do ornaments."

We start working, both of us silent. I want to hear her voice, but I can't seem to think of an easy way to start a conversation. I get on top of the ladder and start to string the lights around the top of the tree. I shift my eyes down to watch her slowly place each ornament on the tree very slowly and methodically.

"Are you OK?" I ask, not knowing if she will answer.

She looks up at me finally. I climb back down the ladder, keeping my eyes on her. I wait for her to respond and, to my surprise, she does.

"Just memories you know," she utters. "Christmas was my favorite time of year."

"Was?" I say, wanting to push her further without hurting her.

"Yeah, well before my dad died. We would always go and cut down our own tree and he would put hot chocolate in a thermos to take with us."

She laughs. I smile in response.

"Which was funny because we never had to travel far from our own backyard to find one," she adds.

So she lived out in the woods somewhere?

"That sounds amazing," I respond.

I hear her sigh, and then add another ornament to the tree.

"What happened?" I ask, immediately regretting asking it. "I'm sorry, I shouldn't pry."

"No, it's kinda nice to talk about it." She smiles. "If

you're willing to listen."

"Absolutely," I say, my heart soaring that she is willing to open up so quickly.

"When I turned 15 my father was diagnosed with Hodgkin's. He was my best friend," she says with a twinge of pain in her voice. She doesn't have to say more for me to understand.

"I'm so sorry, Phoenix," I say softly. "I'm sure that was a hard thing to go through."

She just shrugs.

"I guess everything happens for a reason," she mutters. I don't respond, feeling that information was a lot for her to share at once to basically a stranger.

"Do you like Christmas music?" I ask, hoping she will say yes. She nods.

I had spotted some old records in one of the boxes. I pull them out, blowing the dust off. Walking over to our old record player, I put one on, the music softly filling the room. Heading back over to the tree, I resume helping her put ornaments on, the tree starting to look complete. We are quiet, only the music reaching our ears now. It's a strange feeling. I don't feel like we are in the hospital anymore, but two people just hanging out. Doing *normal* things. When we finish the tree we continue to decorate the rest of the room, Phoenix has an incredible eye for detail. For the most part we remain silent, her face changing from joyful to gloomy throughout the process. After what seems like a few hours, we both stand back. The room is almost pitch black now.

"Should we plug in the lights?" she asks.

An idea flashes into my head.

"Can we wait five minutes? I'll be right back!" I say before walking off to the kitchen.

Phoenix

I stand there, my heart racing, wondering where he has gone off to. I inhale deeply, my nerves on high throughout our entire encounter but the smell of the tree seems to calm me slightly. *Smells like home.* I fidget with my hands, impatiently waiting. Walking around the room, I go through the boxes again, making sure we haven't missed anything. When I get to the last box, I overturn it and a bundle of mistletoe falls out onto the floor.

Reaching down I pick it up and hold it between my fingers. I smile, remembering when my father used to give me Eskimo kisses whenever we would pass underneath it. I find the tape and climb up on top of the couch, reaching up to attach it to the archway. Just as I climb back down, Braeden comes around the corner, two mugs in hand. He smiles at me, obviously not seeing the mistletoe. He hands me one of the mugs and I reach out with a shaky hand.

"I know it will never be as good as your father's..." he says, taking a sip.

Looking down I realize what he is talking about. He made me hot chocolate. I fight back the tears, so many memories flooding through me. The record changes songs, the melody recognizable. I look over at Braeden, his hands gripping the handle of his cup tight.

Taking a sip of my hot chocolate, I close my eyes, almost feeling the snow crunching under my feet. When I open them again, Braeden is no longer at my side. I look around the room, making out his figure far off, moments later the entire room lighting up in all colors of the rainbow. It's so beautiful I fight even harder to not let the tears fall. Braeden returns to my side.

"It's so beautiful," I whisper.

"Yes it is," he answers, but his eyes are not facing forward.

Taking another sip of my hot cocoa, I look up once more at the mistletoe, Braeden's eyes following mine. My heart skips a beat, a lump in my throat forms. Leaning forward, I place my lips on Braeden's cheek, feeling the warmth of his skin on my lips, it makes me inhale deeply.

Pulling away quickly, I notice that Braeden's face has no emotion. A flash of panic flows through me, feeling as though I have just made a grave mistake. I can't form words, my body in panic mode. Before Braeden has time to say anything, I turn around abruptly, the hot chocolate spilling over the mug's edge and burning my hand slightly.

Braeden

I stand there, holding onto my mug, my palms sweaty. When "All I Want for Christmas" came on the record player, I panicked internally. Looking down at her, I have never seen a more beautiful person on this planet. It's amazing how far she has come in the short amount of time. Donovan's words swirl around in my head, diverting my attention between her and my fucked-up mind.

"It's so beautiful," I hear her say beneath her breath, taking me out of my trance.

"Yes, it is," I say, unable to hold the words back.

Looking over at her, I see her eyes shift to the ceiling, confusing me. I follow, finally noticing the small batch of mistletoe now hanging from the entryway. I swear my heart skipped numerous beats. Mere seconds later, I feel her lips on my cheek, her skin delicate, that feeling of when we first touched even stronger, now flowing through me. And just as fast as it started, it was over. The sound of sloshing reaches my ears. The feeling leaves me, making me open my eyes. She is gone, nowhere in sight. *She's not a figment of your imagination.* Setting my mug down, I sprint after her, reaching her just as she gets to her bedroom door.

"Phoenix," I breathe out, wanting to touch her shoulder but I refrain. She turns halfway around to face me, her hand still on the door handle.

"Goodnight, Braeden," she says no emotion on her face.

"Sweet dreams," I respond.

She pushes open the door, slipping into the dark abyss. I stand there for a few seconds, not knowing what to feel.

~

When I make it back to my apartment, I am relieved that it's empty, only god knows where Bret is at this hour. Placing my bike against my bedroom wall, I plop down on the bed, my body in both an exhaustive and contented state. I lay there for what seems like an eternity. My mind going over anything and everything it can remember. The way her hair shined underneath the lights of the Christmas tree. The way her delicate fingers placed each ornament on the branches. The way each one of her scars stood out like a bright star in the sky, each a symbol of her survival. Lying in my bed, I think about everything. Every moment since Phoenix Harper came into my life. Was Donovan right? Was I trying to save her because I was too late for my mother? Perhaps she is too late to save. I hear my front door creak open, not wanting to deal with his bullshit at the moment.

I remain lying in my bed, hoping that if I don't move he won't notice me in the dark room. The footsteps stop outside my door. Seconds later I am blinded by light, something being thrown at my stomach.

"Figured you could use these," I hear Donovan say. Reaching down, I pick up the box of animal crackers that are now at my side.

"Thanks," I say, sliding my body up so that I am now leaning against my pillows.

Donovan jogs from my doorway, bouncing his massive form onto my bed.

"Dude get off my bed," I mutter as I open the box.

"Fuck you, man, I'm beat," he says, rolling over onto his back. We both lay there, only the sound of me eating apparent.

"So how'd it go?" he asks. I pop a few more crackers in my mouth.

"Fine," I mutter. He turns over to face me, his hand holding his chin up.

"That's all you're going to say?" he say, clearly not satisfied by my answer. He just flutters his eyelashes, obviously not wavering.

"She kissed me," I say, trying to hide the smile. Donovan shoots upwards, bouncing on my bed with his knees.

"Stop it!" I say as the crackers are being flung across my bed.

He picks one up from the bed, popping it in his mouth, spitting it out immediately.

"Shit tastes like cardboard," he says, wiping his tongue on his shirt.

"More for me then," I say, recollecting them all. He is now at my side, his back against the pillows as well.

"You are too close for comfort," I say, leaning away from him.

"You are clearly not comfortable with your sexuality," he responds. "Just tell me what the fuck happened."

"I told you, she kissed me," I state, stopping there.

"Wow," he states. "I thought for sure you were going to tonsil attack her first."

I roll my eyes.

"It's not like that with her."

"It's not?" he asks.

I sigh.

"I feel protective of her. Plus it was just on the cheek," I correct. Donovan pauses before responding.

"I'm sure that was a big risk for her," he says. "I mean, I didn't even touch her and she flipped. The fact that she touched you, actually *touched* you. That means something."

I hadn't even thought about it.

"Yeah, well, I'm sure our supervisor is going to enjoy seeing that on the security camera," I state.

"Nah, I wouldn't worry about that," he responds, a crooked smile on his face.

I furrow my brow at him.

"I turned the camera angle when I was brining in the tree, pretty sure it was pointed straight at the ceiling for about four hours."

I almost fly off the bed, wanting to give him a hug but I contain myself, realizing how incredibly fucking awkward that would be.

"Thanks, man," I say, nodding my head.

"Anytime," he responds. "But just be careful, I can't always be doing shit like that." I just nod. We both fall silent again.

"So, I have to ask, why her? There has got to be more to her than just her being a suicide patient," Donovan states.

"I don't really know," I respond, pondering the question. "Ever since she got her, she has never left my mind. Whether I wanted her there or not," I continue.

Donovan puts his fist under his chin looking like a child at story time. I laugh lightly.

"When I first met Phoenix in the admittance room, she looked terrified, her eyes barely looking past the hair. At that point, she was just another patient. Just another lost cause." I pause. "But when we touched, it was unlike anything I had ever felt before. It was like I felt everything she felt. I felt her pain and suffering. I wanted nothing more than to take it all away. To make her happy."

I stop again, wondering if I should continue on. It feels oddly relieving to talk about this.

"So, you're like her guardian angel?" Donovan asks. I laugh.

"I don't know." I put my hands to my face, rubbing my eyes. "God, I've gone completely mental," I mutter to myself. We are both quiet for a while. "I just want to show her that her life is worth living, that she can't let her past dictate her future."

"No one better to show her than you," Donovan states. I just give him a crooked smile.

"Do you want to go grab a drink?" he asks, now bouncing up and off the bed.

"I've had a long-ass day. I think I'm just gonna stay in for tonight," I state.

"Alright," he says, heading towards the door before stopping. "Oh yeah, I meant to ask you, since Phoenix was admitted after we took present requests, you got any ideas on what to get her?"

I sit there, it only taking a second for me to think of

something.

"Yeah, I'll take care of it."

"Cool, well, are you gonna be coming tomorrow night for the feast?" he asks.

"Yeah, I'm working a double shift," I explain. Donovan winks at me before exiting my room.

~

The buzzing of my alarm clock reaches my ears, my body exhausted but ecstatic. I didn't do much after my shift, most of it was spent in my room until the day reached its end, the sunset now at sunrise. Pulling my covers off, I spring up out of bed, throwing on a new pair of scrubs. The ride over to the hospital is hasty, not wanting to spend a moment away, excited to see what today will bring me. The hospital is lively. I put my things away, wanting to start my shift as soon as possible.

Knowing that I have to get actual work done, I do my duties first, hoping that I will have some downtime later on when the Christmas Eve dinner is being prepped. But not much to my liking, the afternoon drags on, making every minute without seeing her unbearable. Looking down at my list of duties, I notice that today I have to change the sheets in every patient's room. I don't know if I am happy or nervous. I have changed patients sheets thousands of time without a second thought, but hers, it seems intrusive.

Grabbing a few sets of clean ones, I make my way to

her room, hesitating at the closed door. When I push it open, she is nowhere to be found.

"She's out for a walk," I hear Rain say, her figure coming out from the bathroom. "I think she had quite a night last night."

"What do you mean?" I ask, suddenly worried.

"I'm pretty sure you were there." She laughs.

I'm an idiot.

"Oh," I respond. "Did she say anything about it?"

"She doesn't need to." Rain smiles. "She didn't sleep much though; she tossed and turned for quite some time."

I quickly make way of changing the beds before leaving the room. As I head back to my station, I look behind me, making sure that no one is following me. I stop at a door, sliding my key into the knob and push it open, making sure it latches behind me.

~

The sun is now starting to set, the lights of the city around us coming on. Grabbing my coat I go out into the courtyard, knowing that she hasn't come back in. Once I get outside, even with a coat on I can feel the cold air through it. I spot her immediately, her arms wrapped around herself, her long brown hair whipping in the wind. I make my way over to her slowly, hoping not to startle her. I notice that she is wearing nothing but a thin pair of pants and a t-shirt.

"If you stay out here any longer you may freeze," I

say quietly.

She turns just her head to face me.

"I like it out here." She smiles.

"Aren't you cold?" I ask.

She just shrugs. "I've felt worse."

"I can only imagine," I mutter. She turns to fully face me.

"I'm sure you can't," she says harshly.

Looking to my side to see if anyone is near, I take a step towards her, ending up only mere inches from her.

"Just because I'm not a patient here doesn't mean I haven't felt pain," I snap, not being able to stop the words from leaving my mouth. Things fall silent. "You don't know anything about me, Phoenix."

She looks down at her feet. I've clearly upset her.

"I'm sorry," I say, trying to back track. She brings her head up.

"No, I'm sorry," she says. "And you're right, I don't know you. We've talked plenty enough about me though."

"I'm not that interesting," I say. Her face falls into a frown.

"I'm sure that's not true," she states, biting her lip gently.

"It will take me hell of a lot longer than the five minutes we have, to explain my life."

"Will you promise to tell me about it one day?" she asks.

"Someday," I smile crookedly.

I look back into the windows of the hospital, seeing everyone getting ready to eat.

"I think your dinner is being served, you should probably get in there, and Rain is waiting for you."

She goes to walk around me, but I match her.

"I don't mean to scare you," I sputter.

"You don't scare me," she says lightly. I look down at my hand.

"It's, uh, accustomed that the hospital gives presents to the patients."

I pull something out of my pants pocket. I swallow hard before I speak again.

"And, while it may be totally against hospital policy and I can get my ass fired for this, I think this is something you should have."

I hold it out to her, it sitting delicately in the palm of my hand.

Phoenix

I can't do anything but stare. The gold chain flickers in the moonlight. *He's giving me my necklace back?* The tears threaten to fall and as much as I fight, I lose. The warm liquid flows down my frozen cheeks.

Reaching out, I take it delicately in my hands, feeling as though it may crumble from my fingertips at any moment.

"But why?" I ask, knowing stuff like this is forbidden.

"Because I know how important things like this can be," he says with a twinge of pain behind his voice.

"Thank you so much," I repeat.

"You're welcome. I'm afraid that you can't wear it

though. Technically patients can't have something that they can..." he stops mid sentence.

"...hurt themselves with," I finish for him. He just nods.

"I promise," I say while nodding. "You have no idea how much this means to me."

"I'm glad that I can bring you happiness, Phoenix," he says. "Well, you better get in there."

"OK." That desire builds up again, the same feeling as last night. When I reach the door, I turned back around.

"Just remember, you promised," I say.

He nods.

I give him a large smile before entering back into hospital, clutching the necklace in my hand. I sit down at the table, the smell in the kitchen is nothing short of incredible. With Rain at my side, I feel content. Happy.

As we eat, I get small glimpses of Braeden as he walks by, his eyes always finding mine. The feeling of anxiety is now replaced with excitement. I eat everything on my plate, not having had a real Christmas Eve dinner since I moved from my father's to San Francisco after his death.

"Someone was hungry," I hear Rain say, her eyes on my now empty plate. I just smile at her.

As I sit around watching everyone else eat, I look at the tree that Braeden and I put up and it makes me smile. My eyes then look up at the mistletoe, my smile falling when I notice it is not longer there. I drop my eyes downward, looking at the hair now standing up on my arms. Something subconsciously tells me to look up again and out through the kitchen windows into the direction of the nurses' station. That's when I see him. Them.

I snap my eyes away from his, my heart beating so fast that I fear I may pass out. I remain seated in my chair, every muscle in my body locked. My eyes looking. Searching. I finally spot him outside another window, his back now facing me. It takes everything in my power to not scream out his name, the notion of that even scaring me. I start to gnaw on my lip so hard that a warm, metallic taste reaches the tip of my tongue within seconds. Braeden isn't turning around and it makes me even more frustrated. I search out for someone else, anyone at this point.

I look to my left, the chair next to me empty. I hadn't even noticed she left. Tears start to well up and they cloud my vision. The forcefulness of the tears becomes too great; a slow drop runs down my cheek. I try to peer through the window again, realizing that I have lost sight of them, not knowing if they are still here or not. I feel so helpless. Alone. And the thing is, I'm surrounded by people. The only place I thought I felt safe can't even keep the fear away. Shifting my eyes around the table, all the other patrons are absorbed in their food, no one seems to notice my frightened state. No one ever noticed. Not here. Not ever.

I look over at Braeden again. This time his eyes are on me, not moving anywhere else in the slightest. He's clearly noticed my anxiety and all I can do is shift my eyes in the direction of the nurse's station, hoping that Braeden has picked up mind reading since I last talked to him. My body is trembling, the wooden chair creaking slightly with each quiver. Braeden remains fixated on me until a figure steps in front of him, a white doctor's coat taking up most of my peripheral vision, essentially blocking any and all views of him. I remain locked in a stare, not knowing what else to do.

A large crash reaches my ears, making me jump in my chair, and clutch my chest. Peeling my eyes away from the window, I see two aides wrestling a patient to the ground. I take in all the food that is now thrown across that end of the table, pieces of porcelain plate joining them. I secretly thank my lucky stars for the distraction. All eyes are on the unruly patient, giving me a chance to leave the room unnoticed. Reaching up slowly but keeping my eyes focused upwards, I run my fingers along my silverware. Feeling the curvature of the spoon, the triple prongs of the fork. The small jagged blade of the knife. Wrapping my fingers around the handle, I continue to look upward, waiting for someone to stop me. Someone to rip it out of my hand. But they don't. The metal of the knife is cool against my clammy palms as I drag it towards me. I know what I am doing is wrong, but having it on me feels...*safe*. The knife is incredibly dull, but it will do.

Tucking it into the hem of my pants, it's skinny enough to be concealed easily. Sliding out my chair, I rise slowly, needing to get out of here. I get up calmly. Well, what I think is calm, but I know that if anyone truly saw me, they would know I am far from it. Walking down the length of the table, I reach the edge of the kitchen and stop in my tracks.

Down the hallway from me is a mass of people. People I know. Facing me is Carl, the look on his face couldn't be described as anything less than deathly. Next to him was Elaina. I could see her eyes peering over the shoulders of the figures that were not facing me. But those figures didn't need to face me for me to know instantly who they were. One was clearly Braeden. I could pick him out of a crowd within seconds. The other was the coated figure that had come to Braeden earlier. It's Dr. Harris. He had told me that he would be my attending physician here, but I hadn't seen him around before now.

As I stand there, Braeden slowly turns around to face me, his sympathetic look no longer on his face, a look of rage replacing it. He shifts his head back to the crowd, mumbling something, his eyes looking at Dr. Harris. He then shifts back to me, and starts walking toward me. My heart starts to beat faster, the rate now equating to what feels like the flutter of a humming bird's wings. I watch with tunnel vision as he comes toward me. It only takes a few strides for him to cross the room. He reaches out as though he is going to grab my upper arm, but he stops himself his arm stretched out mid air. He drops it instantly, a small part of me upset by the fact that he won't touch me. Also a new feeling for me. His eyes remain on the floor for a second then dart back up to me. He clears his throat before speaking.

"Phoenix," he says finally looking up at me. "Come with me, please."

He starts to walk away from me and it only takes mere seconds for me to follow. I don't look back. I never want to look back. I follow behind Braeden closely, reaching my bedroom door in no time. He opens the door slowly, allowing me to enter first. We don't say anything, each second ticking by seems like an eternity. He clears his throat again.

"Well, I guess I'll just be leaving. You stay in here until this gets resolved."

He takes a step away from me and I instinctively reach out, my finger tips only grazing the sleeve of his shirt. I retract my arm hastily. He must have felt it because he turns back around. I gnaw on my already tender lip.

"Please, I don't want to be alone when they come in here," I swallow. He takes a step towards me, followed by another one.

"Phoenix," he says, saying it only above a whisper.

The way he says it, the way it flows off his tongue, makes me want to cry. His eyes are piercing into me now, the green in them bright. My mind reviews his previous sentence, realizing there were parts of it I don't understand. *Until this gets resolved.*

"What did you mean by this gets resolved?" I ask. The look on his face is indescribable, it shifts rapidly through several emotions that he doesn't even give me a second to identify.

"I don't want to assume anything," he states, the statement rather vague. I look at him confused. "I want you to know that I'd never pressure a patient into telling me their story. We always know a little bit about them, of course, but we never know the whole thing."

I swallow.

"I know what you tried to do to yourself, Phoenix," he says. "But I know that it wasn't you that caused that pain. The pain that made you think you had no other way out."

My bottom lips starts to quiver.

"And I want you to know...."

There is a loud knock on the door, Braeden stops mid sentence. He walks backwards, opening the door slowly. A flush of panic flows through me, the idea of Braeden being in the room with them. With me. But much to my relief there was only one figure standing in the open doorway, blonde hair shining in the light.

Braeden and Dr. Harris talk in hushed tones, the conversation brief. Before he leaves, he looks up at me, giving me an apologetic smirk before leaving again. Braeden shuts the door, turning back around.

"They're gone," he mutters.

My heart jolts and I am rendered speechless. I do nothing but stare.

"Phoenix?" Braeden asks, clearly noticing my state.

"How?" I ask, it being the only word I can utter. Braeden looks down at the ground again.

"To protect you," he says softly. My stomach does flip flops. "Is that not what you wanted?"

"You are allowed to just stop people from coming in here?" I ask. He clasps his hand behind his back.

"We do what is right for the patient," he states, almost like he is reading it from a textbook. "We may not know the whole story, Phoenix, but it wasn't hard for my father to catch on. The scars. The way your mood changed whenever your parents were around."

"They are not my parents," I say sternly.

He frowns slightly.

"While he may not be, she is, Phoenix."

I huff.

"I know that's not what you want to hear, but according to the state, she is your legal guardian."

The fire burned inside of me. I almost feel mad at my father for leaving me. Leaving me with her. I felt like crying, but I didn't want Braeden to see me like that. I shake my head to distract myself.

"So, you banned them?" I ask.

He nods.

"Well, really only Carl," he says. "But when my father refused to let him through, your mother got very...flustered."

My mother didn't have the ability to be flustered. She was either very calm, or very irate. I've got a pretty good guess of which one she displayed.

"I'm sorry you had to deal with that," I mutter.

"I just glad you didn't have to," Braeden says, a small smile on his face.

My heart jumps. I wanted to ask so many questions, I wanted to know why he was being so nice to me. Was it something he did with every patient? But there was only one thing I could say.

"Thank you, Braeden," I say softly. He just nods and then checks the clock on the wall.

"I have to get back to work," he says in a disappointed tone. "Are you going to be OK?"

"I think so," I respond softly.

He goes to turn around, but I stop him.

"Can you please thank your father for me, too?" I ask.

"Of course," he says before pulling open the door.

"Good night, Phoenix."

"Good night."

I remain in the same position for quite some time,

almost not believing all that had happened. I had come into contact with Carl and came out unscathed. Something that was definitely new. And I have Braeden and his father to thank for that. Within seconds of Braeden leaving, the door opens again, it making me jump a little. I see Rain peek through the doorway, a worried look on her face.

"Are you OK?" she asks, stepping inside and shutting the door behind her.

I just nod. I know I don't have to explain what just happened to Rain, the look on her face already tells me she knows everything. She walks over to me, wrapping her arms around me. It's nice having someone hold me. Someone that I care about, and that cares about me. I put my arms around her as well, remaining in this position until I pull back.

"Sorry I wasn't there," she says. "I had a visitor."

"Your parents?" I ask.

She shakes her head. "Someone way more special."

"Who?" is all I can utter.

"Landon," was all she said.

How did she find time for a boyfriend? Where did she find him?

"You gotta give me more details than that!" I shout, suddenly feeling like a high school gossiping girl.

"Well, I met him last week," she starts.

"He works here?" I ask, clearly confused.

"No, no, no," she says quickly.

She takes my hand.

"You see, when you are...trusted, you are allowed to go out."

I stare at her even more confused than before.

"Rain, what are you talking about?" I ask.

"Outside the hospital, into the real world," she says, making air quotes when she says the last two words. "Along with an aide and a social worker of course."

"And that's where I met Landon," she squeals.

I put my fingers in my ear, fearing the glass in the windows was going to break. When she stops, I pull them back out.

"So, where did you meet this Romeo?" I ask, knowing Rain wants to gush about it.

"Well, I was starving and really just didn't want to eat the food here, so Donovan took me to a diner, along with my social worker, Vivienne."

She pauses and then starts back up immediately.

"So, there I was, sitting in the booth, eating my salad. I accidently knocked my knife off the table. He ran over and picked it up for me."

My heart drops. I had completely forgotten about the knife, now feeling the metal against my skin. I guess between my family drama and my alone time with Braeden I had forgotten about it. I try to pay attention to what Rain is saying, hoping to not give away my inner freak out.

"So, yeah...and then he said he wanted to see me

again...." I hear.

I have clearly missed part of the story.

"That's awesome," I respond.

"You missed part of that didn't you?" she asks laughing.

Right. Can't keep anything from Rain. I hang my head.

"I'm such a shitty friend," I say. I hear her laugh.

"You're a great friend, Phoenix," she says, reaching out and holds my hand. "I know that you have other things on your mind."

"Wait, what's that?" she adds. I panic.

Could she possibly know? Is there an outline of it?

"Phoenix?" she asks, her head bobbing back and forth as though she is looking for something. I look at her.

"What's what?" I ask, trying to not lose my composure.

"On your finger," she says pointing.

I look down, opening my closed fists. I can't hold a smile back. I had forgotten that I wrapped the necklace around my finger, the heart pendent held in my palm.

"It's my necklace," I mutter, not able to get rid of my smile.

"And where did you get that?" she asks, clearly knowing the answer.

"Is there anything you don't know?" I ask. She laughs.

"I don't know everything," she says. "I can't tell you exactly what's going to happen next. I mostly just feed off people's emotions. And I can feel when there is going to a large shift in those emotions. After that I'm a really good guesser."

She stops.

"I'm not making any sense am I?" she asks.

"Actually, it kinda makes perfect sense," I say. "I'm just not used to be around people can gauge emotions...like at all."

I think about Elaina, all the times I would come downstairs, my eyes bloodshot from crying. She never even flinched. She never even looked my way.

"So, when are you seeing Landon again?" I ask, trying to keep my concentration this time. She shrugs.

"He said he would come back to visit me sometime, not a specific date."

"Oh," I respond.

We both fall silent for a second.

"Can I ask you something? Something...intrusive?" I say.

"Of course!" she says with glee.

"When do you get to leave here?" She laughs slightly.

"I choose to be here," she responds. *Who would want to be here, under their own will?*

"Why do you stay?" I ask, trying to understand.

"I feel safe here," she explains. "Plus, I don't really

have anywhere else to go."

My heart sinks.

"I am a shitty friend," I repeat. I realize I never asked her about her.

"There isn't really much to know," she starts. "Parents both...do you really want to hear about this?"

"Yes. I do. If you want to tell," I declare. I didn't want to pressure her, knowing from firsthand experience how hard it is to air your dirty laundry to strangers.

"It's really pretty simple, my parents had me sent here and then they decided to take off..."

"Take off?" I ask, her choice of words...vague.

"They moved out of the country," she says, no emotion on her face.

I put my hand to mouth.

"I'm so sorry," I say, walking over to her, putting my hand on her back. I see a single tear form in the duct of her left eye. I don't know what to say or do. I've never comforted anyone before.

"It's for the best," she simply states. "Even though they were my family, I never felt connected to them, especially after the things that they did." My heart jumps.

"Which is..."

"My parents...were unorthodox. They don't believe in modern medicine, so they tried different ways to rid me of my demons."

I jerk my head back, trying to understand what exactly she was talking about. I didn't have to say anything before she answered my questions.

"Exorcism..." she states.

I don't even respond, not knowing what to say. *Didn't they only do that in cheesy scary movies*? I can only imagine what that entails.

"And when that didn't work, much to their surprise," she rolls her eyes. "Then they went a little more abrasive."

"Do I even want to know?" I say.

Her hands leave her side and find their way to the hair behind her ear. She moves it away slowly, exposing small scars behind her earlobe.

"Electric shock therapy," she states.

That is something I do know about. I had learned about it in school, but knew it was popular back in the 40's and 50's. The fact that her parents thought this was good for her makes me sick to my stomach. How could anyone want to cause physical harm to their own child? I have to hold back a laugh, realizing the hilarity in that thought.

"I'm so, so sorry," I say, knowing my apology doesn't change anything. She flattens her hair so that the scar is now gone again.

"It was a dark time in my life," she says. "And I don't ever plan on going back there again."

This great urge to hug her overcomes me, wanting to

show her that I am there for her, just like she has been for me since I have been there.

I wrap my arms around her, her doing the same. We stand there for a few minutes in silence, nothing but the sounds from the hallway reaching my ears. Lesson learned for the night? There has been two broken hearts in this room all along. After a few minutes Rain pulls back.

"I think I am going to go to bed," she states.

"OK," I say softly. "I am going to go take a shower."

Rain is the closest thing I had to family since my father's death. Sliding into my closet, I reach down, pulling the knife from the pants. I hold it in my hand, staring at it. What the hell am I going to do with it? If I turn it in I know they will think I am suicidal again. I choose to hide it in an old sweatshirt, realizing I have never seen them search our closets before. I jump into the shower, the warm water relieving some of the tension I had been holding onto. When I finish I hop out quickly, throwing on a pair of pajamas before the frigid air can hit my body. When I make it back to the bedroom it is pitch black, the sound of Rain's breathing reaching my ears. For once, the silenced darkness is welcoming.

Braeden

With my hand propping up my head, I attempt to read what's on the page, but my eyelids protest, drooping constantly as every second passes. I have been at work for 15 hours now, a part of me wishes I hadn't agreed to this double shift. But another part of me doesn't want to be anywhere else but here. My mind shifts to her as it frequently does now, thinking about the moment I gave Phoenix that necklace. The smile on her face was indescribable! It felt fucking incredible to give someone that much joy. I couldn't care less if I got fired. That smile alone would be worth it. Shaking my head, I try to pay attention to my book again.

"Fuck," I mutter to myself. "I've read this sentence

seven goddamn times."

I let out a heavy sigh, slamming the book shut and pushing it away from me. I only have a little over a week left before school starts up again and let's just say I haven't done much of my winter break reading. I'm exhausted just thinking about it. Medical school isn't what I would call easy and it doesn't come as natural to me as it did for my father. But now I couldn't see myself doing anything else. When my mother passed, I knew exactly what I wanted to be when I grew up. Not too many eight year olds know what they want to be, but I did. I wanted to save people. I never wanted anyone else to feel the pain I did when my mother took her own life. Pushing my chair back I stand up, I stretch my hands up over my head, letting out a large yawn, knowing I have to get back to work. I shift to look up at the clock on the wall. Nine a.m.

Most of the patients should be up, breakfast currently being served. I exit the break room and head into the nurses' station, trying to remember what duties I have left. Just as I am about to start, I feel a tap of my shoulder. I turn around to see who it is.

"Braeden, I need to speak to you," he says, flicking his finger in motion for me to follow him.

I set the clipboard down, my stomach doing flip flops. *Had he found out?* I follow behind, reaching his office door in seconds. He pushes it open, letting me enter first. I sit down in one of the chairs opposite his desk. He walks around the length of it, sitting down in his large, brown leather chair, his hands folded in front. I can feel my heart racing. I know this can't be good. The look on Victor's face is as hard as marble. We both remain silent for a second, his body shifting in his chair, the silence eating me.

"Braeden," he starts to say. "How are you feeling?"

I furrow my brow.

"Fine, sir," I respond. He continues to stare at me.

"You know that I don't like to meddle in people's affairs, but when it comes to our patients and our aides..." he says.

Here we go. We both fall silent again. He lets out a sigh and pulls out a chart, reading through it. The room is so quiet you could hear a pin drop.

"I see that we had an incident last night?" he asks, almost as a rhetorical question.

I swallow. "Yes."

"Do you mind explaining that to me?" he says harshly.

I sit up in my chair. "I felt that a patient was at risk," I say sternly. "Is it not my job to protect them?"

My anger is starting to rise.

"There is no need for an attitude," he states. He continues to read the chart, not responding.

"And what about the mother?" he asks.

I don't respond, eventually making him look up.

"I asked you a question," he says harshly. I become

nervous, feeling as though we are prying in someone else's business.

"I suspect only the step father has caused her physical pain," I say in a monotone.

"And what makes you suspect that?" he asks.

"The look on her face when she saw him," I mutter.

He narrows his eyes a little. "And my father also suspects," I add quickly. "He was actually the one who suggested that he be removed."

He looks down at the chart again. I can feel my fingers becoming twitchy, wanting to read that chart for myself. I know whatever she has told the doctors and psychologist would be in there. But I could never invade her mind like that.

"I have noticed you have become close with..." he looks down at the chart again. "Miss Harper."

My heart skips a beat. I can't lie. Nor do I want to. I just nod. He doesn't respond and the room falls silent again.

"It's today isn't it?" he asks.

"Excuse me?" I ask, not understanding.

"It's today's date right?" he says softly, his hard expression changing.

I look at the paper calendar on his desk. *How could I have forgotten?* A lump in my throat greatens. I nod.

"Thank you, Braeden, that's all I needed to know," he says, waving me off.

Getting up from my chair, I exit his office, closing

the door behind me. I stretch out my hand, then close it again; realizing they were clenched the whole time. And just as I'm about to be lost in my own head, a faint sound of laughter echo's down the hallway. I don't need to second guess whose it is. Following the sound, I find myself walking by the recreation area, my eyes instantly finding her. She is laughing, a wonderful sight that quite nearly breaks through my sullen mood. I notice that she's wearing makeup, her long hair flowing down the curvature of her back. She is facing me, her eyes finding me quickly. She is still smiling, and as much as I want to return one, I can't.

Phoenix

I shift around in my bed, pulling the covers over my head, the air in the room cold. Can't they turn the damn heater on? Moments later I feel a poke on my shoulder, knowing exactly who it is.

"What?" I say in a whiny voice.

"Come on," she says, poking me in the shoulder again.

Throwing the covers off, I flip around to look at her, giving her my best "don't fuck with me" look, but as soon as I see her, I can't do it. Rain is standing by my bed, her hair perfectly straight. The makeup on her face is immaculate. *How the hell did she always look so good?* I lean up slightly while continuing to look at her.

"Do you have your own makeover fairies that you're not sharing?" I ask, a sly smile on my face.

Rain's eyes become large, a smile coming across her face.

"No," I say sternly, grabbing the blanket and pulling it up and over my head again.

"Please," I hear her beg.

How can I say no to her? I let out a heavy sigh.

"Fine, do with me what you will," I say, pulling my body out of bed, not able to deny Rain anything that would bring her joy. I hear a small squeal escape her lips, her body now bouncing off the floor. I stand there, waiting for her instruction.

"You took a shower last night, right?" she asks me.

I nod in return.

"Perfect!" she exclaims. "Your hair will be just greasy enough." I grab my hair in my hand to one side, looking at it. "My hair isn't greasy."

Rain giggles. "I didn't mean you had dirty hair, it's just easier to style when it's not freshly washed," she explains.

She grabs my hand, taking the spare wooden chair in the other. She sets it up in the bathroom in front of the mirror, leading me over to it. I plop my body down, a sigh escaping my throat. It's now that I realize how nervous I am. I wasn't allowed to wear makeup in Elaina's house. She always said I didn't need to look like a hooker under her roof. It's not like my father even knew where to begin when it came to girls stuff. I can remember when we went shopping for my first bra. A small laughter escapes my lips.

"What's so funny?" Rain asks. I look up her in the mirror.

"Nothing," I say still smiling.

"Doesn't look like nothing," she says.

"I was just thinking about my dad," I explain. She just smiles.

"It's nice to see you smile when you talk about your family for once." I reach up, running my hand along the back of my neck.

"He's the only one I consider family," I explain. I look up at her again, a pout on her lips.

"Well, of course you, too," I say smiling. She giggles then puts the brush in my hair, slowly running it thorough my strands.

"We'll be each other's sisters," she says softly, her demeanor changing slightly.

I can tell she is lost in thought as much as I am. Reaching up, I place my hand on top of hers.

"We'll be the family we never had." I smile, Rain's returning.

"I'd like that very much," she says through a cracked voice.

I let go of her hand and she resumes brushing, it actually feels fantastic. When she finishes, she sets the big brush down, picking up a large round one.

"I'll be right back," she exclaims.

She leaves the bathroom, coming back moments later with a blow dryer in hand, and an aide trailing behind her.

"He has to watch us use this and then I have to give it right back," she explains.

She picks up the round brush again and flicks on the blow dryer, my thoughts being drowned out. I watch Rain in the mirror, trying to follow what she is doing but her hands move like a whirlwind. Minutes later she switches it off, a large smile on her face.

"You have incredible hair, Phoenix," she exclaims. "You should be a model! Don't you agree, Donovan?"

I had almost forgotten he was here. The fire in my cheeks is burning hot.

"You don't have to answer that," I mutter to him.

"I think you're smokin'."He laughs. *Now I can die of embarrassment.*

"Uh, thanks?" I respond, not really knowing what to say.

We both hear Rain huff.

"Donovan, you don't say smoking, you say beautiful. Women like it when you call them beautiful," she says sternly.

"Got it," he says as though he was truly listening.

Rain coils up the cord, handing it back to Donovan.

"Thanks," she says.

"Anytime, pipsqueak," he responds.

"See you ladies around," he says before giving both of us a smile and leaving the room.

I just smile at him as he leaves.

"You can just talk to the aides like that?" I ask her. She shrugs.

"Most of them are pretty relaxed, plus I've been here long enough to get to know them personally."

"Oh," was all I could respond with. Does she know Braeden...personally?

I am quiet for a moment, thinking out how I am going to do this. A part of me wants to - no has to - know Braeden's story. There is clearly something there and it's eating me up inside. I swallow before opening my mouth.

"So Rain..." I start out.

"Mmm hmm..." I hear her respond, her attention fixated on my hair.

"Has Braeden ever told you his story?" I ask, feeling like I am prying into his life.

She stops what she is doing and looks up at me in the mirror. Her face changes from ecstatic to somewhat worrisome.

"No," she responds. "But I can always tell something is off with him. And whatever it is, it still very much hurts him to this day."

A million things run through my mind, trying to guess what it is. Rain resumes her work. After what seems like an eternity, she steps back to let me look at myself in the mirror. And that's all I can do. The figure standing in front of me is not me. I don't recognize this person. Her skin is porcelain like. The dark circles from under her eyes are gone. Her eye lids are a dark smoky color, making the color in them pop. Her hair looks soft, large barrel curls surrounding her face. And the scars gone. My lip begins to quiver, trying everything in my power not to cry. I turn to Rain, a large smile still on her face. I wrap my arms around her.

"Thank you," I say, still fighting the tears.

"You're very welcome," she says as I pull back. "You look beautiful, Phoenix."

As much as I fight, tears start to swell up. Rain reaches up, wiping them quickly away.

"You're messing up my masterpiece!" she giggles.

I help wipe them away, not wanting to waste all of her hard work. I turn around, taking one more look in the mirror. I feel...beautiful.

I notice that Rain has left the room, leaving me to my own thoughts. After one more glance in the mirror quickly, I head out, flicking the light off when I leave. Rain and I leave our room, arms linked just like my first day here. When we reach the hallway, my mind instantly switches. My eyes searching.

"So, what do you want to do today?" she asks nonchalantly.

I laugh. *Like there are so many options*. Turning my head, I take a peek outside. The wind is strong, dark clouds lingering.

"Maybe we can just watch some TV?" I suggest.

We walk into the recreation room, a few other patients mingling about. Rain and I sit down on the couch, her handing me the clicker. I spend the next ten minutes flicking through the hundreds of channels, amazed that there is nothing on. As I continue to search, I stop when something catches my eye. I watch the group of sweaty shirtless men bouncing the volley ball back and forth, all of them hooting and hollering like bunch of animals.

"He's really hot," I hear Rain say, her clearly watching it as intently as me.

"I'm more of a Val Kilmer girl," I admit.

"Nothing wrong with that." She laughs. We both go back to watching it. A few minutes later I hear someone speak.

"Phoenix likes herself some sweaty shirtless men," Donovan says, his body standing behind us on the couch.

I pick up the remote, it fumbling out of my hand and falling to the floor. Reaching down I find it, hitting the power off button, the TV going black. Donovan laughs.

"I didn't mean to interrupt you ladies," he explains.

"You weren't," I mutter. Donovan comes around the front of the couch.

"Can I sit?" he asks, ushering to the space next to me.

"Of course," I say.

I scoot over closer to Rain, giving him more room. He plops down, letting out a big sigh. We all sit there for a few minutes not saying much. I can feel the heat off his body, it making me nervous. I start to pick at my fingernails, the silence making me on edge.

"Do you guys want to play cards?" Rain asks.

"Sure," I say.

"Absolutely!" Donovan exclaims.

Rain flies off the couch, grabbing a pack of cards. She comes back, shuffling the new stack in her hands.

"So, what do you want to play?" she asks, looking at both of us. I immediately look up at Donovan. "Have you ever played cards, Phoenix?"

I have a flash back, my father and I playing Go Fish on the kitchen table.

"Just Go Fish," I say quietly.

"I fucking love Go Fish!" Donovan yells, it making me jump.

"Sorry," he says sympathetically.

"It's OK." I smile. "I know you don't mean to do it on purpose."

Rain starts dealing out the cards. I pick mine up, holding them close to my body.

"Phoenix, you go first," Rain says. I look down at my cards.

"Rain, do you have any...three's?" I ask.

She huffs, handing me two cards. We continue to

play, the stack of pairs in front of me growing. That's when I realize I'm having fun. It's Donovan's turn next.

"Phoenix, do you have any five's?" he asks me.

I giggle, shaking my head.

"What the hell," he says, looking down at his cards again. He then leans over, clearly looking at mine. I gasp.

"Are you cheating?"

We all start laughing, it feeling incredible. I take my eyes off of Donovan, looking up, Braeden standing behind him. I find myself smiling harder when I see him, but it instantly falls when I realize something is wrong.

"Hey, man," Donovan says, turning around to face him. "Wanna join?"

"Nah," he says. "You guys look like you are having fun."

"We are!" Rain exclaims. "Phoenix is winning!" I can feel that burn returning.

"Well, I better get back to work," Donovan says getting up.

"Thanks for playing with us," I squeak out.

"Anytime, Phoenix." He smiles.

He goes to walk away, but stops and turns around to face us again.

"You do look beautiful."

I see Braeden's head snap in Donovan's direction. I look down at my cards again, diverting my eyes from the uncomfortable moment. Out of the corner of my eye, I see Rain get up.

"I'm not feeling so well, I think I'm going to go lie down," she says, leaving so quickly that no one can respond.

When she is out of view, I lean over, starting to pick up the cards that are sprawled all over the floor.

"Here," Braeden says, leaning down and helping me.

We both pick up the cards, making small piles in our hands. When we get to the last card, we both reach out at the same time, our hands stopping mere inches from each other. We aren't actually touching but I can feel the electricity in the empty space between them. Braeden recoils his hand slowly. And it upsets me. *Did I want him to touch him?* I pick up the last card and stand up, Braeden doing the same. He reaches out, silently asking for my cards. I hand them to him, looking around the room. My stomach starts to do flip flops. I turn my head back to him, his eyes on me nervously.

"I was thinking about going for a walk," I say.

"It looks cold out," he says, glancing out the window.

"I like it out there," I respond.

"Yes, I know." He smiles. "You told me."

"Oh...yeah." I gnaw on my lip a little, the feeling of nausea growing. "Do you...want to...join me?" I ask, not knowing if that's even allowed.

"I'd love to," he says, his voice strong. "I'll meet you

out there in a second."

I give him a short smile, and turn around, heading out the back doors. The weather outside is indeed cold, possibly the coldest in a while. I continue walking, heading to the right, leaving the small courtyard. Wrapping my arms around myself, I wait. Moments later, I feel him behind me.

"Where do you want to go?" he asks.

I turn around. Looking in both directions.

"That way?" I say, looking in the direction that takes us the furthest away from the hospital. He nods.

I start walking, Braeden always keeping his distance from me. The wind is whipping through my hair, the scent of his cologne swirling around me. We walk silently for what seems like an eternity, eventually reaching the end of the property. There is no one in sight. Just him and I. I stand there facing him, his face hard. Worrisome. I swallow the lump in my throat. *It's now or never.*

"I wanted to thank you again for yesterday," I say. "You have no idea what that means to me."

"It was no problem, Phoenix," he says softly. "I wish it could be more than that." My heart skips a beat.

"Why would you say that?" I ask, confused.

He sighs. "I can't do this anymore," he says, almost as though he is out of breath. I look at him puzzled. "I can't pretend anymore."

My heart is now pounding so hard I can hear it in my

ears. *Did he not want to talk to me anymore? Had I done something to upset him?* He takes a small step forward.

"Something about you, Phoenix," he starts. "I am drawn to. And I can't explain it."

He pauses.

"Ever since I heard your name, ever since I first laid eyes on you. You have been in my every thought since."

I swallow. He stops and stares at me, gauging my expression.

"And I know that this is beyond wrong, and I know you don't feel the same," he says.

"That's not true," I quickly say.

He remains still. I take my eyes off of him, his gaze too intimidating.

"I can't explain it either," I mutter. "I've never felt this way before. With anyone."

The goose bumps on my arms are now a result of our conversation, not the frigid air.

"And what way is that?" he asks. My eyes snap back up to him.

"Safe," I say.

"You've never felt safe?"

"Not in quite some time."

His body is now close to mine, but I can tell he is keeping a distance between us.

"What did he do to you?" he asks sternly, the direction of our conversation turning.

I shake my head.

"I can't talk about it," I respond. "Not yet."

His face relaxes.

"OK," he responds. "Do you promise one day?"

I smile slightly.

"I promise." We both fall silent again, I shift my eyes around.

"I don't even know what I am doing," I admit. "I've never…is this even allowed?"

He shakes his head.

"It is strongly against hospital policy," he says, it making me nervous.

"I can't let you take that risk," I say shaking my head. "Plus you barely even know me." He looks down, his hand fidgety.

"I would risk a lot more than my job if it meant I got the spend time with you, Phoenix," he says.

My heart swells, so many emotions flowing through my body at this moment. Before I know it, a tear starts to stream down my cheek. Braeden reaches out, hovering his hand in front of my face. Waiting. I stare at it, my heart racing. I lean in slightly, his finger coming into contact with my cheek, the tip of his finger brushing the path of the tear, wiping it away in its entirety. His touch is soft, the feeling foreign to me. It still amazes me how much I am at ease with him. While he makes me nervous, I feel *different*.

"You *are* beautiful, Phoenix," he says as he wipes it

away, then moving his hand away slowly.

Those words coming out of his mouth have a thousand times more impact. I stand there, staring at him. Amazed that this beautiful creature has come into my life. Like I was handed my very own knight in shining armor. My savior. I sit down on the bench in the nearby corner, all the emotions still running through me, feeling as though I will wake up from this dream at any moment. Braeden sits down beside me, both of us silent, watching the traffic and people go by. He speaks again.

"Today's the anniversary," he speaks. I look over at him confused.

"What?" I ask softly.

"The day my mother died," he says. My heart drops.

"I'm so sorry, Braeden," I respond.

"I had completely forgotten," he says as he runs his hands through his hair. I don't know how to respond.

"To be honest, I am surprised that I hadn't received a call from my father," he adds.

"Maybe he didn't want to upset you," I say.

"Maybe," he mutters.

"How long has it been?" I ask.

"16 years," he declares. My eyes widen.

"It still hurts huh?" I say, more as a statement then a question. He turns to look at me.

"Like the day it happened."

"Were you close?" I ask, wanting more information.

Wanting to know as much as I can about him.

"Very," he explains. "Our whole family was." I can now feel his pain behind his tone of voice. "Well, that was before she decided to leave us."

I furrow my brow at him. "Decided?" I squeak out.

"She took her own life, Phoenix," he says, his eyes now looking off in the distant. Involuntarily my hands fly to my mouth.

"I am so sorry, Braeden," I say behind my fingertips.

"It's not your fault," he says. "It was a long time ago."

Something inside me wants to reach out and comfort him, that idea scaring me. He looks down at his watch, his body straightening.

"I have to go," he says to me.

"OK," I respond.

"Do you want me to walk you back?" he asks.

"I would like that."

We both stand up. We walk side by side, our bodies closer together than before. Our arms swing side by side, his finger tips grazing mine every so often. I can't hold back the smile on my face. When we get closer to the back door Braeden drops back behind me a little. Looking up, I notice the security cameras around the back doors. Always being watched. Walking up the back steps, Braeden shuts the door behind us. He steps beside me.

"I'm sorry, that was a lot to unload at you at once,"

he says softly.

"It's fine." I smile.

"Well, I have to go, but I will be back tomorrow night," he says."OK," I say, a little disappointed.

"Have a good day, Phoenix," he says, sounding as though he wants to say more.

"Bye, Braeden."

He starts to walk away from me, a sight I am beginning to not enjoy. When he is out of view, I go sit down on the couch, our whole conversation running though my head. I feel a range of emotions. Happy. Nervous. Scared. I had never had a...boyfriend before. *Is that even what he is?*

After a few minutes I stand up and walk over to the window, knowing that I will be able to see him leave, part of me wanting one last glance. Moments later, I see him, his uniform now covered up with a jacket, his hair sticking up in every direction. I can't help but smile when I see him leave. When he gets to the curb, my smile instantly disappears.

A tall figure with long red hair runs up to Braeden, her arms wrapping around his neck, her lips on his within seconds. I instantly become sick to my stomach, running from the window, needing to get away. When I make it to our room I fly into the bathroom, emptying the contents of my stomach into the toilet. For once I am grateful that Rain is no where around. When my stomach stops heaving and there is nothing left to throw up, I reach up, pulling the handle on the toilet, slamming to lid shut.

All the happiness I had been feeling moments prior are gone, a confusing emotion replacing it. I begin to cry, the tears falling fast. Holding onto my knees I rock back and forth, replaying the same image in my mind over and over. *How could I be so stupid? What would he ever want with someone like me when he has someone like her?* I scramble up off the bathroom floor, heading into my closet. I find the sweatshirt, unrolling it until the metal of the knife appears. Throwing the sweatshirt onto the floor, I hold the knife in my hand. My chest is heaving up and down, my head light. Tears start to flow, knowing I would end up here again. Lowering the knife, I press it to my skin, the blue veins in my wrist pulsing. I drag slowly, the first pass not breaking the skin.

I feel as though I may vomit again, but I press on. Flashes of him come across my mind but I immediately dismiss them. The second pass is a little harder, but the skin refuses to break. I scream out in frustration. I quickly do it again, using all my might, a sight of red coming into view. I smile. *It will all be over soon.* I hear a loud bang, the door to the closet flying open. Rain is standing in the doorway, tears rolling down her face. I drop the knife instantly, realizing what I've just done. I have people that care about me now. But then her body is moved to the side abruptly, a massive form coming at me. I start to panic, seeing Carl's face coming at me. I scramble to my feet, the room spinning.

"Stay away from me!" I scream.

I can feel his hands on me, the feeling making me nauseous. I start swinging my arms around, hitting everything and anything I can. I kick my legs out with all my force, it coming into contact with the figure multiple times. Moments later, I can no longer move my arms and legs, my body weightless. I can feel multiple hands on me now, my body still trying to fight. I try to wiggle out of their holds but it is useless. I don't know how much time passes, it feels like an eternity. I feel my body being raised and lowered, but I keep using all my energy I have left to try to free myself. And then my mind and body goes black.

Braeden

Just as I reach outside the parameter of the hospital, I feel something slam into me. Before I even have time to react her lips are on mine. I panic, reaching up and pulling her body away from mine, our lips detaching.

"What's up, lover?" she says smiling.

"Wh...What are you doing here?" I ask, clearly confused by her presence.

"I wanted to see you," she says. "Plus it isn't really hard to find the retard hospital. Are you ready for round two?" A large smile comes across her face.

"No," I say sternly, still holding her away from me. "That was a one-time thing." She gives me a fake pout.

"You seemed to enjoy yourself at the time."

I let out a big sigh.

"It was...fun," I lie. "But I don't feel anything for

you."

"What the fuck ever, Harris," she huffs. "When the hell did you get so fucking boring?"

I just sigh, knowing I won't get anywhere with her. When I make it clear that we aren't and never will be anything she turns around and leaves. I knew that was a fucking mistake. I look back at the hospital into the recreation room window, a soft light illuminating from it. I start walking down the block, the sound of thunder reaching my ears. I walk a few blocks but then abruptly stop.

"Fuck," I mutter to myself, remembering my text book on the table.

I turn around and head back to the hospital, getting their quickly in fear that it may start to rain soon. Pulling open the back door, I step inside, shouting and hollering reaching my ears instantly. Life as a medical aid is unpredictable, especially when it came to mentally impaired patients, times of chaos not exactly a rarity. I go into the break room, my book sitting in the same spot that I had left it. I grab it, sliding it into my backpack and exit the room.

When I finish zipping up my backpack, I look up, my feet frozen in place. In front of me is a mob of aides carrying Phoenix. Her body is thrashing about, her left arm dripping with blood. I instantly feel sick to my stomach. I want to run up to them and scream for them to get her hands off of her. I want to soothe her. But I know I can't. Just as soon as I see them, they are gone. I almost feel as though it was all my imagination. I had *just* left her. She was happy. I was happy. Even though they are out of sight, my legs still protest to move. There is now no one else in the hallway, it extremely quiet. After a few minutes I begin to inch forward slowly, knowing exactly where they have taken her. When I come around the bend, my body slams into a hurrying figure.

"Braeden, what are you doing here?" he asks.

"I should ask you the same thing," I say.

"I came by to drop something off," he responds. "And then..." he stops.

"What happened?" I sternly ask.

"She's OK," he says.

"That's not what I asked."

"They called a Code Green." *Psychiatric emergency.*

A lump in my throat appears, trying to swallow all my emotions.

"So she's..." I ask. He nods slowly.

"She's restrained but she's fine. We gave her a shot of Ativan to calm her down. The cut on her arm isn't deep and she didn't hit any main veins."

I let out the large breath that I didn't know I was holding in. He puts his hand on my shoulder.

"I know this is hard for you, son, but there is nothing you can do for her. You need to go home and get some sleep."

"No," I say sternly.

"Braeden," he says, his voice demanding. "Go. You've been on duty all night. Phoenix is surrounded by people who know what she needs and how to take care of her. I know she's a special patient for you, but you need to go home."

I feel sick to my stomach, wanting to be near her, a selfish part of me thinking this wouldn't have happened while I was on shift. I would have kept more of a watch on her. But would I be able to restrain her?

"I promise to keep you updated," he says.

I turn around, much to my dismay, and head back down the hallway. Worried. Sick. Angry. But before I get too far, I turn around back to face my father.

"Did you know it was today?" I ask.

He nods. I don't say anything else before heading down the hallway and out the back door. When I make it back outside the rain has started to fall, the small drops seeping into my clothing, soon reaching my bare skin underneath. I couldn't care less.

I stand outside the employee entrance of the hospital, staring at the door, the only thing blocking me from running back inside. The scene replays in my mind over and over. Hands all over her, the way the blood streaked down her arm like a flowing river. I had never felt a surge of anger like that. Anger at myself. Anger at those touching her, even knowing full well they were only there to protect her. Protect her from what *she* had done.

I replay our last encounter in my head, a weight being lifted off my shoulder when I told her how I felt about her. And not only did she not run away screaming, she confessed the same to me. That was the first time in a long time my heart felt...hope. I don't know what that meant for us, how would this work? Many questions came to my mind, but no matter the question, the answer was always the same. We will find a way.

I think tonight marked the first night I didn't want to leave my shift. I wanted to talk to her, get to know her more. Stare at her beautiful face for hours. But I knew that if I stuck around things would become more suspicious, a small part of me thought Victor already has his suspicions. As I continue to stand there in the rain, my entire body is now soaked, my scrubs wet against me like a second skin. But I don't care. I stay where I am, squinting as my eyes are being bombarded with rain drops. If I can't be in the room, I can at least be near her. After an unknown amount of time, the back door flies open, startling me out of the trance.

"What the fuck are you doing out here?" the figure standing in the doorway asks.

"I....I..." I start to say, not able to complete a sentence.

The figure steps down, pulling up its hood up and over its head. He walks over under the awning, pulling out a cigarette and lighting it.

"Will you please just come the hell out of the rain," he says. "You look like a drowned rat."

I start to make my way over to him, leaning against the building wall. He hands me the cigarette, and I take a long draw from it before handing it back. I don't usually smoke, but this night calls for it. Looking out at the passing traffic, I slowly let the smoke leave my lungs, mixing into the rainy air. Donovan doesn't saying anything else. I suspect he is waiting for me to break first. It only takes a matter of seconds.

"I feel like I'm going to fucking throw up," I say, my nerves still getting the better part of me.

Donovan takes another puff, handing it back to me. Each draw relaxes me a little.

"Just relax, man, you flipping out isn't gonna help the situation."

"You have no idea how much strength it's taking me to not barge back through that door," I state. He turns to face me.

"You care for her right?" I nod. "And you want what's best for her right?" I nod again. "Then you need to stay away. Her mind is obviously not in its best state right now."

"You sound like my father," I mutter.

I notice that the cigarette is at its end and I flick the butt out, the tip snuffed out in the rain in seconds.

"Well, he's right."

We both fall silent again, the sound of raindrops

hitting the roof overtakes the stillness. I notice that he is shaking his head slightly, his face lost in thought.

"What?" I ask.

"I guess I know how you kind of feel," he admits.

"In what way?" I ask confused. He hesitates. "Just tell me."

"I don't know, man," he starts. "I mean we've dealt with a lot of attempted suicides over the years, but seeing the...seeing her like that. Something about it affected me more than normal."

My stomach begins to churn. I don't respond. I honestly didn't know whether to yell at him or thank him.

"How did you know to go in there?" I ask. He laughs a little.

"Rain," he states. "She was about to go grab some food and the next thing I know she is bolting to her room, grabbing my arm on the way. She kept saying 'Phoenix' over and over, almost like she was in a trance, man. It was fucking weird."

I get chills, the hair on my arms stand vertical. Maybe Rain really is psychic after all.

"Did Rain say anything about Phoenix beforehand?"

"Nah, but hadn't you just left her? I saw you two coming out from inside and then you left right?"

"Yeah."

That's when the panic sets in, nausea growing. She saw me. *Us.* I put my hands up to my face, rubbing my face up and down.

"Fuck!" I scream out.

Turning around I slam my fist in the concrete wall, pain radiating through my fingertips.

"Woah, man," Donovan yells, pulling his body off the wall to face me. "You wanna tell me what the hell that was all about?"

"Fucking bitch," I whisper to myself. Donovan stands there facing me, not saying anything.

"I gotta go," I say as I start to walk away. Donovan reaches out and grabs my arm.

"Here," he says, handing me his coat.

"Thanks," I mutter.

And that's when I notice his shirt. It's splattered with red. In blood. Her blood. Taking the coat I swing it over my body and break out into a run, leaving a silent Donovan behind. I continue to run, the rain pelting me in the face, the cold reaching far down in my throat, my vocal cords freezing over. As much as my mind tells me to stop, my body can't. I just run, not exactly knowing where to go. After what seems like an eternity, I stop, my body bending over, my throat begging for air. Once my breathing returns, I stand up, slowly walking now down the path I was headed. When I reach it, I pull the door open and hold it, letting a woman exiting leave first.

"Thank you," she says awkwardly, probably noticing my disheveled state. I just nod in response.

I enter the shop, the scent reaching my nose. I take a deep breath, it calms me slightly. I walk over to the refrigerated case looking at all the options.

"May I help you?" I hear a voice say to the right of me.

I turn to face the direction, a petite women standing beside me. She has to be well into her seventies. Her eyes are taking in my form, realizing now that a pool of water was gathering at my feet.

"I'm so sorry," I say backing away from it, the water only following.

"It's no worry," she says. "Anything I can assist you with?" she asks again.

"How do you know which one to choose?" I mutter, turning my attention back to case.

"Is it for someone special?" she asks.

"Yes," I explain.

She helps me pick one out and I pay for it quickly before heading out of the shop again. Heading west, I walk down the street; the heavy rain has changed to a light sprinkle. After walking a few more blocks, I reach the wrought iron gates, slowly pushing them open. The place is quiet, it makes me nervous. I walk down the familiar path, the bouquet tight in my hands. I take in my surroundings, a few colorful umbrellas off in the distance. They are so vibrant against all the dark stones. After a few minutes I find it, my visit is clearly not the only recent one. Kneeling down, I place the small bouquet of roses up against the stone, making sure to not cover her name.

Sophia Harris. Always loving. Always loved.

The wet grass seeps into my already drenched pants and I just look down at the ground. I don't know what to say. But yet, I want to say everything. I want to tell her about Phoenix. I want to tell her I royally fucked up the only good thing that has come into my life. I want to tell her about the unexplained pull I have to this human being, a pull not even I can explain. Reaching down I wrap my fingers around the grass blades, pulling them out one by one, slowly making a small pile in front of me. I finally decide to speak.

"Hi," I say softly. I pause, almost as though she is going to respond. Or anyone for that fact.

"Sorry I haven't come by lately...but I see that dad has been here," I say as I look down at the dozen white roses propped up against the headstone.

They were always her favorite. My dad gave them to her every year on their anniversary. White roses stand for heaven, purity and innocence. It wasn't a surprise when my father adopted the nickname "Seraph" for her. He always believed in the afterlife and that she would be taken care of in heaven. He refused to think that taking one's own life was considered a sin. I silently begged to differ. I clear my throat, it echoes between the trees.

"What do I do?" I ask.

Of course there is no answer. I replay the scene in my head again, the red on her arm, the fire that burned inside of me, the hopelessness I felt returning. *What was I to do?* How could I ever explain to her who that woman was? Would telling her the truth only further bury me in the bed of quicksand I fear that I am in?

I smile. Remembering our walk prior to the incident, and how she had told me that she felt the same for me. I knew that it was hesitant, but she had the courage to tell me, to meet me halfway. And that was music to my ears.

While I was lost in thought, I felt a bright light hit my eyes, making me squint a little. Looking up and beyond the trees I could see that the dark clouds had separated, rays of sunshine beaming through the leaves and branches. The warmth was welcome. Leaning up, I soak it in, keeping my eyes closed in the process. *Thanks Mom.* I know exactly what I have to do. I have to tell her that girl means nothing to me and that she is what I want.

Phoenix

Calm. Relaxed. Fire. Retrained.

My eye lids are so heavy that I can't seem to keep them open and, to be honest, I don't know if I really want to. Opening them would take me back to reality. Moving my arms and legs slowly, I realize that I can't go far. I can feel the soft cloth against my skin. Bits and pieces of hours earlier flash before me. My heart begins to race. I can't exactly remember everything that had happened or how I came to be in these restraints, but I do remember what got me here.

I swallow the growing lump in my throat as I deny my body the tears it so desperately wants to produce. My mind is still in a blur, but Donovan and Rain's faces appear, my mind slowly remembering everything else. A large wave of guilt overcomes me. Donovan was the one who stopped me. My mind and the fear mistook him for Carl.

I remain trapped in my thoughts, wanting nothing more than to get out of there. I can feel the fence around my heart that I had let down for a split second harden up, the base of it now set in concrete. Moments later, I hear the door being pushed open and my heart rate increases. I try to lift my head up to glance at who it is, but it feels as though it weighs a million pounds.

"Phoenix," I hear, not able to place the voice because of my drowsiness. I can feel the figure coming closer to me, the mixture of rage and nervousness washing over me.

"How are you feeling?" I hear before anything comes into view.

I have the incredible sense of déjà vu, remembering the first time I met this figure back in the emergency room. My heart can't seem to return to its natural pace.

"OK," I squeak out. I pause. "A little bit drowsy."

"That would be a side effect of the shot of Ativan we gave you earlier," he responds.

"How long have I been here?" I ask.

He looks down at the watch on his arm. "About an hour and a half," he states.

I remain lying still as Dr. Harris asks me more questions, only giving him brief answers.

"When can I leave?" I ask abruptly. He takes his attention off my arm, looking at me.

"Well, once I am done with this exam, you may head back to your room," he states.

"No, I mean here," I say, shifting my eyes all around the room. He gets a concerned look on his face.

"Phoenix," he starts before pausing. "I think it will be better if you stayed a while longer." I don't respond.

"This..." he says, pointing to my arm, "is not helping. I cannot sign off on your release until I have complete confidence that you are no longer a threat to yourself, or anyone else for that matter."

I just stare at him, wanting to argue but I can't. We both fall silent and Dr. Harris continues to write in what I can only assume is my chart. I find myself curious about what could possibly be written in there. A spike of nervousness flows through me before I speak again.

"You know I..." I start. "I wasn't trying to kill myself."

Neil gives me a small smile, his mood darkening.

"I know," he says softly. "You just wanted the pain to stop." I feel as though he took the words right out of my mouth.

"Yeah," was all that I could respond with. He finishes up his work quietly, his demeanor still sad.

"I will let Donovan know to come undo your restraints," he states. "I am also going to put you on a dose of anxiety medication."

"OK," is all I say. Dr. Harris starts to walk away from me, but pauses and turns around to face me again.

"I know that I have no right, it's not any of my business, and... it's completely inappropriate. I shouldn't be supporting any of this... but I'm gonna say it anyway. You need to be surrounded by good people right now, Phoenix. People who can help you pick up the pieces and heal from the things..." He cuts himself off. "You have someone who cares for you. Give him a chance. I haven't seen him happier than when he talks about you. You may need each other more than you think."

Without another word he leaves the room, the door swinging behind him. I lay my head back again, my mind more confused than it already was. What the hell am I going to do? Just as soon as Dr. Harris leaves, the door swings open again and Donovan's massive figure approaches me. I squirm a little bit.

"How you doing in here?" he asks, a large smile on his face.

"Peachy," I say sarcastically. He just laughs. He reaches his arms out slightly, stopping before he actually makes contact.

"I'm going to remove your restraints, OK?"

I nod in response. He works quickly, releasing each restraint slowly. When he finishes, he backs up slowly and stands there. *I have to apologize.*

"Donovan," I say softly.

"Mmmm?"

"I just wanted to apologize," I state.

"For what?"

"For, you know, earlier...." He waves his hand.

"Hate to say it, Phoenix, but you're not the first, nor will you be the last." I look down as I fidget with my fingers.

"Doesn't mean I'm not embarrassed, you have been nothing but nice to me." He gives me a smile. "All of you have."

Donovan crosses his arms and stares at me.

"So, you wanna tell me what's up," he states.

My heart races. I shake my head. "No, not yet."

"Well, whatever he did, I will gladly kick his ass for you."

I can't help but laugh. "Thanks, but that won't be necessary."

We both drop the subject.

"You ready to go back to your room?" he asks. I nod.

"OK, do you think you can walk?" he asks me.

"I don't know," I admit. "I'm still pretty groggy..."

"OK," he says. "I guess I'll have to carry you."

He slowly places his hands underneath me and I feel my body being lifted in the air. When we make it to my room, he places me on top my bed, my eyelids becoming heavy again. Just before sleep completely overtakes me, I can only think of one thing. His beautiful green eyes looking back at me.

Braeden

I lay in my bed; the sound of rain pelting the window is growing more irritating. I guess the weather is matching my mood at the moment. It's late afternoon and I am still in my damp clothes from earlier. I have no desire to get up and change. When I got back from the cemetery, I turned off my cell phone, not wanting to be bothered by anyone. But I know it's only a matter of time before someone shows up to check up on me. My bet is Donovan.

As I continue to lie there, I know I'll never fall asleep. Restlessness is a notion I've become familiar with since Phoenix came into my life. I reach my arm down to the bedside floor, my finger extending out to find the string. When I feel it, I hook it around my fingertip and pull up. The box is already half empty, which angers me slightly. Popping one into my mouth, it doesn't achieve the same calming effect it normally has. Closing my eyes anyway, I continue to eat the cookies, remembering back to a happier time.

~

"It's OK, sweetie, you tried your best," she said as she stroked the back of my head. The tears continued to stream down my face.

"But I let my team down," I said sniffling.

I had just single handedly made our baseball team lose the championship by striking out. She looked down at me, her brown eyes sympathetic.

"What have I always told you?" she asked, her hand now on her hip.

"Go in there and do the best you can. That's all you can do," I muttered.

"And did you do that?" she asked me. I nodded.

"There is always next time, sweetie," she said.

We both walked to the car, her arm wrapped around me still. Most boys would be mortified by such public displays of affection by their mother, but I didn't care. She was my best friend. My father barely made it to any of my games because he was always so busy with work, so she was my cheering section. When we made it home, I was still pretty bummed, knowing that I would probably get teased at school on Monday. I went

upstairs and changed and came back down to put my
dirty uniform into the washer. My mother taught us a
lot of household skills that most other men still can't do
to this day. She always wanted us to be self-sufficient.

When I came into the kitchen, the room was quiet.
The house was quiet. I walked into the living room
where the sound of muffled crying reached my ears. I
walked towards the sound, my heart starting to race.
Then the sight of them came into view. My dad was
facing my mother, his arms on both her shoulders, tears
running down his face. I ran to the side of the wall,
hoping that he hadn't caught me yet. I stood there,
continuing to stare at them, my mother's profile facing
me. She was not crying, her face in a frozen state. My
father shook her slightly and I could tell from his lips
that he is repeating her name over and over. I put my
hand on the table, leaning in, hoping to listen better.
My gut told me not to, but a bigger part of me needed
to understand what's happening. But as I leaned in
closer my body hit a picture frame, the glass smashing
to the floor with a loud crash. My father looked up, his
hands dropping from my mother's shoulders as he
backs away. Something in my mother snapped back, her
eyes on me. My father walked away and she came back
in through the patio door.

"I'm so sorry you had to see that, sweetie," she said,
rubbing the top of my head.

"What was happening?" I asked, still confused.

"Maybe I'll tell you someday," she said. I furrowed my brow.

"Are you hungry? I'm sure you are after that big game you played!" she said, her smile now back on her face as though nothing had happened. I just nod.

"Then why don't you take a seat," she said as she rooted around in the cupboard.

I do as I'm told, pulling out a chair at the kitchen table. Moments later, I noticed she has two small boxes in her hand. She set one down in front of me. "Now, I have a challenge for you," she said. "I want you to write down every animal that is in this box, which one is your favorite and why."

I smiled, the challenge of it excited me. Over the next hour my mother and I talked and ate our crackers. My favorite is the elephant and hers was the bear. It's then that I realized all the worry I had previously had been eliminated.

~

It was that night that my dad convinced my mother to admit herself. Digging into the box again, I realize it's empty, tossing it back onto the floor. Moments later, I hear voices, recognizing only Bret, the other female voices unknown. Grunting, I pull the comforter over my head, wishing that I could just disappear.

~

I fling the blanket off my body in a panic and sit up straight. The room is pitch black and I glance over at the clock. 11:07 p.m. I don't know exactly how much I slept, but a small part of me feels refreshed but my brain only takes seconds to remind me what had happened. The anger and grief comes back to me quickly, knowing I will never truly run away from it.

I don't go back to the hospital for another twelve hours, but I know I will be useless until I can talk to her. To tell her what she mistakenly saw. That is if she will believe me. Pulling the covers off, I walk slowly through the dark room, grabbing my phone to illuminate it. I open the door slowly, remembering the voices I heard earlier. Not wanting to talk to anyone, I decide to not search them out. Opening the bathroom door I peer in, happy to see that no one is currently occupying it. Turning on the shower, I close the curtain while waiting for it to warm up. Looking up in the mirror, I barely notice the person looking back at me. It's even worse than the last time. My face is beyond scruff and I can't actually remember the last time I shaved or took a shower.

Pulling off my once-damp, now crusty, scrubs I pull open the shower curtain again and step inside. The warmth calms me and relieves the tension in my back a little. After a few minutes, I start to shave, smoothing the cream all over my face. Once I finish, I set the shaver down and pick up my body wash. I start to wash myself, my hand grazing over my nether region, a surge of tension emanating through my body. Grabbing my body wash again, I squeeze a hefty amount out onto my hand, placing my hand back, it instantly hardens. Wrapping my fingers around it, I pump up and down, feeling fucking incredible. My breathing becomes hitched and I lean my other arm on the wall to rest my head against. I continue to pump and as soon as I close my eyes, all I can see is her. As much as I try not to, I just can't keep the vision at bay.

Picturing everything about her makes me jerk harder. Her eyes. Her lips. Her smile. The way she laughs. I shake my head, knowing this isn't where she should be. I continue to stroke, the body wash now frothy, making the stroking easier. I can feel it, the intense knot in my lower abdomen. I am close. After a few more strokes the pressure is released and I come, the sticky substance mixes with the body wash and falls to the shower floor. Stepping back into the spray of the water, I finish washing myself off before I turn off the shower and grab my towel. Its only when I finish drying off that I realize how much I needed it. Wrapping my towel around my waist, I finish getting ready and realize that lying around here might not be the best thing for me. Grabbing my phone I quickly send out a message. Pulling open the bathroom door I exit, only getting a few steps outside before my body slams into something. Before me is standing a petite redhead, her body wrapped in nothing but a sheet. She leans into me closer.

"Well, if I had known that you were in there taking a shower I would have come in sooner," she says, her words slurring a little bit.

I don't respond, not really wanting to give her the satisfaction of a reply. Instead, I hold on tighter to my towel and squeeze myself out. When I get to my bedroom door, I close it and lock it behind me. I dress in a pair of skinny jeans, a dark grey, hooded sweatshirt and grab a pair of mis-matched socks, along with my well-worn lace up boots. In the middle of lacing them, I hear my phone chime. I open it while laughing a little, respond and then slide it into my pocket.

Walking over to my window, I peer out onto the street. It's still pouring out so I grab my black beanie before unlocking the door and heading out into the living room. I take a quick scan of the room, glad to see that Bret has taken his party to his own bedroom. Leaving the apartment, I pull my beanie on over my head. It's only a few blocks to the bar but I decide to take a cab, not wanting to walk around in wet clothes again. Within a few minutes I arrive and toss some cash at the driver. When I exit, I spot him outside immediately. I walk up to him, not knowing who is going to speak first.

"I'm surprised you don't have a cast on your arm," he states. "You punched that wall pretty hard." I give him a sideways smile.

"It does kind of hurt," I say, stretching my fingers

outward.

"Is it not manly to say that I was worried about you when you took off?"

I laugh. "A little."

"Well, whatever," he shrugs. "Let's go get a drink."

We walk inside, glad that it's not the other bar we frequent, realizing I can never go back there. Donovan and I each grab a seat at the bar and order our respective drinks. I decide on something a little harder than beer, hoping to drown out my own thoughts. Taking a sip of it, the vodka burns as it travels down my throat, but I like it. The pain matches the pain that is currently flowing through my body. I wish that I could just talk to her. To tell her everything that she needs to hear. But I know that if I show up there while I'm not on shift everyone will know and I don't think she is ready for that. Taking another sip, I can feel my nerves easing up and my tense shoulders relaxing a little.

"Good huh?" Donovan asks.

I just nod. "Yeah, this might just be exactly what I needed."

"Good to hear, man," he responds, putting his lips to his own glass.

"I guess I owe you an apology," I mutter so quiet I almost hope he doesn't hear me.

"For what?"

I let out a sigh. "For earlier, man, I sort of just snapped."

"That's alright, not like I haven't been there over a chick before," he explains.

I just shake my head, my inner thoughts taking over my mind again. "I just can't believe she saw us," I mutter to myself, then realize that I had just said it out loud. I hear Donovan's glass slam down to the counter, his eyes wide.

"And what do you mean by *us?*" he asks, a pissed look on his face.

I swallow, not wanting to tell him. Not wanting to believe that I am the one who fucked things up. Me and my fucking cock.

"Remember the bartender…the one I…." I let my voice trail off.

"…that hot one you fucked?" Donovan so eloquently finishes my sentence for me. I just nod.

"Well, she showed up at the hospital just as I was leaving," I continue.

"Dude," Donovan responds.

"And she assaulted me with her mouth, I didn't even have fucking time to react," I defend. "I have a horrible feeling that's what caused Phoenix's breakdown. I think she saw us."

We both fall silent, Donovan's non-responsiveness putting me on edge. "There is only one way to find out man," he finally says. "You gotta tell her."

What the hell am I going to say? Would she even listen to me? I start picking at the coaster underneath my drink.

"How was she when they released her?" I ask. Donovan shifts his head from side to side slightly.

"She was pretty loopy, the Ativan had her pretty jacked up and it was still clearly in her system. She just apologized and pretty much sacked out once I carried her to her bed."

A spike of jealousy runs through me. I know that Donovan would never try to go for her like that, but it always seems like he is there for her and I can't be. We spend a few more hours in the bar, both of us just chatting about various things, trying to avoid the elephant in the room. I'm surprised that I can hold a conversation considering there is only one thing on my mind.

~

The loud sound of a buzzer reaches my ear, an instant groan leaving my throat. I can feel the pounding in my head, an obvious sign that I had way too much to drink last night. I continue to lay with my head on my pillow, almost forgetting why I have my alarm set. My heart starts to beat and I instantly spring out of bed, the room spinning slightly.

"Fuck," I say grabbing my head.

Pulling a new set of scrubs out of my closet I head to the bathroom, deciding to take another shower, considering I smell like a dirty bar. Within ten minutes, I am dressed and heading towards the hospital, my heart beats fast and a thousand words repeat inside my head. After a few blocks of walking fast I pull out my cell phone, realizing that I may have left a little too early. I continue to walk down the street a little slower now and the sound of guitar strings reaching my ears. I walk towards it, a young man busking on the side of the sidewalk with an open guitar case in front of him. It's scattered with some coins and a few paper bills. I watch him play; his handwork is good for someone so young. I run my fingers over my own calluses, remembering when I started playing, almost the same age as him. My father said it would be good therapy, to get my mind off things. Reaching into my pocket, I grab my wallet, pulling out a twenty dollar bill.

I toss it into the case, the player giving me a nod without breaking his concentration on the song. I continue to walk down the street, coming across a small novelty shop. I decide to go in, needing to kill a few more minutes. The shop is filled from head to toe with small trinkets, making it somewhat claustrophobic and overwhelming. I mindlessly peruse the shelves, my mind only on her. My stomach is tied in knots. I don't know how this will turn out but all I know is that I have to tell her everything.

Just as I am about to leave the shop, something catches my eye. On one the shelves closest to the door is a small porcelain seal. I pick it up, remembering reading Phoenix's account of her jump from when she was first admitted. When she described something swirling around her feet I knew exactly what she was talking about. She wasn't the first suicide survivor to tell this story. There had been urban myths and legends about animals saving people's lives in times of dire need. In Phoenix's case it was a seal. I knew it instantly when she described the way the water swirled under her feet, the seal working hard to keep her afloat. Grabbing the trinket, I pay for it quickly and rush out of the store, hoping that this will be enough for her to let me talk to her. A possible icebreaker.

After a few more blocks the hospital comes into view and my heart starts racing even more. I quickly find my way to the staff lounge. As much as I want to run to her room, I know I can't make a big scene about it, for fear of scaring her or losing my job. Sliding the seal into my pocket, I make myself busy with my tasks. Time is moving too slow during this shift. I keep one eye peeled, looking and hoping to see her. To see her beautiful face. To know if she is OK. When I finish a few things I look down on my duties cart, seeing the words "linens." Never has such a simple word make my stomach wrench. I was hoping that I would get to see Phoenix on neutral grounds. I didn't want to invade her privacy like that. I laugh to myself. *Privacy? Here?*

Looking up at all the security cameras that clutter the hallway I fear the bedroom is the only place that we can do this. The only place in the hospital that cameras are not allowed. Walking into the linen closet, I grab a pair of fresh sheets and slowly make my way to their door.

I hesitate and stand in the doorway trying to gather my thoughts, but my nerves get the best of me. Wrapping my fingers around the door knob I push it open slowly, the hinge squeaking a little. The room light is off but there is enough light coming through the shades for me to see inside.

Shutting the door behind me I set the sheets down on the small table. The room is quiet and I instantly see her form lying in her bed, her long hair sprawled across her pillow. I take small steps to get closer to her, her beautiful face coming into view. She looks so peaceful, it makes me heart soar. All the pain from her face is gone, her lips turned slightly upward.

She is smiling. I continue to stare at her, absolutely mesmerized by the creature in front of me. If only I knew what was bringing her such joy I would try my hardest to make it come true. Knowing that I could never awaken her, I pull the porcelain seal from my pocket, setting it gently on her nightstand and quietly leave the room.

Phoenix

Breathing is becoming difficult. My lungs are working overtime and my throat begs for oxygen. I look at myself in the mirror and notice that the color in my skin has vanished. *A ghost.*

I slowly side down the cabinet wall, my body giving up, no longer having the energy to stay vertical. As I heave against the wall I feel warmth flow from my arm, the familiar sight of spewing blood running down it and onto the tile floor.

I watch as it flows through the grout like a river, each line meeting to create an even bigger puddle. The gash in my arm grows bigger with every pulse, the severed veins coming into view as they work overtime to pump more blood. But instead of the usual feeling of happiness I have when I do this, I realize I am filled with fear. An extreme thirst for life fills me and my eyes instantly well up with tears.

Reaching over with my right hand I try to plug the hole, but my fingers are not wide enough to cover the ever growing gash. I start to cry furiously, begging God for one more second chance. The darkness and silence I longed for just moments ago is far from what I desire now. I want to travel the world; I want to feel the sun beat on my face as I lay in the grass on a warm summer day. I want to feel someone's love. I want to love someone.

My fingers are deep inside my arm now, finding the severed veins in hope of stopping the blood, but there is no luck. The bathroom floor is now a permanent pool of crimson red. Knowing that it's a lost cause, I retract my fingers, laying my head back against the cabinets. Closing my eyes I try to talk myself into remembering this is what I always wanted. What I always asked for. As I lay there I can feel myself slipping, my mind blank, no memories or visions from my soon-to-be past life coming. Complete silence. But then a touch. A slight tickle graces my arm, snapping me back into reality. It takes my mind a few seconds to process this touch, but when it does my eyes snap open instantly. Once I can focus I see a figure standing before me, both of its hands clamped onto my wound, an immense burning coming from their touch. It sends me into an agonizing pain. I scream out but the hands do not remove themselves. My whole body shakes, trying to get away from this thing that is hurting me. A pain much worse than Carl has ever inflicted upon me. It feels as though my whole body has been set on fire under my skin and sealed shut.

I decide to look up at the figure causing this, my heart instantly breaking. The hands belong to Braeden, his green eyes look demonic, the always-compassionate look on his face departed. But he isn't concentrated on my face, his eyes are looking only at his hands that remain on my arm, a sweat breaking on his brow. I realize that since I saw him, I no longer feel the need to scream and a sense of calm comes about. I take in his apparel. He is still wearing his scrubs, but instead of them being the usual green they are stark white. White in a sea of red. My eyes continue south, now realizing that the blood around his feet is non-existent, almost as though the blood retreats anywhere he touches. He grabs onto my arm even tighter, snapping me back. The pain is even more excruciating than before and I fear I may blackout. I start to plead for him to stop, confused about what he is trying to do. *Was he sent here to finally end me? To put me out of my misery?*

I fall back out of consciousness again, the darkness and silence returning. The pain becomes nonexistent. Just as I fear that I am slipping again, a brush on my cheek awakens me. I fight again to open my eyes and when I do, Braeden's face is mere inches from me.

"I thought I had lost you," his soft, velvety voice utters.

I try to find words to say, but my mind and mouth will not work together. His fingers continue to brush my cheeks, calming me slightly. *Why is he prolonging it? Did he want me to suffer more?*

Prying my eyes away from him, I notice the entire bathroom is now completely white, all the red gone from the room. Even my clothes are white. Grabbing my arm I see that the hole is entirely closed with no sign that it was ever there. The pain, however, lingers. It's not as strong but it's a low burn, almost as though my bones have been extinguished from the flames but the damage still remains. Moving my hands slowly, I reach upwards and my once-still heart beats rapidly. I continue to move slowly, fearing that he is merely a mirage that will disappear at my lightest touch. But when my fingertips come into contact with his skin I try to hold back a smile but I can't.

When he sees my smile he mimics it, his pearly whites matching the rest of the room. As my heart continues to beat, the knot in my stomach grows. Leaning up slowly, I continue to stare at his mouth until I can feel his hot breath on mine, the knot growing into desire. We both hold still, our breathing moving in sync. Not wanting to wait any longer, I put my lips to his, tasting his sweet breath instantly. My lips move with his, his arms now wrapped around my body and pulls me onto his lap. His touch is somewhat harsh, his fingers clutching onto my shirt tight but I am not afraid of it and I feel as though I crave it. When I pull back from his kiss I can't help but put my fingers to my lips, feeling the small tingle on them. When I look back up, Braeden is gone.

~

I snap my eyes open, my heart still racing, my mind still in the dream. Reaching up I touch my lips, feeling nothing but dryness. No tingle. No warmth. Tossing my body over, I lay on my side, replaying the whole dream in my head. It still seems so real. Bringing my arms out in front of me, I run my fingertips over the stitches still in my arm, the incision slightly inflamed. *Of course it was only a dream.*

Pulling them back into my body I spot something on my nightstand that wasn't there before. A small porcelain seal is staring at me, its lips slightly curved up as though it is smiling. Reaching out I gently pull it from the table, cupping it in my hands. I smile as I look it over. Flipping over, I place it back on the corner of the nightstand. I continue to smile but then it hits me. He was here? I know where it must have come from and that makes me instantly nervous. I know I'll have to talk to him eventually, this place being so incredibly small. But the thought of talking to him makes me scared and I wish I had never put myself in this situation. *What was there to say?*

My heart begins to race just thinking about it. I want nothing more than stay in this bed forever, to hide from the world. It will only be a matter of time before Rain comes and pulls my ass out. We didn't talk much about the incident once I was released from the restraints, Rain probably didn't want to upset me, but I know everyone thinks it was all because of Braeden. But it wasn't. *OK, it was a little about Braeden, but it was mostly about me.* I was mad at myself for thinking that Braeden and I would run off together when I got out of here and live happily ever after. Or that he was anything close to being mine. I wouldn't even know what to do with him if he was.

Once my father died, I instantly put a wall around my heart. It kept me safe. It kept me from getting close to anyone and never feeling the pain of loss all over again. Something about Braeden slowly made that wall crumble and it scared me. Fairy tales are bullshit. There was no prince to rescue me. There was no spell to make the big bad wolf disappear. This was real life. *My life.*

Pulling my cover off, I get out of bed slowly. I grab the seal in my hand, a sudden irritation flowing through me. I walk into the bathroom and, holding my hand clutching the seal out over the wastebasket, my palms become sweaty. As much as I want to release it and drop it into the trash, I can't. Its eyes seem to bore into mine.

"Fuck," I mutter as I retract my hand.

It bugs me how much he is still under my skin, even though I plead and beg for my body and mind to forget about him. He doesn't even have to be in the room for me to feel him. Grabbing a few sheets of toilet paper, I wrap the figurine up and place it in the back of my closet. After getting dressed I hover at our bedroom door, not wanting to leave the confines of the room. As I stand there, I can hear my stomach grumble, not having eaten in quite some time.

Putting my trembling hand on the door knob I pull it open, the bright lights from the hallway blinding me. When my eyes adjust I instantly scan the hallway. He is nowhere in sight. I feel like I exhale for the very first time. Walking slowly to the kitchen I grab myself a plate and notice that my appetite is returning, slightly. I sit down and eat a few bites, mostly pushing the rest of it around my plate with my fork. Just when my nerves have calmed, I look up and scan the room, wondering what Rain is doing at this moment. It's only a matter of time before my eyes find him.

He's looking down at something in his hand; I assume what could only be a patient's chart. After staring at him for a few seconds he looks up, our eyes instantly connecting. I quickly retreat, putting my attention back on my plate of food. My heart now starts to race. I could just get up from the table and exit the room through the other entrance, but some unexplainable force keeps me planted in my chair. I can feel him coming closer but I keep my eyes down until he is standing on the opposite side of the table, his fingers gripping the back of the chair opposite me. I look up from under my eyelashes, noticing that his knuckles are turning white. He's nervous. That makes two of us.

"Phoenix," his tone is eerily similar to what it was in my dream. Dropping my fork down on my plate, I slowly look up at him. The look on his face is heartbreaking, even to someone who is incredibly mad at him. He looks lost.

"Yes, Brae..." I pause. His eyes look down at the table instead of looking at me.

"Can I talk to you?" he asks.

I lick my lips before responding. "About what?" I ask, clearly knowing what I am doing. I hear a sigh leave his throat.

"Please," his voice begs. I realize how torn I am at this moment, wanting nothing more than for this to all be over. Standing up, I grab my tray in my hands. Braeden's hand drops off the chair, a look of defeat in his eyes.

"Remember where..." I swallow hard. "We talked earlier, out in the yard?"

He nods. "Be out there in 5 minutes."

He just nods again and leaves the kitchen. I slowly

walk over and put my tray in the window. My heart still beats fast as I doodle around the day room, each minute seeming to last an eternity. When I think that enough time has passed I make my way to the patio door. The wind is blowing so hard that it takes all of my might to push it open. When I get outside, an instant chill runs through my body. I usually like the cold, having lived in cold places for all of my life, but not tonight.

I slowly make my way down, out of the security camera's eye. When I round the corner he is already there. When he sees me he takes a hurried step forward, making me instantly take a step back.

"I'm sorry," he mutters as I retreat.

Wrapping my arms around myself, I wait for him to speak. To plead his case. Braeden remains standing where he is and I can tell he is thinking carefully about what he was going to say next.

"You shouldn't have seen that," he says first, his words shocking me.

"Seen what, Braeden?"

He sighs. "I don't want to lie to you."

"Then don't." I get antsy at the silence. "You know what, Braeden, I don't need to know," I snap.

"But I want you to," he says, trying to take a step forward this time. I don't move back.

"I want you to know that she means nothing to me," he says only above a whisper. "Nothing."

"Who is she?"

He swallows. "Someone I've slept with," he admits, shame in his voice.

I can feel tears prick at my eyes, but I refuse to let them fall. I look off to the side hoping to hide my emotions from him, but the idea of Braeden's hands on her makes my stomach turn. And I have no reason for feeling this way.

"If she meant nothing to you why was she here? Why did she have her hands on you? Why did you kiss her back?" I ask quickly, my emotions getting the best of me.

"If you had stayed and watched you would have seen me push her away," he says defeated. I continue to cross my arms and stare at him.

"All I can say is I am sorry, Phoenix. If you just give me a chance..." I interrupt him. I have to end this now.

"I think that it would be better if we were just friends."

His eyes turn sorrowful. "Friends?" he asks, his tone in disbelief. "Please don't let this ruin everything."

"Ruin what?" I ask confused.

"You know what," he says, his tone becoming harsh.

I shake my head. "We could never be anything, Braeden," I state, my eyes now looking at the ground. "I was stupid to think we could be."

"But you said that you felt something for me," he says, his voice getting louder.

"Please, I beg of you. It was nothing."

He takes a step closer to me, his body extremely close. I remain silent. He takes a few seconds before speaking again. "I could never explain the way you make me feel," he starts. "And I still can't to this day. But something about us is connected. The past few weeks have been incredible. Something inside me lit when we met, Phoenix. And I know it's the same for you."

"And how do you know that?" I ask, trying to be stern.

"Because I can see it. You are different around me than you are with others. I know that I make you nervous, but I also know that you feel something for me. Something you have never felt with anyone else."

I can now feel his breath on my face, his chest rising and falling.

"I can see it now," he continues. "You don't let Donovan get within 5 feet of you without flinching and here I am, standing mere inches from you."

I look up at him, his eyes intense. "It's too late for me, Braeden. I am broken beyond repair," I say, my throat tight. "You deserve better. You deserve someone you can touch. Who has the capability to…feel."

I back away slowly so that I can come out from under this spell his has over me. "Goodbye, Braeden," I whisper.

Turning around I run back to the hospital, leaving him alone in the frigid cold.

Braeden

"Goodbye Braeden," is all I hear as she retreats back to the hospital.

I remain planted, my mind frozen. This wasn't how we were supposed to end. Things hadn't even really started. Then I spring forward, my body in full action. When I catch up to her I know that we are extremely close and within the eyes of the security cameras, but I don't care. I reach out for her hand and lock my fingers in with her, her eyes widening instantly.

"Braeden, they will see," she says, her voice in a panic.

"I don't care," I admit, my tone harsh. "Do you not understand the feelings I have for you?" She remains silent. I hold up both our hands, our finger intertwined."Tell me you don't feel that and I will leave you alone. Forever."

I can see tears forming, her eyes becoming glossy. Reaching up with my free hand I touch her jaw gently and I feel her face lean into it slightly.

"I'm sorry," I say as I lean into her, placing my lips gently on hers. I keep my eyes open to watch her reaction, noticing that hers close instantly. I wait for her to panic but it never comes. I pull back, her eyes opening instantly. Now I see the fear. The panic.

Shit. Her fingers pull from mind, her fingers tracing the line of her lips. A small smile develops behind her hand.

"I'm so sorry," she says, her voice in a panic.
And just like that she runs off again.

Phoenix

Two weeks. It has been two weeks since I have talked to him. I have spent most of that time in my room. *Guess I really am a coward.* I hear a sigh echo through our room.

"What, Rain?" I mutter from under my comforter.

"Don't you want to eat something?"

"No, not really," I respond.

"But..." I flip my covers off, my body now facing hers.

"I really appreciate your concern but getting out of this bed sounds fucking awful right now."

Rain flinches at my use of vulgar language. Sometimes I swear she acts like my mother. To be honest, I have spent most of my time in my room, wanting to spend as little time out there. Of course I do have to go out at some point, but it's mostly for food and to show everyone that I am OK. I laugh out loud and Rain instantly reacts.

"What?" she says, a smile on her face.

"Nothing," I say, shifting back over to face the wall.

Who was I kidding? I was far from OK. But I was used to it.

~

I must have fallen asleep again because when my eyes open the room is completely dark and Rain's soft breathing reaches my ears. I sit up, pulling the covers off me, my body instantly breaking out into a sweat. Standing up, I stare over to where I know Rain is sleeping and a pain in my gut grows. I know that I have treated her like shit for a while now. She's the last person that I should be doing that to.

When Dr. Harris took me off my medication, I instantly felt my emotions heighten, everything pissing me off. But the tiredness stayed. Stumbling my way to the bathroom I sit down on the toilet, my bladder feeling as though it's going to pop. As I sit there I try to count back the days since we talked. As much as I tell myself I won't think about him, when things get silent he always sneaks into my thoughts. Which is a lot lately. Once I pulled away from his kiss I had ruined everything. I saw him a couple times after that, but he never looked my way. He never spoke to me. *Why would he?* He told me everything. He never lied once and yet I still refused to believe him. As the days stretched on I saw less and less of him. I overheard Donovan and him talking about his medical school so I assumed he was spending more time there and less time here.

When I finished, I got up and washed my hands, splashing a little on my face in hopes that it will wake me up. Feeling along the wall, I walk into the closet and try to grab things from memory. Slipping them on I walk back into the room and hear Rain snoring loudly. It makes me laugh and always amazes me how something so loud could come out of something so small. Opening the bedroom door slowly I peek across the hallway, happy to have the nurses' station so close. On the wall behind is a rip-away calendar. Looking up I smile. It's Tuesday.

Braeden doesn't work Tuesdays. I shake my head, realizing how pathetic I have become. A few days after the incident I found a copy of the employee schedule on the floor, committing it to memory before putting it back. Just as I am about the exit the room a tall figure flashes before me, scaring me instantly.

"Oh, good, you're awake," the figure says. I just nod in response.

"If you could please come with me," he says.

Opening the door more I slip out and then shut it

gently, making sure not to wake Rain. I follow behind him, my fingers intertwining in a nervous manner. My mind goes in a million different directions and I don't notice that he stops, my body ramming into him. I instinctively flinch. He turns around, giving me a wide smile.

"I'm sorry," I plead.

"That's quite alright, Phoenix, I know you didn't do it on purpose."

He pushes open a door, my heart racing.

"You may sit wherever you like," he says, ushering me in without touching me. A wave of nervousness comes over me, a feeling I have never had with Dr. Harris before. But I know why it's different this time. Walking into the room I sit in an over-sized arm chair. It's the most comfortable thing I have sat in a long time. Shimmying myself so that I sit upright, I watch Dr. Harris walk around his desk, setting some paperwork down. He looks up, giving me a small smile. He starts to make his way over, but stops at a high counter top. I see him pull out some scissors, my heart racing. He continues over, putting on a pair of rubber gloves.

"Is it OK if I sit down?" he asks, pointing to the ottoman across from my chair. I nod. As he sits down I am now eye level with him, it seeming to calm my nerves a bit.

"I am going to remove your stitches," he explains. "It may pinch, but it shouldn't cause you any great discomfort."

I laugh inside. If he really only knew how many times I have had this done. Reaching over gently he takes my arm in his hands, the six stitches displayed outright. He looks puzzled.

"They seem to be a little inflamed for how long it's been." I bite my lip, not responding. I've always had a thing for picking at things. Stitches and scabs included.

"But the wound seems to be healed," he says, continuing to snip them one by one. The room falls silent. When the procedure is done he wipes it with an alcohol swab.

"Do you want me to wrap it?" he asks.

I shake my head no. He nods slightly in return. As he goes to get up I notice that he is moving slowly, obviously for my benefit. He walks back over to the counter top and puts his utensils in a sterilizing bucket and washes his hands.

"Are you thirsty?" he asks, walking over to the mini fridge behind his desk. It makes me smile, not having pictured Dr. Harris as a mini fridge guy.

"Please," I mutter. He looks back in the fridge, shouting out what he has.

"I have sparkling water, iced tea or regular bottled water."

"Uh, iced tea, please," I say.

"Good choice." He smiles as he hands it to me.

"Thank you."

"You're very welcome, Phoenix."

I begin to wonder what he wants. Dr. Harris has never been mean to me but this was a little much.

"Is there something that you need?" I ask, hoping to get a roll on things.

"In particular...no," he states abruptly. "I just wanted to see how you are, considering I am your attending physician."

"I'm great, doc," I say, saluting my tea to him before taking a sip. *Mother of God this was good.*

"I'm sensing some sarcasm." He laughs. Ding. Ding. Ding. One point for the doctor. "Perhaps I should reword that, how are you feeling?"

Fan-fucking-tastic. "Much better," I lie.

"And without the medication?"

"Fine," I lie again.

"Cause you know there is no shame if you want to go back on it." I laugh inside. Maybe I should so I can be a zombie the rest of this shit they call life.

"I don't know," I say, looking down at my hands.

"Well, we'll just take it slow, it's only been a few days since you have been off it."

"Ok." Things fall silent again until a phone ringing fills the room, it making me jump.

"Excuse me," he says as he goes over and silences it. The room falls quiet again. He picks up what I think is my chart. "So, I see that you have been going to all your therapy appointments," he states, not really to me in particular. "She has quite some good things to say about you, you've made quite progress since your first visit."

If he really only knew how much of it was all bullshit. One could say I was a master of putting on fake faces. He goes to open his mouth again, but is stopped short by the sound of his phone ringing again. I even hear him sigh.

"I don't mind if you answer it," I say, hoping to get a small break from talking. He picks it up and answers it.

"Yes," he states.

I furrow my brow. That's an odd way of answering his phone. I look at the other side of the room, my eyes finding Dr. Harris' bookcase. Looking back over at him I realize his back is now facing me. Getting up from my chair I make my way over, running my hands along the spines of them. Most of them are rather thick medical books but when I start to read the titles I realize they are all about psychoanalysis. I grab one at random, opening it up. The text seems like a foreign language, most of them long medical terms. I skim a few pages, the illustrations intriguing.

"OK, Braeden," I hear Dr Harris mutters underneath his breath, probably because he didn't want me to hear. I didn't know if Braeden had told him anything, but part of me knew he did.

"I'm sorry," I say as I shut the book.

Looking up at the bookcase I try to remember where

it went, the once great hole where it sat now closed. *Shit.* Dr. Harris walks over to me, taking the book from my hands.

"We are never so defenseless against suffering as when we love." I snap my head up at him. He laughs lightly.

"Freud," he says, holding the book up.

I look back down, the burn in my cheeks growing.

He slides the book back in its spot but continues to stare at the bookcase as a whole.

"Have you read all these?" I ask, trying to make conversation.

"Yes," he says turning to me. "My wife used to say I was obsessed."

My heart drops at the mention of his wife. I forgot her death not only affected Braeden.

"Little did she know it was only research," he says quietly. I swear I hear his heart break. I mutter a sorry to him, a small smile returning on his lips.

"That's quite alright, Phoenix, it was a long time ago."

I continue to scan the bookcase, noticing two smaller books in the far corner, vastly different from the others. Dr. Harris must have noticed and reached back to pull them out, but only chooses one.

"This was her favorite book," he says handing it to me.

I look down at it. "Gone With The Wind." The cover

is cracked and thin, it apparent that it has been loved for many years.

"She used to sit in the windowsill all day long and read this over and over. She always smiled. It was the most beautiful thing I have ever seen."

I can feel my lip start to quiver. Sometimes I forget I am not the only person that has lost someone special.

"She seemed really incredible," I say, not knowing what else to do.

I go to hand him back the book but he doesn't reach out for it. "You should read it," he states. "That is, if you want to."

I look down at the book, feeling as though I would be invading her privacy. "I can't do that, it's hers...I mean yours...."

"She would be honored for you to read it, she was always making everyone else." He laughs. I couldn't say no to him with that smile so I just nod.

"I will take really good care of it, I promise."

"I know you will, Phoenix."

Clutching the book to my chest I leave his office, our discussion done for the day. When I got back to my room I immediately stash the book away, wanting to make sure nothing happened to it. I don't know why Dr. Harris has chosen to let me borrow it. Would it hold secrets about Braeden's mother? What about it had her so entranced? But somewhere in the dark corners of my sick mind, I knew what I was truly doing. I was keeping my connection to Braeden alive without directly seeing him.

After our discussion I immediately went back to bed, not really wanting to do much else. I felt emotionally drained. For once I hadn't been the only one in the room with painful memories. It was hard to miss the brokenness in Dr. Harris's eyes when he spoke about his wife. Braeden never told me the whole story about his mother's death, but he didn't have to for me to understand the hurt behind it. I miss my father every day, but fortunately my father didn't choose to leave me. Braeden's mother had gone willingly, by her own hand. She'd had people that loved her; people that did everything to help her. I had no one. I have no one.

~

When I woke up this morning I felt surprisingly refreshed. The haze in my head was gone, the tiredness vanished. In my new-found happiness, I sprung out of bed and got dressed quickly. Grabbing the book from my closet, I flung open the bedroom door and was greeted by the sunshine coming in from outside. The weather here was always so unpredictable, but I like to think the sun today was just for me.

Bounding for the patio door I push it open, finding a small spot on the ground underneath a tree. I sit down Indian style, the book gently settled in my lap. Somewhere between Scarlett, Ashley, Rhett and Charles, I become lost in their world of love and deceit.

Hours passed before I look up. I can feel the weather starting to shift, the warm sun starting to hide behind the thick fog.

I knew it was too good to be true. I can see why this was Sophia's favorite book. Scarlett is strong, overcoming adversity through brute strength of will. Scarlett is cunning and manipulates men with ease but she is also weak, insignificant things breaking her. But the most important theme of this story strikes me hard. The characters were most successful when they depended on no one but themselves. Did Sophia feel as though no one but herself could make things right?

As I continue to read I feel a figure standing over me, blocking my reading light. A long chill runs down my spine and I hesitate to look up. When I do, I see Dr. Harris standing over me, a crooked smile on his face.

"I see that you are enjoying it," he states, looking at where my finger is currently bookmarked, more than halfway through the mammoth novel.

"I am, very much," I respond, looking down at it as well, my tooth gnawing on my bottom lip. He lingers for a moment, making me antsy. I can tell that he is uncharacteristically uneasy as well.

"Did you need something?" I ask, my tone tentative.

"I just wanted to let you know you have a visitor."

My heart drops, bile rising in my throat. I feel light headed, like all the oxygen from the world has been removed. He doesn't have to tell me who it is.

"She has been here for quite some time actually," he states, his eyes looking straight into mine. "We've been talking."

She has been talking to him? Is she alone? I suddenly become very protective; an odd sensation.

"She would like to speak with you," he says softly.

He pauses. "He's not with her," he adds, as though he could read my mind.

My nerves calm a little but of the idea of being alone with Elaina still unsettles me. As much as I want to refuse, I know I need to channel a little Scarlett and try to be brave enough to handle her. I have to be strong. I get up from the ground, dusting the dirt off of me. Following him back into the building I stop at my bedroom door.

"Is it OK if I just put this back real quick?" I ask.

"Of course," he responds, waiting outside.

I run into the room, putting the novel in my closet. My hands are shaking, my breathing erratic. *It's just Elaina.* Shaking my body, I try to stop the nervousness, but it never completely goes away. Walking back out, I see Dr. Harris talking with a nurse, turning his attention back to me instantly.

"Ready?" I nod.

We make our way down the long hallway, each second passing slowly. We stop just outside his office door.

"It will be OK," he assures me. "I won't be far."

I watch him put his hand on the knob, my body trembling. Pushing it open he allows me to enter first. When I come around the corner, I spot her immediately. She is sitting in the same chair I had sat in not 24 hours ago. And for some reason that angers me. I feel like she is intruding. Intruding the one place I feel safe. Well, safe from them anyway. When I get fully into the room, my eyes fixate on the bookcase as though it's another person. Elaina's eyes fixate on me. A smile blooms on her face. *Fake.*

I look closer at her eyes, noticing that they are bloodshot and red, and the skin around them puffy. There is a tissue in her hand. *Who knew she had emotions.* She goes to get up from her chair but the purse that was on her lap falls to the floor, the contents spilling everywhere.

"Oh, I'm such a klutz," she says through a broken voice.

She bends down, trying to pick everything up quickly. Dr. Harris, who must have been behind me this whole time, walks around me, helping her. I remain frozen, laughing to myself on the inside. *Typical dramatic Elaina.* When they finish up, Dr. Harris calls me over. When I go to move my foot forward I feel myself kick something. Looking down there is a can of pepper spray settled between my feet. Picking it up, I walk over to the other couch, holding it out to her. She gives me a crooked smile and takes it from me. What does she need that for? The room falls silent and I start to chew on the inside of my cheek. Dr Harris remains standing and looks over at me.

"Your mother..." *She's not my mother.* "Would like to talk to you. And I think that you owe it to her to listen."

I involuntarily give him my biggest bitch face.

"It doesn't seem like I have a choice," I snap.

"Phoenix," I hear Elaina say.

"Don't call me that," I respond, my voice angered.

"I can't call you by the name that I gave you?" she says harshly.

"You didn't name me, dad did," I say, hoping to hurt her.

"Don't bring your father into this," she says.

I hear her sigh then close her eyes. "I didn't come here to fight with you," she adds.

Her eyes are now open again and she turns to face Dr. Harris. "Can I have some alone time with my daughter?"

I snap my eyes up at him, silently begging him to stay.

He clears his throat before speaking. "I'll be right outside if you need me."

To be honest, I don't know which one of us he's talking to. Once he leaves the room things remain silent until she speaks first.

"How have you been, sweetheart?" she asks, her

body now shifted to face me.

"Why are you here?" I immediately say, not answering her question.

"I wanted to see how you are."

"That's bullshit," I mutter under my breath.

I hear her sigh again, her face dropping. A twinge of guilt runs through me. *Don't play into it.*

"So, how have things been with Mr. Charming?"

I don't even want to say his fucking name. Elaina looks back up and reaches over, setting her hand down on top of mine. I stare down at it for a second before moving back so that it falls off.

"He's gone, baby," she says, a smile on her face.

I laugh. "Good one Elaina."

"God damnit, Phoenix," she hisses. "Stop it."

"Stop what?" I say calmly, knowing it's pissing her off.

"Why do you do this to me?"

I laugh. "Do what to you?"

My voice escalates to match hers. Elaina takes another deep breath. "I am your mother, whether you like it or not. And I came here to get you back, sweetie," she says as she gets up and sits next to me on the couch. She reaches out and grabs my hands again, holding on tight so I can't pull away.

"I came here to apologize." Tears start to gather in her eyes. "And that I know. I've always known, but I've been too cowardly to do anything about it. And I'm so, so sorry, baby," she adds.

I look at her confused. "Know what?" I ask. I wanted to her say it. Out loud. I wanted her to admit that she has knowingly allowed her disgusting man put his hands on me. And that she never did anything to stop it. Nothing. Removing her hands from mine she starts to take her scarf off, and I now realize how many layers she was actually wearing. I can't help but stare at her as she removes it slowly, my eyes focus on the bruises. I think I gasp. I can't be quite sure. Some kind of noise comes out of me. From deep in my gut, where I feel like I've been punched.

"Mom," I say, reaching out.

I put my hand up to my lips, shocked that I even knew how to say that word. The marks on her neck are all too familiar. I can tell that they are slightly yellow around the edges, a sign that they are starting to heal.

"When did this happen?" I ask, still surprised by my own compassion. She reaches up putting her hand over it.

"Oh, a few weeks ago." I look down at my hands. "But he's gone now, baby."

The anger in me starts to return. I stand up, my body towering over her. "So, it took him hitting *you* for you to kick his ass to the curb?"

A sorrowful look comes across her face but doesn't answer. "Why didn't you ever believe me?" I ask, trying to calm myself. "I never gave you a reason not to trust me."

"I know, sweetie," she answers, her voice cracking. "I wouldn't exactly call myself mother of the year."

I bite my lip to refrain myself from the venom my mouth wants to spew at her. She scoots even closer. "But from here on out, I want to make things better. I want to start anew."

I look at her confused. "Dr. Harris is releasing you, baby," she says reaching up and brushing my cheeks. "You get to come home."

Tears start prick at my eyes and as much as I try to stop them I can't.

"Ahh, sweetie," she says as she wipes them away. "Are those happy or sad tears?" Honestly, how can she even ask?

I turn my head so I no longer face her. I can't look at her anymore. My eyes land on the bookcase again. My mind goes to Sophia. To him. To them. *Family.*

"He said that I could leave?" I say turning back to her.

"Uh huh!"

Just like that I was free? How could he think I'm ready for this? I hear a knock on the door, Dr. Harris entering.

"Everything going OK in here?" he asks as he shuts the door behind him. I wipe away the tears I've been silently shedding from my face, suddenly embarrassed.

"Of course!" Elaina says her tone all too confident.

"Great," Dr. Harris says as he crosses his hands. "Well, if you don't mind I would like to speak to Phoenix alone."

Elaina nods and reaches over to give me a hug, my body stays rigid.

"I love you, sweetie," she whispers in my ear before kissing the side of my head. I don't respond. I haven't said those three words to anyone since the day of my father's death. She lets go of me and gets up, leaving Dr. Harris and I alone. I shake my head slightly, realizing I feel safer with him than I do my own flesh and blood. Dr. Harris sits down in the chair opposite me.

"How are you feeling, Phoenix?" he asks.

"Fine," I say confused by his question.

"Well, I am sure that your mother told you, but I have signed your release paperwork." Those words coming from his lips scare me even more.

"Dr. Young and I have talked quite extensively and we feel that your time here is no longer a necessity. However, I do strongly suggest that you continue intensive outpatient therapy."

I don't respond. My mind going in a million different directions.

"Since you are older than 18, I can't force you to go to your mother," he continues. "But I feel that rebuilding your relationship with her will be very beneficial."

I bite my lip. He stops talking, allowing me to gather my thoughts.

"I'm scared," I blurt out.

"I know you are. You have a long road to recovery, Phoenix. But you're ready to face the outside world. You can't stay in this bubble forever. Part of recovering is learning to be on the outside again. Learning to deal with fear and anger from everyday situations. You're ready for the next step," he says. "Your mother and I have talked at great length. I wouldn't be releasing you if he were still in the picture."

"OK," I say while nodding. I can stay with her until I find a job and then be on my own.

"Great," he says then stands.

"Do I have to go now?" I ask my nerves still high.

"No, she will be back tomorrow morning to pick you up. Give you some time to get your things together and to say goodbye."

Goodbye? My mind goes instantly to Rain and immediately I don't want to go. I stand up and nod.

"Thank you, Dr. Harris," I say.

He smiles. "How many times have I told you to call me Neil?"

"Not enough." I respond with a smile.

"Good luck to you, Phoenix," he says holding his hand out. "I'm always a phone call away."

I look down at his hand and then take it in mine. His handshake is firm. For some reason I feel like I am saying goodbye not only to him. Exiting the room the hospital looks completely different. Foreign. Didn't I just think of this as my safe place? I am glad when I see Elaina is talking with a nurse, so I just slip past her and head immediately for my room. When I open the door Rain is sitting upright, her outfit and hair perfect. A pout forms across her face and I can't help but laugh and shake my head.

"Of course you know," I say as I enter the room.

She stands up and puts her arms around me. "I am so happy for you, Phoenix."

"But what about you?" I ask.

She pulls back and waves it off. "I will be fine, just think how much bigger my room will be again."

I laugh as we both sit down on my bed. "So, she showed up, huh?"

I nod. "Was it weird seeing her?" I nod again. Unable to speak without the emotions crashing down again.

~

The last night in the hospital was my most restless. By around two in the morning I had given up and decide to roam the hallways which were eerily quiet at this hour. I haven't seen Donovan in a really long time. I wish he was here for me to say goodbye, but that would probably only make things worse. Turning the corner I decide to head outside, the building becoming stifling. As usual it's freezing out but I couldn't care less.

Walking the length of the courtyard all I can think about is him. When I reach the fence I look out over the bay, seeing the lights of the Golden Gate shinning. I find myself staring at it, probably longer that I should have. It's in that moment I realize how much life has changed. How much I have changed. Maybe things really can be different. Maybe I can be a little like Scarlett.

I look up at the sky, almost hoping for an answer or something. Pulling myself away from the fence I head back inside, my arms wrapped around myself. Just as I reach inside I hear a large roll of thunder, it jarring me slightly.

~

Ten came way too fucking quickly. Elaina had left behind some clothes for me yesterday and I would be lying if I wasn't excited to see my favorite shoes and a hooded sweatshirt. Maybe she has changed. When I had finished packing I gave Rain a hug, promising her that I would come back to visit her. Dr. Harris ushered me out, but stopped before we reached Elaina, who was now outside waiting. I can tell something is off with him and that worries me.

"Is everything OK?" I blurt out.

He smiles. "Yes, I'm sorry. I don't wish to worry you," he says as he pulls out a piece of paper. "I know that this may be very untoward, but I wanted to give you my phone numbers."

I look down, taking the piece of paper from him. He

clears his throat before continuing. "There is my number for here..." he points to the first one. "And then at the bottom, my personal cell and home number. Please don't ever hesitate to call me if you need anything."

I look back up at him. *Was there some "Save Phoenix" program I didn't know about?*

"Thank you," I say, oddly warmed by the gesture. "Oh and I almost forgot." I reach around grabbing the book out of my bag. "Here, this belongs to you."

Dr. Harris takes it in his hands, a smile on his face. He traces his fingers across the cover as though retracing a memory and hands it back towards me.

"You take it. You haven't finished it have you?" he asks

I shake my head. "Well, then it's settled. Bring it back to me when you're done with it. I'd love to hear what you think of the story."

I reach up slowly taking it again. "Thank you... Neil," I say, a smile on my face. "I will take good care of it."

"You're most welcome, Phoenix. Take good care of yourself too."

When we make it through the automatic door, I immediately spot Elaina. She's sitting in the car and I must say I'm not surprised to see the white, piece of shit El Camino. I turn around to give Dr. Harris a smile before Elaina spots us, jumping out of the car to grab my things. She looks truly happy. I take one last scan of the hospital, knowing what I am looking for. When I don't see it I slide into the passenger's seat, Elaina shutting it behind me.

"Goodbye, Braeden," I whisper as we pull out, the view of the hospital out of sight.

~

As soon as we pulled out I could feel my nerves rising, the signs of a panic attack becoming apparent. Reaching over I crank the window down, the fresh air feels good. I close my eyes, knowing every turn from the hospital to the house, it being only a ten-minute drive. When I feel the vehicle come to a complete stop I keep my eyes closed for a prolonged period of time before opening them, one by one. The house looks exactly the same and for some reason that unsettles me. Elaina jumps out of the car and walks over to my door, opening it. I know that she is putting on a show and I try to not get caught up in her games. She goes to reach for my bag but I grab it first, not wanting her to tarnish it. When I stand in the driveway, I look over at the oil spots on the concrete where Carl's truck is usually parked.

Biting my lip, I make it up the steps to the front door, Elaina already inside. I'm glad she's not hovering. Once I get inside things start to feel foreign. I had only spent thirty days at the hospital, but it seemed like an eternity. I spot Elaina come out of the kitchen, two glasses in her hands. I know instantly what she has.

"It's still your favorite right?" she asks, handing one glass to me.

I shrug. "I didn't have much other than water in the hospital," I say taking a sip.

I didn't know whether to be happy or sad. This was my father's favorite drink when there was no beer in the house. But he did always tell me that Elaina used to make them for him. He always liked the way the sparkling water fizzed the orange juice. I take another sip, an awkward silence overtakes the room.

"Well, I think I am going to just go up to my room. That is, if it's still there."

I hear Elaina huff. "Of course it's still there."

I just nod while holding the drink up in the air. "Thanks for the drink."

I clutch my bag in my hand as I make my way up the stairs, keeping my eyes forward, fixated only on the direction of my room. I find myself becoming antsy so I start to take two steps at a time, reaching my door within seconds. Slamming it behind me I lean against the back of it, my chest heaving. When I have calmed down slightly I put my bag on my bed, looking around at everything. It all seems so unfamiliar. Like another version of me lived here previously. Pulling the book out, I reach over, opening my nightstand drawer, a small flask clanking against the side. I pick it up, unscrewing the lid and lift it up to my nose and inhale.

Vodka.

Grabbing my cup, I empty its contents; figuring being drunk at this moment could only help things. I walk back over to my bed, grabbing the rest of the contents of my bag in my arms in one big fabric mess. Walking over to my closet I slide the doors open with my foot. As I go to throw them in I feel a sharp pain hit my ankle. Dropping the pile I look down, a small ball of toilet paper lies just to the left of my foot. Reaching down I feel its sharp edges, my heart instantly sinking. With it still in my hands I walk back to my nightstand slowly and grab my cup, downing it without taking a breath.

I sit down on my bed, slowly unwrapping it, sheet by sheet, until the figure is exposed. Holding the seal in my hand, all the emotions I had been holding onto break loose. I heave, the tears coming too fast, my breathing not able to keep up. I instantly start to feel like I may pass out. Throwing the figurine onto my desk I pull the door open, heading to the bathroom. I turn the cold faucet on, splashing water on my face. When I start to feel a little better I sit on top of the toilet, my elbows rested on my knees, holding a damp towel on my face.

"Sweetie, are you OK?" I hear.

I pull the towel down to see Elaina standing in the bathroom doorway.

"Yeah," I mutter. "Just swallowed my drink down the

wrong tube."

"Oh! I hate when that happens," she says before bouncing off.

"Yeah, me too," I respond, rolling my eyes.

I look around the room, seeing a faint burgundy stain on the wall. I sit up immediately, realizing they never replaced the mirror. Reaching up I feel the 3-inch scar along my clavicle. Getting up from the toilet I sprint out, slamming the door of the bathroom shut behind me, trying to close off the memory.

I spend the rest of the afternoon in my room, not really wanting to be with Elaina quite yet. Grabbing the last of the contents in my bag I fish out the chain, holding it between my fingers. Turning over the heart pendent, I read the inscription I now know by heart.

You are always my reason to smile.

Clasping the necklace onto my neck I can feel his love flow through me, warming my heart.

~

I spent as much time in my room as I could, but I knew I would have to go down for dinner eventually. I walked into the kitchen where Elaina was seated at the kitchen table, a glass in her hand.

"Whatcha got there?" I ask.

"Oh, Phoenix, I didn't hear you come in," she says, getting up from the chair and empties her glass into the sink.

"I see that you still drink," I say harshly.

I could still feel the warmth of the vodka flowing through my veins. Liquid courage. I know I am a hypocrite for taunting her about the very thing I resorted to, to calm my frayed mind but it just feels good to be bitchy to her right now. I need to maintain my wall of animosity. Whatever, she has it coming.

"I really am trying, sweetie, it's just hard...ya know?"

I roll my eyes while facing in the opposite direction. Pulling open the fridge I am not surprised by what I see.

"And I guess I will have to go grocery shopping."

"I figured we could go out!" she says, suddenly excited.

"I'm a little tired to go out in public, Elaina," I lie. I could find something to make here. I was experienced with making dinner out of nothing. Grabbing a thing of hamburger meat out of the fridge, I check the date. Surprisingly it's still good. Opening the pantry I grab a box of noodles and a jar of spaghetti sauce. When I finished cooking, I slid a plate to Elaina, who had yet to move from her spot at the table.

"Thanks, sweetie!" she exclaims. "You were always a better cook than me."

"You have to actually *cook* to learn how to cook," I snap.

She looks at me as though disappointed. Picking up my fork, I shove a huge amount of noodles into my mouth, hoping to stop the word venom. We eat mostly in silence, except for Elaina who feels the need to ask petty questions. When I clear my plate, I immediately stand up and wash it before putting it in the dishwasher.

"You know you don't have to wash it first, that is the purpose of the actual dishwasher."

I don't respond. "Well, I am going to bed," I shout as I round the corner of the kitchen, not waiting for her to answer.

When I get back to my room I shut the door behind me, locking it. *Habit.* I look over my room again, it feeling no more familiar than before. Pulling my body away I reach into the first drawer of my dresser and pull out a pack of matches. Striking one, I light the candle beside my bed and the one on my desk. Walking over to my windowsill I plug in the blue twinkle lights that I had hung years ago. Sliding open my nightstand again I pick up the book before lying down on my bed. Finding the place that I had bookmarked, I get lost in the world of 1861 Georgia all over again.

~

The smell of a snuffed out candle reaches my nose, it instantly awakening me. Looking over, I notice that the small votive on my nightstand has been blown out. I yawn loudly and stretch, pulling the open book off my chest. I reach over to set it down on my nightstand when I sense movement. I slowly shift my eyes to where my closet is. Looking back at me is a pair of eyes, his tall dark form now hovering over me.

Braeden

I can't seem to hold my eyes open any more. Grabbing my phone next to me I turn it on to check the time. It's way past when I was planning on going to bed. A deep yawn leaves my throat as I slam the textbook shut, officially having met my knowledge quota for the day. Getting up from my chair I pull off my shirt and jeans, sliding into bed, the cool sheets refreshing. Reaching over I click my light off, the room falls into complete darkness. Even though my body and mind are tired, I can't seem to fall asleep quickly. I can't shut my brain off. School has been incredibly exhausting, so I had to cut my hours back at the hospital. It's probably for the better. I haven't seen much of Phoenix since the day outside. I'm sure she's been avoiding me and at this point I've learned that it's better if I just move on. I would be lying if I said I didn't think about her often.

~

Pulling open my bedroom door, I sleepily rub the palms of my hands on my eyes, trying to wake myself up. I grab onto the banister just like my mother has always told me. However, I become confused when I look down at my arm, it's covered in black hair. Rushing down the rest of the steps I find the mirror in the foyer and I am immediately shocked at what I see. I am in my parents' house but I am present day age, not the young version of me I am usually. The house is quiet and moonlight shines through the living room windows. I start to walk towards the backyard, my feet almost having a mind of their own. For some reason, I am conscious of what I am about to find, tears already streaming down my face. When I make it outside, I see a billow of smoke, the shed completely engulfed in flames, the crackling of timber reaching my ears. Running over I try to pull the door open, but it won't budge. Taking off my shirt I punch the window out, the glass only repairing itself with every hit. Tears are still running down my face and I let out an angry scream into the wind. Something inside me tells me not to give up. It only takes me a second to realize she is near.

"I can't get in," I say through cries.

"I have faith in you, baby. She needs you."

I take another deep breath as I collect all of my anger, letting all of the fear leave my body. Taking a few steps back so that my feet are practically on the edge of the pool, I start to run, leaning my shoulder out first. Within a fraction of a second my body collides with the building and it explodes. The walls and floor boards fly off in every direction and I fall back, the force too strong. When I have the ability to get back up, the sight before me makes me instantly heave and I vomit in the grass next to me. Most of the building is gone except the ceiling boards which are magically still afloat, the ends of the boards glowing from the embers. And from it hangs Phoenix. Her delicate body swaying back and forth in the wind.

~

I fly up out of bed, my clothes drenched in sweat. It takes me a few seconds to gather where I am, the details of the dream replaying over and over in my mind. And then I feel it. A sick feeling in my gut that something's not right. Jumping out of bed, I grab my clothes from the floor, putting them on in a flash. Grabbing my wallet off the counter I run out of my apartment.

"Taxi!" I scream out as soon as I get out of my apartment building.

Of course there is no response. Unfortunately this isn't the city that never sleeps. Breaking into a run I go for as long as I can until I spot a cab and run out in front of it, its breaks screech as the vehicle comes to a halt. Pulling open the door I see the pissed off look on the driver's face. I couldn't care less.

The rest of the ride my mind is lost inside itself. I don't even know if anything is wrong, but in my gut I feel like there is. When we pull up to the hospital I pull out some cash, not even knowing if it's enough. Sprinting up to the front entrance I continue down the hallway, my body screeching to a halt outside her bedroom door. *I've gone insane.* Leaning my head on it, I contemplate if I should just go home, but I know I won't be able to go back to my apartment without knowing. I need some kind of reassurance. Some kind of proof that I am truly now as insane as some of the patients we help here. I slowly open the door, the room is completely dark.

"Phoenix," I whisper.

No response. Reaching on the wall, I find the light switch, flicking it on. And my worst fear becomes a reality. Phoenix's bed is empty, the sheets and comforter are made up nicely. I go to leave the room again, until a figure comes out of the bathroom.

"Rain," I shout, running up to her. Her face is white, her eyes distant. "Rain," I repeat. "Where is she?"

She finally looks over at me. "She's gone..." she says.

My heart races even more. *What kind of gone?* I leave the room in a hurry, knowing immediately my next stop. Grabbing the door handle I fling the familiar office door open, and glare at the figure sitting behind the desk.

"Where is she?" I shout as I come around to face him.

A concerned look spreads across his face. "Braeden, what is going on?"

"Where. Is. She?" I repeat, not answering his previous question. He walks out from around his desk, placing a hand on my shoulder.

"She's gone, Braeden," he says.

"Will everyone please stop fucking saying that. What the hell does that mean? She's fucking dead isn't she?"

He looks at me puzzled again. "What? Why would you think that, Braeden?" he pauses. "No. She's been released."

I can't tell if that makes me relived or more irritated.

"I mean...who...when..." I start to mutter as a million things runs through my mind, pissed that I wasn't on shift today.

"She left with her mother," he starts to say as he looks down at his watch. "What would be yesterday morning..."

"You let her leave with *them?* How could you fucking allow that? I swear sometimes you can be so goddamn stupid," I snap.

"Braeden, why don't you come over here and sit down. You're going to give yourself a panic attack."

"Honestly, how can you think her leaving with them

would do any good for Phoenix?"

My father's body tenses, his face hardening. "Last time I checked I was Phoenix's doctor. You have no right to decide what is good for her or not. She is an adult, whether you want to believe it or not. She is of age, Braeden. I didn't force her to go, she chose to."

My mind starts running in a million different directions.

"But what about your suspicions? I mean you got him banned from here... you had to know..."

He shakes his head slightly. "That's just it, Braeden. They were just suspicions. Until Phoenix admits out loud that her stepfather abused her we can't do anything," he grumbled. "I won't lie to you. Part of me okayed the release because I thought maybe she'd say no to going home and would finally admit to Dr. Young what was happening. She was getting very far with her in their sessions. But she went...with little hesitation."

My blood boils through my veins. I didn't need confirmation from her lips. The way Phoenix acted around men was enough evidence for me. I have to make sure she is OK. If these doctors refuse to protect her, I will. But then is dawned on me. She left because she didn't want to see my anymore. *She would rather go back there than be around me?* My mind instantly shifts when I spot her chart on his desk.

"You know what, dad, I think I could use a glass of water, do you mind getting me one?"

"Sure, son," he nods, leaving the room.

As soon as I hear the door latch shut I reach over his desk, thumbing through it, heading to the last page. Emergency Contacts.

Grabbing a pen from his desk I write the address on my palm, my hand shaking so bad it's barely legible. Hauling the door open I break into a sprint down the hallway, my father's voice shouting my name behind me. I felt ashamed for deceiving my father but he will understand eventually. I thank my lucky fucking stars when I see a cab parked out front, pulling the door open.

"Bryant Street," I say quickly.

The cab takes off without any conversation; him obviously noticing my desperate state. I keep my head down and choose to not look out the window. My stomach does flip flops, every scenario running through my mind. *Or like I have been saying, you're insane.* When the cab pulls up to the curb, my head snaps up and looks at the house. Grabbing another wad of cash I hand it to the driver.

"There is some extra in there for you, can you please wait for a few minutes?"

The driver takes the cash and nods, pulling out a magazine. I exit from the vehicle, shutting the car door behind me quietly. Making my way up the driveway I put my hands in my pockets, realizing how cold it is. To my left is a large white truck, the engine making tinkering noises, a sign it was running not too long ago. When I get halfway there I stop and wait. Listening for anything.

Phoenix

My heart rate jumps and a familiar feeling of nausea overtakes me. I go to scream but his hands are over my mouth within seconds.

"Ahhh...you should know by now that screaming only makes things worse."

Tears are falling down my face and I still try to scream but it's too muffled. I try to kick and punch him with all my might but he is too strong. He leans over me and puts his leg on top of mine so that I am pinned to the mattress. I look up at him, his eyes are glossed over and red. A clear sign he is drunk. His face is hard, the anger in them more intense than I have ever seen. I still continue to try to scream out.

"Shhh shhh shhh, you don't want to wake your mother now, do you?"

I scream out a garbled "fuck you" underneath his hand, surprised by my own internal strength. After that comment his eyes narrow and he becomes even more outraged.

"Your mother thinks she could get rid of me?" he says through gritted teeth. "You are both going to pay for that mistake."

He removes his leg from mine in an attempt to shift his weight. Giving all my strength I flail, getting half my body out from underneath him, his hand slipping from my mouth.

"HELP!" I scream out at the top of my lungs, my voice cracking. My feet find the floor and I try to get away. I lunge for the door and manage to get my hands on the knob and fumble with the lock, my hands shaking violently, my vision blurred by my tears.

"I see that you are making this fun for me," he breathes into my ear, the smell of his hot breath makes my head spin. "Let's try something new."

I hear the slow decent of a zipper and I cry out. Instinctively I throw my elbow backwards but it collides with his stomach and not the place I was aiming for. I feel intense pain in my scalp. Reaching back I try to pry his hands from my hair, but his grip is tight. The next thing I feel is my body being hurled forward, my head slamming into the metal door knob. My body crumbles to the floor, a loud ringing in my ears now apparent. My vision starts to blur but I keep my eyes on him. He glides across to the other side of my room, grabbing the still lit candle off my desk. His mouth is moving but I can't make out the words.

"Moooom," I cry out before everything goes black.

Braeden

My body heaves as it tries to recollect oxygen, but my nerves are still on high. The night is eerily quiet. I watch the steam come from my breath. My ear catches a sound. I swear I heard her voice. Looking up at the house, I squint, seeing something off in the distance coming from the upper bedroom window. And then I smell it. *Smoke.*

Before my brain has time to process my legs are running forward. I climb up the steps, taking them two at a time, reaching the front door in a millisecond. My mind immediately shifts to my dream, the emotions flowing through me right now match those in the dream. Backing away from the door slightly I run straight at it, my body collides and it flies open, smacking against the opposite wall with a loud bang.

The veins in my body fill with adrenaline. Consciously trying to slow myself down, I take in my surroundings, the downstairs is completely quiet, nothing but the glow of a TV filling the room. But the strong odor of smoke fills my nostrils, it making my heart race even faster. Pulling up the collar of my shirt, I try to block myself from inhaling it and ascend the stairs. My eyes begin to water intensely due to the smoke, my vision almost completely dark.

"Phoenix!" I scream out, hoping that she will hear me.

Nothing. Feeling my way around I find an opening and wipe the water from my eyes, the room illuminated by a fire that is currently billowing from the curtains by what looks like a desk. I don't know what told me to pick this room first but from what I can tell by the things on the floor, it's a girl's room. As I continuously wipe my eyes I make out a rather large form on the floor. I don't have to think twice about what it is. I fall to the ground beside her body, the heat from the flames excruciating. Her eyes are closed, her body gravely still. My mind tells me to do a million different things at once, it resulting in my muscles frozen in place.

"Phoenix," I scream again, jolting her body.

Nothing. But finally something in me kicks on, my mind clear on what I have to do. Reaching my hands underneath her I pick up her delicate body and make my way downstairs, trying to find an exit through my burning eyes. When I find the front door again I bound down the stairs and set her and myself on the sidewalk. Laying her out flat I tilt her head back, listening for normal breathing. I rub my hands on her face, waiting for her to open her eyes, my uneasiness not settling.

I know now that I have to have to give her CPR. My lungs are already on fire, wondering if I even have any oxygen left to give. Placing my palms on her sternum I push, trying to remember the right repetition. I finish pushing after thirty, then immediately place my lips on her, blowing as much oxygen into her lungs as I can.

"Come on!" I scream, my anger now taking over. Nothing. "You can't do this to me. You're not dead. You can't leave me too."

I don't know how many times I repeat the process but I'm well aware of tears running down my face. They are not the result of the smoke anymore. But I continue to give CPR until every muscle in my body becomes weak. Just when I am about to give up, I hear something. *My mind must be playing tricks on me.* But when I pick my head back up I see her eyes looking back at me. They are full of fear. Pulling my hands from her chest I scoot even closer to her, my hands automatically rubbing her forehead.

"Phoenix," was all I could breathe out.

Her eyes instantly start to swell up with tears, the

vision absolutely heartbreaking.

"Are you hurt?" I ask.

She nods. I go to put my arms underneath her to lift, but she starts shaking her head violently, her body fighting my every move. I can tell she is trying to talk.

"What?" I ask, trying to understand what she wants.

Phoenix puts her shaky hand to her throat. "Mmmmyyy mmmoooommmm," she says, her voice harshly disfigured.

"You want me to get your mom?" I ask, my voice partly shocked.

Part of me wanted nothing more than to get as far away from here, but the look in Phoenix's eyes were desperate. Pleading.

"Are you going to be OK out here alone?" I ask clearly concerned. She just nods. "I will be right back, OK?" I say, squeezing her hand.

Getting up from the sidewalk I run back into the house, the smoke ten times more intense. I hated having this distance between us again, my mind always on her as I navigate. Walking over to the sliding door I open it, ventilating the downstairs slightly. Finding the stairs again I bound up them, but move slower than before. The house is quiet except the crackle of the flames. But then I hear a cough that's too feminine to be his. I try to think back to Phoenix's chart, but my mind is fuzzy. But then it snaps.

"Elaina?"

The cough becomes louder. And then I see her. Walking over I bend down so that we are face to face. I can see a river of blood flowing from her nose, her right eye almost swollen shut.

"Can you walk?" I ask.

"I don't know," she says.

Leaning down I put her arm around my shoulder and lift her up. Luckily she seems to not stumble badly as we stand and begin heading back to stairs.

"OK, were going to take one step at a...."

My words are cut off when I feel an excruciating pain in my shoulder, my grip on Elaina faltering, her body leaving my fingertips. Turning around I see him behind me, a knife in his hands, its tip drenched in my blood. Within seconds his hands are around me and my body is being tossed back and forth. Every time I land on the ground I cry out, my whole body in agony. Getting back up I look at his face, an eerie smile across it. The *fucking sick bastard is getting joy from this.* I can feel blood start to slide down my face, my right eyebrow on fire.

"Got a little blood there," he taunts, wiping his own eyebrow.

"Go fuck yourself," I spit, my new found rage shocking even myself. His smile widens as he looks over the blade again. It's now that I realize I am against a wall, his massive figure towering over me.

Phoenix

Pain. That's all I could feel.

My mind tried to put everything together but it was one big broken puzzle. I could only remember bits and pieces. One thing was for sure. Braeden was here. Braeden had pulled me out. But what I didn't know was what he was doing here. I continue to lay there on the sidewalk, my mind not being able to concentrate but on only one thing. Every second he was gone I began to question myself. Why would I trade his safety for hers?

~

I don't know how much time passes but I began to get uneasy, the smoke billowing from the house, the flames disintegrating the curtain on the upstairs window. I can't just sit here and wait.

I grip the right side of my abdomen as I lift myself

off the ground, my whole body screaming in agony. After what seems like an eternity of mostly crawling I reach the opened front door, once again entering the fiery building. I can feel the adrenaline flowing through my veins now, it subsiding the pain slightly. As I stand in the middle of the family room I can't do much but listen. I cry out when my ears pick up on something. I hear voices but I can't make out what they are saying. But in my gut I know one of them is Braeden's. Looking around the room I try to find something. Anything. And then I see it. I pick it up in my hand to test its weight. I'm satisfied when it feels quite heavy. I plan out what I know has to be done. I can't let anything happen to him. He doesn't deserve it.

When I make it to the bottom of the stairs I can't see much but I stop and listen, hearing his labored breath and follow it. I start up them slowly, the bottle grasped tightly in my fingers. When I reach the top I put my arm up and put my face into my elbow, hoping to block out some of the smoke. That when I see him. His figure is facing away from me and I smile inside. I am breathing hard at this point. When I get mere inches from him I drop my elbow and grip the bottle with both hands and swing with all my might, the bottle colliding with the side of his head, the noise is loud to my ears. I cry out in pain, my side hurting immensely. Carl's body goes limp and he drops to his knees for a second, before toppling to the floor in the fetal position. I stop, every part of my body frozen. Time stands still.

"Phoenix, we have to get out of here!" I hear someone scream at me.

But I can't move. I just stare. Stare at the lifeless body at my feet. I get joy from the flowing red. I feel a brush on my cheek, snapping me back to reality. All I see is his eyes. The beautiful emerald green I have been longing for. And then the sound of sirens drowns out my thoughts.

Braeden

At this point I have one concern. Get Phoenix out. I can feel the flow of the blood making my shirt stick to me and I begin to feel lightheaded. Her body and mind are completely frozen from the shock. Grabbing her hand I pull her down the stairs, knowing it may be any moment before the fire reaches this hallway. When we reach outside our bodies slam into someone else.

"Are you two alright?" he asks.

"I, uh...." I stutter not really knowing how to answer that.

"Is there anyone else in the house?" I contemplate telling him no.

"Her mother." I stop myself. Grappling with knowing I have to tell them about him, but really not wanting to.

"We've got her, she's already being treated in the ambulance."

"There is one more, upstairs," I state. As much as I wanted to, I can't be that evil. Plus he deserves nothing more than to rot in jail the rest of his pitiful life. That is if he lives.

"OK," he responds

Once we reach the driveway I am blinded by red flashing lights. It's absolute chaos, both policeman and fireman running amuck. That's when I see my father.

"Braeden," he says running over to me.

"I'm fine, I'm fine," I assure him.

"Medics!" he screams, paramedics running over to us immediately.

I look over to Phoenix, our hands still intertwined, tears rolling down her face.

"You both need to be treated," he says. Phoenix squeezes my hand harder.

"We can both go to the same ambulance," I state rather than question, pleading with my eyes to my father. He nods. Leading us to the open ambulance, I swing Phoenix around so that she enters first and I follow, never letting go of her hand once. The paramedic gets in after us, holding the oxygen mask out. I shift my eyes to Phoenix and she slides it onto her face gently. Her grip on my hand never falters.

"I'll see you two at the hospital," Neil says before slamming the doors shut.

Phoenix remained silent throughout the ride, her hand still gripping mine tightly. I don't take my eyes off her until the ambulance comes to a stop, my heart racing immediately. I go to get up but Phoenix doesn't move.

"Phoenix?"

She doesn't respond. The paramedic goes to shift her so that she can lay down on the gurney but Phoenix flinches, her eyes now fixated on the restraints.

"Just stop," I tell the paramedic, suddenly angry that they are causing her distress.

"We need to get her inside," the paramedic responds. "She shouldn't walk."

Swinging myself around, I take Phoenix in my arms and carry her out of the ambulance. When we reach just outside the lobby, a nurse awaits with a wheel chair. Setting her down in it gently, her fingers find mine, her grasp strong again. We walk back inside, waiting for my father to show up. Minutes later, he and a team of nurses come around the corner.

"I'm going to have to let go." I bend down and whisper into her ear, snapping her out of her zombie state.

"No," she says, a tear running down her face. Reaching up with my other hand, I brush her cheek lightly, afraid she may recoil from my touch.

"I promise I am not going anywhere," I say. "Do you trust me?"

She nods. I start to unlock my fingers from hers, our hands releasing. Phoenix returns to her comatose state.

"Dad," I utter, still facing Phoenix.

"Yeah, Braeden?" he says, pulling his attention away from a nurse.

"Can you be the one who treats her?" I ask swallowing. "She trusts you." He nods and ushers her away and I watch until they are no longer in view.

~

"Fuck!" I mutter under my breath. I can feel each swoop of the needle as the doctor stitches up my shoulder, the anesthesia is not really helping. 13 stitches. Lucky fucking me.

Once he is finished, he leaves the room, leaving me to my own. My body and mind are both worn out. I can't seem to relax, my mind keeps going over every second of the night, constantly returning to her. I lay my head back, pleading my body for any amount of sleep. Moments later, I hear the door swing open. I sit up immediately.

"How is she?" I blurt out.

"She's OK," he says plainly. I sit there, waiting for more. He picks up my chart and starts reading it.

"Andddd?" I say when the silence becomes too long.

"You know very well I can't tell you...."

Patient doctor confidentiality. "You have got to be fucking kidding me," I mutter. "I think we're a little past that notion."

A sigh leaves his throat.

"She is suffering from a pretty decent amount of smoke inhalation. She has two bruised ribs, from what seems to be excessive CPR. Minor cuts were treated."

My heart sinks. I have caused her pain.

"Do you even care to hear about yourself?" I shake my head.

"Braeden," he says apprehensively. "She'll be fine. Time heals all wounds."

I get the vibe he's not talking just about the physical ones. "I just don't understand...how...why?" I start to mutter, my mind going in a million different directions.

"There are a lot of different reasons why people chose to abuse others. It can be a result of a mental health issue or disorders. Or some were abused themselves." *I wasn't asking for a medical lesson.*

I scoff. "Still doesn't excuse him from what the fuck he did!" I say in a heightened voice.

"Braeden, calm down," my father says.

My knuckles instantly clench, my mind thinking about how very much I'd like to have five more minutes in a room alone with that monster.

"Is she awake?"

"No, she's on some strong pain medication right now; a lot of sleep is only natural. I think you should do the same son."

"I'm not tired."

He shakes his head.

"So stubborn. Just like your mother. Well, I am going to be around, please try to get some sleep," he begs again.

When he leaves I try shutting my eyes, but I know sleep is useless. Staring at the clock on the wall, an hour passes before I know I have to see her. Throwing my covers off, I exit my room, wondering how long it will be before I get caught. I only get a few feet before I feel something pinch my arm.

Grabbing the pole, I slowly make my way down the hallway, thankful her room is close to mine. I push the door open slowly, the room is dark except for a small amount of light coming through the blinds. I walk over to her bed, her eyes are closed. I take the time to look at her, all the cuts on her face have been cleaned, one of them required stitches on her forehead. I realize now how dizzy I am becoming. I grab a spare chair, pulling it up to her bedside. She is tightly tucked into her sheets, only her upper body and arms showing. She is hooked up to an IV also and an oxygen nose tube. Looking back down at her arm, I slide my hand into hers, holding it tightly. Then I wait.

Phoenix

I shift my weight, my abdomen on fire.

"Ow," I breathe out.

Before I open my eyes, I know exactly where I am. I can tell by the smell. But there is a new sensation. Warmth. Turning my head over I see him, his face down on the bed side, his body bent in half. His hand is still in mine just like he always promised. I can't do anything but stare at our hands intermingled, my body free of the normal urge to recoil. I take this time to look at him, his auburn hair disheveled. I look down at what I can see of his body, corners of white gauze sticking out under his hospital top. When he doesn't move, I squeeze his hand slightly, making him stir. He slowly raises his head and I can tell he is trying to get his bearings. And then he finds me.

"You're awake," he says with a smile. "How are you feeling?"

"How long have you been here?" I ask through a scratchy throat.

"I don't really know. Are you OK?"

"Medicated," I say with a smile. "And tired."

His head drops, something apparently wrong.

"What?" I ask.

"It's all my fault."

I look at him confused. "What do you mean?"

"The reason you are hurt is because of me."

Still not helping me understand.

"You're not making any sense."

"You have two bruised ribs, Phoenix, and I caused it."

I sit up further, holding my wince in internally. "No," I say harshly. "You saved me, Braeden. I would be dead if it was not for you." He cringes at my harsh words. "I had to. I couldn't let him harm you anymore."

I grip his hand tighter. Braeden shifts around in his chair, his face displaying he is also in pain. I start to panic.

"Braeden..."

"I'm fine," he assures me.

"No. You're not."

I am the one that caused *him* pain. I never thought

my hate for Carl could increase. My mind hastily shifts to my mother. Braeden must have noticed my shift in emotions because he stands up, his grip on my hand tightening.

"Phoenix, what's wrong?"

"My mom."

His face falls. "Let me go find out," he says.

"No," I say sternly. "I don't want you to leave. Not yet."

He gives me a crooked smile. "OK, I'll stay."

He goes to sit back down but I squeeze his hand, effectively making him stop midair. My heart begins to race and I gnaw on my bottom lip. I shift my eyes from him to the empty space in the bed beside me.

"Are you sure?" he asks.

My heart skips a beat. Maybe he doesn't want to be that close to me.

"I...uh..." *Don't be a coward.* "Yes."

Scooting over a little, Braeden lowers himself onto the bed, his body is still above the sheets, mine still nestled underneath. We both lay there, not saying anything important, the sounds of nothing but our breath fills the room. I watch as he lays there, his eyes finally closing. I soon follow.

~

When I woke up from my nap Braeden was gone from my bed. I panic for a moment thinking all of it was a dream. But I inhale, smelling his scent on the sheets. An intense feeling of dread overwhelms me, the tears falling fast, my emotions on a roller coaster. *Everything's gone.*

Reaching up, I feel the emptiness of where my necklace should hang, my hands start to shake. I sit up slightly, looking around the room. I breathe a sigh of relief when I see it sitting on the table beside me. The door pushes open and Braeden walks through holding two cups. He is smiling until he notices my state of panic.

"What's going on?" he says as he sets the cups down and rushes over to me.

"I've lost it," I utter.

"Lost what?" he asks, clearly confused.

Tears start to fall again, my chest hiccupping with every breath.

"Breathe," he says as he runs a finger across my cheek.

"Your mom's book..." He continues to look at me confused. "Your father allowed me to borrow your mother's book, it was in the nightstand when..."

"Shhh, it doesn't matter," he says.

I start to respond but something catches my eyes in the door window. She is looking at me, her black eye frightening me. She smiles, but there are tears in her eyes. She puts her hand up to her mouth and blows me a kiss. I remain frozen in my bed, not able to move. With a blink of an eye she's gone. There is something so final to her figure no longer being in sight. I instantly know. That would be the last time I would see Elaina. And to be honest, I don't know how I feel about it.

~

The days in the hospital blur together, Braeden and I lost in our own world. I would be lying if I said they weren't some of the greatest days I've had in a long time.

"You are totally kicking my ass," I hear Braeden say, sitting in a chair across from me. I smile.

"King me," I say through laughter.

Braeden stacks a checker on top on mine. The board is mostly red, my pile of black checkers expanding.

"I used to play this with my dad all the time," I giggle. "I think he always let me win."

My heart sinks a little at my own mention of my father. Braeden notices.

"Everything OK?"

"Yeah, just thinking about my dad," I sigh.

"I bet you wish he was here huh?" Braeden asks.

I nod. I go to speak but Dr. Harris enters the room, a nervous look on his face. I instantly feel on edge.

"Are you ever going to leave Phoenix's room?" he asks Braeden, who looks at me and smiles.

"Not until she gets sick of me," he says. There is silence for a moment.

"Well, son, I'm afraid I am going to have to order you to leave."

I shake my head. "No. Whatever you have to tell me, you can say in front of him."

Dr. Harris nods his head slightly. "You're mother's gone, Phoenix," he blurts right out.

A lump in my throat forms as I try to hold back the tears. Why am I even surprised? I knew. Maybe it's the confirmation.

"And she's not coming back," he adds. "I promised her...I promised her I would take care of you..."

A wave of anger flows through me. Did she think I was just a fucking puppy she could pawn off onto anyone she liked?

"That's wonderful," Braeden says, his eyes shifting from Dr. Harris to me. "She can live with me. I can keep her safe."

My heart skips a beat.

"No," Dr. Harris says sternly.

Dr. Harris walks away from the door to foot of my bed. "I know that you are of age Phoenix, but I promised your mother your safety. And in your... condition...I don't think you moving in with Braeden would be a great idea."

Woah. I hadn't even agreed. I'm still trying to process everything.

"That's bullshit," I hear Braeden say under his breath.

Dr. Harris turns to Braeden. "If you are going to be a fucking child about this you can leave."

I inwardly gasp. I've never heard Dr. Harris swear before. Braeden doesn't respond as he crosses his arm. He turns his attention back to me.

"As I was saying, moving in with Braeden, I fear, will be a mistake. He is your first..." Dr. Harris pauses. "What are you exactly?"

I almost laugh. I hadn't even really thought about it. Braeden's eyes find mine as he waits for an answer.

"I don't really know," I say as I bite my lip. "We care for each other..." I utter almost as a question. Braeden smiles. Dr. Harris just nods.

"OK," he says. "And you care for her?" he asks Braeden.

"I do," Braeden says without hesitation.

"Then I feel what's best for Phoenix is that she lives with me."

A spike of nervousness runs through me. Braeden stands up abruptly.

"I need to speak to you...outside," Braeden says sharply.

Dr. Harris nods at me and follows Braeden out of the room.

Braeden

"Are you fucking kidding me?" I say loudly when we get outside of Phoenix's room. He grabs my upper arm and squeezes it.

"My office, now."

I don't say anything until we reach the confines of it.

"Are you fucking kidding me!" I repeat, my anger stronger.

"I demand a little more respect than that, Braeden. When did you become so goddamn hot headed?"

I don't answer. To be honest I didn't even know. I take a deep breath before continuing. "Do you really think her living with you is a good idea?"

My dad leans his body against his desk, crossing his

arms. "Yes, I do."

I shake my head.

"What? You think her living with you is such a good goddamn idea?" he says sharply. "Please tell me how her living with you and that fucking disgusting thing you call a roommate is better. Tell me how her staying home alone at your house with a male stranger while you are at school is a good idea."

I go to open my mouth, but he doesn't let me talk.

"I understand that you have feelings for her. You wouldn't have been involved last night if you didn't, but you need to start thinking more with your head than your heart, Braeden. You could have died last night. Do you even care?"

"No," I respond. "As long as she is OK, that's all that matters."

"You're being blinded by lust," he says.

I laugh out loud.

"No one even gets it," I say shaking my head. "Would you even believe me if I told you it's not like that with her?"

The anger in my father's face diminishes.

"So you care for her on a deeper level?" he rhetorically asks.

"Yes."

"And you would do anything to help her along, do what's right for her?"

"Yes." I begin to get what he is saying.

"Phoenix has lost both her parents, Braeden. While Elaina may not be deceased, she feels that she can no longer be in Phoenix's life. She doesn't think she deserves her daughter anymore. Walking away is her way of punishing herself although I'm not really sure I agree with her. We need to do what's right to help her along."

"OK," is all that I could utter.

"It may not be the situation you want, but with her at my house I can keep an eye on her. Things are going to tough for a while, Braeden. She has suffered both physical and emotional trauma. This situation is going to force her to talk about things and face things she didn't want to before. Things aren't going to be perfect."

"They never are."

He stands up from the desk and walks over and puts his arms around me.

"You know I love you, son," he says. "You're scaring the hell out of me. But, I'm proud of you."

"Thanks," I mutter into his shoulder. "I love you, too."

~

I leave my father's office, immediately heading back to Phoenix's room. I'm frustrated dragging this fucking IV stand around and when I see no one is around I start to pick at the tape, slowly removing the needle from my arm and ditching it in the closest red "sharps" box hanging on the wall. Pushing the door open I find her,

her face immediately lights up and I can't hold back the smile that comes across my face. And to be honest, I don't want to.

I can't explain how Phoenix makes me feel or why I feel that way, but anytime I am near her it feels as though there is an invisible string between us. She instantly makes me happy. Her smile disappears, a look of worry coming across her face.

"I'm sorry," she blurts out.

I'm confused. What else could she have to apologize for? "And what are you apologizing for now?"

From the nervous look that spreads across her face I realize my response may have been harsh. I bow my head.

"Shit. I'm sorry, that was rude of me."

Phoenix seems to compose herself again.

"I owe you an apology for everything, Braeden," she says only above a whisper. "I should have believed you and I didn't. I didn't even give you a chance...."

I walk over to her bedside, my need to comfort her growing, but I hold my hands back. I open my mouth but shut it again.

"I had no right to even question who she was. It wasn't any of my business." Now I can't hold back. I pick up her hand gently in mine.

"I never want to hurt you, Phoenix...." I start. "And seeing that I had caused you pain was one of the worst feelings I had ever experienced in my life."

Her brown eyes stare into mine as she listens to every word.

"I don't know what told me to come after you but I am so happy that it did. Seeing you unconscious on the floor is something I never want to see again." I swallow the lump on my throat. "I wanted to kill him."

She lets go of my hand as reaches up to brush the edges of my gauzed shoulder.

"I still want to," she mutters. My face becomes serious.

"He will never come near you again, that I can promise you."

Her face falls serious also.

"You can't save me from everything, Braeden. Things are going to happen that are out of our control."

"Not if I can help it," I say quietly.

I take a deep breath.

"Apology accepted." I smile, her returning one.

She starts to gnaw on her bottom lips, her eyes shifted down.

"So what do we do now?" she asks.

I smile.

"Whatever you want to do," I say softly.

I pause before continuing.

"You know that you don't have to stay here. You are over 18. If there is some place you would rather be..."

Her eyes snap up to look at mine.

"I don't want to go anywhere, Braeden. Wherever

you are is where I want to be."

I think my heart does a back flip. "You have no idea how happy that makes me, hearing you say that."

She gives me a sly smile, her fingers playing in and around mine.

"Can't describe how amazing this feels," she speaks. "I've never had anyone care for me like you do."

"That's a shame," I respond quickly. "You deserve so much more than that."

"Do I?"

I lean over her so that our faces are close but I make sure to do it gently, afraid that she might retreat from my touch.

"Yes," I say softly as our eyes are locked on each other.

We hold our position and I can tell she is nervous, but I want her to make the first move. I made the mistake of pushing it on her the first time and I won't be doing that again. I can feel the heat of her breath on my face, its oddly intoxicating. But I hold still. I start to count the number of my heartbeats when I suddenly feel force against my lips. I hold back the smile, my hand coming up to cup her cheek. I start to move my lips against her, the waves of ecstasy flowing through my body. After a second, her lips start to move in unison with mine. I've kissed lots of women, but it's never felt quite like this. I don't know how long it lasts, but I refrain from sticking my tongue in her mouth, fearing that may be too much. I then swear I feel her moan in my mouth, and it's the most incredible fucking turn on I have ever heard in my life. She must have realized it too considering she pulled her lips off mine, her hands coming up to her mouth.

"That was incredibly involuntary," she whispers.

I just smile at her.

"That should have been our first kiss," I say, almost ashamed of myself.

A light smile comes across her face.

"I thought that was," she laughs.

Seconds later, a nurse comes bounding through the door.

"I've got some great news! You two get to go home today!"

Phoenix gasps.

Phoenix

Home?

Where is home?

My body was in a state of bliss after that kiss and I silently curse the nurse out for interrupting. The idea of leaving this hospital scares me. Almost the entire time I have known Braeden, I've always been confined to some sort of hospital room. Would he still want me when we leave here? Will I still be the same person? Would he? This thing between us is was different. But how well do we really know each other? A million things start to run through my mind, sending me into a silent panic attack. I feel Braeden's hand slip into mine, almost as though he can sense my uneasiness. I give it a light squeeze and a probably not-so-convincing smile.

"Oh, and Miss Harper, Dr. Harris would like to speak to you in his office whenever you are ready."

Braeden shoots me a glance, probably trying to gauge my reaction. I'm assuming this is about what he and his father discussed earlier.

"OK," I respond.

When she leaves again, Braeden and I return to our bubble. I shift in my bed, swinging my legs over until they reach the coldness of the tiled floor.

"Are you OK?" he asks, a concerned look on his face.

I can't help but smirk. He is always so worried.

"You're going to have a heart attack at such a young age if worry about me all the time."

He clutches his chest.

"I might have already experienced one." He laughs.

My smile falls from my face. Braeden's hand comes up to my face, his thumb rubbing over my cheek bone.

"Don't frown, Phoenix," he says softly. "I love it when you smile."

And just like that I am happy again.

"Well, I'm going to go take a shower," I say softly. "And then go see your father."

"Do you want me to go with you?"

I begin to panic and I hear Braeden laugh.

"To my father's office." He laughs. "Not to the shower."

"Oh," I respond. "I think I want to go alone, is that

OK?"

"Of course, my Seraph," he utters.

My heart begins to race for the millionth time since I have met him.

"What did you just call me?" I ask softly.

"Seraph." He smiles. "It's another word for angel."

"Oh," I say, feeling the burn in my cheeks.

"Too soon?" he asks hesitantly.

I shake my head.

"No, I like the way it sounds."

"Me too."

Shutting the bathroom door behind me, I lean against it and let my heart come down to its normal rhythm. Did he just call me his angel? I reach up and pull on my lip with my finger and get lost in thought. When I am finally able to peel myself off the door, I reach up and pull off my hospital gown, running my fingers over the bandages wrapped around my upper body. Reaching my fingers up slowly I start to unravel them, the black-and-blue skin unveiled. I run my fingers over the delicate skin and wince slightly. But something inside me changes. I am pretty used to seeing cuts and bruises on my body so often that I hardly notice them, but this time is different. They are there because he saved my life.

He came after me. I still feel like I may wake up from this dream at any moment. Or was it a nightmare? The butterflies in my stomach start to dance just thinking about him. And that feeling scares me sometimes. I had never been in a relationship before and I fear that I might not be what he needs. What if he wants something that I can't give him? What every man needs.

I grip the counter of the sink, the walls around me becoming blurry, tingling sensations running through my body. Using the sink as support I lower myself onto the toilet lid and concentrate on breathing in and out of my nose. I fight to have this feeling leave my body, not wanting to be crippled by it anymore. I am safe now. Peeling myself off the toilet, I walk over to the shower knobs, my knees still feeling a bit weak. Turning on the shower I step inside, the hot water feeling incredible. It's been the first time I have been able to take a shower by myself, the past few times have been observed by a nurse. I grab the bottle of shampoo and I stick my nose up at the smell. It's so…medicinal. Squirting some into my palm, I go to reach up to put it in my hair, the pain radiating through my body.

"Fuck," I say loudly, clasping my mouth shut.

Within seconds I hear a knock on the door. The figure doesn't have to speak for me to know who it is.

"I'm fine," I say out loud.

"Are you sure?" he asks.

I laugh to myself.

"Yes, I promise," I shout out.

I stand there for a few more seconds until I don't

hear anything and resume my washing. Slowly. I don't know how long I am in the shower, but when I look down my fingers are pruney, a sign that it has probably been too long. Stepping out, I wrap a towel around me, still telling myself to move slowly. I hear a knock on the door again and I roll my eyes.

"I'm fine, Braeden," I call out.

I hear a female laugh. "It's Chelsea."

Turning around I open the door open enough for her to slide in. Held in her hands are clothes and more wraps and tape. She works quickly and before I know it I feel like I am wearing a straight jacket again. Holding the clothes out to me I pick one up at a time and put them on, they are incredibly feminine. She must have noticed my confused state.

"Dr. Harris sent me out to pick some things up." She smiles.

My heart jolts. "Thank you," I say.

"Of course my dear," she responds.

There is a moment of silence.

"They are both pretty incredible, huh?" I ask.

A genuine smile comes across her face.

"I have known Dr. Harris and Braeden for quite a long time now. They are both very sweet men."

I can't help but smile too.

"And I know that you don't know me, but I just want you to know that Braeden does care about you. I've never seen him look at anyone like he looks at you."

I can feel the fire in my cheeks starting.

"Not since she was here," she says quietly.

Her.

"I bet she was beautiful," I utter, not really being able to stop the words from leaving my mouth.

"Beautiful doesn't even begin to describe her. She was an incredible human being, both inside and out," she explains. "A life lost too early."

I can hear the pain behind her words. It's like it's still an open wound when they all speak about her like that. When we finish up she opens the door and exits before looking back at me to smile. When I get through the door, I see the reason for the smile. Braeden is no longer in his hospital clothing. His body is now adorned in a white, long-sleeve, waffle-knit shirt and black skinny jeans. His body is slumped down in the chair, his eyes closed. *He sleeps.* We both sneak out of the room quietly, shutting the door behind us.

"I'll take you to Dr. Harris' office if you want," she says putting her hand on my back.

I just nod my head. After we go through a series of hallways and doors we arrive to at his office. She reaches up and knocks on the door slightly.

"Come in," I hear from the other side.

She pushes the door open and ushers me to enter. I spot Dr. Harris behind his desk but he immediately gets up and walks over to us.

"Thank you, Chelsea," he says to her.

"You're very welcome, Neil...I mean, Dr. Harris," she responds, a nervous look on her face.

I shift my eyes around, the room suddenly becoming uncomfortable. She gives me a small squeeze on my arm before leaving, shutting the door behind her. I look around his office, it very different than the one at the psychology office. There is nothing personal about this one, everything's so white and sterile. I look back over at him and he just smiles at me.

"So, how are you feeling?" he asks me.

"Good," I lie. *I'm scared shitless.* I'm pretty sure he doesn't believe me.

"So, as you can imagine I had the same discussion with Braeden, even though it's really none of his concern."

"I want Braeden to know everything, he's important to me."

"I think I'm beginning to gather that," he grins. "Now, I know that I have already mentioned that you are more than welcome to stay with me. But I want you to make that decision without the pressure of Braeden present."

I stand there silent for a few minutes, my mind racing in a million different directions.

"Okay," I say only above a whisper.

Dr. Harris nods. "I know that this is a tough time in your life right now, Phoenix, but things will get better. I can promise you that."

I start to gnaw on my lip. "I don't...have...
anything," I say nervously. "I can't just live in your
house and expect you to pay for everything."

"I was thinking that we could make a deal." He
laughs lightly.

My heart begins to race.

"The hospital can always use volunteers."

"Uh, I don't have any hospital training," I explain.
His smile stays.

"I know that. I was thinking you could help with
visiting patients. Move around items, deliver flowers."

I smile.

"You want me to be a candy stripper?" I ask.

"I don't think it's been called that for quite some
time, but essentially yes."

"OK," I agree.

"And, as we discussed before, I think it would be in
your best interest for you to continue to seek therapy."

I nod. He claps his hands together.

"And in return I will pay for anything you absolutely
need. But anything more than that will have to get my
easily persuaded son to buy."

"I can get a job," I explain.

"Maybe someday Phoenix, but as of right now I
want you to concentrate on getting things in your life in
the order *you* want them in."

This overwhelming sensation to hug him flows
through me but my muscles remain in their frozen state.

"I have no words to express how deeply appreciative I am, Dr. Harris," I utter.

He continues to smile and shakes his head.

"And that's one more condition..." he says.

I become confused.

"I am forbidding you from calling me Dr. Harris in my household. From now on it will only be Neil."

I fly my hands up to my mouth.

"Oh. Well...thank you, Neil."

"You're very welcome, my child," he responds.

I slowly make my way out of his office and when I get the door closed I find myself leaning against it, letting out the breath I didn't know I was holding in. I look up to see Braeden leaning over the counter talking to Chelsea, her hand on his shoulder, both of them laughing. I can't help but watch them, it making me smile in return.

A few moments later Braeden's eyes find mine, his smile widening. He says something to Chelsea and then makes his way towards me. I can smell him instantly, the woody aroma taking me back to my father's house. *Home.* When he reaches me he immediately runs his finger across my cheek and I don't recoil, surprised at myself.

"Are you OK?" he asks.

"I've never been better. Thanks to you," I say as I lean up on my tippy toes, placing a small kiss on his lips.

Braeden

When Phoenix's lips hit mine a rush of pleasure runs through my body and I have to stop my hands from wanting to run themselves all over her. This is going to be a test of my patience. Moments later she pulls back and I inwardly whine. I can see the red spreading across her cheeks, and I am beginning to think she feels the same when we do this. Reaching down I interlock my fingers in hers.

"Let's get the fuck out of here," I whisper close to her ear.

She responds with the most beautiful smile I have ever seen. We make our way out of the series of doorways and hallways. I've been in this hospital millions of times but I've never been in such a hurry to get the hell out of here. I can see the front door in sight and my heart starts to race. *Freedom.*

As soon as that thought enters my mind I feel Phoenix stop dead in her tracks, a heavy anchor in the ground. I stop in front of her, my face finding hers. She looks terrified.

Reaching up I brush my finger along her cheek. "Seraph?"

But not even my sentiment snaps her out of her comatose state. Her hand clenches onto mine tighter and I become surprised by her strength. Instinctively I follow her eyes and then I see it. *Her demon.*

Just outside the hospital front door there are two police officers and Carl in handcuffs. I instantly become outraged that this piece of shit is still here, but a small part of me is happy that I get to see his miserable face as he is being shoved into the back of the cop car. I think I even find myself grinning ear to ear as I notice the obvious pain on his face, a large bandage wrapped around his head. But my mind switches back to Phoenix. I step in front of her, essentially protecting her from his harmful glare.

"Phoenix," I say sternly, her eyes finally looking back at me. "I want you to go back to my dad's office and I want you to stay there until I come get you, do you understand?"

She nods her head as I slowly release my fingers

from hers. I watch her walk away until she is out of sight. Jingling the keys in my hand I veer off to the right and out the employee's exit, finding my father's car instantly.

Hitting the unlock button on the fob I slide into the driver's seat. I go to start the engine but instead I grasp the steering wheel, my mind overtaking my ability to move. I start to think how I could run him over with this beast of a car. My father has impeccable insurance. I wonder if he would fly up and over the hood or if his body would be mangled underneath.

I shake my head as I scare myself with my own thoughts. Putting the car in reverse I back out of the spot slowly and round the corner of the hospital and I let out the breath I didn't know I was holding. The cops, the car and Carl are all gone. Good fucking riddance. Pulling up under the overhang I put the car in park and shut it off and head back inside for Phoenix. When I reach my father's office again I see a large man standing in front of it, my father talking to him. I start to pick up my pace.

"What's going on?" I ask to both of them, wondering who will answer me first.

"Just protocol," the tall man says. He doesn't have to even tell me he's cop, I can just tell.

"They had a few last questions to ask her before you two left."

I huff. "Yeah, speaking of leaving....why was that

asshole still here? Wasn't he supposed to have been gone days ago?"

"I don't think that's any of your concern, son," the cop responds.

"Don't fucking call me 'son'," I snap back at him.

"Braeden," I hear my father say but I don't peel my eyes from the blockhead standing before me.

A few seconds later the door opens, another cop exiting, Phoenix following behind him at a slowed distance. I push myself around them, grabbing her face in my hands.

"Are you OK?" I ask her softly.

She just nods her head but remains silent.

"Are we done here?" I say harshly, not wanting her to suffer through another moment of this shit. The one that was interviewing Phoenix nods his head.

"If we need anything else for her we have her contact information."

I can feel Phoenix tense up. With our hands still intertwined I pull on her, making her feet move.

"I'll see you both at the house," I hear my father call out from behind us. I wave my free arm in the air silently telling him OK. We walk the same path to the front door again. She is moving slowly so I drop my hand from hers and instead slide my arm around her shoulder pulling her in close, silently telling her that I will protect her no matter what.

"He's not here anymore, Seraph," I bend down and

whisper into her ear. "He's going to spend the rest of his miserable life behind bars. Paying for what he did."

She looks up at me and I give her my best reassuring smile. I get lost in the depth of her eyes, both now a mixture of terror and excitement.

"He's gone," I repeat as I lean down, placing my lips against hers, thirsty again for that feeling. When it starts to become overbearing I pull back.

"Let's get you home," I tell her.

"Home," she says softly. "I like the sound of that."

We make it to the front of the hospital and I reach down, opening the passenger door for her. Sliding myself into driver's seat I start it up, pulling slowly out, the hospital getting smaller and smaller in the rear view mirror.

Phoenix

Watching that hospital get smaller in the side mirror was one of the best visions of my life to date. For once I feel optimistic. When I saw Carl being ushered into the police car, I was terrified. I could feel his eyes boring into mine and it felt like every scar on my body had been immediately ignited. Fear flooded my mind again. *What if he gets released? What if they don't believe my testimony? What if he escapes?*

Before I had time to talk myself out of this nonsense, every muscle in me froze. I hated that he still had this effect on me. But just like always, Braeden was at my side, always so in tune with my emotions. When the police officer came into Neil's office, I started to panic but I swore I heard Braeden's voice telling me to calm down. I found myself zoning out through most of it, answering the man's questions with short answers. When he asked questions about my mother's whereabouts I remained silent. In truth, I didn't care at the moment.

~

I must have zoned out for most of the ride because a short time later, Braeden pulled the car into a steep driveway. I didn't realize how nervous I was until I looked down, my hands white knuckled against the leather of the seat. I found myself frozen again. Before I realize it, Braeden is on my side of the car, his hand held out for me to take.

"Phoenix?" he states, noticing my zombie state.

I look up at him and I find myself staring in his eyes and I swear they are even a deeper green than usual.

"Are you ready?" he asks.

I nod my head. Braeden leans down and into the car, his long arm reaches around my torso and unhooks my seatbelt, his upper body hovering over mine. All I can do it stare at his muscular arm wrapped around me, the way his shirt clings to his upper back. Once its unhooked he leans back up and then takes my hand, lifting me out of the chair with ease. We walk together, hand-in-hand, out of the garage. The door shuts automatically behind us.

The house is all white and I see that there is a large

porch on the back, adorned with multiple rocking chairs. A thought of Braeden and I sitting hand in hand in them invades my mind. I can't help but smile. Braeden slides the keys into the lock in the side door, pushing it open and ushering us inside. I scan the rooms as I walk through each of them. The house is minimalistic without a lot of clutter but it's warm and inviting. Much like Neil and Braeden. When we reach the living room, Braeden stops. I can tell that he is a little bit on edge at the moment but he's trying to hide it.

"So...this is home. Well, my old home," he says as he scans the room.

"It's really nice, Braeden."

"Yeah...it is," he responds, his voice flat.

I get the sense there is something he's not explaining but I choose not to push it. Moments later I hear a car door slam and jump instinctively, a small squeal escaping my lips. Braeden squeezes my hand.

"It's just my dad, Seraph," he assures.

I hang my head a little.

"Sorry."

I feel his finger slide out under my chin, making me look at him.

"Don't ever apologize," he explains. "Especially for something that is so far fucking out of your control."

"OK," I say softly, still wishing for a day where I won't jump at every single noise.

A few seconds later, I hear keys being jingled and

the front door being pushed open. Dr. Harris approaches us with a smile, which instantly warms me.

"You two doing OK?" he asks.

"As good as can be expected I guess," Braeden answers sternly. "How'd you get home?"

"I took a cab," he explains.

A twinge of guilt flows through me. *Always putting others out.*

"I'm sorry," I blurt out.

Braeden shoots me a look. I mutter another "I'm sorry" before I even have time to catch it.

"You gotta make her stop apologizing for everything while she's here," Braeden says, a curvaceous smile coming across his lips. He looks over at me and winks.

"Well, I'm starving," Dr. Harris says while looking at Braeden. "Why don't you go make us something while I show Phoenix her room."

Braeden starts to object but the silent look his dad gives him shuts him right up. He lets go of my hand and gives me a smile, then heads into the kitchen. I look back up at Dr. Harris.

"If you wanna follow me," he says before turning around and heads up the stairs.

As I ascend them I can feel my heart racing, everything so foreign. When we reach the top there are three rooms, two of them are closed shut. We walk down the hall, Dr. Harris remains silent until we reach the only open door. He clears his throat before speaking.

"So, this will be your room," he explains letting me enter first.

My eyes well up with tears instantly. The room is absolutely gorgeous. It's small but it feels inviting. In the direct middle is a queen-sized bed, the comforter adorned with pink flowers.

"I hope you like pink." He smiles.

The rest of the furniture is a simple painted white, making the room seem vibrant. I stand facing away from him, trying to talk my body into getting a god damn hold on its emotions.

"I know that it's not much right now but I figured you could make it more personable," I hear him say. "I had Chelsea pick some things up and they are all in your closet."

I finally spin around the face him.

"I don't even know where to start to thank you," I choke out. "It's a thousand times better already."

"Well, that makes me happy," he responds. "But, just remember, we have a deal." I nod. "I know that this is not very conventional. But I want you to feel safe here. My room is downstairs, far enough away for your own privacy but close enough in case you need me for anything."

"Thank you Dr. Harr…Neil," I say as I catch myself.

We then both hear a collective banging of drawers and plates and I can't help but laugh.

"Maybe we should go help him," I suggest.

Neil nods and we both start to make it back down the hallway, my eyes falling upon the two closed doors as we pass them. When we make it back to the kitchen, it looks like a tornado went off.

"Do you know you don't have shit to eat in this place?" Braeden says, to what I am assuming is his father. Neil grins and looks down at me.

"I guess I'll have to go shopping huh?" He smiles.

I just smile in return. On the table is a large salad and a few sandwiches. *Impressive.* We all sit down at the table and eat in silence, my stomach thanking me for the nutrients. It may be only a salad and half a sandwich but it's a thousand times better than the food served at the hospital. After a few minutes I hear a phone ring, Neil sighs as he pulls it from his pocket.

"Dr. Harris," he answers.

I can hear murmurs on the other end but try my hardest not to eavesdrop. He hangs up, taking another big bite of his food before standing up. He walks over to a pad of paper and starts scribbling something down. He rips the piece off and hands it to me.

"I have to head back into work for a while, here are the hospital's numbers, I am always reachable," he explains.

"OK," I respond, getting a huge feeling of déjà vu.

"I shouldn't be too late," he explains. "But if I am, I want you to set the alarm if you become worried."

"Thank you, Neil," I explain, feeling as though the words are so inadequate.

"It's my pleasure, Phoenix." He smiles before taking another bite from his standing position. He turns to face Braeden.

"Make sure you show her how to set it and remember that you have class in the morning. Professor Waleton has been nice enough to let you make up what you have missed because of the circumstances..."

Braeden just nods and, like a whirlwind, he is gone again. The room falls awkwardly silent again and I start shoving forkfuls of food into my mouth, realizing that I am alone with Braeden. No one else around. No nurses to pop in at any moment. I can tell even Braeden is still a little on edge.

"This is really good," I finally say, my mouth still a little full.

It makes Braeden smile. "Thanks."

Things fall silent again for a moment. *Why does this feel so weird?*

"Are you sure you want to do this?" Braeden asks, the question throwing me off guard.

"Of course," I answer sort on confused. Maybe he's changed his mind about me. "Do you not want me to stay here?" I ask, my nerves becoming uneasy.

"Well, as much as I would love for you to be with me always, I know this is what's best for you."

"Maybe we can have a sleepover sometime," I

suggest, feeling the burn in my cheeks as soon as the words leave my mouth.

Braeden smiles wide, making my look down at my plate. "I'd like that."

I finish up my plate and get up from the table, picking up the rest of the dirty plates on the way. Braeden immediately stands up and I have to hold back a flinch.

"Sorry," he says.

I look up at him and grin.

"I thought we weren't apologizing?" I laugh.

Braeden shakes his head slightly.

"OK, you got me," he says as he takes the plates from my hands. "But you don't have to do the dishes."

I go to reach back over to take them from him again but he holds them over my head, making me jump for them. I start to laugh because with every jump Braeden reaches up higher, the dishes always out of my reach. Before I know it, Braeden's back is flush against the wall, my chest pushing against his.

I look up at him, his eyes intense, and the smile gone from his face and in its place a look of fervor. Reaching over, Braeden sets the plates down on the counter and immediately wraps his long fingers around the back of my neck, sending a shiver down my spine. Both our chests rise and fall in unison and I want nothing more that to taste him against my lips. Stepping up on my tippy toes I place my lips on his, his mouth immediately responding. I feel the tip of his tongue trace where my lips meet, begging to enter. I part them a little and feel the warmth of it on mine and I follow his lead, both of our tongues begging for dominance.

I clench the fabric of his shirt in my hands and I lean up and press harder into his chest, my emotions taking over any logical thought. Braeden's hand that was once behind my neck slowly travels south and plants itself against my lower back, making my hips gyrate into his. And then I feel hardness against my stomach and it makes me gasp, stopping our kiss. Pulled away from our make out session, Braeden looks down at me.

"You OK, Seraph?" he asks.

I gnaw on my bottom lip, suddenly embarrassed by my overreaction.

"I'm great," I respond as I lean up to resume but his hands on each side of my shoulders stop me.

"I don't think I can take anymore at this point, without taking advantage of you," he responds.

Unhooking my fingers from his t-shirt I take a step back. I can instantly see the bulge in his pants and I find myself staring for probably what would be considered too long. My thoughts are confirmed when I hear Braeden clear his throat. I look up at him, a cocky smile on his face.

"See something you like?" he says.

I just awkwardly laugh, not really knowing how to respond to that. He starts to laugh, his arm wrapping around my shoulder, his lips kissing the top of my head.

"Let's go watch some TV," he says, ushering us both out of the kitchen and into the living room.

As we watch, I observe as the day sky turns to night, my nerves building with every moment. I always hated the dark. But it's been a long day and I feel my eyelids drooping, sleep taking over.

Braeden

Just when I thought kissing her was the best feeling in the world she had to fall asleep against me. The glow of the TV was the only thing that filled the room, the light accentuating the features on her face. She looked so peaceful that I never wanted to leave from this spot. Instead of watching the TV I decided to watch her instead. I scan every portion of her face and notice the occasional smile and brow furrow that comes across it. My arm starts to burn but I don't dare move, not wanting to cause her any discomfort. I don't know how much time passes, but I hear the garage door go up, knowing that sound anywhere. My dad comes through the side door, putting his keys on the kitchen counter. When he enters the living room he immediately stops.

"She fell asleep," I explain.

"She's had quite a rough couple days," he says softly. "As have you, Braeden."

I look back down at her.

"Her whole life has been rough, Dad," I whisper. "She's too young to have experienced this much pain."

The room is silent again, nothing but the light from the TV still on.

"So, is this what it feels like?" I say out loud, my heart racing. My father doesn't have to guess what I'm talking about.

"The best gift that a man can get is a woman's heart," he says smiling down at me. "I am truly happy for you, Braeden."

He leans down and squeezes my shoulder.

"I'm going to try and get some sleep. You should probably get her to bed and head home."

We both know I'm not leaving tonight. I just nod, and then watch my father head upstairs. I turn my attention back to Phoenix, watching her chest still rising and falling methodically. I hesitate for a second before the words leave my throat.

"I think I'm in love with you, Seraph," I whisper, brushing a piece of hair that has fallen in front of her face.

I stare down at her, wanting her to respond, but instead the soft sound of her breath leaves her lips. Just the hope of her saying those words to me someday makes my heart jump. Sitting up slowly I turn around and slide my arms underneath her body, not wanting to interrupt her peaceful sleep. She is light in my arms. *Too light.* I haven't known Phoenix for a long time, but I can see that the stress takes a toll on her. Her appetite is nonexistent at times.

When we reach her room, I push to door open with my foot, thankful that there was moonlight coming through the window. Setting her down on the bed, I slide the comforter up and over her. I find myself staring at her. Just being in her presence makes my heart race. I look up for her and scan the room, it brings a smile to my face. Never in a million years would I have imagined something like this would have happened. Walking out of the room I go into my father's office, finding a piece of paper and pen, jotting something down before folding it in half. Going back into Phoenix's room, I place it softly on top her night stand, knowing it will be the first thing she sees in the morning. Quietly exiting I head back down the hallway, stopping in front of the closed door. My hand hovers over the knob, shaking. Letting out a deep breath, I lean my forehead against the wood, slamming my fist into it. *After all these fucking years.* Pulling myself off of it I head back downstairs, pulling a blanket off the back of the couch before settling myself down on it. She's safe. That's all that matters. I find myself becoming drowsy and it's only a matter of moments before sleep finds me.

~

My eyes pop open and I momentarily forget when I am, my brain taking a few seconds to process my surroundings. Sitting up I let out a yawn, finding the clock on the wall. 5:58 a.m. Grunting, I pull my body off the couch and stretch my arms above me. Rubbing my eyes, I walk into the kitchen and feel my body jump at the unexpected form sitting at the table.

"Jesus Christ," I say clutching my chest.

"Well, good morning to you too, son," my father smirks, his head still looking down at the papers sprawled across the table.

"How long have you been awake?" I get out through another loud yawn.

"About two hours," he says as he highlights a few things on his paper.

"Jesus, pops, how the fuck do you work on two hours of sleep?"

He holds up his coffee cup and salutes me with it. I shake my head. I don't know how he does it honestly. My father and I haven't always seen eye to eye on things but I would be lying if I didn't say he was the fucking hardest working person I'd ever seen.

Walking over to the cabinet, I look at the coffee cups, one in the back brings a smile to my face. Grabbing it, I pull it out and fill it with coffee. No cream, no sugar. Turning around I lean back against the counter with mug in hand and just watch him. After a few minutes, I hear my father sigh.

"You do realize it's a quarter past six right?" he asks. "Don't you think you should get ready for school?" He finally removes his eyes from the document and starts to look up at me, but they stop when they reach the mug.

"I didn't even know we still had that." He laughs.

I look down at my mug and I smile at the four green turtles on the front.

"Teenage Mutant Ninja Turtles was the shit." I laugh, taking another sip.

Memories of sitting in front of the TV eating pancakes every Sunday flood my mind. I remember drinking my milk out of this cup, wanting to be just like my parents.

"Not much has changed around here since everything happened," I mutter.

"And yet, quite so much has," he croaks out.

We both take a sip of our respective mugs.

"Did you ever think about moving?" I blurt out.

A small smile comes across his face.

"Never."

"Doesn't it hurt though? Everywhere you turn there's a memory..."

"Braeden, I know that you are new to this whole love thing, but I want you to know something. Love is hard. Love is rough. It will viciously rip open your chest, leaving your heart vulnerable. At times things will be perfect, and at others they will be worse than you can even imagine. But, in the end, even the bad turns into the good."

I find myself staring at my father. Hanging on every word. Taking the last sip of my coffee I walk over to the sink, rinse it out and put it in the dish dryer.

"Why don't you take that home with you," my father suggests.

I look back down at it. "Nah, I'll keep it here."

My father nods.

"It was really nice having you here last night. It's been too long since you've spent the night here."

I smile. "It was nice," I say looking in the direction of her bedroom. "I'm afraid you'll be seeing more of me now."

"Braeden, this is your home. You were always welcome. I hope you know that."

I just nod. "Thank you, Dad," I start. "For everything."

"Everyone deserves a second chance," he states.

Walking over, I put my hand on his shoulder.

"Including you," I say. "You've got to stop blaming yourself."

He just gives me a sideways grin. His lack of response worries me.

"I guess I'll see you later," I say heading out the door.

"See you, son," I hear him respond.

~

When I get back home I have a little over an hour to make it to class. I let out a huff when I notice Bret is sprawled across the couch, a bong on the floor. I walk up to him, smacking the bottom of his boot.

"I told you not to smoke that shit in here anymore," I tell him with a raised voice.

"Ah, man, lighten the fuck up," he says, his eyes heavy. "Hey, by the way, where the fuck have you been lately?"

I roll my eyes. "Why do you care?"

"The landlord came by yesterday, rent's due."

"Then pay it!" I yell as I walk away from him, taking off my shirt and throwing it in the hamper.

"But what about your half?"

I stalk back out to him.

"You have never bought a fucking thing for this place. Furniture...mine. All the groceries...mine."

Picking up the small ziplock bag that on the table, holding a few buds left.

"And this is fucking mine," I say clenching it. "You can fucking pay all of the rent this month or you can move your fucking ass somewhere else."

"It's not like you were fucking using it. You haven't smoked in months."

Grunting, I turn around and head back to the bathroom and jump in the shower, knowing I need to make it fast. By the time I'm done and dressed I have only about twenty minutes but I couldn't care less. Just as I start to leave something catches my eye. In cash is the exact amount needed to pay rent.

Phoenix

Snapping open my eyes I sit up in my bed, confused for a second as to exactly where I am. I scan the room and a smile comes across my face when I spot a small note placed beside my bed. Reaching out, I grab it with shaky fingers.

Good morning, my Seraph. As much as I want to spend every moment with you - day and night - I fear I can't.
But I promise I will be back after class.
Love, Braeden.
P.S. Put on something nice.

I run my finger over the word "love", my smile

remains, but my body is laced with anxiety. Setting the note back down I get up from my bed, stretching out, temporarily forgetting about my ribs.

"Ow," I breathe out.

Carl may be in jail but he is still taking a toll on my mind and body. Walking over to my closet, I slide the door open and my jaw drops. It is filled with clothes, most of them simple and just my style. Comfortable. Grabbing a change of clothing I head off into the direction of what I think might be the bathroom, but I don't exactly remember which is which, as I come across the two closed doors. My heart starts to race. Turning around to look behind me, I become satisfied when I see no one.

"Hello," I call out, just to make sure.

Sending my attention back to the two doors, I stare. *What's behind door #1?* My eyes shift to the other door.

I instantly go to the right, knowing I am completely invading their privacy, but something is screaming at me from the other side. Sliding my hand over the knob I turn it clockwise, the door jamb makes a large cracking noise and I can tell it hasn't been opened in quite some time. The room is stark black within and I feel along the wall till I find the light switch. I flick it on. My eyes widen at what I see.

At first glance, the room looks normal except everything in it covered in a thick layer of dust. Confirming no one has stepped in this bedroom for years, possibly decades. I take a few steps inside, looking at everything above and below me. I can tell that it is a boy's room. Walking over to the dresser, I see a few photo frames. Taking one in my hand, I wipe my fingers across it. I squint, making sure that my eyes are seeing what I think they're seeing. In the picture are two boys, both golden brown hair, eyes as green as emeralds. Two identical boys.

"Phoenix," I hear a female voice call out, my body jumping. Startled, my fingers spontaneously let go of the frame letting it fall to the floor. I rush out of the room and shut the door behind me.

"Hello?" I hear the voice repeat.

My mind races trying to think who the hell it could be, a flash of my mother coming up the stairs takes over my mind. *That voice is too sweet to belong to Elaina.* I then see Chelsea's blonde hair coming up the stairs. Pulling my body away from the door, I drop my clothes on the floor pretending like I wasn't just snooping. Standing back up I lock my eyes with her, her smile dropping.

"What's wrong, sweetie, you look like you just saw a ghost."

I think I did.

"Oh, umm," I sat looking down at the floor. "I guess I'm just still not feeling that well."

She holds up a bottle of pills and a smile on her face.

"Precisely why Dr. Harris sent me."

"Oh, thanks," I say, hesitantly reaching out for the bottle. But she holds onto it. I look at her confused. Popping open the bottle she hands me one, giving me a sorrowful look.

"Guess I can't be trusted with them, considering my past history," I say putting the round pill in my mouth, swallowing it dry. She smiles lightly.

"Wait," I say looking around. "Did he really send you here to babysit me?"

Her smile widens. "He just wants to make sure that you are OK, this being a new and awkward place to you."

I gnaw on my bottom lip.

"Would I sound insane if I say that I have never felt more at home then I have staying here?"

"Not at all," she responds.

My eyes shift to the closed door and part of me wants to ask her what she knows. She has seems to have been a big part of the Harris family for quite some time. I can't make the words leave my mouth. My stomach sinks a little, realizing I don't know as much about Braeden as I thought. Things remain silent for a second.

"Well, it looks you were about to take a shower before I barged in." She laughs. "I'll be downstairs and then you and I are going to have a girls' day! I have a little surprise for you, too."

My face drops. *I have a surprise for you.* I can hear

her voice in my head. Surprises were never good when it came to Elaina. It usually resulted in her doing something completely stupid, me paying for her mistakes.

"Phoenix?" I hear Chelsea say.

I snap out of my daymare.

"I'm gonna...go take a shower," I say heading in the other direction passing my bedroom, the bathroom next to my room.

Setting my clothes on top of the counter, I reach over and turning on the shower head. Stepping inside I let the warm water soothe over me. Letting the warm water run down my face I close my eyes, the picture frame taking over my memory. My mind runs in a million different directions. What is he keeping from me? Fed up with not being able to relax I hop out, towel drying myself off. Slipping on my clothes I make my way back downstairs, finding Chelsea in the kitchen. I watch her as she moves about the room and I can tell she is comfortable, knows where everything is. As she turns around her eyes catch mine.

"That was fast," she says standing up. "Are you hungry?"

The table is piled with a hill of food. It looks like take out.

"Yeah..." I say staring at it. "But are we...."

I go to continue, but my ears pick up on a voice coming from the living room.

"Where the fuck is everybody?" the loud voice booms.

A smile instantly breaks across my face.

"And there would be your surprise," Chelsea smiles.

Pushing back through the kitchen door, I lay my eyes upon the massive figure standing in the foyer.

"Hey there, little one!" Donovan booms.

I walk up to him and I can tell he is excited and apprehensive at the same time.

"You can hug me, Donovan." I laugh.

He doesn't need a second invitation. He bounds toward me, scooping me up and swings me around.

"Ahhhh!" I scream out, pain radiating out from my chest.

"Jesus, Donovan!" I hear Chelsea scream out. "She has two bruised ribs!"

He sets me down gently and backs away from me slowly.

"It's OK, Donovan, you didn't know."

I hear a light giggle that definitely didn't come from him. Shifting my body to peer around him, my eyes fall on another figure.

"Rain!" I screech out, my eyes almost not able to believe what they're seeing.

"Surprise!" she squeals out.

Taking large, quick steps, I close the distance between us, wrapping my arms around her.

"I can't believe you're here," I say into her ear.

"I'm sorry I couldn't come sooner. I was so worried about you, Phoenix," she squeaks out.

"How...I mean...why are you here?" I ask.

"Remember? I told you I was allowed day visits," she reminds me. "Donovan is my aide."

I wrap my arms over her again, knowing I won't be able to do this every day. I hear her laugh as I pull back.

"You look good," she tells me.

I roll my eyes.

"I feel like I've been run over by a truck for the past decade."

"You look happy..."

I smile. "For once I can say I am."

The room falls silent and my heart soars. People are here because they care about me.

"Well, I'm fucking starving and I can smell the food," Donovan says.

We all laugh and pile into the kitchen, grabbing plates of food. Walking back into the living room, I notice the chairs out on the porch.

"Let's go sit outside," I tell Rain.

She smiles and nods, following me out the sliding glass door. We settle ourselves in the chair, eating quietly at first.

"So, tell me, how are things with you?" I ask, not wanting to spend my time with her in silence.

"A lot less fun since you left," she says with a sigh.

"I'm sorry," I say, feeling slightly disappointed.

"Have you ever thought about leaving?"

My heart races as I wait for her to answer.

"I have," she admits. "I just don't have a knight in shining armor to save me."

I give her a crooked smile.

"He loves you," she states, my heart skips multiple beats, my fork slipping through my fingers.

"What?" I ask, knowing I must have heard her wrong.

She looks down at her plate, pushing her food around.

"You should have seen his face when he came looking for you. He knew..." she explains. "He may not have had all the pieces put together, but he knew you were in danger. He looked so...broken."

I cringe at her words.

"I think we both were," I explain. "When he went back into that house there was a part of me that felt I was going to lose him."

As shiver runs down my spine as the emotions from that night bubble up.

"That should be proof enough." She smiles. "Has he said anything yet?"

I shake my head and her brow furrows. "Rain?" I ask, confused by her change of emotion.

She just looks up and gives me a smile, putting her fork in her mouth. We sit out for quite some time and we hear the slider open, both our heads turning. A smile comes across my face when my eyes meet Braeden's. His body stands relaxed in the open doorway, a small smile on his face, but I can tell something is off. My mind shifts to the picture frame. Rain stands up from her chair, looking in between us, and smiles before heading back inside.

"Hi, Seraph," he says smiling. "Are you having a good time?"

I smile back and nod.

"It's really great to see Rain," I explain.

His smile widens.

"Let me guess, it was your idea." I laugh.

"I figured you could use some girl time before you get too tired of always being with my sorry ass."

Setting my plate down on the side table, I pop up out of my chair and bound towards him, my fingers wrapping up in his shirt as I try to climb his tall form. My lips find his instantly, a moan escaping both our lips. I pull back, suddenly embarrassed by this uncontrollable desire I have for him.

"You don't know how much I missed that today," he says, bending down and placing a small kiss on my lips.

"How was school?" I ask, trying to remember his schedule.

"It was fucking boring as hell, pretty sure I didn't hear a damn word the professor said." He laughs. "You were the only thing on my mind, Seraph."

I lick my lips, feeling the warmth creep up my face.

"Are you far behind because of...ummm...the incident?"

"Don't worry, I'm a fast reader," he says as he reaches out lightly, taking my hand in his. "Did you get my note this morning?"

"I did!" I squeak, excitement taking over. "But why do I have to wear something nice?" *I don't own anything nice.*

"That's for me to know and for you to find out."

Hearing giggles coming from the living room, both Braeden and I turning around and head back inside. I scan the room, realizing now that Dr. Harris has joined us. He and Chelsea sit together on the couch eating and laughing. Braeden and I stand there just holding hands.

"He looks happy," I whisper into Braeden's ear.

Braeden studies his father.

"That he does," he says quietly.

~

Too soon everyone has to return to their respective jobs. I give Rain a hug before walking her out to the car, Donovan is already smiling and waving from the driver's seat. The house quickly goes from being full of activity to the quiet solitude of just Braeden and me. I keep myself busy by cleaning up all the dishes from lunch and I find myself content with the idea of a lazy afternoon. As I swirl the brush around a dirty plate, I feel hands slide underneath my arms and settle on my hips. I try to hold my anxiousness, knowing his touch will never be harsh. I feel his lips on my neck, my body suddenly feeling like it's on fire. Dropping the dishes and the brush I spin around to face him, gorgeous green eyes staring down at me.

Two identical boys.

"Are you ready to go out?" he softly asks.

My eyes widen.

"Were going…" I swallow the lump in my throat. "Out?"

His eyes change from passion to worry.

"Oh, fuck," he mumbles. "I didn't even think about how you would feel about going out after all that has happened."

I smile. "Braeden," I sternly say trying to get undivided attention again. "It's fine…"

Reaching up I run my hand through his hair.

"I would love to go out with you." I smile and I can see his worry settle.

"I just want you to feel safe," he explains.

"I always feel safe when I am with you," I explain while stand up on my tippy toes giving him a kiss. "Just give me a little bit of time to get ready, OK?"

Slipping out from under his grasp, I bound up the stairs quickly, my eyes staring down at the ground as I pass the closed doors. Walking over to the closet I really take the time to go through each and every item hanging, thanking my lucky fucking stars Chelsea picked out stuff that I would actually wear. I settle on skinny jeans and a t-shirt, pulling the extra fabric to the side and tying it in a knot. Reaching back into the closet I find something for warmth, my mouth dropping when my fingers come across leather. Pulling it out, I scan over the jacket. Remind me to thank Chelsea...again.

Sliding it on I walk into the bathroom, brushing my teeth and hair quickly, not wanting to be one of those girls who take forever. When I feel satisfied, I make my way downstairs, my eyes falling on Braeden immediately. He is in a completely different outfit, now sporting dark jeans and a black button up shirt, his hands in his pocket. I have to grip the banister so I don't fall flat on my face. He turns around to face me and I look down at the floor, suddenly feeling incredibly nervous.

Braeden

"**Y**ou look beautiful," I state, noticing how incredibly amazing she looks in that outfit. Walking up the first few steps, I slide my hand in hers.

"Ready?"

She nods. Leading her out the front door, we walk down the street, crossing a few blocks before we reach the underground transit. Most people don't have the need for a car living in the city and taxis tend to be expensive. As we descend the escalator, I pull her close to me, feeling her fingers tremble in mine.

"He's not here, Seraph," I whisper in her ear. "I won't let anyone hurt you again."

She looks up at me and gives me a light smile before

nuzzling her face into my neck. Once we reach the bottom, I walk over to the machines, putting twenty dollars on a pre-paid card for her.

"This is yours," I say handing it to her. "I want you to keep it. You're going to need it for when I'm not with you. "

Her eyes widen as she takes it from my hand. I can tell the thought of being out alone terrifies her. A small wave of anger flows through me every time she looks this vulnerable, knowing that asshole caused her broken state.

"Come on, Seraph, let's go eat."

We stand on the platform for a few minutes, my form behind her, my arms wrapped around her tiny frame.

"Have you ever ridden the subway before?" I ask into her ear.

I see her head shake. I guess that's a dumb question. When our train comes, I push on her to move forward, still holding onto her from behind, knowing people on here can be quite pushy. I maintain my hold on Phoenix as we remain in the standing position, all the seats already taken. Curling my left arm around her back, I hold her into my chest, my right arm hanging onto the handlebar above me. After a few stops we filter out and head back above ground, only a block away. We reach the restaurant quickly and I open the door, letting Phoenix enter first.

"Braeden!" I hear my name being called out, the owner of the restaurant coming over to us. "It's so nice to see you!"

Letting go of Phoenix's hand I shake his.

"It's really nice to see you too, Salvatore." I smile.

"And who is this beautiful creature you've brought with you?" he asks, his eyes finding Phoenix's.

I smile. "This is my Phoenix," I say, wrapping my arm around her. Salvatore brings her hand up gently, placing a small kiss on top of it. If he wasn't almost old enough to be her grandfather I would be jealous. "We have the best table for you two," he says, ushering us to follow him.

When we reach the back room I notice we're going to be seated alone, a table for two in the middle of the room, a small candle lit in the center.

"Thank you," I say to him as I walk around the table, pulling out a chair for her.

Salvatore nods and leaves us alone.

"Thank you," she says shyly as she sits. "This is beautiful, Braeden."

I smile at her as I sit down across from her.

"I have been coming to this place for a long time. It was my family's favorite restaurant."

The waitress brings us our menus. I don't have to even look at it to know what I am going to order. I take this opportunity to watch Phoenix, her eyebrows scrunching as she reads over the menu, a small smile coming across her face. After a few minutes, she sets her menu down and looks up at me, catching me staring at her.

"What?" she asks, red rising on her cheeks.

My heart begins to pound in my chest. Before I have time to answer the waitress comes up to our table, losing the moment.

For the rest of dinner Phoenix and I talk about everything and anything. I am relieved by her happy mood and Salvatore's chef seems to know the secret to awakening her appetite. After dessert we walk along the streets of the city, my hand in hers. After a few blocks, I feel a shiver run down Phoenix's arm, different than the fearful kind I'm used to.

"Are you cold?" I ask her.

"A little bit," she admits shyly.

I look at what street were on, knowing the café is close.

"Come on," I say tugging on her, an idea popping into my head.

When we reach the front door I stop her.

"Since I want to be completely honest with you, when we go in this café the women working here might seem...odd."

She laughs lightly. "It's OK, Braeden. I see how women look at you."

I roll my eyes. "Don't let that shit get to you, Seraph, I only want you," I say leaning down and pressing her lips to mine.

Pushing the door open, I hear the bells on the handle chime, my eyes immediately finding Lacey, her eyes wide. Grasping Phoenix's hand, I walk up to the front counter, pulling out my wallet.

"Two hot chocolates, please," I say pulling out a twenty, keeping my eyes on Phoenix, a smile coming across her face.

Out of the corner of my eye I see Lacey throw her broom on the ground and leave the room. A girl I've never seen before starts to makes our drinks and I'm grateful I don't have to deal with any bullshit. When they're done I slide a lid and sleeve on each and head back out the door, still hand-in-hand with Phoenix. I watch her take a sip, a look of enjoyment spreads across her face.

"Good?" I ask.

"Very." She smiles.

Things fall silent for a second.

"She looked really mad," Phoenix laughs as she puts her lips on the cup again. "Did you two have a thing?"

I scoff, almost ashamed that she would think I would date *that*.

"Never," I say looking into her eyes. "I wouldn't touch that with a ten foot pole. That woman is the definition of fugly."

"Braeden..." I hear her scold.

"No, I don't mean it like that, baby," I go to explain.

"Inside, she is as black as night."

"What about me?" I hear her ask softly.

Leaning down I put my fingers under her chin, making her look at me.

"You are the most beautiful person I have ever seen, Phoenix. Both inside and out. You have been broken multiple times over, but here you stand. Willing to open your heart to me when you trust no one else."

She doesn't respond but instead curls into my chest and we walk the rest of the to the subway station. Once we get home I open the side door to my father's house. I'm not surprised to see all the lights off. The house is vacant. Shutting the door behind me I watch her start to head upstairs.

"I'll be right back," she says before running upstairs and out of sight.

Walking over to the couch, I set myself down on it, turning on the TV hoping to cut up the silence. I stare at the screen, an unknown amount of time passing before my vision becomes blocked, everything dark.

"Count to ten and come find me," I hear her voice whisper in my ear.

Before my eyes have time to adjust she is gone like a leaf in the wind. I slowly rise from the couch.

"One..." I call out loud. "Two. Three."

I start to walk around the family room.

"Four."

"Five."

"Six."

I peer into the kitchen, her figure nowhere to be seen.

"Seven."

"Eight."

"Nine."

"TEN!" I shout out, bounding more into the kitchen, pulling open the door to pantry.

Empty.

I feel like a kid again, memories flooding over me. Heading back into the living room I check every crevice and closet, all of them coming up empty. I look up the stairs but decide to stay on the first floor since I didn't hear any telltale creaks coming from the stairs while I was counting. After minutes I gather that she's not downstairs, only leaving one place. Outside.

Walking up to the glass slider, I reach up with a shaky hand, pushing it open. Looking down at the ground, I secretly pray that she is sitting on one of the chairs on the porch. I am grateful for the motion censored lights illuminating the backyard. Swallowing, I take the first step out, peering out into the backyard.

"Phoenix," I call out, no longer wanting to play.

When I hear no answer I take another step, my body slowly descending the stairs. And then I hear it. A crash comes from the shed, my body jumping.

"Phoenix!" I shout out as I run over to it.

I go to put my hand on the handle but my hands are

trembling so bad that I can't clasp onto it. I can hear a giggle come from within.

"Phoenix! Get out of there now!" I scream, my voice echoing through open space. Moments later, I see the shed door being pulled open, Phoenix's form coming into the light. Grabbing her arm harshly I drag her back up the steps of the patio and slam the back door closed behind us. As I lean against it, I feel my body becoming weak and my legs buckle out from under me, my body hitting the ground.

I hear Phoenix scream out my name before everything goes black.

Phoenix

Stumbling forward I go to stop Braeden's lifeless body from crumbling to the ground but my strength cannot match it.

"Braeden!" I ear-piercingly scream out.

We both crash to the ground in a pile. Getting our arms and legs untangled, I center myself on my knees, my face hovering over his.

"Braeden! Can you hear me?" I say, running my hands across his cheek. When I don't hear a response I can feel the tears begging to fall. *Fuck! What do I do?*

"Dr. Harris," I say out loud to myself as I pull myself from the ground.

Sprinting into the kitchen I find the card with his

hospital numbers on it. Dialing the number my fingers are so shaky I hit multiple buttons at once.

"Fuck!" I scream out, the tears flowing down my face.

Trying to calm myself I focus on the buttons, finally getting the right number. Putting it up to my ear I listen, the silence between each ring feels like hours, not milliseconds. Just as I am about to hang up I hear a female voice come over the phone.

"Sarah speaking," her happy voice declares.

"I need Dr. Harris," I squeak out, my voice shaky.

"I think he might be with a patient but let me go check."

"Please hurry, it's an..."

I hear a moan coming from the other room and the phone slips out of my fingers and bounces on the counter top. Pressing my legs forward, I bound back into the living room. Braeden's body remains on the floor but his hands are now on his head, his fingers methodically running through his hair.

"Braeden," I cry out.

His eyes snap open. They are dark as night.

"Are you OK?" I ask, my heart still pounding in my chest.

"Yes," I hear him mutter.

He goes to sit up and I rush over, putting my arm behind his back. When he stands up he seems taller and I feel my body on edge and I instinctively take a step back, my arms hugging each other. He immediately notices my retreat.

"Seraph?" he voice cracks, his hand extended in the space between us. I can't hold back the tears anymore and they fall even harder, my chest heaving.

"I'm so sorry Braeden," I cry out, suddenly feeling that this is my entire fault. *Isn't it always?*

"Phoenix," he says softly. "This has nothing to do with you."

I look up into his eyes suddenly confused. He remains silent for a moment as he steps closer to me, removing my arms from each other, his fingers grazing where he once had firm a hold of me.

"I promised myself that I would never touch you harshly," he says, the tone of his voice disappointed.

I look down at his hand on my arm. "Braeden, it would take a lot more than that for you to hurt me," I whisper.

He lets out a sigh and leans his forehead on mine, our hot breath mixing in the space between us.

"I guess I have some explaining to do."

"Only if you want to."

"I promised I would never lie to you," he whispers, his eyes now on the ground.

Grabbing his hand in mine I lead him upstairs, wanting to be in the confines of my room for this discussion. We both ascend the stairs, remaining quiet, nothing but the squeak of each step filling the still air. I look at Braeden as we pass the closed doors, hoping that my questions about what I thought I saw will be fulfilled tonight. Opening my door I lead Braeden over to the bed and I climb onto it, never letting our grip falter. He remains standing beside it, his eyes dark and distanced.

"Braeden," I say yanking gently on his arm. "Please sit."

His eyes find me as I pat the bed beside me. I scoot over as Braeden climbs up, both our backs up against my pillows, our hands still interlocked. We sit there in silence for a while and I don't want to push him. *He'll talk when he wants to.* I stare at the wall, the stillness in the room slowly eating away at me.

"It happened so long ago but why does it seem like no time has passed?" I hear him softly say.

That one sentence crumbles my heart into a million pieces.

"Because trauma blocks you from happiness," I say out loud. "You want to move on but you can't. No matter how hard you fight to forget it, it's always there."

I realize I'm not just talking about Braeden. I feel his hand grip mine tighter.

"What happened, Braeden?" I ask softly.

"There was an accident," he say, his words heavy. "There was so much blood."

My stomach churns at his words but I remain silent.

"I was seven years old when I lost one of the most

312

important people in my life. We were the exact same age but Thomas always seemed older. He was my best friend, my protector."

I squeeze his hand as the picture of the two boys flooded my mind.

"You were a twin," I whisper as a statement rather than a question. He nods.

"He was born six minutes before me," he said with a small laugh. "He always said that I had to do whatever he said because he was the big brother."

A flash of Braeden's whole family at the kitchen table smiling and laughing comes across.

"What happened?" I ask.

"It was an unusually warm night for the city and I insisted Thomas play street hockey with me."

Braeden

"*Come on Thomas!*" *I shout from downstairs, my stick and pads in my hands.* "*It's going to be dark soon!*"

I hear the creak of the stairs moments later.

"*Hold your horses, Braeden.*" *He laughs.*

My brother walks past me and into the kitchen. I get flustered and follow him in, my stick hitting the doors and walls as I move.

"*Braeden, watch where you hold that stick,*" *I hear my mother say.*

"*Sorry, Mom,*" *I mutter.*

She smiles and walks over to me, placing a small kiss on my head.

"Moooom," I whine.

She just laughs.

"Someday you are going to miss my kisses." She smiles as she stirs the pot on the stove. She looks out the window and then at the clock on the wall. "Dinner is going to be ready in 30 minutes. You two better go play now."

"OK, Mom," we say in unison.

"Jinx, you owe me a Coke," I say quickly.

Thomas just laughs.

We both filter out the side door, grabbing our nets from the garage. Setting up in the middle of the street we start playing.

Phoenix

"**I** don't know how much time had passed, but I remember that being one of the best days of my life," he says, his voice cracking. "I remember laughing so hard that I had tears in my eyes. Thomas was always so supportive of me and would always be there for me to practice. He was of course always naturally good."

I see a small smirk come across his face and then it quickly disappears.

"And then all I heard was screeching of breaks and it was all over."

I begin to feel sick.

"They said it was a drunk driver," he says quietly. "I don't remember much but they told me the car hit him first and that he was dead upon impact."

I squeeze his hand even harder as I feel his pain.

"But that means he didn't suffer, that's good right?" I say, needing to comfort him somehow.

"I guess so," he admits. "And then the car struck me."

Tears start to well up in my eyes but I try hard for him to not to let them fall.

"By the time it hit me they weren't going as fast but I apparently got dragged through shards of broken glass."

I cringe. Braeden lets go of my hand and I worry that our conversation is over. But instead his hands go to the bottom of his shirt and he lifts up, exposing his torso. I shimmy myself on the bed a little trying to not be uncomfortable with a half-naked man in my bed. *It's not the time for that.*

Braeden turns his body a little and I gasp. Straight down the length of his entire back is a large scar, the skin raised and slightly pink. I reach out and touch it, making Braeden jumping a little.

"Did it hurt?" I ask, knowing it's a stupid question.

"I don't really remember most of it," he admits. "One minute I was laughing on the street with my brother and the next I was in a hospital bed alone."

My eyes fall upon a scripture tattooed into his skin, the words are broken up by the line of the scar.

"Death captures the dying, but sorrow steals from those left behind," I read out loud.

There are also two birds in midflight adorning it.

There is a moment of silence between us. "And after

his death, the life I always knew crumbled in more ways than I could ever have imagined. Not only did I lose a brother on that day, little did I know I was starting to slowly lose my mother as well."

He turns back around and is now facing me.

"I'm so sorry, Braeden," I say as a betraying tear escapes, flowing down my cheek.

Unfortunately, I know that this nightmarish story isn't over.

"Every day since his death, the days drug on, days turning into weeks, weeks turning into months. I remember being on my own a lot. My mother started to lose all interest in everything and severe depression crippled her. I couldn't even make myself go back into our room that we had shared. From the night of his death, I stayed in the guest bedroom. My whole family fell apart that day."

I run my thumb over the top of his hand.

"My father did what he could for me, but between the hospitals and my mother's depression there was no time for me. Sometimes I would come home and she would just be staring out the front window. She was a ghost with nothing of my loving mother left inside that shell."

"She still loved you, Braeden, you have to know that," I assure him.

He shrugs. "Is it wrong that I was mad at her?" he asks.

I shake my head. "No," I admit. "She left you alone when you needed her the most. But don't blame her. Being crippled by depression is something I hope for no one to experience. You feel like you can't control anything. Like the only way out is death."

He gives me a worried look and reaches up and brushes a finger down my cheek.

"It breaks my heart when you speak like that, Seraph," he whispers.

"But it was my life," I explain. "Like you want to forget how much pain your mother and brother's death have caused you, I do as well, but it will never happen for me."

Putting my forearms out in front of us so that the scars are on my arms are visible to both.

"As long as we bear these scars we will always be reminded."

He reaches out and runs his fingers along them, then bends down and puts his lips gently to each. He shifts again and I see the bright red slash across the top of his shoulder. I reach out and touch it.

"And now you bear a new scar because of me," I utter with a tone of disappointment. He looks over his shoulder at it.

"I could never regret my decision that got me that one, Phoenix," he says, the mention of my name sending shivers down my spine.

He takes his hand in mine and silently tells me to

come over and I settle myself in between his legs, my back to his chest.

"How did she die?" I ask nervously.

I feel his chest rise and fall more quickly.

"She hung herself," he says into my ear. "In the shed."

Fear runs through my body and I can't hold back the stream of tears that leave my eyes. Now I know exactly why he panicked when he found me.

"Braeden, I'm so..." I start to say before he cuts me off.

"Shhh, Seraph," he says while running his fingers through my hair. "You had no way of knowing."

I quiet myself down, the sound of my small sniffles filling the room.

"And then after that it was just my dad and I," he explains. "My father spent a lot of time blaming himself that he couldn't save her. I know that he loved her and tried everything he could but she just wouldn't hold on enough to try. We both loved her so much but at some point we were almost relieved. Does that sound too selfish?"

"Not at all," I admit. "You both had watched her suffer for so long."

Putting the pieces together from what Braeden had previously told me, three years had passed between the death of his brother and his mother.

"You just wanted her to be at peace right?" I ask.

"Yes," he breathes out.

"She is, Braeden," I assure him as I look down at our hands interlocking. "She got the peace that she always wanted."

Braeden

As I talked about my family to Phoenix each reveal seemed to have lifted weight off my shoulders but in the end I felt physically and emotionally drained. I didn't want to burden her mind with my tragic past but after my scene out in the backyard I knew I had to. She would eventually see the scars and the tattoo. I know she would never push me into explaining, but I owed it to her. She needed to know everything. Everything that made me the man I am today.

With her back still laid upon my chest, we remain silent for a moment, I assume both of us taking in what I had just told her. My mind races in a million different directions, wondering what she's thinking. Feeling.

"Tell me what you are thinking," I ask her.

She doesn't say anything for a moment and I fear that she is starting to break down.

"Seraph?" I ask again worried.

"I was just thinking about my dad," she says, her voice soft.

I give her a light squeeze, remembering I'm not the only person who has lost someone. Phoenix has in more ways than just death.

"He was my best friend," she starts. "My whole world crumbled when he took his last breath."

I hear her sniffle and I know she is trying not to cry again.

"Let the tears fall, baby," I say as I lean down, putting my lips on top of her head.

"I was so young and all we had was each other," she starts. "When I was born my mother took off after a few months leaving no note, she didn't even leave anything for me to remember her by. My father worked full time, but I was always his number one priority. He wasn't the best at everything but he did his best to care for me."

I hear a sigh leave her lips.

"I remember lying in my bed every night imagining my mother coming home to us, our broken family once whole again. But she never came."

My heart breaks a little.

"I remember the exact day that my whole life fell apart. My father told me he wouldn't be picking me up after school and that I was to go home with Mary, our neighbor, because he had an important appointment he had to go to. I knew something was off when he woke up that morning, something was wrong. I could just tell in his face."

I run my thumbs over her knuckles, silently encouraging her to go on.

"It was later that night he told me he was dying. I was pretty mature for my age and my father and I never lied to each other. He didn't want to sugar coat it for me."

I want to comfort her more, but I find myself frozen.

"It was the first time in my life that I truly felt alone," she starts up again. "He only had six months to live and as much as I don't want to admit it, they were the best of my life. My father was very reserved but he took this time to spend even more time with me than he already did. Every day he would pick me up from school and we would go do something, whether it was simple like getting ice cream or taking me to the zoo for the afternoon."

I could hear the smile in her words.

"But things were incredibly different. After a few months, the roles reversed and I became the parent. My father was strong but the disease was stronger. He lost a lot of weight and, much like your mother, he was a hollow form of what he once was. He couldn't walk much anymore due to the excruciating back pain. "

"You and him were all alone?" I ask.

"No, there were neighbors that came around a lot and dropped off food and helped me clean but, to be honest, I enjoyed it most when it was just me and him," she explains.

Things fall silent again and I wonder if she is done.

"And then, just after four months, the disease over took his body and he spent the rest of his life in a hospital bed, which, thankfully, was only a few days."

She lets out a sigh.

"I spent every waking moment with him in that hospital room. We ate every meal together and watched our favorite shows. And then I knew that our time together was dwindling at a rapid pace by the look on doctors and nurses faces every time they would look at him. At the end of the third day he passed away."

I can hear her sobbing, her chest heaving up and down. Putting my arms around her, I drag her body up to mine and I cradle her in my arms like a child, her face nuzzled into my neck. I don't say anything and just let the tears fall, knowing like me that this has been bottled up for quite some time. After about five minutes, she pulls back and looks at me, her eyes puffy and blood shot.

"And if my life couldn't have gotten any worse, Elaina showed up at the hospital the next day along with a social worker and I was informed since she was my mother that I would be handed over to her."

I cringe at the word handed, it was so...unloving.

"She never wanted me," she continues. "She thought she had gotten away from me when she left my father. She constantly reminded me that I was a burden to her. Before I was even born I had ruined her life."

How could anyone not want her? Not love her and see the wonderful human being that I see?

"And then Carl came into the picture," she says quietly.

My whole body goes rigid, the mere sound of his name sending anger through my body.

"Phoenix, you don't have to talk about it if you don't want to."

"We're showing our skeletons, right?" she asks me.

All I do is nod slightly.

"I was fifteen when Carl started abusing me," she says slowly. "I remember exactly how it started."

She points to one scar on her arm, it the most faded, but still very apparent. It was round and raised a little bit, but I knew exactly what it is, it fit the size and shape perfectly.

"He burned you with a fucking car cigarette lighter?" I ask in disbelief, my heart breaking all over again.

She nods.

"The three of us were out grocery shopping, which I was dragged to because Elaina was all about appearances. I didn't realize how close the car next to us was and I bumped the door into it."

She runs her finger over the raised skin.

"I knew it was coming," she says, her voice dripping with pain. "That was the worst pain I had ever felt in my life. Well, up until that point."

My knuckles clench, my desire to have this man dead increasing by the second.

"But then it just became the normal for me. It was everyday life."

"Why didn't you try to escape? Why didn't you tell someone?" I ask, not knowing if that was a fair question.

She shrugs.

"I was scared," she admits. "I knew that if he ever caught me he would give me the worst beating of my life. He wouldn't kill me because that would be too nice. He would beat me to the edge of my life but never let me slip off it."

I can feel tears start to well up, something that hasn't happened to me since my mother's death.

"But I did get away once."

I don't have to ask to know what incident she is talking about.

"It was the first time I had control of my own life. No one knew I was there except the cars zipping by but they didn't even care enough to stop. I was scared when I climbed up on the railing but there was an eerie sense of calm flowing through me. Peace was within my grasp."

A shiver runs through my spine, imagining Phoenix's body falling over the rail, her eyes closed and peaceful.

"But even then I wasn't granted it. The one decision I made for myself and it didn't work."

I understand her frustration for a moment, her need for the pain to stop.

"But I guess everything does happen for a reason," she says, a small smirk coming across her face. "I can't regret that now."

Wrapping my arms around her again, I hold her tightly.

"I would have found you anyways, Seraph," I say into her ear. "We were meant for each other. You belong to me and you always will."

Shimmying us both so that we are both laying on the bed, we face each other, the heaviness of both our words weighing down on us. Once she calms down I lean forward putting my lips in hers, my fingers running through her hair, finding the back of her head.

We kiss in the darkness of her room and I realize this is where we both belong. She is my home now. I would die for her. After a few minutes she pulls back, her body shifting so that it is on top of mine. I can feel her hot center on me and I try not to think about it as she leans down and kisses my chest. Leaning up I wrap my arms around hers, planting kisses on her neck, my fingers going underneath her shirt in the back. I hear a moan escape her lips.

"Yes," she breathes out.

I trail my fingers up the length of her back, feeling raised skin every so often. We both start to breathe hard and I pull back from her, our eyes meeting.

"Braeden, I want to…" she starts to say.

My heart rate spikes.

"I don't know if I can, Seraph," I admit. "It's going to hurt, I don't know if I can live with that."

"Please?" she begs, her voice desperate. "I know that you would never hurt me intentionally. For the first time in my life I don't feel alone and scared. I need you, Braeden."

I contemplate it for a moment but I know I could never deny her. Reaching up I lift up her shirt and slide it off, her creamy skin exposed. I place my lips on her chest while I reach around slowly and unhook her bra with one hand, her beautiful breasts coming into view.

"You are beautiful, Seraph," I say into her skin.

Shifting my body so that she is now underneath me I continue to kiss, my tongue landing on her breasts, both of them standing at attention to me. When I encircle my lips around one peak I hear another moan leave her throat, her way of telling me it's OK. I continue down her torso until I come to the button on her jeans. I stop and look up at her, silently asking her if I may continue. She gives me a nod. With shaky hands I reach for it, sliding the zipper down slowly. At this point I am rock hard as much as I don't want it to. I want this to be all about her, about the pleasure she deserves.

As I get her jeans off I pull myself off the bed. Phoenix's eyes turn to worry.

"It's OK, baby, I'm not going anywhere," I explain.

I start to undo my button and zipper, my pants falling down to the floor. Phoenix's eyes find it immediately, her eyes widening. Reaching down to the floor I pick up my t-shirt and walk over to the bed.

"Lift your hips, baby," I say softly.

She does as she is told and I slide my shirt underneath her hips before she lowers back down. I take a deep breath, my whole body buzzing. I had slept with a few women, but none of them meant this much to me. Knowing that I will cause her pain only makes it worse. Sliding my underwear off I keep them in my hand as I climb back on the bed, hooking the string of her underwear in my finger tips and slowly slide it down.

Placing one finger in between the folds of her lips I can feel her wetness seep around my fingers and I twitch with sensation. I gently slide one inside her, her hips bucking while I do. A loud moan escapes her lips and I pray to god that my father isn't home at the moment. After I pump a few more times I pull out, Phoenix's eyes still locked on mine.

"Are you ready?" I say through shaky breath.

He bites her lip and then nods. Grabbing myself with my hand, I line myself up and slowly run the tip of it through her slit, before pushing inside her slowly. I hear her gasp and I withdraw a little.

"No," she says through gritted teeth. "It's OK."

I resume to pushing slowly as I watch her fingers grip the sheets beside her. After a few more thrusts I am all the way in, all the pain leaving her face, a small smile coming across her face. Just when I thought I couldn't love her more she lets me worship her body, letting me take something so important to every woman. The rest of it was a blur but after some time we both reach our climax, mine coming into my boxers. Watching Phoenix's orgasm come from my touch is my new favorite vision and I know it will be replayed in my mind for days to come. I go to slide off of her but she stops me, our eyes interlocking.

"I love you, Braeden," she says softly, a blush creeping across her face.

At that moment my heart explodes into a million pieces.

"I love you, too, Phoenix," I respond. "I think I have since the moment I first saw you."

Phoenix

"No, please don't," I choke out, his grip on my neck getting tighter as each second ticks on. I can feel the tears starting to well up.

"You think that you can get away with this?" his voice growls, his mouth mere inches from mine.

My eyes shift to a figure in the corner. Her hair matches mine but her eyes are cold, her mouth turned up in a devilish grin. This person is not here to help me. With his hands still around my neck, he pulls me off the wall and I instinctively put both my hands around his arm, trying to pry it from my throat. It doesn't budge and he slams be back into the wall, this time so high that my feet dangle off the ground. My eyes shift to the female figure in the corner again, her hands reaching deep inside her pocket and pulls something out. The small light in the room shines from the silver of the blade. I instantly start to flail, trying everything I can to get away from them but the fingers around my neck tighten, my wind pipes completely cut off. The female form takes long strides towards me and the two figures are now side by side.

My eyes shift between the both of them, a wicked grin begins to sprawl across their faces and then things move so quickly. The feeling of warmth flows down torso and I feel around, the handle of the dagger flush against the skin on top my ribcage, an eruption of pain coursing through every inch of my body. When I look back up the figures have vanished almost like they were a figment of my imagination. But the pain and blood is all too real.

Without the support of his fingers around my neck, my now weak body crumbles to the floor, my back flush against the hardwood floors. The only thing in my sight is the handle of the dagger. With my blood-soaked hand, I wrap it around the etched wooden handle, but as soon as my skin comes in contact with it, the dagger thrusts deeper into my skin. I scream out at the top of my lungs, my vision no longer clear due to the tears falling down my cheeks.

I don't know how much time passes, the pools of blood on either side of my body growing with each second. I feel my eyes starting to become heavy and I know it will only be moments before I am taken from this world. But instead of the sense of calm that is always hoped for, it is replaced with dread and longing. I lay there staring at the wall, feeling so lost and alone. But then a soft light starts to fill the room and I lean up to see another female figure standing before me. Her facial features are soft, her presence instantly comforting me. She walks over to me on what I swear is air, never seeing her actual feet touch the ground. I remain lying still on the ground, only my eyes moving. The figure makes it to the side of my body and slowly leans down, her hand hovering over the dagger.

"NO! Please," I cry out. "It will kill me."

She doesn't listen and continues to reach for it, her fingers never actually touching it. The dagger then slowly starts to ascend from my body, drops of blood dripping from its pointed tip. I squint my eyes, noticing a dark tar-like substance wrapped around it. I remain still, still afraid to move. The dagger spins slowly underneath her command before it completely disappears before me. Her eyes find mine and I inhale sharply, the blue in her eyes is so vibrant that I swear they glow.

"You may sit up," her voice echoes through the room.

I hesitate for a moment but start to raise my head. As I do, I see the blood pools traveling back towards my body, a series of small rivers retreating back to the stab wound. Once in the blood returned, the wound starts to heal itself and, soon, there is no evidence of where the dagger was once immovable.

When I get fully seated upright, the figure only smiles at me before reaching out, her fingers close to my skin. I can feel every hair on my face and neck stand on end, but her touch is warm.

"You are safe now, my dear," she speaks again.

I go out to touch her, knowing she must just be another figment of my imagination. Much to my displeasure, my fingers go right through her arm but the same sensation that was on my face is now flowing through my fingertips.

"Who are you?" I ask nervously.

"I was sent here by someone who desperately loves you, Phoenix," her velvet voice explains. "You have many people who deeply care about you, both walking on this Earth and those that aren't."

"So, are you like, my guardian angel?" I ask, my voice shaking.

A smile comes across her lips, a smile that seems all too familiar to me.

"I will always protect what is important to my family," she explains. My heart beat quickens.

"You're...are you?" I mutter, not knowing what to say.

Her head slowly starts to nod.

"I'm so sorry, for everything you had to experience..." I cry out, suddenly feeling her pain.

"Shhh," she hums. "You are now what is important to him. He shouldn't grieve over me anymore."

The warm tears start to flow down my face, a few of them entering my mouth, the salty taste on my tongue.

"He has what he needs now," she continues on. "You both do. You both should live the life you always deserved and never look back."

She then puts her hand over my heart and I feel a jolt through my body, my back arching off the floor from the force.

~

I snap my eyes open, the feeling of warmth sprawled across my stomach. The room is bright, being the complete opposite of my dream. Shifting my body so that I am now facing him, I find myself only being able to stare. Stare at the heavenly creature next to me. My mind becomes a jumbled mess of visions from last night and my dream. Had we really bared our souls to each other?

I had never talked to anyone about my father before, not even when my mother would pretend to care and ask me. Not even to the psychiatrists at the hospital, most of them were always blinded by the cuts and bruises. And then those bright blue eyes come across my vision and my heart rate spikes. I hastily pull down my shirt a little to look at my upper chest, a sigh of relief coming over me when I don't find anything there. But what I do find is that a feeling of something inside me is gone. The once dark hatred that haunted me has vanished. I see Braeden stir, his eyes opening slowly, confused by the severity of my movements.

"Seraph?" he says sitting up, noticing my confused state. "What's going on?"

My face changes, a smile coming across my lips.

"I'm...happy," I say, almost confusing myself.

He returns with a smile.

"Can I ask you a question?" I blurt out suddenly.

His fingers find mine and they intertwine. "You never have to ask if you can ask me a question," he says softly.

"What color eyes did your mother have?" I ask, already knowing what the answer is.

"A very light blue," he responds. "Why?"

I smile even wider while looking down at our hands intertwined.

"She's OK, Braeden, I want you to know that," I start. "She is happy and so proud of you. Of us."

I see his eyebrows crunch together.

"It's a long story." I laugh.

Instead of continuing on, he tugs on my arm gently and I push my body into his, both of his arms around me tight.

"That was the best night of my life," he whispers into my ear.

I can feel the burning growing in my cheeks.

"It was mine too," I say softly. "It was better than I

could have ever imagined."

We both collectively hear the garage door open, it pulling us out of our serene moment. My body goes rigid, almost forgetting about Dr. Harris. I go to try to pull away, scenes of Dr. Harris finding us here together going through my mind. I then hear Braeden laugh.

"Stop squirming, you're ruining the moment," he kids.

"But what if he finds us?" I ask.

"He won't come up here, he wouldn't want to invade your privacy like that," he explains.

"That's ridiculous, it's his house."

"He doesn't come up here much," he says sadly, and I instantly understand why.

I go back to face him and he plants a kiss on top of my lips before letting me go.

"Why don't you go take a shower and get dressed, I'll head down and make us some breakfast."

I just smile and nod. His fingers reach up and gently graze my cheek, my skin responding the same as it was in the dream.

"I love you, Seraph."

My heart skips a beat.

"I love you, too."

After placing another kiss on his lips I bounce out of bed, grabbing my towel on the way out.

Braeden

I pull myself from the bed, silently cursing in my head. I want nothing more than to stay in this bed with her the rest of our lives. Just she and I, the rest of the world could stop spinning for all I cared. Fumbling around on the floor for my zip up, I slide it on, my t-shirt no longer wearable. Pulling open the bedroom door I can hear my father walking around downstairs, wondering if he was coming or going. When I reach the bottom of the stairs my father immediately notices me, my presence making him stop dead in his tracks.

"Braeden," he states, his face looking the most exhausted I have seen in a long time.

"Long night?" I ask, already knowing the answer.

"Like you couldn't believe," he says shaking his head.

"Do you wanna talk about it?" I ask, concerned that he is always taking on too much.

"You know I can't talk about patients," he says almost sternly. "But I do need to talk to you about something else."

My heart skips a beat, wondering what it could be. I now notice that he has a brown paper bag in his right hand. He closes his eyes and lets out a deep breath.

"I know that this situation is...different," he starts. "And I have prescribed this to a lot of women but I don't want her to feel uncomfortable having that talk with her."

I stare at him confused for a moment until my brain decides to play catch up.

"Oh," was all I blurt out.

He hands the bag out towards me and I take it from him.

"Uh...thanks," I say, suddenly feeling uncomfortable myself.

"I know that you two are serious, but I am way too young to be a grandfather." He laughs.

I crack a smile.

"You don't have to worry about that anytime soon," I respond.

We silently realize our conversation is done and both make our way towards the kitchen. "Hungry?" I ask.

"Famished," he calls out behind me.

Opening the fridge I am shocked about how much food is in here, a clear difference from just a few days ago. Pulling out some eggs and vegetables I quickly make a scramble for the three of us, portioning it out between the plates, setting one down in front of my father.

"Thanks, son," he says with a sigh while picking up his fork.

"Anytime," I say, my eyes catching a figure in the doorway.

"Good morning, Phoenix," my father says, a smile across his face.

She smiles back but I can tell she is nervous, or embarrassed. I leave the table side and wrap my hand around her lower back, placing a kiss on her forehead.

"Morning, Seraph," I call out.

A loud clanking sound fills the room and I turn around to see my father had dropped his fork, his eyes on us. It's only now that I realize what I had said out loud.

"Is everything OK?" Phoenix asks, clearly confused by the change of atmosphere.

I look over at my father, a tight smile coming across his face.

"Everything is fine," he assures. "Both of you eat before it gets cold."

My eyes find my father's and I apologize silently, his

eyes telling me it's OK. We both grab our plates and sit down at the table, all three of us eating in silence. After a few minutes my father finishes up his plate, gets up from the table, placing his dirty dishes in the sink. He then walks back over to the table, both of our eyes looking back at him.

"I'm heading into my office to do some paperwork," he starts. "Phoenix, when you are finished there is something I need to give to you."

"OK," she says softly, her face looking instantly nervous. He then steps out of the room and I instantly wrap my hand around hers.

"Don't be nervous, I'm sure it's just nothing," I assure her.

"I know," she admits. "Still, gotta get used to being able to trust people," she shrugs, putting another forkful in her mouth.

Leaning over I place my lips on hers, the fire running through my body, still amazed at how the simplest of touches sends my body into a frenzy. When I pull back I spot the brown paper bag on the counter. Releasing my hand from hers I get, grabbing it I suddenly feel embarrassed.

"My father, uh," I start, realizing how uncomfortable my father would feel talking about this with her. "He thought this would be a good thing."

I hold the bag out to her and she reaches up, taking it from me. She slowly unrolls the bag, her eyes sort of widening as she goes over the contents.

"You just have to take it once around the same time every day, its low hormone so you shouldn't have many side effects," I explain, the medical side of me kicking in.

She laughs lightly.

"I know what birth control is, Braeden." She smiles.

I let out a breath.

"Do you think he knows?" she asks suddenly, a blush creeping across her face.

"I think so," I admit. "My father is incredibly good at reading people. Guess being a doctor for twenty years probably helps."

She looks down at her plate.

"Don't be embarrassed," I whisper in her ear. "Was it what you expected?"

I instantly become nervous.

"It was better," she says while now looking back up.

She starts to stand up from the table but instead of walking past me, she wraps her arms around my torso tight, the side of her face plastered against my chest. I instinctively wrap my arm around her back, my other hand brushing her hair.

"Thank you, Braeden," she says. "For everything."

"You don't have to thank me," I whisper.

"I would be dead if it wasn't for you," she says softly into my chest.

I don't know how to respond to that, instead letting

my body answer, my grip around her tightening. The thought of her dead makes me instantly nauseous. We remain in the silent kitchen, nothing but the tick of the clock reaching our ears. After a few minutes she pulls back and looks up at me.

"Well, I guess I better go see what your dad wants," she says as her arms fall from my waist. I inwardly protest at the loss of her touch, always wishing for the ability to stop whenever she is in my arms.

"I'm sure it's nothing," I assure her again.

She stands up on her tippy toes, placing a kiss on my lips before leaving the room.

Phoenix

I walk to the back of the house and down a hallway that I have never seen before. I swear every time I turn around this place has a new room. When I reach an open door, light emanating it, I knock on the door frame.

"Phoenix," Dr. Harris responds. "Please come in."

As I make my way into the room I sit down in a chair, waiting for him to speak first. When he turns around to face me I instantly relax.

He would never harm me.

"So, how are things going?" he asks.

"They are good," I answer, sort of thrown off by his questions.

"I'm happy to hear that."

Reaching back he opens a drawer in his desk, pulling something out and setting it on his lap.

"Do you remember our agreement?" he asks.

"I do," I answer.

"This is for you," he responds, handing me the folded garments on his lap. "You start tomorrow." I take them from him and nod, suddenly feeling very nervous.

"You won't be responsible for anything medical, but your job as a volunteer is extremely important," he starts complaining. "I don't think people understand how much companionship is important in the healing process."

I give him a small smile.

"Chelsea will be there to help and train you," he says. "I really hope you end up liking it, but if you don't I will not force you to stay. If you are upset about anything, please come to me with no hesitation."

I just nod.

"One more thing. Did Braeden give you..."

I nod my head again fast. "Thank you," I blurt out suddenly.

"Do you have any questions for me?" he asks.

"How am I going to get there?" I panic at the thought of getting there myself.

"Well, since I am not sure you or I feel comfortable with you taking the subway alone at this point in time, I will come back and get you at eight."

"OK," I say a nervous tone in my voice.

We both fall silent. I open my mouth to say something, but close it again. Dr. Harris notices.

"Please don't ever be afraid to tell me something," he assures. I gnaw on my inner cheek for a moment.

"I just wanted to say I'm sorry," I hesitate. "For your loss of Thomas and…" I stop myself, realizing I don't know her name.

"Sophia," he says softly.

My heart drops, putting a name to her makes everything so much more heartbreaking.

"Thank you for your condolences," he says. "I'm glad Braeden felt comfortable to tell you about them."

"We both did some secret sharing last night," I say softly.

Things fall silent again.

"Well, that's all I have for you at the moment." He smiles. I stand up from the chair.

"Thank you," I say.

"You're very welcome, my dear." He smiles reassuringly.

Once I leave his office I head back up to my room, setting the outfit on top of my dresser. I hear a knock on my door, walking over and pulling it open.

"Everything go OK?" he asks, before taking a bite from the apple in his hand.

"Yeah," I assure him. "He just had to give me my outfit for the hospital."

Braeden looks down at me confused. *Oh I guess I never discussed it with him.*

"When your father talked to me about letting me stay here I promised him that I would volunteer at the hospital."

A wicked smile comes across his face, spotting the red and white garment folded on my dresser.

"Fuck, Seraph, you're going to be a candy striper?"

I gnaw on my bottom lip a little.

"Maybe," I say shyly.

He takes a step towards me, his free hand on the back of my neck. His lips smash to mine and I can taste the essence of apple on his lips. When he pulls back, I slide my tongue over my own lips, tasting even more of it.

"I've always had a thing for nurses," he whispers in my ear.

A shot of pleasure runs its course through my body, my knees becoming weak, my mind wandering to last night.

"I want you again, so bad," he says.

I look up at him, my body and mind wanting him also.

"I want you too," I respond, my fingertips finding the space of skin between his pants and his zip up.

"Fuck," he says through gritted teeth. "I don't know how the simplest touches..."

He stops talking mid sentence and takes a step

towards me, kicking the door closed with his foot. He continues to walk, my body moving backward in unison with him before my knees buckle against the soft bed. I feel the heat coming off his body as he presses his chest against mine, his hardness pressing against my inner thighs.

We continue to kiss until I hear his phone ring in his pocket but he continues to ignore it, the vibration tickling me. It finally stops, only for it to start up again a minute later.

"I think someone is trying to get a hold of you." I laugh.

"I really couldn't care fucking less," he says sternly, placing another kiss on my lips.

After its third ring he groans and reaches down, grabbing it from his pocket and answers it.

"Mmm," is all he utters, his lips on mine. "Mmm huh."

I can hear the voice talking on the other line but I can't make out what they are saying. Finally pulling his lips from mine he hits end and puts the phone on the bed beside us.

He lets out a sigh.

"I have to go, Seraph."

"Really?" I ask, suddenly depressed.

"I really don't want to," he says.

Leaning up I press my lips to his hard, my arm hooking around his neck for leverage.

"Stay," I beg.

"You are making this really fucking hard," he says then smiles. "No pun intended."

I respond with a smile.

"But I have to go, my professor is going to have my ass handed to me if I don't finish this paper."

"OK," I say as I start to climb out from underneath him.

The look on his face is heartbreaking. Reaching up I put my palm on the side of his face.

"I'm not going anywhere, Braeden." I laugh. "I'll be right here when you get back."

He gives me a smile.

"I was actually wondering if you wanted to come see my place tonight. Maybe we can grab some food and just get out of this house?"

"I'd like that."

He leans back down and places a kiss on my forehead.

"I'll be back before you have time to miss me."

Once he leaves the room I lay back on my bed, having only what I can imagine as the girl equivalent to blue balls.

Braeden

Her dark brown eyes. Her upturned smile whenever my body presses against her. The way she licks her lips after we've kissed. The feeling of her chest rising and falling beneath me. I feel something bounce off the side of my head, it pulling me from my Phoenix-induced daydream.

"What the fuck?" I call out, trying to see who threw it.

"Jesus, man," I hear Elliot say. "You think you can pull yourself away from whatever wet dream you are having at the moment so we can finish this shit?"

I shift uncomfortably in my seat, my ever-growing hard on becoming apparent. *Thank fuck that I am sitting under a table.*

"Yeah, sorry, man," I respond as I run my fingers through my hair. Elliot lets out a laugh.

"It's all good, must be nice to have pussy on the brain," he says seriously. "Is it that chick from the bar?"

I cringe just thinking about her. My life has changed so much since Phoenix walked into it.

"You want to hear an interesting story?" I say to Elliot, knowing I can confide in him.

~

"So, yeah," I say through winded breath.

"Holy shit, man," he responds with widening eyes. "Where the hell do you find time for shit like this?"

Running my hands through my hair again I let out a deep sigh.

"So, you fell for the mental patient? Does she even know who you are? What if she wakes up one day and thinks you kidnapped her ass." He laughs.

"Don't make me fucking punch you, asshole. I'm not above that."

"I don't know, dude, seems your girlfriend has to beat people up for you," he kids. "But he fucking deserved it."

"That was one of the greatest yet terrifying moments of my life," I explain. "I wanted to kill him more that I could ever describe, but seeing that bottle break over his mother fucking head was priceless. I've never been so proud of a person in my entire life."

"When do I get to meet this chick that now owns your balls?"

I shrug.

"I don't know if she's ready for your crazy ass," I grin.

"I am as sweet as fucking candy." He laughs.

"Right," I say picking up my pencil again. "Can we just finish this shit so I can go home?"

We both fall silent, our attention back on our textbooks.

After a few more hours I've had my fill of this fucking library and of Elliot. Slamming my textbook shut, I stuff it in my messenger back.

"I'm out," I say, clasping Elliot's hand in mine, shaking it. "I'll see you in class."

"Sounds good, dude," he says looking up. "Have a good time with your lady."

He gives me a wink before I walk out. When I step outside of the library, I notice the sun starting to set, the sky various shades of red and orange. Walking over to the bike rack I bend down, unlocking my bike lock. Pulling my bike from the rack I hop on it, I weave in and out of traffic, wanting nothing more than to wrap my arms around Phoenix. By the time I reach my father's house, I am winded and out of breath. The hills of San Francisco are not so kind to us bicyclists. Hoping off of it, I set it against the porch and pull open the front door. What greets my eyes causes me to stop and smile. My father and Phoenix are on the couch sitting side by side, coffee mugs in both their hands. A smile on both their faces. I remain still until Phoenix's eyes find mine, her smile widening even more.

"Hello, son," my father says.

"What are you two up to?" I ask as I set my book bag down in the foyer.

"We were just talking about Gone with the Wind," he explains.

"How was the library?" she asks, her voice soft and quiet.

"It was fucking boring, Seraph," I breathe out.

Phoenix's body grows rigid as the words leave my throat. Walking over to couch I sit down on the other side of her.

"It's OK," I say grabbing her hand.

"I don't want to make anyone feel uncomfortable," she mutters as she looks down at her hands.

"It's completely fine, Phoenix," I hear my father say. "I would be lying if I wasn't flattered that he chose what I called his mother. I think it is quite fitting," he explains.

My eyes snap up to him, my father is not usually one for the touchy-feely conversations.

"Thank you," I mouth to him.

I look back down at Phoenix, who is now looking back up at me.

"You ready to get out of here?" I ask, wrapping my

fingers around hers. My father goes to get up from the couch, taking one last swig from his coffee cup.

"What are you two up to tonight?" he asks.

"I was thinking of taking Phoenix to my place, get out of this damn house for a while."

I hear my father mumble something into his cup but I don't catch it. I'm kind of glad about that. My father has never approved of my choice of living arrangements. I'm beginning to think I agree.

"Well, just make sure she's back by 11," he says as he walks away.

"Are you fucking kidding me?" I blurt out.

My father stops in his tracks, and slowly turns back to face us.

"Braeden, it's ok..." Phoenix starts to say.

My father sets his coffee mug on the side table and I know I am about to get the wrath of Dr. Harris.

"I know I don't have to explain this to Phoenix because she knows not to question authority, but this is my house, and when someone is under my watch they will abide by my rules. I don't know where you get the sense of entitlement from, but as long as she is living here she will do what I say," he says sternly.

I look down at Phoenix, her eyes now down on her hands again, her body shaking ever so slightly. When I look back up my father's eyes are now closed, his breathing deep.

"Please, have her back by 11, she has a very busy

day tomorrow," he repeats before pushing the kitchen door open and disappears from sight.

"Seraph?" I say wrapping my arm around her back. "You OK?"

She nods but doesn't say anything.

"You know he doesn't mean that, right?" I assure her. "You can do whatever you want. He just wants you safe."

When those words leave my mouth I feel like a complete jackass. If it wasn't for my father who knows where Phoenix would be.

"Let's go," I say as I pull her off the couch.

We both walk to the front door, I grab my book bag on the way out. Both of our eyes fall on my bike, my mind trying to figure out how she could ride with me.

"Let's just walk." I laugh.

A smile spreads across her face and I curl her under my arm, every moment of being around her is breathtaking. We walk a few blocks before I see the subway station approaching.

"Got your card?" I ask.

She reaches into her back pocket and pulls out her fare card, a large smile across her face. I hold out my hand, ushering her to the turnstile. She walks in front of me and I get a small glimpse of her ass in those jeans and I think a whimper leaves my throat.

She puts her card in the slot and enters through into the crowd of people on the other side, no signs of distress visible. I'm so fucking proud of her. Putting my card in, I come up behind her, wrapping my arms around her waist, placing a kiss on her neck.

"I love you," I whisper.

She spins so that she is now facing me.

"I love you, too," she responds.

That is something I will never tire of hearing. She stands up on her toes, putting her lips on mine. This kiss is like no other, it's full of passion and lust, not the shy kiss I usually receive. Wrapping my hands into the fabric of her shirt I press against her harder. The whole world seems to stop, the people around us becoming nothing but blurs. The only thing that reaches my ears is the soft murmurs and moans leaving her throat and entering my mouth. But something pulls me back, the loudspeaker for the station calling our train's arrival.

"Fuck," I say as I pull my lips from hers.

"What is..." I hear her say but I grab her hand in mine and bolt for the stairs. I push through gobs of people, probably shoulder checking them a little harder than what is considered appropriate. I hear Phoenix laughing behind me, it causing me to smile. When we get to the bottom of the staircase I see the train pull up, its door opening to allow people to enter. I know I have very little time to get our asses on that train. Swinging Phoenix around so that she is now in front of me, we continue to push our way through.

"Push em," I call out to Phoenix.

She whips her head around and gives me a "no fucking way" look. *Tell her to touch strangers. That's smart asshole.* When we reach the doorway my grasp on her tightens, not even wanting to think about what would happen if she got separated from me. We finally get inside the train cabin, packed in like a bunch of fucking sardines. I grab onto the bar above my head, Phoenix too short to grab it herself.

"Just hold onto me," I say as I lean down a kiss the top of her head.

She does as I tell her, both her delicate arms wrapping around my torso. Her head is now laid upon my chest.

"I can hear your heart beat," she says smiling.

"Well, I hope so, Seraph," I joke. "Cause if you didn't we'd have a cause for concern."

She looks up at me and shakes her head. When I look back up I see a man staring back at us, but his eyes are purely on Phoenix.

"You got a fucking problem?" I blurt out, not liking how this asshole is looking at her.

The guy shifts his eyes away from us and I calm down a little.

"Braeden..." she scolds.

"What?" I ask confused. "I don't like the way he was looking at you."

"He wasn't doing anything," she states.

"He didn't have to," I explain. "Believe me, I know

what he was thinking."

"So, are you just going to hide me from the entire world?" she asks laughing.

"Yup," I say as I fumble with the zipper on my jacket before zipping her up in it with me.

I can hear her giggle from underneath my jacket, it makes me fucking grin ear to ear. I swear to fucking god, Phoenix's laugh could brighten anyone's darkest day. When I look back up I realize we have quite the audience. After a few more seconds I unzip it, Phoenix's head poking back out.

"If you didn't smell so good I would have to punish you for that," she smirks.

"And what that might entail?" I ask, suddenly curious.

I can see the blush start to creep up her face and I absolutely love it. The apprehensive sexual side of her is trying to break through. After a few more minutes, our stop comes and we filter off the train and up into the night air, now completely dark. We walk down the busy streets hand in hand just talking about random things, Phoenix's fear of working at the hospital, my schooling. When we get about a block from my apartment, Phoenix stops dead in her tracks. I start to panic at what it could be but my eyes find what she is staring at.

"Do you draw?" I ask as I watch her stare into the front window of the art shop.

She just shrugs.

"I guess so, just kind of doodling here and there."

I stare at her for a while, the admiration for the art before her apparent in her eyes. After few minutes we continue on, waiting at a street corner for the light to change. I spot something out of the corner of my eyes and I try my best to cover her body with mine before it gets to her, the wave of water soaking my entire back.

I look down at her, her hair is soaked, my protection not serving much purpose. I try to gauge her reaction, but then she opens her mouth and a roar of laughter leaves her throat. I match her and peel myself off, our clothes slightly sticking to each other.

"I tried," I admit through laughter.

The light finally changes, I grab Phoenix's hand in mine, and we hastily make it to the rest of the way to my apartment, the cold wind whipping through our waterlogged clothes. By the time we reach my front door we are both exhausted, but then something shifts inside of me. The need for her mouth to be on mine becomes an obsession. I watch Phoenix's chest rise and fall, my eyes finding her bottom lip gently tucked between her teeth. Her eyes then find mine, the look in them telling me she is feeling the electricity running between our bodies. Taking a step forward I press her up against the door frame, my hips pinning her. Once I press my lips to hers I feel my need being filled but, yet, I feel like I can't get close enough. Phoenix's hands find their way into my wet hair, her fingertips gently tugging on the strands. My left hand comes out between our bodies and I find the bottom line of her shirt, slowly peeling the fabric away from her soaked skin. I hear her gasp, making me smile against her lips.

Kissing her makes me feel like a teenager again, everything is so innocent. Every touch feels as though it's the first time every time. I don't think I will ever not need it. I crave it like a vampire hungers after blood. I would cease to exist without it. My fingertips continue to travel north, finding the line of her bra. I go to slip my fingers underneath it but suddenly both our bodies fly forward, my body crashing on top of her.

"Fuck," I scream out.

Once I get my bearings, I look up, seeing Bret standing over us, a grin on his face.

"What the fuck?" I say to him, as I reach my hand out to pull Phoenix up from the floor.

"What?" he says, a dumbfounded look on his face. "How was I supposed to know you were making out with some fucking random chick on our front door?"

I huff, and then notice that Phoenix is staring at Bret, a mixture of hatred and fright. Bret eyes her with a look of shock on his face.

"Whoa! You're sleeping with suicide girl?" he blurts out.

A surge of anger rushes through my body and I have to hold back from wanting to bounce his fucking head off the opposing wall.

"Shut the fuck up," I spit out as I grab Phoenix's arm, leading her into my bedroom. After a second I hear the front door shut, happy that he chose to leave. Walking over to my closest I pull out a towel, handing it to Phoenix, a smile back on her face.

"Thanks," she says taking it for me.

"Sorry about that, he can be....a fucking asshole," I say, finding no way to make it more eloquent.

"It's OK," she says softly. "It's only true what he said about me."

I take a step towards her, grabbing the towel from her.

"I never want to hear that out of your mouth again," I whisper between us. "Do you understand me?"

She looks up at me from underneath her eyelashes and nods. Opening up the towel I put it in her hair, massaging it gently.

"You know what Rain calls him?" she asks.

I almost forget that Phoenix must already know him.

"What?" I ask suddenly curious.

"The devil," she says just above a whisper.

A laugh escapes my throat.

"Fitting," I admit.

Phoenix slowly takes the towel from my hands and starts to move around the room and I suddenly become embarrassed by its current state.

"I should have cleaned it a little more," I say as I run

my fingers through the air.

She turns around to face me, a smile enveloping her lips.

"I like it, Braeden, it feels very...you," she says.

"So, I'm dark and I smell?" I ask.

Dropping the towel she makes her way back over to me, our bodies pressed together once again.

"No," her velvet voice rings out. "Warm and safe."

I wouldn't normally call those words extremely sexy, but coming from Phoenix they might as well be verbal porn.

"I think I need to go take a shower," I utter, partly because I need to cool down my skin that is now on fire, and because my wet jeans are starting to chafe.

"Feel free to change into anything you want," I say.

"OK," she says shyly.

"I'll be back in a jiffy." I place a kiss on her nose.

Walking into the bathroom I peel off my wet clothes, throwing them in the pile in a corner. Reaching into the shower I turn on the faucet, the hot steam filling the room after a minute or so. I step into the shower, the water bouncing off my shoulder blades, the grime from the dirty water leaving my skin. Grabbing my body wash I squirt some into my palm, doing the usual routine, but when I get to my lower regions it begs for some attention. Knowing that this can be done fast I wrap my hands around it, letting the body wash encase it...my hand gently gliding down its length. Just after a few pumps I can feel it's at its maximum hardness. When I close my eyes, nothing but Phoenix floods my mind.

I pump harder until I hear a gasp reach my ears, it pulling me out of my state of bliss. Snapping open my eyes I see Phoenix's peeking inside the shower curtain, her body wrapped in a towel.

"I'm so...sorry," she says as she tries to flee but I catch her wrist just in time.

Pushing open the curtain more I get a full view of her, her delicate ivory skin barely covered by the towel. She turns back around, her face a color of red I've never seen before.

"Come in," I say tugging on her arm gently.

She continues to stare at me, but not at my face. I let out a laugh. I don't know whether to be embarrassed or flattered. Dropping her hand from mine she reaches up and starts to unravel the towel from under her arm. I can't do anything but watch. It drops to the floor in a pile at her feet, all of her exposed.

"God, you are so fucking beautiful," I declare, holding my hand out to her.

She takes it delicately and I lead her into the shower. She looks incredibly nervous so I place my hand on the side of her face.

"It's me, Seraph," I assure her.

I want to bring her into my chest but there is something in the way. She looks back down at it.

"Have you ever, um…masturbated?" I ask her, already knowing the answer to that.

She shakes her head.

"Do you want to feel good, Phoenix? Do you want me to show you how?"

She gnaws on her bottom lip and I pull her into to me, tucking myself in between us, silently telling it to behave itself. I walk us under the water so that she can get clean first. Pushing her hair to one side I expose the skin of her neck. I lean down pressing my lips to it, my need for her being fulfilled again. I hear her moan, the muscles in her neck and shoulders relaxing. Reaching out, I cover Phoenix's hand with mine. Bringing it close to her center I put our hands between her lips, her own fingertips grazing her herself. I can feel myself harden and I'm not even the one touching her. A moan leaves her mouth and she drops her head back so that it is resting on my chest. I move our hands in a circular motion and watch Phoenix's chest start to rise and fall rapidly.

"Holy shit," she breathes out, her back arching away from me.

"Does that feel good?" I whisper in to her ear.

I see her head nod fast, her mouth now open.

Picking up the pace even more I feel her body start to vibrate, so I bring my other arm down against her torso, pinning her against me even more, to make sure she doesn't fall. Putting my lips back to her neck, I plant numerous kisses, keeping my hand on hers as we circle her, but then move her fingers downward.

"Put a finger inside you," I say into her ear.

I feel her fingers shift under mine until she inserts a finger and I hear her take a sharp breath. I instantly become jealous, wanting nothing more than for my fingers to be giving her pleasure. But this is about Phoenix, not about me.

"Now curl your finger in a 'come hither' motion," I tell her and I know she has listened when a loud moan leaves her throat.

"That's your G-spot," I explain to her, wanting her to explore every part of her anatomy.

I replace my finger on her as she pumps in and out, it only a matter of seconds before her orgasm cripples her and I feel her slump over in my arms. With a smile on my face I lean down, placing a kiss between her shoulder blades. We stand still for a moment, allowing her to regroup before she turns back around to face me.

Phoenix

Holy fucking hell. Holy shit.

Every fiber of my being feels content. Relaxed. If Braeden wasn't holding me right now I would melt into a puddle on the floor. I can feel my heart beating so fast that it sounds like a hummingbird's wings. To be honest, I knew people masturbated but I was never brave enough to try it. I had definitely played in the sand box in the past, but never stayed more than a few seconds. When I knew that Braeden was in the next room naked, something inside me wanted to be with him. Needing to feel his touch. When I regain some of my composure, I feel his hands release me and I silently whine, wanting his hands on me always. When I turn around I look up at him and smile.

"I take it that felt good?" he asks.

"Holy shit," is all I was able to breathe out.

Little tingles start to fill my fingertips, my desire to touch it greatening, but I hold back.

"You don't have to," he says above a whisper.

I instantly realize that I am over-reacting, my desire to make him feel what I just felt growing.

"I want to," I admit while gnawing on the inside of my cheek. "I just might be horrible at it."

A small smile comes across his face and he leans down so that our foreheads are touching.

"Just having your hands on me feels fucking incredible, Seraph, so I can only begin to imagine what..."

I put my hand on it, his voice cuts off mid sentence. Running my hand up and down its length, I keep my eyes on his face, watching his eyes slowly close, his head leaning back underneath the water. And then I panic, stopping my motions. Braeden's head snaps back up, finding me in my state of distress.

"Can...you show me?" I ask nervously.

I feel Braeden's hand come over mine again and his fingers mold around it, and he slowly starts to move both of our hands up and down. After a few strokes his hand abandons mine and I continue the motion, watching the muscles in his body tense up, some of the soap from before travels down, making the gliding easier. Braeden's eyes stay on me this time and I can tell it's making him feel good, boosting my confidence.

"Faster," he breathes out and I pick up the pace, the muscles in my arms responding.

I continue at this quickened pace until I see Braeden's eyes slam shut.

"I'm going to come," he says through gritted teeth and a moment later I see a white substance come out, it immediately being washed away by the water.

When he opens his eyes again he leans down, putting his lips on mine.

"That was fucking incredible," he says. "Hell of a lot better than my own hand."

I start to giggle.

"I love you, Braeden," I say through laughs.

Braeden's hand comes across the back of my neck, his beautiful green eyes staring back at me.

"I love you more than I ever thought possible," he says softly. "You've saved me in a way that I can't even begin to explain."

~

By the time we get out of the shower our hands are wrinkled, a towel tightly wrapped around my body again. Braeden and I return to his bedroom.

"Let me get you some clothes to change into," he says as he places a kiss on the side of my head.

I watch him walk over to his dresser and I find myself watching the muscles in his back move. This man has to be a descendent of a Greek god. While he digs around for some clothes, I take the opportunity to inspect more of the room, a corkboard full of various things pinned to it. Taking a step closer I examine each piece of paper, some in his handwriting, others not. He must have noticed my inquisitiveness, his figure now by my side.

"What's this?" I ask, still looking at each one.

He shrugs. "Things that I find, quotes that have meaning to me. If I have an emotional connection to something I put it on the board."

"That's nice," I respond, reading the quotes to myself in my head.

I continue to examine them until I spot one in particular and it makes my heart stop. Reaching up, I glide my fingertips over a paper that is all too familiar to me.

"That is one I found most heartbreaking," Braeden says, leaning up and unpinning it from the wall. He brings it down to our level.

"Can I look at it?" I ask, my voice shaky.

"Sure," he says as he holds it out to me.

Taking it between my hands I run my fingers over the pressed pencil lines, over the shape of the heart. Tears start to well up in my eyes and I look down more, trying to hide my emotions from Braeden. *How could this be? How could my suicide note end up in the room of the only person that has been able to save me?* The only person that makes me feel the opposite of what I wrote inside this very note. It's only a matter of seconds before he picks up on my mood change.

"Seraph?" he asks, his arm touching mine.

I look up at him, the tears now falling freely, my chest heaving slightly.

"This is mine," I blurt out.

He looks at me confused, his eyebrows crunched together.

"You're not making any sense," he says.

I take a breath. "I wrote this," I say holding it out to him. "I drew this. On the day I was going to..." I don't have to continue on for him to understand.

His eyes widen as he begins to catch on.

"Where did you find this?" I ask.

He smiles. "I like to think that it found me," he explains. "I was walking home from work one day and it wrapped around my leg and it wouldn't let go."

My heart starts to beat again and its pace picks up. He takes the piece of paper from my hand, his eyes looking it over again.

"Everything happens for a reason. Always remember that what's meant to be will always find a way to come about."

I look up at him as he smiles.

"My mother used to always say that." He smiles. "It's just more proof that we were made for each other, Phoenix, that someone has a greater plan for us than we could have ever imagined."

Phoenix

I take another look in the mirror, not recognizing the girl looking back at me. My face is bright, the once-dark circles that haunted underneath my eyes are gone. The cuts and bruises on my inner arms have healed, leaving only faint scars left in their spot. Picking up my brush I run it through my tangled hair, pulling it into a high ponytail on top my head. Grabbing the small makeup bag from my dresser I dump out the contents of it, looking at each piece with a wary eye. I haven't had much experience with makeup. I was too young to wear it when my father was still alive and my mom would never spend money on something so frivolous, as she would put it. I shake my head slightly, trying to shake her from my memory. I take time trying on the different things, reading the small instructions on each to get a sense of their intended use.

"Fuck." My eyes are watering like a son of a bitch as I pick up some metal thing that looks like a medieval torture device. "There is no way this thing is going anywhere near my eyelashes," I say, tossing it straight into the garbage.

Glancing backwards in the mirror I realize I am getting short on time. Leaning back, I grab my sweater off the bed and head downstairs.

~

The ride to the hospital is silent, my nerves have taken over. I don't know if it's going back to this place, or the idea of the unknown, but my stomach has been doing back flips since I left the house. Neil parks the car and comes over to my side, opening the door for me.

"Thank you," I say softly as I exit, fixing the skirt of my dress.

As we make it through the employee entrance, the overwhelmingly familiar medicinal smell of hit my nostrils. I'm instantly nauseous. I try to block every memory of this place from my mind, but all the feelings come flooding back. Neil turns around and notices my distressed state.

"Are you OK?" he asks stopping suddenly.

I can do this. I nod quickly.

"There is no reason to be nervous, Phoenix," he says as though he can feel my fear. Braeden always said he was good at reading people.

We make it through a series of hallways and I become lost, not knowing what's up or down. We make it to the nurses' station and I instantly spot her, my lips turning up in a smile!

"Phoenix!" she shouts as she rounds the counter top, her long arms wrapping around me in seconds.

She squeezes so tightly I fear I have re-broken a rib.

"I am so excited that you're here." She smiles as she pulls away.

Her eyes look at me up and down, the fire burning in my cheeks.

"You look smoking hot in the get-up, might I add."

"Thanks," I whisper, suddenly hating all the attention on me.

I hear a throat clear behind me.

"I'll be back around five to take you home," he says, now in doctor mode

~

The next few hours are a blur, a series of instructions that become a jumbled mess in my brain. I am happy to be trusted with things less life threatening. I followed closely behind the other volunteers, watching how they interact with the patients. Once we finish visiting all the rooms, I am told we get a break. I am more than ready for some air. Leaving the nurses area, I head toward what I think is the exit, but it only takes me a matter of seconds to get turned around in the labyrinth of corridors that all look the same. I've always had a horrible sense of direction.

I aimlessly walk around the hallways, figuring I'll make it back somehow. But something tells me to look right, my eyes finding a semi-dark room, sunshine from partially-closed blinds illuminating it softly. I stop at the corner of the door frame and peer inside, feeling like a total stalker. In front of the window is a petite fragile frame sitting in a chair, the profile of her face bruised. My mind screams for my feet to move forward, but I can't move. I am frozen. I watch this little girl move around in her seat, a wince coming across her face with every movement. I know that there are a million things that can explain her injuries. Maybe she had an accident. Maybe she tripped and fell.

But I know. She didn't cause this herself. Her head turns in my direction, my presence is no longer invisible. Realizing I'm invading her moment of privacy, my feet finally move me away from her room. After a few more twists and turns I find myself back at the nurses' station, ready for the rest of the day.

~

By the time Dr. Harris and I pull into the driveway, the sun has already set for the day. When I notice that he doesn't pull the car all the way into the garage I look toward him.

"I have something else I have to take care of," he explains, his eyes not looking straight at me.

Since it's none of my business I just nod before exiting the car. I stop when I hear him call my name out again.

"I might be home late, so I want you to set the alarm," he explains. "Do you remember how to do that?"

"Yes."

I swallow the lump in my throat, my nerves getting the best of me.

"You are perfectly safe here," he assures me. "He'll never be free."

My heart skips a beat, an image of Carl behind bars flashes across my vision. He nods and I shut the door, watching the light from his headlights disappear from my sight. Grabbing the spare key that Braeden showed me on my first day, I slide it into the key hole, pushing the front door open. I quickly get inside and lock the deadbolt. Punching in the code, I see the light switch over to green. I let out a deep breath that I didn't realize I was holding in. Dropping my bag on the floor, I scan the room, everything quiet and peaceful. My eyes find themselves peering out into the backyard, the shed illuminated by the backyard lights.

A small part of me wonders why they keep it. Why burden themselves with that memory every day? I yawn loudly, realizing how beat I am. Heading up the stairs slowly, I reach the door of my bedroom but the door is closed. Not how I left it. Taped to the front of it is a piece of paper, with Braeden's handwriting. Reaching up I peel it off, unfolding the paper.

I felt like your walls could use something special.

I look at the paper, confused, and shake my head, knowing he is up to something. Pushing open the door I instantly see what he did. On the floor of my room is a massive stack of art supplies, tears blurring my vision. Typical tears of joy. Drawing was something I always loved to do. My father encouraged the artistic vision I always had when I was younger. We used to have drawing contests on napkins whenever we went out to eat but, like everything else in my life, when he was gone, so was any encouragement of my creativity. Kneeling down I run my fingers across all the paint cans, picking up the brushes, feeling the soft bristles underneath my fingertips. Putting my fingertips to my mouth I effectively hide my smile, shaking my head slowly. On top of the pile is another piece of paper. Reaching over I grab it, opening it slowly.

I can't wait to hold you in my arms again.
I love you Seraph.

Clutching the piece of paper against my chest I can feel my heart soaring. I thought only men like him existed in fairy tales. I often wonder what I did to deserve him. Getting up from the floor, I walk over to my nightstand, sliding the note into the drawer. Walking over to my closet, I slide off my dress and find my favorite pair of yoga pants and an over-sized t-shirt that I stole from Braeden. Sliding myself on top of the bed I feel my eyes becoming heavy, sleep overtakes me quickly.

~

I snap my eyes open and turn over to glance at the clock. It's incredibly early in the morning, the sun not due to rise for hours. Pushing the covers off of me, I slide on my robe because the house is frigid. I head into the kitchen, grab the water kettle and fill it with water from the faucet. Clicking on the burner, I watch the blue-and-orange flame crawl up the sides of the kettle, the warmth flowing to my face. While I wait for the whistle, I look around the kitchen some more and start looking for a spoon but instead I find a stack of dusty pictures. I pull them out and my heart instantly aches at the sight of them. They are all various stages in the family's life. Some of when Braeden and Thomas were babies, all the way up to what seems like less than a year before the accident. In each one of them everyone is smiling or laughing. Everything about them is perfect.

I hear the whistle of the kettle, so I slide the pictures back to where I found them and head back over to the stove, pouring the hot water into the already-dispensed cocoa mix. Stirring it with the spoon, I pick it up, smiling at the turtles staring back at me. When I make is back upstairs, I take a sip of hot chocolate and stop, finding myself staring at the large, blank wall to the left of my bed.

Setting my mug down on the dresser I bend over, gathering multiple brushes and paints in my hands and set them on the ground next me. Looking back up at the wall I smile wide, only one thing coming to mind.

I work until the soft lights of the morning sun creep through the window, both my body and mind exhausted. After a few more soft strokes of the wings I step back, even amazed at myself at what is looking back at me. Setting the brush back down in the paint can I stare at myself in the mirror and smile, seeing that I am speckled in paint from head to toe. Stripping down, I climb back into bed hoping to get a few more hours of sleep before my day begins.

Braeden

Work and school on the same day fucking sucks. An entire day without Phoenix was torture. I couldn't concentrate at all and most of my work at the hospital was lacking. Even being here is tough; there are memories of her everywhere. Every corner of the hospital seems to have a little piece of her there. But I hate myself for missing those moments. I need to keep thanking god she isn't still here. That she's not the broken girl that he created anymore. I pull out my phone and check it, for the thousandth time in the past hour, wanting to hear her voice, needing to know how her first day alone is.

"You're going to break that damn thing," I hear a

voice over my shoulder.

"I wish that she would just call me," I snap back.

"She's busy, man," he says. "Don't you remember how stressful your first day was here?" Donovan asks.

We both laugh a little, my first day on the job was nothing less than disastrous.

"Now just think how she feels," he says softly.

"She must be fucking mortified," I say softly, running my hands through my hair.

An idea pops into my mind, making me smile. "I'm gonna take my lunch," I say as I bolt out the back door and hop on my bike.

~

When I get back to work my nervousness only increases, now my mind wants to know what she'll think of her gift. When I saw the look on her face in front of the art shop I could see the love in her eyes. I could definitely tell her past was trying to claw its way out. Sometimes I wish she would open up more. I want to hear more about the good in her life. I love watching her tell me about the times with her father. She's always her most happiest at those moments. The minute hand on the clock on the wall moves at an insanely sluggish pace. My patience for being here is wearing thin. Once it hits 6:59am I dart out the back entrance, hop on my bike again and pedal back to my father's house. When I reach the front door I put my key in and push it open, a loud buzzing reaching my ears.

Stumbling into the kitchen I reach the key pad, my brain not functioning as well as it should, exhausted from my ride over here. Fumbling with it I hear the beeping becoming more consistent, knowing my thirty seconds is running thin. After my third attempt, it stops. Shutting the door on the pad I bound out of the kitchen and up the stairs, wanting to see my baby girl more than anything else in the fucking world.

When I reach her door I can smell the fumes from the paint, a wide grin coming across my face. Pushing the door open slowly I instantly find her form curled up in itself, her eyes closed. I walk over slowly, my vision in a tunnel, as it always is whenever she is around. I stare down at her angelic state, I reach out and brush the soft flesh of her cheek, making her stir gently but not awaken. Just when I thought I couldn't love her more, my heart literally soars at the simple sight of her. Lifting my eyes from her I look up at the wall, the painting staring back at me weakens my knees. Moving around the span of the bed, I walk over to it, my eyes going over every line of the painting. It's absolutely breathtaking.

"I hope you like it," her soft voice fills the room.

I can't even look back at her, my eyes glued to this amazing piece of artwork.

"You painted this?" I ask.

"Yes," she says, her voice nervous.

I finally peel my eyes away from it and they fall

upon her again. She slides herself off the bed, the dark circles underneath her eyes again, a sign she was up all night. She walks over and wraps her arms around me and I lean down, placing a kiss on top her head.

"Thank you," she announces.

"For what?"

"For the art supplies," she says shyly.

"You don't have to thank me, Seraph."

"You're too good to me," I hear her mutter.

Pulling her body away from mine, I look into her eyes, small flecks of paint surrounding them.

"You deserve more than I could ever give you, Phoenix, but I will try my hardest to give you the world."

"Braeden, you give me everything just by being here. I wouldn't be able to stand if it wasn't for your faith in me."

I can tell that she is starting to get choked up, so I just pull her back into me, both our eyes back on the painting.

"So, what made you want to paint an angel?" I ask.

"It's not just any angel." She laughs. "It's a seraphim angel."

I look down at her confused. She just shakes her head and smiles.

"A seraphim angel has six wings instead of two."

I look back up at it and count the wings. Six. I notice a single word written in the feathers of each wing.

Nelson, Sophia, Thomas, Neil, Braeden and Phoenix.

I look back down at her, a wide smile on her face.

"What's with the names?" I ask.

She looks back up at the painting.

"They're my family." She smiles. "The wind beneath my wings."

At that moment I want to drop to the floor, begging her to be mine forever. But I knew that she would be, whether I asked or not.

"Thank you," I hear her utter. "Thank you for being my savior."

Phoenix

You know the saying time flies when you're having fun? Well, for the first time in my life, I truly understand what they meant. Before I know it, Braeden and I fall into a routine. I stay busy volunteering at the hospital, Braeden continuously busy between school and work. Days turn into weeks, weeks turn into months. The days start to grow exponentially longer, the heat of every day rising. Summertime in San Francisco isn't that hot to begin with, but the sun soaking into my body is a welcomed notion.

Shimmying my glasses on my face, I pick up my drink on the side table next to me, the condensation falling off the bottom and rolling down my chest. Moments later I feel a fingertip between my breasts, wiping up moisture. I let out a giggle.

"That tickles." I laugh.

I look up at Braeden, who is now straddling my body on the chaise on the deck. I gaze over his exposed upper torso, all of its glory out for me to see. Leaning up, I hook my arm around his neck, pulling him closer to me, his lips pressed against mine. I wonder to myself if the feeling I get for kissing him will ever waiver, each of our kisses as great as the first. My body is then lifted off the cushion and thrown over Braeden's shoulder. I don't even have to guess where we are headed.

When I first came here, it was apparent that neither Braeden nor Dr. Harris had set foot out past the balcony since her death. But over the past couple months I convinced him to come out here slowly. His long legs bound down the steps in seconds and both our bodies fly, the cool water reaching my skin. I inhale sharply, hoping not to swallow half the pool as I go under. My feet touch the bottom of it and I push off, shooting myself to the surface.

Wrapping my arms and legs around Braeden, I place my lips on his, our bodies bobbing in the water. When he opens his eyes again I see them shift to the direction of the shed, it making me nervous.

"Babe," I say softly, hoping to distract him.

"Do we really have to go tonight?" he whines. "I just want to stay in tonight with my arms wrapped around you for the whole night."

Maybe we shouldn't go. "But it's important," I try to explain. "Plus, we told your father we would go."

I hear a low grumble escape his throat. "My father will just want to show me off to all of his colleges," he whines.

I shake my head and laugh. "Yes, how terrible to have a son that you are proud of and want to show everyone *how* proud he is of you."

Braeden rolls his eyes. "I haven't graduated yet," he explains.

"Doesn't mean that he's not proud of you," I add. "Or that he is the only one that is."

He slyly smiles. "You're proud of me, Seraph?" he asks.

I bite my lip while nodding excessively. His grip around me tightens and we remain silent for a second.

"I could never spend another day without you in my life," he whispers into my ears.

I pull back, putting a hand on each side of his face.

"I'm not going anywhere," I tell him, my eyes boring into his. "I'm yours, always and forever."

We pull ourselves from the pool once our fingers become pruney, our dip easing the burn of the unusually-hot weather. Wrapping my towel around my body I head inside, instantly spotting Chelsea coming through the front door.

"Hey!" she says as she walks into the family room, two large black garment bags slung over her shoulder.

"Hey," I respond, slinging myself onto the couch.

Her eyes find Braeden coming through the back door, a towel wrapped around his waist, water from his hair dripping off and rolling down his chest. A grin envelopes on Chelsea's face and I don't know whether to laugh or be jealous.

"You two have a nice swim?" She laughs and I instantly know what she's getting at.

"Har har," I say before getting up from the couch.

Chelsea takes one of the bags off her shoulders and throws it at Braeden.

"We better get started." She smiles and heads off into the direction of my room. "Give us...a few hours..."

I widen my eyes at Braeden, silently begging him to stop her but instead he just smiles.

"See you soon," he says as he leans in, placing a kiss on top my head.

"Lord help me," I mutter as I walk away from him.

"Phoenix, get your ass up here right now!" I hear Chelsea scream from upstairs.

When I get there, I widen my eyes at the amount of makeup and hair products that are now laid upon my dresser.

"Here," she says as she hands me a variation of bottles. "Make sure you rinse your hair good, that chlorine is horrible for it."

I look at her confused, never using anything but shampoo. Before I came here I had to wash my hair with bar soap. Spinning me around she pushes me towards the bathroom.

"And make sure you shave!" she calls out. "Everything!"

Over the past few months Chelsea and I have become quite close despite our age difference. She is sort of like the mother I never had. Once I finish in the shower, I am already tired. Braeden's idea of staying home sounds pretty damn good about now. As soon as I re-enter my room the next unknown amount of time flies by, a mixture of hairspray and perfume filling the air.

"Just about...perfect," Chelsea says as she pins the last stray hair. "You look gorgeous."

I look at myself in the mirror, a whole new person looking back at me.

"Holy shit," I call out. "Where did you learn to do this?"

She shrugs.

"I had a lot of free time when I was younger," she explains. "Both my parent's worked at lot and I had no siblings." *Even having both of your parents, you can still be alone.*

"You didn't want to do it as a profession?" I ask, her skills clearly up to par. She shrugs.

"I wanted to do something that would help people," she explains. "I don't think I would save a lot of lives by performing Brazilian blow outs."

"So, what made you want to become a nurse?"

"When I saw the amazing things that they can do," she answers. "When I was around 15 my grandfather fell incredibly ill, in which he had to spend the rest of his days in the hospital. My grandmother had died a few years prior and although we tried to visit as much as we could, it wasn't possible for someone to be with him 24/7."

She takes a breath, the story obviously still having an effect on her.

"But then we met Rachel. She became my grandfather's confident until his very last breath and in that moment, I knew I wanted to be a nurse," she finishes abruptly. *Everyone has a story.*

Once we finish cleaning up I start to walk down the hallway, my heart beating erratically as the satin of the dress swings around me. Although the dress is floor length I have never felt so exposed. Rounding the corner to the stairs I take a deep breath, praying to god that I don't fall. These shoes are clearly the tallest I have ever worn. But then I see Braeden at the bottom, a large smile on his face. *Now I'm definitely going to fall.*

Taking one step at a time I reach the midway point before Braeden takes a few steps himself, holding his hand out to me and guiding me down the rest of the way. When we reach the bottom I get a really good look at him. He looks tall and slender in his suit, his tie matching the color of my dress perfectly.

I silently laugh when I see that he has chosen to keep the small amount of stubble on his face, his hair still disheveled in its natural way.

"Picture time," I hear Chelsea say, turning around to see a camera in her hand.

"This isn't prom," Braeden whines, clearly not wanting his picture taken.

"Just shut up and stand together," she waves on.

We do as we're told, Braeden and I standing side by side. As we look to the camera I feel Braeden's arm come around me, light touches from his fingertips graze my exposed shoulder, goosebumps adorning my skin. After a few more snaps she finally puts the camera down.

"Ready?" she asks. Braeden nods.

"I think we're gonna walk," he explains. "It's only a few blocks."

My heart rate spikes at the thought of walking in these things for more than a few feet.

"Plus, I want to show you off," he says close to my ear. *Blisters are worth it.* Chelsea heads out once more and soon it's just Braeden and I.

"You look beautiful, Seraph," he says, placing his arm around my backside again, pulling me close into him. "Like a true angel."

"You don't look so bad yourself." I laugh.

Luckily, the walk to the banquet room was short and I would be lying if I said that I didn't feel like

Cinderella in this dress, hoping that, at the stroke of midnight, the fairy godmother wasn't going to take it from me, prince and all. When we reach the building, it is utter chaos. A sea of colorful gowns and suits filling the grand ballroom. Braeden notices my uneasiness. His grip on my hand tightens.

"I won't let go," he says as he picks it up, placing a small kiss on top of it. "Are you ready?"

I nervously nod. We make our way through the crowds of people, my eyes scanning every face I can see. *He's not here. You'll never see him again.*

We stride over to the opposite side of the room, spotting Dr. Harris immediately. His eyes find the two of us and he excuses himself from the group.

"Phoenix?" he asks jokingly. "You look beautiful."

I lean in giving him a hug. "Thank you, Neil," I say before pulling back. "Who knew Harris' could rock a suit so well," I kid to both of them.

"We have been known to clean up once in a while."

Neil turns his attention back to the group, introducing Braeden and I. My mind soon becomes a mixture of doctor's names, not really knowing who's who after a few minutes. Braeden excuses us and heads into the direction of the bar.

"One beer, one champagne," he says.

I go to protest but Braeden squeezes my hand. We walk away from the bar, Braeden handing me the fluted glass.

"Believe me, it will make the night better," he says before putting his own glass to his mouth.

I look at the glass, the small bubbles floating up the sides of it. Putting it to my lips I push it back, the cold liquid filling my mouth. We continue to mingle into the gobs of people, more introductions being made and before I know it my glass in empty, the bubbly liquid flowing right through me. I go to excuse myself but then I see a pair of hands come around me and before I know it I am being lifted up into the air, my feet far off the ground. A large scream leaves my throat which gets the attention of multiple patrons around us.

"Put me down," I scream out, trying to not let my crippling fear escape.

"I guess I should have asked first, huh?" I hear the voice say behind me.

Once I get set on the ground I turn around to see Donovan's massive form standing over me.

"Yeah, maybe you should," I spit out, the tone in my voice not even recognizable to myself.

Straightening my dress I look up at Braeden, an angry expression on his face.

"Can you not act like a fucking idiot for one moment in your life?" he snaps.

"Braeden, I'm fine," I assure, putting my hand on his arm.

I see the look on Donovan's face, it absolutely heartbreaking. "Sorry, I keep forgetting," he says shaking his face.

I give him a smile now that my nerves have calmed down.

"Will you take a hug?" I ask, holding my arms out to him.

His face lights up like a child at Christmas. He softly steps forward, wrapping his arms around me. I let out a laugh as he lets go. *Will I ever not do that?*

"No date?" I ask, looking around him.

"Pffft," he responds. "I got the hottest date here."

He turns around and that's when I see a tall women strutting towards me, her red hair accentuated by the fire in her dress. She looks familiar. And then my mind reminds me of who she is. I turn to Braeden, who is now conversing with an older, balding man. I instantly become nauseous, my feet wanting to carry me far away, but the alcohol inhibiting me. My mind is transferred back to a sight of what seemed like another lifetime ago, her lips on his. I fidget with the glass in my hand, a weird desire to throw it at her head overcomes me. When she reaches us Donovan puts his arm around her.

"Lillian, this is Phoenix," he says introducing us.

She smiles at me and holds her hand out. I stare at it for a moment before holding out mine. We shake hands, her grip firm and tight.

"Hi," I say softly, my eyes now on the ground.

After the introductions I feel Braeden's presence at

my side, the same pissed off expression from moments earlier on his face.

"What the hell are you doing here?" he asks her and I'm even surprised by his tone, it throwing even me off guard.

"I didn't know you owned this fucking building," she snaps back.

I think my mouth drops open. Braeden's eyes look at Donovan's.

"Seriously?" I hear Braeden ask, it making the moment even more awkward. "You bring her to this?"

Lillian looks aghast and I don't know what to feel.

"What?" Donovan asks, a true look of confusion on his face.

But something shifts, his eyes telling me that he is finally making the connection with the rest of us. This girl separated Braeden and I last time and I refuse to let it happen again.

"I'm going to go to the bathroom," I announce, pushing past everyone.

"I'll go with you," I hear Braeden say behind me.

I turn around to face him, a concerned look on his face.

"I'm fine, Braeden," I say. "I'm just going to the bathroom, I'll be right back."

"Promise?" he asks, a worried look on his face

I give him a sly smile before walking right up to him, the alcohol serving as liquid courage. I place one hand into his hair and the other on his ass, my lips slamming against his. As we continue to kiss I stare at her, her eyes gazing into mine. I suddenly feel so childish, never having these feelings before Braeden came into my life. After a few more seconds I pull back, a smile on his face as he catches onto my game.

"I'll be right back, handsome," I say as I turn around and head in the direction of the bathrooms and I as I do I can feel Braeden's eyes on my ass so I do a little shimmy as I walk away, Braeden laughing behind me.

When I get out of the main area I look around, trying to remember where I saw the sign for the restrooms but I quickly become lost with my stellar sense of direction, finding myself going down a large hallway. When I get towards the end I go to turn back around but a sound of giggling reaches my ears, it making me peer down a fork off the main hallway. I instantly inhale at the sight before me.

Dr. Harris is leaning against the far wall, a drink in his right hand which is at his side but his other hand is wrapped around Chelsea's back, his fingertips toying with the knot keeping her dress together. I remain peering around the corner, not believing what my eyes are seeing. Her mouth is close to his ear, Dr. Harris clearly enjoying whatever she is saying. When I am able to pull my eyes away, I realize that I am prying into someone's privacy. When I go to turn around my hand collides with the wall, it knocking the glass from my hand, a loud shatter ringing through the once-silent hallway.

I panic, finding the first unlocked door and throw it open, my head banging against various objects. Shutting the door quickly I remain quiet, listening for any sound. I exhale when no one comes searching. After a few minutes I realize I haven't been discovered and what I had just witnessed. Two things were sure. Dr. Harris and Chelsea are definitely more than just associates and that Braeden was going to flip.

After a few more minutes I slowly push open the door, checking both sides of the hallway to make sure the coast is clear. Pulling myself from now what I realize is the janitor's closet I re-arrange my dress and head back to the party. *Shit. I still have to pee.* Once I leave the hallway I see a figure coming towards me, his hands running through his hair. His once-tight tie is loosened somewhat, the top button on his dress shirt undone. He looks deliciously disheveled. When he gets close enough his lips are instantly on the exposed skin of my neck, his kisses fiery. As I inhale, I can smell the alcohol on his breath, it obvious that he had a few more drinks while I was on my adventure. Reminds me of what Carl always smelled like.

"I was afraid you ditched me," he mutters into my skin. "I missed you while you were gone, Seraph."

I laugh lightly. "I wasn't gone that long was I?" I ask.

"I stood outside the bathrooms waiting for you but

you seemed to somehow sneak past me."

"I guess I got a little lost," I lie. *Well it's half true.*

"What's this?" he asks, a small amount of pain radiating from my hand, a small scratch across it.

"Oh, I must have caught it on something." I lie, digging myself deeper.

He pulls back and is now standing facing me.

"Are you mad?" he asks.

My heart races, wondering what he's talking about.

"At what?"

"Donovan bringing her."

"Oh," I start. "No, just shocked that's all. I wasn't expecting that."

Braeden's hands come around my backside, pulling me into him.

"I love you so much," he announces. "I love that we can be honest with each other. We have no secrets, everything is always out in the open."

I swallow the lump in my throat.

"Braeden..." I say, the tone in my voice changing.

He must have noticed the change because his hands come around to my forearms, the sly smirk gone from his face. I go to open my mouth but I can't seem to form the words, feeling like it's not my rightful place to tell him this.

"I had a really good time tonight," I coward, wrapping my arms around him.

I hear him laugh, probably not believing my horrible

acting skills.

"It's not over yet," he announces. "I haven't had the chance to dance with you yet."

I pull back, my eyes widening.

"Braeden, I can't dance...like at all."

"Come on, it's just a slow one, all you have to do is hold onto me."

I smile. "I think I can do that."

He takes his hand in mine and I have tunnel vision, only seeing the beautiful man in front of me. Once we step onto the reserved dance floor his body immediately wraps around mine.

"Put your arms around my neck," he commands.

I do so, Braeden's hands coming around my back again. The song starts slowly, a female's voice filling the room. Braeden's begins moving and in that moment I get lost. There is no one else in this world besides us. Nothing else even mattered. Nothing could come between us. It was just Braeden and I.

Braeden

I wake up in my bed feeling the cold sheets beside me. Sitting up slowly, my head is cloudy, the four drinks I downed last night certainly weren't helping. Once I saw Lillian coming behind Donovan, I had never felt so enraged in my life. All of the visions and feelings from our last encounter came flooding back into my mind. I almost lost Phoenix because of a careless fuck and I wouldn't let that happen again. I refused. I didn't know who to be madder at, myself or Donovan. He knew what bringing her would do and in that moment I hated him. I wanted to wrap my fingers around his massive throat and watch him gasp for air. But I couldn't peel my eyes away from Phoenix's, waiting for her to walk out that door and never come back.

But when she pressed her body against mine, her mouth claiming mine I could feel her insecurities, but she was fighting against them instead of letting them rule her like they always have in the past. When she returned from the bathroom, something had changed, something shifted. I wanted to ask her about it, but pressing the issue was not something I felt like doing.

Pushing the rest of the comforter off me I let out a huge sigh, feeling as though I had not gotten one minute of sleep. Standing up I stretch out, my head slightly pounding.

Perhaps drinking wasn't such a good idea. I look at myself in the mirror, realizing I am still in my dress shirt and slacks; both of them slung open, exposing all of my chest and torso. I slide off my shirt and then my pants, coming to the conclusion I needed a shower badly. I grab my towel and make my way to the bathroom, hoping a shower will somewhat waken me. Stepping under the warm spray, my mind travels back to the night and the look on Phoenix's face. A look of hesitation.

That was the first time I felt like Phoenix was hiding something from me. I finally decide to pull myself out of the shower and get dressed quickly, realizing how late in the day it is. When I make it out to the living room I grumble at what I see.

"I should kick your fucking ass out of here," I spit, grabbing an apple from the basket.

"Dude, I forgot..." Donovan snaps back. "But don't put the blame on me. You're the one who slept with her."

My stomach churns just thinking about it. I lean my body against the countertop, putting the apple to my lips and bite down.

"But why the fuck did you bring her?" I ask. "To a medical fundraiser full of civilized people?"

I see his hands turn into fists, his knuckles turning white.

"I like her," he announces.

I look at him confused. "You like her?" I ask. "Every time you two are around it's like cats and dogs."

"Dude, did you never go to fucking high school?"

I roll my eyes, never understanding the ridiculous games some people play.

"So, are you two dating?" I say with a pause, never thinking I would say dating and Donovan in the same sentence.

He shrugs. "We're spending time together," he explains.

"Do you want to sleep with other women when you are with her?" I ask aggravated.

He shakes his head. "That's the definition of dating," I say shaking my head.

We both fall silent for a moment, both collecting our thoughts.

"How's Phoenix?" he asks.

I shrug. "Something's off," I admit. "But I don't think it was because of your plus one."

He stands up and walks over in my direction.

"You still want to go through with today?" he asks.

I finally smile for the first time today.

"Absolutely."

Phoenix

I stand under the water, trying to wash out the gobs of hair spray out of my hair. By the third wash, it starts to soften, the natural state of my hair returning. I didn't get much sleep last night due to my untimely discovery, running a million different scenarios in my mind on how I could tell Braeden. Every time I talk myself into it, I talk myself right out of it. Pulling myself from the shower I wrap my body in my robe, the soft fibers a welcomed feeling against my skin. When I get back to my bedroom I plop back on the bed, not having much to do today. It's my day off from the hospital and Braeden told me he was going to be busy the first half of the day.

After a few more minutes of staring at the ceiling I

pull myself up and grab some clothes, opting for my comfiest set I can find, a pair of jeans and a simple button-up shirt. I put on my sneakers, my feet still hurting for the high heels. When I am finished getting ready I make my way downstairs, moving slowly and praying to God I don't run into Dr. Harris. I breathe a sigh of relief when I see that the downstairs is vacant and calm. I look out the back windows, the typical fog rolling back in, the warmth of the sun gone. I aimlessly walk the perimeter, realizing how painstakingly bored I am.

Grabbing a light jacket I throw it on and walk down the front steps into the open world. When I get to the end of the walkway I peer off in both directions, choosing to go left, not knowing exactly where I am heading. I walk aimlessly for an unknown amount of time but I begin to admire the city around me, not having much freedom to explore on my own.

However I am unable to break the habit of looking at every face that passes by me, searching for similarities in their eyes. My heart has been beating erratically ever since I stepped foot off that porch. When I feel as though I have had enough exposure I go to turn around but within blocks I am confused, each street I pass by seeming identical to the first. I break out into a run, my body brushing past shadows of people as I pass them. They are so close that I can feel the heat on my skin. I continue to run, the hills of the city making my muscles burn. As I continue to run I feel a long shiver runs its course through me body and then I see why.

I slow down, my body coming to a slow stroll, my fingers grasping the yellow tape as I reach it. Looking out at the property it is hard to believe that a house once stood here. I look to my side and make sure that I am alone before ducking under the tape. The charred wood crunches under my feet, my shoes instantly cover in the grey ash. It has been months since the incident but the city seems not interested in cleaning up the rubble hastily. As I walk through it all the memories come flooding back. I can feel the phantom pain in my scares.

I kick around the rubble, looking for I don't even know what. There is nothing from this life I hold valuable, nothing that I would want to remember this time. The darkest moments of my life. When I have had my fill I start to walk back to the street but something catches my eyes. Pushing the planks of wood off of it I reach down, picking up the small figurine in my hand.

I stare at it, almost as though it may crumble from my existence with any slight movement. I had completely forgotten about it that night, and part of me makes that sad. I continue to stare down at it, its expression making me laugh.

I never asked him why he gave me the seal, but I don't care. Putting it in my pocket I walk out of the rubble, never looking back.

I have to tell him.

Braeden

"**A**aand we need this," Donovan says, placing even more bottles of alcohol in the cart.

"She's not even old enough to drink," I explain.

He just shrugs. "More for me then. Plus what kind of friend would I be if I didn't contribute to the delinquency of a minor?"

I roll my eyes as the obscene amount of shit that starts to pile in the cart.

"OK that's enough," I scold him like a child and start heading to the checkout line.

I make him load the shit onto the conveyor belt. I watch the screen as the numbers jump.

"Jesus Christ," I mutter under my breath, handing

the card out to the cashier.

There are a few minutes of silence.

"Braeden Harris?" I hear a voice ask.

I look back up, the cashier looking down at my card and then back at me.

"Yeah?" I ask confused.

I look over at name tag. Dylan.

"Holy shit," I blurt out.

He comes out from around his station and we instantly wrap our arms around each other, not giving a fuck what anyone else thinks.

"How the hell are you?" I ask as I pull back.

"Good man, living the fucking dream." He laughs.

"I can see that."

I hear a throat clear beside me, drawing me back to reality.

"Dylan, this is my friend Donovan," I say.

They both shake hands.

"He was my brother's best friend," I explain, even saying that has a twinge of pain behind it.

He hesitates before speaking again.

"I'm sorry we lost touch after the accident," he explains. I shrug.

"It's alright," I respond. "I heard you went to live with your dad shortly after."

"Yeah, just had to get out of town, ya know?"

I nod. "But now I'm back!" He smiles.

"Well, it's great to fucking see you," I say as I start to

bag my groceries. Dylan walks back around and finishes the transaction.

"Someone's having a party," he says, scanning over the groceries.

"Yeah," I respond. "Hey, you should come. Were just having a small birthday party for my girlfriend, the more the merrier."

"Young Harris is whipped huh?" he says turning to Donovan.

"He's so pussy whipped it's ridiculous," he answers.

"First of all, assholes, we're all the same age, and second, I am not pussy whipped, I am in love."

They both "oooh" and "awww" together.

"You both are uninvited," I joke as I grab the bags laughing.

"Good to see ya, man," Dylan says as he holds his hand out to me.

"Same here. I'm serious man," I say grabbing a piece of paper and jotting down my number. "You should definitely come."

"Alright, I'll try and make it."

"Sounds good," I say before heading to the door.

When we make it back to the apartment, I am completely winded, the bags of the alcohol weighing a lot.

"This is all your shit, why aren't you carrying it?" I whine.

"I got the decorations," he shows me.

I start to take things out of the bags, setting them on the counter.

"You got three bottles of vodka," I announce.

"I don't see a problem in that," Donovan responds.

I work to put all the food together, Donovan spending his time cracking open the case of beer while his fat ass channel surfs. Looking outside I can see that the sun is beginning to set. Donovan eventually comes up to the counter, looking over the food.

"You're going to make a wonderful wife one day."

"Bite me," I respond. "Listen, I'm going to go pick her up and I want you to take all this to the roof. Do not eat any of it."

He goes to eat a piece of bread and I smack his hand away.

"Yes, mom," he says as he picks up the trays.

"Everyone should be here within the next 20 minutes. I will be back with Phoenix at eight o'clock sharp."

"Gotcha," he responds.

I leave the apartment and hail a cab on the curb, thankful that one comes quickly. Sliding myself into the back seat I start to become nervous. The ride over to my father's is short and I am conscious of the time.

"Can you wait here for a moment?" I ask the cab driver as I leave it.

He just nods and leaves the car running. Pushing open the front door I scan the room, look for her.

"Seraph?" I call out.

I hear movement upstairs so I walk towards it and bound up the stairs. Within moments our bodies collide, my arms immediately coming around her back, holding onto her tight. After a minute we pull back. I look into her eyes, the look from last night gone.

"Hi."

"Hi," she responds. "I missed you."

She presses her lips to mine and its forceful, the taste of her mouth intoxicating. Once she stops I smile down at her.

"We need to go," I announce.

"Where are we going?" she asks. "You just got here."

I smile and grab something from my pocket, letting the fabric dangle in front of our face.

"Do you trust me, Seraph?"

~

When we get back to my building I help Phoenix from the car. Handing some cash to the cab driver I turn back around, placing my hands on each side of her hips. I push her forward, maneuvering her to the back of the building. When we reach the stairs I release her and stand in front of her, my body facing hers.

"I'm afraid there are steps," I explain.

She fumbles the first few, but soon gets a rhythm and we are on the rooftop in no time. When we reach it I do a once over, making sure that everything seems to be in order.

"Braeden?" Phoenix says when she doesn't hear or feel me.

"I'm right here," I say, standing in front of her.

I lean in, placing my lips on hers, our kiss becoming more intimate than I expected, especially in front of a crowd. Low giggles reach my ears.

"I love you, Seraph," I start. "And happy birthday."

Reaching around I untie her blindfold quickly and a loud "surprise!" rings out through the night air. Phoenix's eyes grow wide and a nervous smile spreads across her face. She leans forwards and curls into me, her face hiding in my shoulder. A panic sets into me, hoping I didn't make a bad decision.

"Seraph?" I ask leaning back, hoping to see her face. When I do my heart drops.

"Are you crying?"

She looks up at me, her eyes wet. And then she smiles again, it the most glorious thing I have ever seen.

"I didn't even know it was my birthday."

Phoenix

My heart begins to race when I see the fabric dangle in front of my face. A small wave of panic flows through my body but I try to dismiss it quickly. *It's just Braeden.*

I look up into his eyes as his arms come around my head, my vision going completely dark. When we make it into what I assume is a cab I try to follow the turns in my head but soon become lost and disoriented. As I sit beside him with our hands intertwined, and I begin to calm down, my curiosity overtaking my fear. When the cab stops I inhale and I feel Braeden's hand tug on mine, his hands helping me guide my way.

"I'm afraid there are steps," I hear him say. I feel his

hands slip onto my hips and my stomach clenches, always loving the feel of his hands on my skin. I lift my foot but miss the first one, both of us laughing a little.

Once I get a rhythm I try to listen to familiar sounds, only hearing the cars passing by and sound of creaking metal. When I feel that we have reached our destination I feel his fingers slip from my body and I begin to panic.

"Braeden?" I call out.

"I'm right here," he calls out.

I feel his lips against mine, his mouth hot and minty. Wrapping my arms around his neck I press harder, wanting, needing to be close to him. He pulls back and I feel his breath against my ear.

"I love you, Seraph, and happy birthday."

I hear a loud "surprise" and then the darkness is gone, my eyes adjusting to the sight in front of me. The roof is lit with string lights and candles. Standing before me is a group of people, recognizing most of their faces. I panic momentarily and curl into Braeden's chest, being the center of attention is not something I am used to. And then the tears start to fall but they aren't because I'm upset, but quite the opposite.

"Seraph?" I hear Braeden say, his arm wrapped around my back.

I pull away from him and look up.

"Are you crying?"

I look up at him, wondering what I did to ever

deserve him. Then I can't help but smile.

"I didn't even know it was my birthday," I blurt out, only because it's true.

I look back at the crowds of people, all them have a worried look on their faces.

"Thank you."

Then the crowd breaks out into a loud chatter again, some of them coming up and hugging me. After a few minutes of mingling I turn around to find Braeden and I wrap my arms around him tight and I feel my feet lift off the ground.

"I love you," I whisper into his ear. "This is the first time since my father's death that I have celebrated a birthday. Thank you."

"It was my pleasure, Seraph," he responds. "I hope you like it."

I turn around and scan then area. The lights wrapped around the railing twinkle in the night sky, tables covered with food trays, adorned with small candles flickering.

"Where are we?" I laugh.

"On top of my apartment building."

"You did all this?" I ask.

"With a little help, but yes." He smiles.

~

Braeden and I mingle with all the people but when we reach Donovan things seem odd.

"Happy birthday," he says nervously.

I smile. "I don't get a birthday hug?" I ask with a fake pouty look on my face.

I feel his strong arms come around me, my breathing being cut off.

"I'll be right back," Braeden says as he leans in close to me.

"OK. I'll stay with Donovan," I tell him.

We both stand there silent for a moment until Donovan speaks first.

"I'm really sorry last night. I didn't mean to cause problems."

I shake my head. "You didn't," I admit.

We both fall silent again for a moment.

"Are you two dating?" I ask.

"According to Braeden we are." He laughs.

I look over his shoulder.

"Is she not here?" I ask.

"Braeden didn't want you have to deal with that tonight."

I frown. "You should call her. If she's important to you than I think I can live with it."

He just smiles at me and I wink in return. I leave Donovan and make my way over to the food table, realizing how hungry I am. On my over I spot a table with a mountain of presents on it, a wave of guilt taking over me. I spot Braeden and walk up behind him, wrapping my arms around his torso.

"Having fun, Seraph?"

"I am!" I exclaim.

Walking around the side of him I grab a plate and when I shift my eyes upward I see Dr. Harris coming up the stairs, Chelsea in tow. I can feel a lump form in my throat, completely forgetting about it until now.

"Happy birthday, Phoenix," Dr Harris says.

"Thank you," I respond, trying to push my feelings down.

I see Chelsea round him and she throws her arms around me. When I go to lift my arms around her I feel a sharp pain in my hand and I withdraw quickly.

"Ouch," I say, looking down at my hand.

"Are you OK?" I hear Braeden ask.

"Yeah, I just got a really sharp pain in my hand."

Dr. Harris takes my hand and leads me under the glow of a candle. He runs his hand along the small cut and I feel the pain again.

"Right there," I say.

Dr. Harris continues to examine it. "You have a piece of glass in your hand," he says.

I look up at him and his eyes find mine. Something in his face shifts. Over the next moment we have a silent conversation, my heart pounding that I feel that I may throw up. He knows it was me. He knows that I know. He lets go of my hand and we both turn our attention back to Braeden and Chelsea.

"I'm gonna need tools to get that out," Dr. Harris

explains. "But it's not critical at the moment."

I plaster on a fake smile and walk back over to Braeden, praying that he doesn't ask any questions.

Phoenix

The rest of night goes by in a blur, trying
desperately to push my feelings down. When it came
time to open the presents I felt drained but so grateful
for everyone's gifts. When the party started to wind
down people were filtering out and pretty soon it's just
Braeden and I left, my nerves growing more with every
minute of silence. When he says goodbye to the last
guest he makes his way over to me, his hands wrapping
around my waist.

"Thank you," I say. "That was the nicest thing
anyone has ever done for me."

He places his lips against my forehead and we
remain silent for a few minutes. *Tell him.* I pull back

and go to open my mouth but Braeden holds something out in his hand. A small box with a red bow on top. I lose my train of thought.

"I wanted to wait until everyone was gone before giving you this."

I take it out of his hands and open the lid slowly, a beautiful bracelet nestled among the cotton. Braeden reaches inside and unclasps it. Sticking out my wrist he works delicately to attach it, the tips of his fingers brushing against my inner wrist, it making my legs seem weak. Once it's attached I turn it over more, now noticing the angel wing charm attached to one side of it.

"It's beautiful," I whisper, holding the tears back.

Braeden's fingers come under my chin, them raising my head slowly.

"Are you happy, Seraph?"

"More than I could ever explain."

"Well, good, because I got one more surprise for you," he says.

Putting his hands on my shoulder he guides to over to a chair and then plants a kiss on my lips.

"You're not going to strip are you?" I laugh.

Braeden shakes his head.

"Maybe later."

We both smile wide and I watch him reach underneath a table. From it he produces an acoustic guitar and my heart beat fastens. He grabs a stool nearby and props himself on top of it, the guitar lying across his lap, his fingers placed delicately on the neck of it.

"This is to my beautiful girlfriend, whom without her I would cease to exist," he states to the nonexistent crowd.

I feel a familiar burn in my cheeks but I can't take my eyes off of him. He starts strumming on the guitar, a beautiful melody filling the night sky. He then starts to sing. The words coming out of his mouth are beautiful and I can feel tears prick behind my eyes, the sight before me too much for my emotions to handle. I continue to just stare at him, every moment of the past few months running in my head. I have a hard time regretting the decision that brought me here. He was my fate. He is my destiny.

When he finishes up the song he leans the guitar against the stool and hops down. Launching myself off the chair I wrap my arms around him tightly. I hear him laugh and his hands find their way to my hair. We both pull back and our eyes meet, our gaze holding.

"That was beautiful."

He shrugs. "Just a little something I've been working on."

"Ready to go inside?" he asks.

As much as I want to stay here in this moment forever, my relaxed body is exhausted, my emotional ups and downs taking its toll.

"Yeah," I say as I place a kiss on his lips.

"Why don't you start heading back down," he says. "I'm just gonna take care of a few things here."

"OK," I respond.

When I reach Braeden's bedroom I immediately plop myself onto his bed, feeling as though my eyelids have weights attached to them. Laying my head on the pillow I watch the minutes click on the clock and once I get to seven the darkness overtakes me.

Braeden

After I blow out the candles and shut off the lights I start to make my way down the alley way, a trash bag in both hands. Opening the dumpster I throw them in. When I turn around a movement catching my eye, it making me jump.

"Jesus Christ," I spit out.

"Don't take the lord's name in vain," he responds.

"I didn't know you were so religious."

"I'm not," he says.

I become confused. "I thought you left a while ago."

"I did, but I came back."

I furrow my brow at him. I instantly know something is up. I can feel it. "What's going on?"

My father's eyes shift around us. "I want you to know that I will always love your mother. And in no way will anyone ever replace her."

My heart sinks.

"But I have been dating someone for quite some time now. I have tried a hundred different ways to tell you, but I never wanted to hurt you. But I guess it's not that much of a secret now."

I become more confused.

"Who is it?"

"Chelsea."

I laugh out loud.

"Isn't she a little young for you?"

"Don't be cruel," my father spits. "Your mother and I didn't raise you that way."

I laugh again. "I'm sure she would love you dating someone that's old enough to be my older sister."

My father shakes his head. "I came here to tell you. I thought you would be a man about this. I was clearly wrong."

He goes to turn around and my emotions are a mixture of rage and sadness.

"Wait," I say, his face turning back to face me. "What do you mean it's not a secret anymore?"

I see my father's face change.

"Tell me," I demand.

"Phoenix found us together last night. I figured she would have told you."

Bile rises in my throat. *The change in her behavior.* How she never showed up in front of the bathrooms. I push past my father, done with this conversation. I bound up the stairs to my apartment and push open the bedroom door, the room completely dark. I slam the door shut behind me.

Phoenix

I jolt upright, a loud bang waking me from my sleep. My heart begins to race as I lean over, clicking on the bed side lamp. And then I see him. His eyes red and puffy.

"Braeden?" I say, pulling the covers off me and make my way towards him in a few fast strides.

When I reach him he doesn't even look at me. "What happened?"

His head finally lifts and his eyes boar into mine. He reaches out and takes my hand gently, his finger running over the cut on my hand.

"Where did you get this cut, Phoenix?" he asks, his voice dark. I begin to catch on. I look down at my hand, hiding my eyes from him.

"He told you..." I mutter.

I hear him inhale sharply. The sound is pure agony to my ears.

"So it's true...I didn't want to believe..."

I remain silent, water pooling in my eyes.

"How could you keep that from me?"

And in that moment my heart breaks into a million pieces. I finally have the courage to look up at him but I have to look away quickly, his stare poisonous.

"I...I..." I try to speak but my word faultier.

"Spit it out," he snaps.

"I was scared, Braeden," I retort. "I thought about telling you a million different times over the past 24 hours. I was terrified."

His eyes soften a little. "Scared? Of me? That's ridiculous."

I begin to get angry, wanting to tell him that he's acting like a child.

"No it's not. I didn't want to be the one that caused you pain. And we all know that your mother is still a sensitive subject."

"You not telling me is what's causing the most pain. I thought we had an understanding. An agreement to never lie to each other. I have always been honest with you, even before you were mine. "

The guilt begins to creep up inside me, tears falling freely down my face.

"I'm so sorry, I am," I cry out.

I put my arms out to grab onto him, wanting badly to go back a day, but his hands shoot out and stop them.

"I just can't right now," he says.

"Can't what?"

"Be in here with you, I need to be alone."

And with that sentence he turns around and escapes out the door, it shutting in my face. I stand there for a while, my mind going in a million different directions. Part of me wants to run after him but my feet remain planted, like an outside force is keeping me still. After an unknown amount of time I go back to the bed, confused on what I should be doing. Laying back I lean over, switching off the light. However this time sleep doesn't come.

~

Each minute he doesn't return more tears fall from my eyes, the pillow becoming damp from them. I hear the handle of the door turn but it's so dark that I can't see anything.

"Braeden?" I call out.

I hear the click of a lock and I now know it's not him. Reaching over hastily, I click on the light, a figure standing against the now closed door. I try not to panic but I can't help noticing his state. His face is sweaty, his clothes disheveled. *The Devil.*

"Beautiful girls shouldn't be alone in their beds," his voice calls out, it causing chills down my back.

"Braeden's going to be back any moment," I say, hoping to scare him away. He just smiles.

"I highly doubt that, he seemed quite angry."

My stomach drops. Things fall silent for a second and he starts to take a step towards me. *I need to get around him.* I remain planted, hoping I can out maneuver him in his state. His movements are slow and methodical. I can hear my heart beat pound in my ears, everything else being drained out. My body begins to shake. And then I see it, my moment to slip past him. Pushing my feet forward I bound towards him, the door getting closer and closer. The cold metal of the door handle reaches my fingertips but he catches me, my grip lost and my body flying backwards.

Within seconds my body is pressed against his, my back to his front. His hands are all over me. I go to scream but his hand covers my mouth, it being muffled.

"Shut up," he demands into my ear. "I've been waiting to do this for a long time."

Tears fall from my eyes, my vision becoming blurry. His other arm comes around my waist and he hoists me into the air and my body is tossed onto the bed and I cry out.

"Please, no," I beg, knowing that fighting him will get me nowhere but more bruises. Something that I learned from Carl.

His hands come up and I flinch as they run through my hair. I am confused by this gesture, it more gentle than the others. His fingers then leave my head and trailer down my body, finding the buttons on my shirt and with one yank it is torn open, the buttons bouncing off in a million directions, my naked breasts exposed.

Braeden

I bound down the stairs taking two at a time, my anger surging through every part of my being. *Or was it confusion?* Once I get outside I feel like I can breathe again, but my chest is still tight. I walk on with no real sense of direction, trying to put all the pieces together. When I round the corner I spot a small park and plant myself among its only bench. I sit for a long time, my head hung in my hands.

My father's conversation replays in my head. But why did I feel so betrayed? Angry? I wish nothing but the happiness for my father but I refuse him someone that he loves? Did he love her? Did she love him? My mind shifts to Phoenix. I know now that my anger towards her was unjust. Would I have believed her if she told me? Would I have been madder if she *did* tell me?

Leaning back onto the bench I feel something brush me from behind. I spin around, a lonely white rose stretched out towards me from the rest of the bush. I lift my hand, feeling the soft petals. It makes me smile.

"I'm such an asshole," I call out into the dark.

Wanting nothing more than to apolôgize I get up from the bench and break out into a sprint back in the direction of my building. I reach the apartment within minutes and halt as soon as I reach my bedroom door, a faint sound reaching me ears.

Phoenix

The bile rises in my throat as his lips press against the skin of my chest. I want to cry out, to scream, to beat him with my hands but I know that I will accomplish nothing. So I lie there. My body frozen, the tears from my eyes rolling down my cheeks. I close my eyes, not wanting to look at him. Never wanting to see his face again.

"Such a good girl," he purrs.

I hear the sound of a zipper and I don't know if it's real or simply a memory. My legs are then spread apart and I cry out against my will. I keep my eyes closed until suddenly I feel his weight being lifted off my body, a curdled scream filling the room.

Flying upwards, I see a tangled mess of bodies and limbs on the floor, Braeden's hands now around Bret's throat.

"I will fucking kill you!" Braeden screams into his face, Bret's face begins turning purple.

I lower my eyes to the mattress, my knees pulled into my chest. The sound of fists hitting bone fills the room, a gurgling sound leaving someone's throat. I remain frozen, even though every fiber of my being is screaming on the inside. Small dots travel across my eye sight, my breathing becoming incredibly erratic. I begin to panic and fight to stay conscious but as always, the darkness wins.

~

Opening my eyes slowly I don't have to look around to know where I am. I remain still, reliving all the details of last night. *Was it last night?*

Sitting upright I glance around the room, realizing I am alone. Putting my face between my hands I start to cry, so tired of always ending back here no matter what I do. I hear the door being pushed open, Chelsea coming through.

"How are you feeling, sweetie?" she asks, sitting in the corner of my bed.

I look over my body, for once it's not covered in wounds. *Only invisible ones.*

"I'm OK," I admit.

"Emotionally?"

A lump forms in my throat and I look away from her.

"I just want to go back," I choke out, not being able

to finish my sentence.

I feel her hand slide into mine and I am surprised I don't pull away.

"I'm just so...tired," I cry out.

We both sit in silence for a few minutes. I soon feel her hand leave mine and we don't speak again and soon she exits again. I remain in my bed, my eyes fixated on the ceiling again. The vision of Braeden's fists pounding into Bret's body replays in my head, it creating more anxiety. My mind shifts back to the birthday party, which feels like a decade ago. It's almost like it was a dream. *Maybe I was too happy. Maybe that wasn't allowed.*

Tears form in my eyes and I push the covers off me, walking over to the closet. I am grateful to see some of my clothes hanging, silently thanking whoever brought them. Sliding them on quickly I know what I have to do. I have to go where people can't get hurt because of me. I have to leave him behind.

Zipping up my sweatshirt, I immediately throw the hood up. I put my ear to the closed door hearing no sounds other than small chatter. With a shaky hand I reach for the door handle, swallowing the large ball that is forming in my throat. Pulling it open slowly I peek out, confirming that at the moment the hallway is vacant. I push myself out of the room, my mind wondering what room Braeden is in, but quickly push it out of my mind. As I slowly go down the hallway, I start to panic but push myself forward, only the sound of my heartbeat pounding in my ears. The ER is busy, everyone too preoccupied to pay attention to me. *This is for everyone's good.*

When I reach the end of the hallway without being spotted I let out a sigh. But it's not a sigh of relief. *Did I want to be stopped?* I hear a door click open and it startles me. I break into a sprint, not knowing or seeing who it was coming through the door. I continue to run and bodies fly by me as a blur, probably catching more attention than I should. Lasts night's encounter runs through on repeat in my brain and I swear I can feel his lips burning against my skin. I instantly become nauseated and I wish that I could erase everything from my mind. My eyes lie upon the side doors of the emergency room and feel that I might faint, my knees becoming weak.

"No," I tell myself, not allowing my body to take over my mind control. With a few more steps I push through them, the cool morning air making my throat string. I continue to jog away from the hospital, my breathing being cut off more and more as the distance grows. And then I stop, my body hunched over, trying to catch my breath. But it only worsens.

I stand there, a mixture of relief and regret flowing through my body. I resort to sitting on the curb, my head in my hands, my mind trying to comprehend everything, but instead it shuts down. I sit there for an unknown amount of time, completely numb, my body becoming desensitize.

"What the fuck are you going to do?" I say out loud, obviously to no one in particular.

But there was one thing I was sure about. I couldn't let other people get hurt because of me. Braeden had risked death twice for me. Everything was my fault. I was the reason Carl hit me and my mother. If I had just been more understanding...if I hadn't provoked him with my nasty attitude. Braeden always was there, willing to give up everything for my safety. What did I have to give up for him? Nothing.

Our relationship was wrong. I took everything and gave nothing back. It wasn't fair to him. He deserved so much more than I could ever give him. Someone who wasn't broken. And in that moment I knew where to go. *The only place where I ever felt safe.* Pulling myself off the curb I push myself farther away from the hospital, my hood still tightly cinched around my face. My mind wonders to what they will do when they see I am no longer there. I begin to feel sick thinking about Braeden. *I am a coward.*

I continue to walk down the street, happy to see the morning crowds are active. I blend into them with ease, following as they filer into their destinations. I continue to walk, my feet starting to ache with every step I take, my mind and body still drained. I continue to push on, ignoring the signs that my body is screaming at me. I smile a little when I hear the sounds of idled engines. I drag on closer to the buses, wanting to just climb aboard. There a lot of people milling about, many of them obvious tourists. I stare at the exhaust exiting the back of the buses, fighting with every strength I have left not to let the threatening tears fall. That's when I realize there is a large flaw in my plan. Sinking down onto a nearby bench I curl into myself, bringing my knees up into my chest, my hood still hiding my face from anyone's view. And in my small cocoon of solitude, the tears start fall, not an ounce of energy left.

~

I must have dozed off because the next thing I feel is a soft shake on my shoulder, it startling me. I flip my head up, a middle aged women looking down at me.

"You can't sleep here," she says. "There's a home just up the street that will take in homeless people."

I laugh softly out loud. I know I look like shit but I didn't think I looked that bad.

"I...I...I'm waiting for my bus," I lie.

She clearly doesn't believe me.

"Let me see your ticket."

I shift my eyes around, not knowing what I'm going to say.

"That's my granddaughter," I hear an unknown female voice speak.

When I look over I see an older women walking up to us, a bright smile on her face. The bus worker looks at her and smiles.

"My apologies," she responds and moves on.

The older lady sits beside me, both of us silent for a moment.

"Thank you," I respond nervously.

The women just continues to stare at me and puts her hand on top of mine, I flinch slightly.

"I've been watching you, are you all right?"

No.

"I'm fine."

"You've been here quite a while. Where are you headed?"

"I don't really know," I admit.

Her grip on me tightens. "Where do you want to be?"

"Home, I want to go home…"

"And where might that be?" she asks.

I think about it for a second. Lately home was wherever Braeden was, but that wasn't an option now.

"Oregon," I squeak out.

"How old are you sweetie?" she asks me.

"I just turned twenty."

She gives my hand another squeeze and gets up from the bench. As I watch her walk away I wonder what that was all about. I feel that I should move on before the worker comes back, but I can't. When I peer down the street again, I see the older woman, her body moving slowly. When she reaches me again she holds out a small bag and an envelope.

"Maybe you had to leave in order to really miss a place, and then only will you truly realize how important your beginnings are."

Reaching up I take the things from her, the same smile on her face.

"God bless you child," she says before walking on.

I sit there in a state of shock. Slowly I open the bag, a large muffin, an apple and a bottle of water inside. I open the envelope next, tears starting to form again. A one-way ticket. I look up to find her again, but she's nowhere in sight. I pinch the skin on my arm to make sure this isn't a dream.

I hear a driver call out my route and I peel myself off the bench, taking small steps toward the bus. When I reach the ticket person I hand it to him, my heart pounding in my chest.

"Thank you, ma'am," he says, handing my stub back to me.

I stare at the first step for a few seconds. *Put your foot forward.* Stepping up into the bus I try to hold back the tears.

"I'm sorry, Braeden."

Braeden

"**J**esus Christ!" I call out, as Chelsea wraps the cloth around my bloody knuckles.

She remains silent, which is unusual for her.

"Spit it out," I say, still in my anger driven attitude.

"Nothing," she mutters, continuing to work.

We both fall silent and the sound of machines and people milling about fill the ER. Within a few minutes I see my father bolt through the door.

"Oh, great, here we go," I mutter under my breath, it making Chelsea look up at me.

Without a word he flicks on the X-ray view box and slides two pictures onto it.

"You have two broken fingers on your right hand," he states harshly.

I just laugh. "I'd like to see what his face looks like."

My father's posture straightens even more. "Please leave, Chelsea."

She turns around immediately and before I know it, it's just my father and I.

"I don't even know how to begin to tell you how disappointed I am in you."

"You've got to be fucking kidding me," I blurt out.

He lets out a sigh.

"Oh, so it was OK that he was on top of my girlfriend getting ready to rape her, but I'm not allowed to leave a few marks on his fucking face?"

"Don't use that fucking condescending tone with me!" he shouts.

"Fuck this, I don't need this shit," I say as I start to get up.

He steps in front of me. "You may not want me as your father, but I am your doctor. You will not leave this room until I allow it!"

His voice is stern and loud now. I remain in place, my hand now throbbing without the proper support. He lets out a sigh.

"This is not the time or place to have this discussion. I will have Chelsea come back and finish your cast."

I don't care about myself. "Can I go see her? Is she OK?" I say, trying to change the subject for now, but I know this conversation isn't over.

"I will not be assessing her, a female doctor will be. That type of case is…sensitive."

I cringe at that word, trying to not get worked up again.

"I will come get you when she is available for visitors."

"Thank you," I respond.

"You're welcome," he says before pushing the door back.

Phoenix

When I get to my seat I slide up against the window, my hood now over my head again so I can recoil from the world, not wanting to watch the city pass by. So, instead, I shut my eyes, hoping that I can drown all my feelings from existence.

I don't know how many hours have passed since I boarded this bus, but when I hear the air leave the brakes I sit up, suddenly feeling disoriented and lost. I look out the window, the sun no longer high in the sky and I know that I am far from San Francisco. Far from Braeden.

Pulling myself slowly from my seat I filter out of the bus, in desperate need of fresh air. When I get outside I don't notice anything in my surroundings, a few people from the bus taking pictures of the surrounding scenery.

"OK, people, you have five minutes then back on the bus," our driver calls out to them.

Walking into the small café I find the bathroom quickly, making sure to go since I don't know when we will stop again. Immediately, I walk over to the sink and turn on faucet. Cupping my hands beneath the water I splash it upon my face, the cold water making me inhale sharply. Reaching over I grab a few paper towels and soak the excess water up off my face. Standing up I catch a glimpse of myself in the mirror. I am not surprised by the girl looking back at me. Her hair is disheveled and knotted. Her eyes are red and bloodshot, a result of too much crying. Her body limp, almost lifeless looking. This was the broken girl I have always known.

Reaching up I run my fingertips across my chest, but no visible marks remain. Instead they are like an endless fire deep under my skin. I almost beg for there to be bruise or cuts, at least there would be some sort of healing. It's as though his lips still remain on me and I can't push the memory as much as I beg my mind to erase that night. Running over to toilet I empty the contents of my stomach but there is not much left. When I stop heaving, I pull myself up again, grabbing a towel to wipe over my face. Without looking back in the mirror I leave the bathroom, flicking off the light and head back outside.

We all start to filter back onto the bus and pull out of

the parking lot, and in that moment I don't know if I am getting closer or farther away from my home. After a few more hours of sleep I am awoken by the sound of my gurgling stomach. Reaching over I find the paper bag from the older lady and dump its contents out onto the seat. Picking up the muffin in my hand I unwrap it slowly, inhaling the scent of the blueberries that are scattered across the top.

After a few bites my stomach seems to settle, my body thanking me for the nutrients. As I continue to eat I look out the window, the sun starting to finally set among the trees and I know the day is coming to an end.

The rest of the ride I am nervously awake, my body so exhausted but my eyes refusing to shut. I continue to stare out the window; small things along the roadside become familiar. *We must be getting close*. And then, all too soon, the bus comes to a halt and the engine shuts off. When people start to filter off I remain seated, my hands glued to the seat around me. *What am I so afraid of?* Before I know it I am the only person left in the bus, the driver staring at me from his rear view mirror.

"Are you heading back?" he asks, frustrated.

"No," I say softly.

Picking up what is left of my bagged lunch, I peel myself off the seat, each step making my knees seem weaker. I set my left foot down on the ground and a strange sense of calm washes over me.

Braeden

I remain lying in my bed, the pain from my fingers now radiating up my arm but I couldn't care less. The anger and adrenaline that still surges through me is serving as a pain killer. All the events of last night are running through my mind. *How the fuck did a perfect night turn to this?*

When I saw him on top of her my whole world crumbled. I was supposed to be there to save her, to keep scum like him and her step-father from touching her. I had failed. And here she was, in the hospital again, hurt.

I soon become impatient, Chelsea nowhere in sight to finish wrapping my cast. Swinging my legs over the bed I push the door open out into the hallway. When I find a nurse who isn't Chelsea I pull her aside.

"Can you tell me which room Phoenix Harper is in?"

She looks at my arm.

"Please," I beg.

She just smiles.

"She's in exam room four,"

"Thank you," I whisper.

Turning around, I know exactly what room it is, having spent a lot of time in this hospital as a kid. When I get to the room I notice that the door is open. I slowly step inside and my eyes lay upon the empty bed, a hospital gown crumbled on the floor beside it.

Everything in the world stops. No sounds reach my ears except for the loud boom of my heartbeat. I don't have to look around. I don't have to check to see if she's in the bathroom.

I can tell she is no longer in this building. The pull I always feel when she's around is gone, my body feeling alone and cold. When I tell my body to move I leave the room, hastily making my way down the hallway.

"Braeden?" I hear Chelsea say as I blast past her, her form a blur in my vision.

My mind is only on one thing. Pushing open the door I see my father seated behind his desk, a phone to his ear. He looks up at me, instantly noticing my state.

"I'll have to call you back," he says, immediately hanging up.

He flies up out of his seat, making his way to me in a few strides.

"Braeden? What's going on?" Why isn't your arm in a cast?"

I freeze, not knowing how or where to start. I hear footsteps behind me and I turn around hastily, hoping to see a pair of beautiful brown eyes looking back at me.

"Phoenix is gone," I hear Chelsea say, her breathing labored.

My eyes find the floor. I cringe at her words, hoping that maybe my eyes were lying to me. I look up at my father, his eyes telling me that he has now caught on.

"She couldn't have gone far," he says as he pushes past us.

My mind screams at my body to move but I remain frozen as a statue. I don't even have the energy to tell them that she's not here. Every second that I am alone in the office seems like an eternity and at some point my body decides to seat itself, my legs curled up into my chest. When I see both their forms re-enter it confirms my biggest fears. It's now that my body decides to react.

"How the hell did she leave without anyone noticing?" I shout rising out of my chair, a new found anger coursing through my body. "Isn't this why there are protocols?"

My father sighs and I know that I am aggravating him again, but I don't care. Phoenix's safety was the most important thing right now. It always was and always will be. Even if she didn't want me anymore, I need to know that she was safe.

"Maybe she went home," I exclaim, making my way to the door.

My father's arm shoots out in front of me, effectively blocking my exit.

"I know that you are concerned right now, but for the love of God can you please get your cast on before you cause further damage to your arm."

His eyes are closed as he speaks this and I can tell he is trying to gain his exposure. All I do is nod.

"Chelsea," he says, allowing her to enter the room, all the components still in her arms. "Sit," he directs to me.

I do as I am told like a five year old who just got put in a time out. Each second it takes Chelsea to wrap my arm I become more impatient. Every second I am here is another second unknown of her whereabouts. As she continues to work we remain quiet like before. I notice that my father leaves the room.

"I'm sorry," I blurt out, Chelsea looking up at me in astonishment.

"For what?" she asks.

"For basically being an asshole," I say almost with a laugh. "You're a good person, and you and my father deserve happiness. Especially him."

"Thank you," she says softly. "And I never want you

to feel like I am trying to take the place of your mother. I couldn't even if I wanted to."

I swallow the lump in my throat.

"I appreciate that."

"Believe me; I know how it is to have new people trying to worm their asses into your life. My parents got divorced when I was young."

"Sorry," I say quietly.

"Eh, I was better off without them," she shrugs. "And you, sir, are done."

She gives it a once over before standing back up.

"Let's go get your girl."

Phoenix

I inhale the crisp, clean air, my brain barely remembering that it once breathed this fresh air. Grasping the very little amount of food I have left I walk away from the bus, my body still not sure that I am actually here. As I walk through the streets of the small town I swear that nothing has changed, even down to the fliers on the windows. Memories of my time here take hold of my mind, seeming as though every inch of this place has one. Memories of my father.

Somehow my feet carry me on, my memory guiding me to where I knew I wanted to be all along. I don't know what to expect. *What if a family lives there now?*

With the turn of a corner my eyes lay upon it. My feet move the rest of the distance and before I know it I am on the front lawn. Or where the front lawn used to be. In its place are weeds as tall as me. Bushes that were once strategically placed have now over grown, their branches climbing up the walls of the house. The paint on it is dull and cracked and it reminds me of a haunted house and not the home I once loved. I look around to see if there is anyone watching and when the coast is clear I walk around back, happy to see the tree still standing near what was once my bedroom window. Swinging my leg up I climb onto the first branch, pushing my weak body up until I reach the window level. When I do I sit there staring at it, the glass so dirty that I can't peer inside. I remember that the lock on this particular window always got stuck. Reaching my fingers out I jiggle the window and after a few forceful slams I hear it unlock, the window going up with ease.

Shoving my front end in first I tumble to the floor, a large scream leaving my throat. When I regain my composure I look around and amazed at what I see. Everything in my room is in its place. It is exactly how I remembered it. But everything is covered in white cloths. And just like that, my body heaves into crying and my head falls into my hands.

"What the hell am I doing here?" I mutter to myself.

After a few more minutes of crying I pick myself up

off the floor, wiping the tears away from my face. My mind still doesn't believe that I am actually here. Leaving my bedroom I walk down the hallway and the sight before me almost causes me to breakdown again.

Rubbing my hand over each picture that is hung against the wall, I expose a new year of school pictures. My dad always hung the new one up every year, all of them in sequential order. I smile for a moment at the pictures of me when I was young, my hair more blonde, and my front two teeth missing. I try to think about, try to remember when I was that girl, but there is little to no recollection of it. Elaina and Carl stole that girl from this world. There is nothing left of her.

Making my way further downstairs I am somehow still amazed that mostly everything is in its place. It's as though I could close my eyes and envision my father coming down the stairs. But that won't be happening. *But why is everything still here?*

Walking over to the couch I pull off the sheet, it creating a cloud of dust in the air, it making me cough excessively. Lying down upon it I realize how exhausted my body still is. I feel as though I could sleep for decades. And just as I suspected, I fall asleep quickly.

~

"Phoenix!" his voice calls out for me, a sense of panic in the tone.

Slamming my brush down I pull open the bathroom

door, flying down stairs in seconds. On the floor of the kitchen is my father, his body crumbled onto the ground.

"Dad?" I cry out.

Next to him is a shattered plate, food scattered all around him. I fly to his side and hook my arms under him, trying everything to help lift him but he is too heavy. Tears started to flow down my cheek and I try to stop them but I can't.

"I'm fine," he says softly, his breathing labored.

"I'll be right back," I say, pushing myself away from him and bound out the front steps to the house next door.

I bang on the door repeatedly, waiting for someone to answer. Soon after the door flies open, an older woman looks down at me, her eyes wide.

"Phoenix? What are you doing out here alone?" she asks.

"My dad fell down and I can't get him back up," I utter through heaves of my chest.

"Mitchell!" she screams and the three of us bound down the steps and back to my house.

When we reach him there is even less color in his face and I start to cry again. I bury my face into the wall, it all too much for me the watch. When they get him in the chair I peer out again, a small smile on my father's face.

"I'm fine, sweetie," he says, his breath short. His

arms spread out towards me. I bound off the wall and
slam my body into him, smelling his musky scent.

"You alright?" I hear Mitchell ask.

"Yeah, I'm fine," he huffs, his arms still around me,
my hand stroking the back of my head.

"Don't leave me," I cry out.

I pull back from him, my vision blurry from the
tears.

"I could never leave you, kiddo," he says. "As long
as I am in here." He points to my heart.

~

I am startled awake by a loud banging on the door
and I realize that the house is completely dark, a small
amount of light being emanated by the street lights. I
panic, my heart racing. A small part of me hopes that it
is Braeden, but I know it won't be. No one knows where
I am.

I walk to the front door and place my ear upon it.
Reaching up on my tippy toes I peer through the
peephole, seeing no figure in front of me, but instead
there are red and blue flashing lights. I muffle a shriek.
There is another loud knock on the door and my whole
body jumps. I almost think about bolting out the back
door but I quickly push aside that. There is nowhere
else to go.

"I know that someone is in there," the voice calls
out. "The neighbors claim they've seen movement."

Swallowing my fears I wrap my fingers around the

door knob, the coolness of the metal pressed against my clammy skin. I pull open the door a few inches, a tall figure looking down upon me. He lifts up his flashlight, the bright light hurting my eyes. I become effectively blind for a moment but I can tell that the figure has not moved.

"Phoenix?" the voice calls out, it sending a chill down my spine.

I remain frozen, my body trying to connect that voice. *I know that voice.* He lowers the light and small dots dance their way across my vision, his full form coming into view slowly. I stare at him.

"Do I know you?" I ask nervously, ashamed that I can't remember.

I see him clutch his chest, the fast movement scaring me.

"I'm hurt that you don't remember me," he responds. "You used to spend a lot of time at my house."

And then it clicks.

"Tate?" I shout, my eyes widening.

"At your service." He smiles, tipping his hat.

We both fall silent for a second.

"Since when did you become a cop?" I blurt out.

He laughs lightly.

"That's a long story. Maybe if you let me in I can tell you."

A flash of panic goes through me; the idea of me alone with a strange man terrifies me. *Tate would never*

457

hurt anyone... let alone me. Listening to my gut I push the door open, allowing him to enter.

"Thanks," he says, taking off his hat. "It's pretty cold out there."

He looks around the living room, realizing it's completely dark. I begin to get nervous. *Was he here to arrest me? Kick me out?* His eyes find mine again and I swear that he can hear my heart beating in my chest.

"We really missed you around here," he says, his face serious.

Tate was my best friend Hannah's big brother. He was only a few years older than us. We spent a lot of time at each other's house and Tate was always nice to us. He wasn't the typical older brother that ignores his younger sister. His whole family was my second family. Another thing I lost when Elaina took me.

I push back the tears trying to fall. He walks over to the kitchen as flicks on the light, the room illuminating. I stare at it like I've never seen electricity before. He notices.

"Did you not try to turn on the lights?" he asks.

I shake my head.

"I figured it would have been shut off. It's been... years," I utter. I turn to face him, my mind curious. "Can I ask you something?"

"Of course." He smiles

"Why is it still here?"   .

His eyebrows furrow.

"What do you mean?"

I swallow before speaking again. "My father died, I...left." *More like taken.*

He shrugs. "I don't know," he admits. "There was some complication about the land after your father's death, plus I don't think anyone in this town would let them touch it. Your father was very important to this town."

My vision becomes blurred and silent tears start to fall down my cheeks. He takes a step forward and his fingers find my cheek, wiping them away.

"What happened to you, Phoenix?" he asks.

I laugh a little. "That's a long story."

"I've got nothing but time," he responds. "It's not like much happens in this town, you're the first call I've had all night."

Braeden

The ride back to the house seems like an eternity, my legs bouncing from the anxiety. When we reach the driveway I push the door open before the car comes to a complete stop, my footing faltering a little. Throwing the front door open I bound inside and start screaming her name but there is nothing but silence. I hear the footsteps of my father and Chelsea coming from behind me. I remain frozen, completely lost.

"What am I suppose to do now?" I say softly.

I feel a hand being placed on shoulder.

"Chelsea, if you could please give us a moment," I hear him say.

My father pushes us into his office and I don't

protest. I have no energy to.

"Sit," he demands.

Finding a chair I place myself inside it and remain silent. My father sits in the chair next to mine.

"Are you OK?" he asks.

I almost laugh at the question.

"I'm peachy," I snap.

"I know that I can be hard on you sometimes and I know that you need a father right now and not a medical professional."

I look up at him, his expression...concerned.

"I appreciate that."

We both fall silent again.

"How could she just...leave?" I blurt out.

I hear him sigh slightly. "I know that you don't understand it now, but this might be what's best for her."

I am aghast by his statement.

"Are you fucking kidding me?"

"Braeden, listen to me," he says, his voice more stern. "People like Phoenix are...different."

I try to calm my nerves but it's not working. He begins to notice.

"Do you love her?" he changes the subject.

I feel like our lives have been shifted back, a sense of déjà vu flowing though me.

"More than I could ever explain," I answer.

"Would you do anything for her? If she had a certain

wish, would you grant it to her?"

"Absolutely," I respond,

"It seems confusing, but Phoenix choosing to leave was what she wanted. I know that you are scared right now, but you have to respect her wish."

"How will I know that she is safe?"

"Phoenix is a smart girl, Braeden. Even with her recent past of abuse, she thrives in life incredibly well."

I cringe at the word abuse.

"What if she tries...?" I can't even finish the sentence.

My father's eyes close and we both fall silent. When he opens them again, tears flow down his cheeks.

"I just don't want you to make the same mistakes I did," he says. And in that moment I know were not just talking about Phoenix. I don't know what to say, so I let him continue.

"I thought I was helping your mom, but I ended up just pushing her further towards the cliff."

"You were just trying to help her."

He shakes her head. "No, I refused to listen to her wishes."

"You did it because you love her; you wanted what's best for her."

"Sometimes what you think is best for them really isn't. I forced her into things she didn't want to do. I had already lost Thomas, and I couldn't bear losing her too. But in the end that's exactly what happened."

I still remain silent. "Do you remember what I told you when you first came to me about her?"

I nod.

"Some people don't want to be saved," I say just above a whisper.

"I'm not saying that you should never see her again, but I beg of you, please, give her space. If she chooses to come back then do not give her any grief for leaving. She is confused more than you could ever imagine."

I look at my father and I really notice his face. I begin to finally understand what he's gone through, the hardships he's had to deal with. The ones I was too young to understand. He goes to get up but I reach out, grabbing his arm.

"Thanks," I say.

"I'm glad that we had this talk, Braeden," he responds. "It was long overdue."

Once my father leaves the room I remain seated in my chair. When I am able to tell my legs to move I find myself immediately heading upstairs, even though I know that it will just cause me pain. Pushing open her bedroom door I scan the room, the light that once filled this room now gone. I close my eyes and inhale, a faint smell of her fills my nostrils.

Running my fingers along her dresser, I pick up various things of hers, the lump in my throat and the burn behind my eyes becomes stronger. I look out the bedroom window and it almost seems unreal that so little time has passed. My body feels like it has been awake for days on end, every second ticking away painfully slow. My father's conversation replays in my head and I don't know whether to scream or curl into a corner and never come out.

But I am numb. I don't feel hatred. I don't feel sadness. *OK, maybe that's a lie.* My mind keeps going back to what she's doing at this moment. *Was she safe?*

Lying down on the bed I curl up into myself, my face in her pillow, her scent now all around me and I become crippled. My body no longer is made of bone and muscle, but of mush. At this moment, I don't know if I can move, fearing that if I try I may fall to the floor. So I stay.

I don't know how long it was before I fell asleep but I'm startled awake by a shaking of my shoulder. I fly up out of the bed.

"Phoenix?" I shout out into the room.

My eyes peer into the darkness of the room but there is no sound. No stirring. No one's here. Laying back down I run my hands through my hair, gathering my thoughts together. It wasn't a dream.

Pushing my feet over the side of the bed, I pull my heavy form out of the bedroom and slowly walk downstairs. As I reach the kitchen I glance up at the wall. 3:18 a.m. I groan as I pull open the fridge, the light inside blinding me. Grabbing the carton of orange juice I flip open the tab. The cool liquid runs down my throat quenching the thirst I didn't know I had. With the carton still in my hand I leave the kitchen and head to the family room. Setting the carton down on the coffee table I go to sit on the couch but instead I am met with a scream. I abruptly stand back up, my eyes shifting to see a massive figure sprawled across the couch.

"Jesus, man, I think you sat on my balls," the figure shouts, his voice strained.

I reach over and flip on the lamp, Donovan's form wrapped in a blanket.

"What the fuck are you doing here? I ask.

He sits upright, the blanket now wrapped around his shoulders. He starts rubbing his eyes. I've clearly woke him up from his beauty sleep.

"Your father called me, wanted me to hold down the fort," he explains.

I huff. "I'm not a child, I don't need any damn babysitting."

"Says the person that is whining like one," he snaps back.

Donovan grabs the orange juice from the table and tips it back until it runs dry.

"Thanks for the drink." He smiles.

I shake my head, smirking a little.

"Ahh, I knew that there was a smile in there somewhere," he teases.

I immediately drop it and the room falls silent.

"So, what are you going to do man?" he asks.

I remain silent.

"I mean, what the hell even happened?" he asks.

I sit down on the now vacant end of the couch and immediately put my head into my hands.

"I should have known," I blurt out. I begin to shake my head. "I should have got rid of his fucking ass a long time ago. No one liked him, not even me."

Donovan remains silent. Pulling my head up I lean back against the couch, staring
up at the ceiling, my fingers running through my hair.

"Fuck, this is all my fault."

"That's not true, Phoenix, would be dead if you two weren't so...fucking destined for each other."

I shift my eyes to the side, now facing Donovan.

"If we're so fucking destined, then why the hell am I sitting here not knowing where she is?" I retort.

He doesn't respond.

"Exactly," I say, the anger building inside me.

"Then why don't you go find her?" he asks.

I laugh inside. "She clearly doesn't want me around."

"That's bullshit and you know it," Donovan says.

"What the fuck am I suppose to do? She left Donovan, no goodbye, no note...if she wanted to be found she would have told me where she is going. I'm not fucking psychic..."

And then something clicks. I jump off the couch and grab one of my father's jackets off the coat rack.

"You fucking coming or what?" I blurt out to Donovan.

Donovan throws the blanket off of him, his form by my side in a few steps.

Phoenix

My conversation with Tate spilled out of me at a rapid rate, my mind and mouth going a million miles an hour. When I had finished I felt like a weight had been lifted off my shoulders. But every time his name came up it felt as though there were tiny needles being inserted into my heart. I finally look up from the ground and Tate's eyes are wide. The burn in my cheeks grows.

"I...How..." is all that he could mutter.

I just shrug.

"These assholes are in jail right?" he asks, his fingers curled into a fist.

"I only know about Carl, the other one I'm not so sure, I left shortly after the incident."

"You have to go back," he says standing up. "They'll need you to testify."

I stand up abruptly, fear coursing through me.

"I'm not going back," I spit. "I have nothing left there. I have nothing anywhere. I am alone and that's the way it should be. No more of people getting hurt because of me. I'm not worth it."

"I think that's for the other person to decide," he says softly. "Plus, anyone would be crazy not to want to be around you, Phoenix."

A voice emits from his radio.

"Negative. No disturbance, coast is clear," he says into it. He looks back at me. "I have to go, people are going to start wondering where I am. Are you going to be OK?"

I give him a small smile. "Yeah. I'll be fine."

He nods. "Maybe you can come over sometime, I'm sure my parents would love to see you."

"I'd like that," I respond.

He reaches over and puts his arms around me. I don't flinch.

"It's really good to see you," he says softly.

I shut the door behind him, locking the handle and the deadbolt, something I never felt was necessary before. With the crackle of the fire now filling the room, I lay back down on the couch, my encounter with Tate running through my mind. And then I think about him. Curling up into myself, I stare at the dancing flames of the fire, wondering what he was doing right now. *Was he mad at me? Was he looking for me? Was he forgetting about me?* I continue to lay there and watch as the sun begins to rise, this time sleep not reaching me.

~

Getting up, I pull the blanket off the couch and wrap it around me. I exit through the back door and the fresh smell of rain reaches my nose, the weather matching my disposition. I sit down in one of the rockers and just stare out into the forest. My body is shaking from the cold but it somehow numbs the pain, making my body calm and my mind blank. A temporary coma. I don't know how long I am out there before movement catches my eye. I look at the figure and quickly look away, my eyes probably playing tricks on me.

"Phoenix?" a delicate voice says.

I look back again, the figure closer.

"Rain?" I say in a hushed tone.

She smiles back at me. Pulling myself from the chair I bound over to her, wrapping my arms around her, her warm body touching my cold skin. I pull back and really look at her. It seems as though I haven't seen her in years with all that has happened.

"What are you doing here?" I ask, still shocked that she is here. "Wait...did you have a vision?"

She laughs.

"No," she starts. "Although when I saw Dr. Harris come in I knew something was wrong." I am somehow disappointed. I snap my eyes back at her.

"Dr. Harris?"

She shifts her eyes around.

"Guess I'm not good at keeping secrets am I?" She smiles.

"He...sent you here?" I ask. "How did you know where to go?"

"It doesn't take a smart person to figure out where you would go, Phoenix. You only really spoke of this as your true home. Plus, someone noticed your picture at the bus station."

My knees become weak at the thought of the Harris' searching for me. I never wanted to cause anyone any grief. But I guess I was too naive. I sit back down in the chair and Rain sits in the one beside me, my eyes resuming their position into the forest.

"So, what, are you here to bring me back?" I ask harshly.

I feel Rain's hand slip into mine.

"I would never force you to leave. I am here for nothing but companionship."

I look back over to her. "I am so happy that you are here, but I don't think I will be great company. Wait....how are you even here? Aren't the people at the hospital going to be looking for you?"

She smiles again.

"I leave the hospital escaping to you," she starts. "I left by choice, Phoenix. Remember?"

I think back to what seems like so long ago, Rain's story about how she came to be in that hospital. She was there by choice, not force. We fall silent again until the grumble of my stomach fills the air.

"Let's go get you some food," she says while tugging my hand.

"I'm not hungry," I say softly.

"Well, I'm starving." She smiles.

We walk back into the house and Rain holds a bag out to me.

"I know that you couldn't care less right now, but you look like hell."

I scowl at her. "Well, then my outside matches my inside," I announce.

She lets out a sigh.

"Just go take a shower, for me?" she asks sweetly.

I grumble and take the bag from her, making my way upstairs.

"I'll be down here whenever you are ready," I hear her voice call out.

When I reach the confines of the bathroom I start to undress when something gets caught on the inside of my sweatshirt. Looking down into it I see that attached to the inside of the sleeve is my bracelet. I had forgotten I was even wearing it. With shaky hands I reach down, unclasping it and set it on the counter top. The silver wings bounce in the light. I place it in the medicine cabinet. *Out of sight, out of mind.*

When I pull myself from the shower I wrap myself in the towel that Rain brought, tucking it underneath my armpit. Opening up the bag some more, I dump the contents of it out onto the counter, grabbing the brush and run it though my tangled hair.

"Ouch," I call out.

When I'm done with it I set it back down when something shiny catches my eye. In a cup near the faucet is my father's razor. I stare at it for a second before taking it between my fingers. My father was always into the old school way of shaving. With my opposite hand I open the straight razor. I look up at myself in the mirror and press the cool metal against my skin. My breathing becomes hitched and I feel like I have been transported back in time. Closing my eyes I concentrate on my breathing, my hands frozen. *Braeden would want you to live.*

The next thing I hear is metal hitting porcelain. Looking down the razor is no longer in my hand, but now at the bottom of the sink. A sense of panic washes over me and I hastily pull on the clothes that were in the bag, slamming the door to the bathroom shut behind me. I fly down the stairs to see Rain trying to tidy up.

"Don't even bother," I say through labored breath.

Rain drops the towel and turns towards me. "You look refreshed." She smiles.

"Ready?" I ask, assuming she still wants food.

"Yup!" She smiles, grabbing her bag.

"Wait, how are we going to pay for food?" I ask. "Never mind, I know the answer to that."

I hated the fact that they were still taking care of me even though there was a whole state between us. I had taken so much from them and I gave them nothing in return. Grabbing the front door handle I pull it open and my eyes are met with a figure standing before me, his arm raised in mid air.

"Tate, what are you doing here?" I blurt out.

His eyes shift from me to Rain.

"Oh, I'm sorry, I didn't realize you had company," he says and starts to walk away.

"Wait, where are you going?" I call out after him.

He stops in his tracks. "This is...this is Rain," I explain.

He turns back around and faces us. I know that he know who she is from my story last night.

"I just don't want to intrude," he explains. "You obviously have a lot to talk about."

"You're not," Rain calls out behind me. "We were just about to go get some food, want to join us?"

A sense of jealousy washes over me, Rain's ability to blend into society despite her past astonishes me.

"I'd love to." He smiles at me.

Tate is no longer in his uniform but sporting a button up shirt and dark jeans. His clothes too nice to be from any shop here in town. Shutting the door behind us I follow behind Rain and Tate. The rain has stopped but the ground is still wet, the smell of damp concrete filling the air. We choose to walk, considering the town is so small there is very little need for a car here. When we decide on a place we slide into the booth, every patron and worker has their eyes on me. *News travels fast here.*

I eat mostly in silence except for the occasional person coming up to me, all of their faces unrecognizable. Rain and Tate fall in and out of conversation but I remain mute, picking at my plate of food. The walk back to the house is sluggish, my body is tired and the small amount of food I was able to choke down is making me feel heavy. When we reach the house again there are three people sitting on the porch. I don't have to second guess who two of them are. When they see me they both stand up, smiles wide across their face.

"I almost didn't believe my son when he told us you were back," her soft voice says as she pulls me close. "We truly missed you, Phoenix."

"I missed you guys, too," I respond as I pull back.

I look over to the figure standing beside her.

"Hey, Mr. Hendricks." I smile.

"It's good to have you home, Phoenix, the house hasn't been the same since you left. Well…since you both left."

I just nod, trying to hold back the tears. My eyes then fall upon the person I don't know.

"Phoenix, this is Mr. Bernstein," Mary explains. I reach out and shake his hand.

I hear Rain clear her throat behind me.

"Oh...ummm...this is my friend, Rain."

"It's so nice to meet you," Rain says, shaking their hands.

"Mom...Dad...you have something to tell Phoenix, right?" Tate pipes in.

Mary looks at me again and smiles.

"Yes I do. And I hope that it will make you very happy."

Braeden

"**D**ude, where are we going?" Donovan continues to complain. "You don't even know where she is."

I huff. "I don't need to know where she is, all I need to know is that she is OK."

I see his confused expression out of the corner of my eye. I don't care. When we reach the hospital I push the door to the cab open, noticing I am alone.

"Are you coming or what?" I call out.

A second later Donovan exits the cab, his form by my side.

"Have you lost your mind? She's not..." Donovan stops talking abruptly. He's finally caught on. "Good thinking."

I don't know if anyone else believed her visions, but after that previous night I would believe anything she would tell me. I remain quiet and enter through the employee entrance, the hospital busy at this time of the day. With my head down I make my way for Rain's room, my heart racing. But when I push open the door all I see is her empty bed. The room dark and vacant. Spinning around I see Lucy behind the nurses' station and I curse silently under my breath. Walking over to her, she looks up and catches my gaze.

"Braeden! What did you do to your arm?" she squeals.

"It's nothing," I begin to say.

She walks out from behind the counter, her fingers trailing up the cast and onto my shoulder.

"Seriously, I'm fine," I snap at her, my eyes closing in frustration. "Listen, I just need to know where Rain is."

"Rain?" she asks confused. Does no one care enough around here to learn fucking people's names?

"Patient in room eight."

"Oh!" she giggles. "I think she left."

I snap open my eyes.

"What do you mean 'left'?" I ask again.

"Like, as in, not here anymore," she says sarcastically. "Are you sure you are all right, Braeden?"

I don't respond and instead turn around, heading back out the way we came.

"Well, that went...unexpected," I hear Donovan say behind me.

"Thank you, Captain Fucking Obvious."

"Where do you want to go now?" he asks.

"Home," is all that I could utter.

~

When we get back to my father's house I notice that all the lights are on, my father's car in the driveway. When I open the door my father is on the phone, something that is becoming a regular occurrence. Donovan walks over to the couch, his body falling down upon it. My father's eyes stay on me.

"OK, thank you very much," he says into the phone before hanging up. "You weren't here when I got back," he states.

"Yeah, I was out," I state.

"I can see that," he declares. "What were you doing?"

"Nothing," I say, hoping that Donovan can keep his mouth shut. All three of us are silent.

"I have some news about Phoenix," my father speaks.

At that moment my body goes through all emotions. *This is where he tells me she's dead.*

"She is safe," he says.

I let out a large breath that I didn't know I was holding.

"And how do you know this?" I ask.

"That's not important," he says.

"Bullshit it's not," I snap.

More pieces of the puzzle snap into place

"That's why Rain is gone isn't it? You sent her to check up on Phoenix," I say, her name causing my heart pain.

His facial expressions tell me yes.

"You wanted to know that she was safe, right?" he asks.

I just nod. "Well, now you do."

For some reason anger rises inside of me, even though I should be relieved - or thankful - I'm not sure which. All I know is that I am not satisfied.

"Where is she?" I say sternly.

Phoenix

I am seated at the kitchen table, stacks of paper sprawled across the top of it. I stare at each one, realizing that most of them contained words I don't even understand.

"What do you mean it's mine?" I ask, looking up at the eyes of the patrons sitting across from me.

Mr. Bernstein gives me a crooked smile. "The property, the house and its contents are yours."

I still don't believe him. Mr. Bernstein laughs.

"When your father passed away he left you everything," he explains. "The only stipulation was that you must be eighteen years of age to obtain your assets."

I look down at my hands, my vision becoming blurry. He starts to rustle through some papers.

"We tried contacting you as of your eighteenth birthday and we spoke to someone named Carl, but he claimed no one by that name lived there."

I snap my head back up, a sudden fire burning through my body. He had taken more from me than I could have ever imagined. The whole room is silent. When I look back up everyone is staring at me with a sympathetic look on their faces.

"Well," Mr. Bernstein says as he stands up. "If you just sign here, we can be done with this."

Picking up the pen in my hand, I stare at it. It feels incredibly heavy. Putting it to the paper I sign my name and I don't know whether to laugh or cry.

"Welcome home, Phoenix." He smiles at me before packing up the papers and leaves.

~

The Hendricks' stay for a little while after, Mary explaining to me what this all entails and that they were here for me whenever I needed them. Soon it was just Rain and myself. Another day here and gone.

"Did that all really just happen?" I blurt out.

She just smiles and nods her head. *It can't be true.*

"I think I'm going to go for a walk," I say. "To you know…process it all."

"Do you want some company?" she asks softly.

"I think I want to be alone," I explain.

Grabbing my sweatshirt I walk out the front door. On my way down the steps I pull it over my head, the hood getting caught around my ears. I stumble forward a little bit and trip over something, a pair of hands catching me. My skin burns where these fingers lay upon me. I pull the rest of it down until my vision become clear, a figure standing before me.

"Braeden."

Braeden

Having her in my arms again felt abnormal. I almost didn't believe that she was standing before me. I take time to observe her state, her eyes telling me that she hasn't slept much. She's still breathtakingly beautiful.

"Braeden," her voice calls out so softly that I swear I imagined it.

We both stare at each other for a second until her eyes start to shift, looking at every direction but mine. I immediately drop my hands from her shoulders. *She's not mine anymore.*

"How did you find me?" she asks quietly, as though she is ashamed.

"My father told me," I answer. "He sent Rain to come take care of you."

She looks up at me. "I figured. But why would he do

that?" she asks, her tone slightly irritated.

"Because we all care about you, Ser..." I stop and swallow. "Phoenix. Did you really think we would just let you go like that and at least not make sure you are OK?"

I remove my eyes from hers and look at the house behind her.

"I'm glad that you have found comfort here," I say softly.

Phoenix turns around to face it for a second before turning attention back to me. The air between us is thick and I don't know what to say or do.

"I just wanted to know that you were safe," I utter, swallowing the lump in my throat. "And now that I see that you are, I guess I can go now."

I turn around, feeling as though my emotions are betraying me. Each step I take away from her is painful, the tie between us stretching dangerously thin with every movement.

"Braeden!" I hear her call out from behind me.

I stop but I remain facing away from her. I can hear her move so that she is right behind me. I can feel the heat radiating off of her body. As I slowly turn around to face her, I am met with her wet cheeks, her eyes staring into mine. Reaching up with my finger, I wipe away the tears that are traveling down her face.

"Don't cry, Seraph," I whisper into the darkness.

Her beautiful eyes continue to look into mine and we

have a silent conversation. All the pain and agony that was caused is gone and we are simply two people. With my palm still caressing her cheek I lean down, placing my lips gently on top of hers. I am afraid that she will pull back and reject me, but she doesn't. Instead, she pushes into me, our kiss turning from timid to passionate. Her hands come around my backside and fist into my shirt and my free arm falls onto her lower back, pushing her even closer into me, my other arm caught between us. *Fucking cast.*

The taste of her mouth is better than I ever remembered, her scent swirling all around us. I don't know how long the kiss lasts but I wanted it to never stop. I wanted to live in this moment forever.

When we both pull back I feel like there is no oxygen left in my body. Phoenix remains silent, her fingertips pressed against her lips, a small smile hiding behind them.

"I've never been able to explain that feeling," she says softly.

Reaching out I take her hand in mine and press it against my chest, my heartbeat thumping underneath her fingertips.

"My heart only does this when you are near, Seraph, and it feels fucking incredible," I say.

She looks up at me, her eyes serious. "Will you take a walk with me?" she asks.

"I would follow you to the end of the earth if you'd

allow me."

With our hands intertwined, she passes by me and pulls me in her direction. She is moving so fast that I have to make my strides wider to keep up, but I don't complain. We walk into the thick forest and the temperature drops immensely, the sun hiding behind the branches of the trees. I soon become lost of our direction but Phoenix seems to know exactly where she is headed.

When we break through a patch of trees, my eyes fall upon one massive tree. Phoenix stops at my side, her eyes looking up to the sky. I follow and see a large playhouse nestled high in the center of branches.

"This was one of my favorite places to be."She smiles. "I used to spend so much time in this tree that my father began building this playhouse for me. I kept asking him to add things and he told me that it would never be done." She pauses. "Unfortunately, that came true," she says with pain behind her voice.

I look up at the tree house again, noticing its diminished look.

"Follow me," she says and walks over to the tree trunk, her eyes looking over the branches. With her left arm first, she grabs the nearest one, trying to pull herself up. She puts her foot up and immediately slips, with only her fingers still gripping the bark. I rush over to her and grab onto her hips, trying to balance her. And then I hear her laugh and it's like fucking music to my ears. Pushing her up, she grips her other arm onto the branch and swings herself onto it. Once she is settled, I reach up high and pull myself up. It's a lot more complicated with one arm in a cast.

"You're not the only one who climbed trees as a kid," I laugh.

We sit side-by-side and stare out into a break in the trees. We are both silent for a while, allowing her to gather her thoughts. The sound of flapping wings and cries of nearby birds in the air reaches my ears. After what seems like an eternity, she speaks.

"I used to sit here for hours by myself thinking about what my life would be like when I got older," she states before pausing. "And never in a million years would I have ever imagined it would turn out like this."

Hey eyes are facing outward, as though she is declaring this statement to the forest itself.

"What do you mean?" I ask.

She finally looks over and her eyes are lost, yet so in love.

"Well," she starts, her teeth nibbling on her lip. "I never imagined you."

I take her hand in mine, my fingertips playing delicately against the top of her hand.

"I never thought someone like you could love someone like me," she adds.

"Seraph," I say quietly. "You are perfect to me in every single way. You were what I was looking for all along. I never had to think twice about my love for you. I was yours from the moment you broke my glasses."

She laughs but looks back out into the sky.

"But I ran away," she said. "I ran from you when you were the only thing that never hurt me. I gave up on us."

My father's conversation flows through my mind.

"But I did hurt you," I admit.

She looks back over at me, her brow furrowed.

"Phoenix, I allowed you to become hurt because of me. If I didn't leave you alone..."

Her hand squeezes onto mine.

"Stop that," she says. "It was nothing you did. It was just another unfortunate time in my life."

My stomach churns thinking about all the "unfortunate" times in her life.

"But I couldn't keep seeing you hurt because of me. My own pain I can deal with, but pain brought upon you...I can't bear it," she says just above a whisper.

I don't know how to respond. We both fall silent.

"So, what do we do know?" I ask.

"Well, there is something I haven't told you," she says, making my heart skip a few beats.

She swings her leg over so that she is now straddling the branch.

"I'm not going back to San Francisco," she states. "I can't ask you to give up your whole life to be with me but it was never truly my home."

"And here is," I say softly.

She nods. "Being here for the past few days reminded me where I truly belong. I could never hate the time I spent in California though, because it brought me to you."

Reaching out I run my fingertips through her hair.

"Then, let's stay," I say quietly.

Her eyes become wide and I can't stop a smile from coming onto my face.

"I can't ask you to do that," she says shaking her head.

"I know you weren't asking, but I will stay…if you want me to. You are my life, Seraph, and the past forty-eight hours have been the worse of my life. I never want to experience that again. It comes down to if you love me or not, the rest is just details."

.

Phoenix

My heart is beating so fast that my hearing is blurred, only the loud pounding of my heart is apparent in my ears.

"I do," I say, tears threatening to fall. "I love you more than I could ever explain."

I scoot closer to him so that my front is pressed against his side. If we weren't so high up I would probably be straddling him. The heat from his body is intoxicating. I press my lips to his and we both fight for dominance, our kiss forceful and heavy.

"Well, then you might just have to show me," he says with a cocky smirk and in this moment I feel like the past has been washed away. It was just the two of us. The way it should have always been.

"Seraph," I hear him say, his mouth still pressed against mine.

"Yeah," I call out, still in my intoxicated state.

"As much as I want to spend every second with my body against you, I don't think we should be doing this so high in the air," he says.

I pull back, my lips pouty. He laughs at my reaction.

"OK," I breathe out.

Braeden slowly jumps down and turns back around, his free arm outstretched to catch me.

"Do you trust me, Seraph?" he asks.

"With my life," I respond with a smile.

I close my eyes and jump from the branch, his arm hugging around me and his grip tight, our faces close together.

"I just want you to know, you can't run away again," he says, his statement making my heart quicken. "I'm here to stay."

"I already made that mistake once," I say softly. "I don't plan on making it again."

I slowly set her back down on the ground but re-lock our hands.

"Come on," I say pulling on her, heading back in the direction we came from.

When we reach the house again I see a figure on the porch, a wide smile across its face.

"Hey, Rain," I say.

She just continues to smile. "About time you got here," she jokes to Braeden.

"I know," he responds.

I see that she is gripping her suitcase in her hand.

"You're not staying?" I ask.

"I figured you guys could use some time alone," she says softly. "Plus, I have the whole world to see."

I let go of Braeden's hand and wrap my arms around her.

"Thank you," I say into her ear. "For everything. Just promise me that I will see you again."

"I will always be with you, in this life and the next," Rain smiles.

I pull back, Rain turning her attention to Braeden.

"Take care of each other. You both need each other more than you think."

"She's my life," he says.

"And you are her guardian angel," Rain smiles. I see him nod.

"See ya," she says before walking down the driveway and soon out of sight.

I turn back to Braeden.

"So, this is my home," I say nervously, it resulting in me chewing on my bottom lip. "It could definitely use some help."

I see him shake his head.

"It's beautiful," he says as he looks over it. "I understand why you like it here."

I see him step forward and put his hand in mine. I let out a laugh as he bounds up the front steps, our bodies soon inside the foyer.

"Why is everything still here?" he asks, confused as much as I was when I got here.

I smile. "My father left it to me," I explain.

"Wow."

"Yeah, it's a long story. They kept it from me," I state.

Braeden's hands come up on either side of my face.

"I never want you to think about them again," he says.

He then puts his lips to mine. Our kiss is deep like before but now I can feel the burn between my legs and the tightening in my stomach growing. He slowly leads us against a wall, his hips thrust into mine, effectively pinning me against it. His hand travels over every inch of my torso and my hands tease along the hemline of his shirt. His hands find my bottom and he cups them, making my legs interlock around him.

"Jesus Christ," he says between us, it clear that he is feeling what I am feeling.

I need more of his touch, my body craving everything that he can give me.

"Braeden?" I call out.

"Hmmm?" he says, his lips pressed against my collar bone.

"I need you," I say shyly.

I barely have time to finish my sentence before my body is peeled off the wall and I am thrown over his shoulder, his grip on me even tighter. We remain in the open for a second, our bodies spinning around. We both laugh.

"Where the hell do I go?" he asks.

"That way," I say pointing to stairs.

We bound up them quickly and I swear that he is taking two at a time.

"Left!" I shout out when he starts to make his way towards what was once my father's room. *That would be horrific.*

Pushing open my bedroom door we stand in the middle of it, Braeden taking his time to look around. He puts me down slowly. His eyes fall upon my nineties boys band poster. I walk over to it, trying to cover it up with my body. He just smiles.

"Don't worry, I won't love you less because you had bad taste in music," he jokes.

He continues to look around and I get antsy, his attention running away from the task at hand. I decide to take matter into my own hands. I pull my shirt and sweatshirt up and over my head, thankful for the clean clothes that Rain had brought me, which included a match bra and panties. Braeden's eyes are immediately back on me, his fingertips now trailing around my stomach.

"You are so beautiful, Seraph."

Once we are both on the bed, he situates himself between my legs and my body waits, needing and craving him like an addict. He enters me and I gasp, my hands finding each side of his hips. With every thrust I feel as though I may begin to cry. Grabbing one of Braeden's hands I place it over my heart.

"This is what *you* do to me," I explain.

His hand then travels over my breasts, my nipples being pinched between his fingertips, making my hips buck and inviting him to enter me even deeper. I don't know how long we are at it, the notion of time seems non-existent. I feel the pleasure build up inside me and I may spill over at any time.

"I'm so close," I call out.

With that statement he begins to thrust even faster.

"Come for me," he speaks. "I want to feel you come around me."

And just like that, I do. My eyes slam shut and the pleasure rips through every ounce of my body, flowing from my head to the tips of my toes. Sometime between my state of bliss, I feel Braeden come, too, and I can't help but smile, knowing that I can also bring him pleasure. Once we finish, we lay side-by-side in the small bed, both our chests rising and falling rapidly.

At some point we must have fallen asleep, a deep chill runs through my body and wakes me up. I look out the window, the sky is full of different hues of orange and red. I look back down at Braeden, his naked form still resting.

"I love you," I say so softly that it doesn't waken him.

Reaching out, I run my fingers through his hair and begin to trail down his back. A reminder of what happened.

"Something that can be healed," I say to myself.

Just then, a ruthless pain rips through me and I grip my chest as I begin to fall backwards, screaming out Braeden's name as I do.

Phoenix

Pain.

There is so much pain that I'm surprised I don't lose consciousness from it. It feels like every bone in my body has been shattered and every inch of my skin bruised. I try to open my eyes but I can't. Something is keeping them shut. I begin to panic and try to move my arms and legs but they are weak. *Am I paralyzed?*

An ever-increasing beep reaches my ears and I concentrate on it, since it is the only sound I can hear. Someone's hands are on me and I cry out, not being able to see them is terrifying me.

"Shh," is all the voice coos. It's quiet and comforting.

I feel something being pulled away from my eyes and I pop them open, the bright light harsh. My eyes are extremely dry and I blink rapidly to regain some moisture.

I now see whose hands are on me and it's a face I don't recognize. She holds a flashlight in her hand, taking turns shining it in each one of my eyes.

"Do you know where you are?" she asks, her voice distant and muddled.

I shake my head.

"You're at the hospital," she states.

I look at her confused.

"Do you know where you are?" she asks.

I nod.

"Oregon," I say through a dry and scratched throat.

She is the one now looking at me confused.

"No," she says while shaking her head. "You're in San Francisco."

I begin to get upset. This nurse does not understand what I am saying.

"Do you know your name?" she asks again.

"Phoenix...Harper," I say, pausing to swallow between words.

"Good," she says.

She continues to look over me, touching and feeling all over my body.

"Are you in a lot of pain?" she asks.

"Yes," I respond.

"I'll have your doctor increase the amount of morphine," she starts. "Can you lift your arm for me, Phoenix?"

I look down at my right arm, concentrating on my muscles until it lifts off the bed slightly, it shaking immensely.

"Good. That's a good sign." She smiles at me.

I continue to stare at her, confused by *everything*.

"Where's Braeden?" I ask. "Can I see him?"

She looks into my eyes again.

"Oh, is that your boyfriend?" she asks with a smile. *How does she not know who Braeden is?*

"Yes," I explain, repeating my question "Can I see him?"

"I think the doctor just wants to make sure your progress is well enough for you to have visitors." She smiles.

Turning off her flash light she pulls the blanket back over my body again.

"OK," I say with disappointment. "What happened to me?"

"The doctor will be in shortly," she says before exiting the room, her eyes sympathetic. "He will explain everything to you."

I take this time to look around and I see a long curtain separating the room. I hear a steady beeping that is not coming from my own machine. The room falls quiet again except for the constant beeping of the machines. I don't know how long they were gone, but every moment ticking away painfully slow. I jump a little when I hear the door being pushed open, someone coming through it. I think I smile a little when I see who it is.

"It's so nice to see you awake Ms. Harper," Dr. Harris says, his eyes warm and gentle. I am confused by his formalities.

"How are you feeling?" he asks, looking down at what I assume is my chart.

I ignore his question as I look up at him. Something about him is so different. His hair is darker. His eyes the wrong shade of blue.

"Ms. Harper?" I hear him repeat.

I snap my attention back and I begin to cry, tired of not knowing what's going on.

"Where's Braeden?" I cry out, wanting and needing his comfort.

I start to thrash around, my limbs somehow regaining strength. I feel two sets of hands on me, the nurse from earlier is back.

"Please, just calm down," Dr. Harris calls out.

"Why am I here?" I call out between cries.

"If you calm down I can tell you," he says, his hands still on me.

I slow down my movements and keep my eyes on him.

"You've been in a coma, Phoenix," he says with

regret.

I become paralyzed by his words, my body now remaining still.

"What?" I cry out. "How?"

He stands back up, his hands now off of me.

"You tried to commit suicide," he says.

"No, I didn't," I call out. "You're lying." He pulls open the chart, reading some more.

"You tried jumping off the Golden Gate Bridge," he reads. "You were pulled from the frigid waters seven days ago; you've been unresponsive until now."

Everything in the world stops. I feel so lost, my mind not being able to comprehend what he just said.

"That can't be possible," I say to myself.

I hear Dr. Harris say something to the nurse but I don't make out what it is. I reach down and grip the blanket with my sweaty palm, pulling it off of me.

"Miss Harper," Dr. Harris says, his hands back on me.

"Stop calling me that!" I scream out. "You know who I am. You know me!" I continue.

I notice that a new nurse has entered the room, a needle in her hand.

"No!" I scream out. "Please, no," I beg him.

"Wait," I hear him say to the nurse, his hand reaching out towards her. The nurse stops in her tracks.

"Please...just get Braeden. He can explain this," I say.

"Braeden, who?" he asks.

I am confused once again.

"What do you mean? Your son…"

Now he looks at me confused.

"How do you know my son?" he asks.

My knees go weak and I fall, his hands are the only thing supporting me. He sets me back on the bed and turns to the nurses.

"Leave us," he says to them.

They both leave and it's soon just him and I.

"Please, lay back," he says. "You've had a rough time. You shouldn't be moving so much."

I do as I am told, even though I want nothing more than to leave this place. As I lay back, he grabs a chair and sits beside me. We are both silent until he speaks first.

"It's normal for someone who's just came out of a coma to become confused, to not understand a series of events prior to the injury," he starts.

I don't care what he has to say and I'm starting to think he's the one with the head injury.

"Now, I'm going to ask you a question and I want you to think about it really hard."

"OK."

"What was the last thing you remember?" I think hard.

"I was at my home, with Braeden, and I felt a sharp pain in my chest."

He opens my chart again. "Impossible," he says stern like.

"What?" I ask nervously.

"You were seen at your home here in San Francisco an hour before your incident by your mother…an Elaina Collins." *He's lying.*

"And you say my son was with you?" he asks, his eye brows furrowed.

"Yes!" I respond, becoming even more agitated.

He sets my chart down on the bed beside me. "Do you think you can stand again?"

I just nod. He stretches his hand out towards me.

"I need to show you something."

Putting my hand in his, he helps me to raise slowly, the pain still very much apparent in my body. We walk a few steps and I become even more confused when we do not exit the room. Instead, we walk around the curtain, my heart racing. *Why is he taking me over here?*

As I round the corner my eyes fall upon a blanketed form, the face of this figure not within eyesight. Their side of the room looks the same to mine, the body attached to numerous monitors, obviously where the extra beeping was being emitted from.

"This is my son," he says, his voice heavy.

My eyes widen.

"He's been in a coma for a little while longer than you," he states.

I feel like I am going to faint.

"What happened?" my mouth utters before my mind even has time to catch up.

"He was attacked by one of his patients," he explains. "A war veteran suffering from extensive post traumatic stress."

And in the moment every hair on my body stands up, goosebumps breaking out everywhere.

"We've had a few responses, spike in his heart rate monitor but he hasn't opened his eyes since."

A single tear falls down my cheek.

"There is something that we have been monitoring for a while though," he declares. I look up at him. "It could be nothing more than coincidence, but every time your heart rate increased, his did as well."

A chill runs down my spine.

"Maybe you could talk to him? Tell him to wake up…" he says, a small but painful smile on face.

Neil steps out from beside me, his form approaching the bedside. He reaches out and runs his hand through his son's hair. He leans down and kisses his forehead before standing back up. I can see tears in his eyes.

"I'm sure he would like the company," he states. "Maybe a pretty girl's voice will help him wake up." He continues to walk right past me. "I'll be right outside if you need me."

And then I am alone. I remain in my standing position, staring at the bed. I couldn't say how many minutes pass. I take one step forward.

Then another.

And another.

As I get closer I feel a tingling sensation flow through my body, it's exciting and frightening at the same time. Maybe he doesn't understand. Maybe it's a different Braeden. And then I see him. I look over his lifeless face. But much like with Neil, something is different. Odd.

The grooves in his face are different, his hair a different shade of brown. His face is covered in facial hair and I am sad that I can't see his eyes. I look over at the table beside his bed, a pair of black framed glasses folded on top of it.

"Phoenix," I hear the sound of my name so soft that I swear I imagined it.

I look back down at him, his lips now parted ever so slightly. *There's no way.* And then in one swift movement, his body jerks, his right arm coming up and gripping his chest. I rush closer to his side, placing one of my hands onto his clutched hand to steady him.

"Braeden!" I call out.

As soon as his name leaves my lips, his eyes fly open and, in return, I am met with the most vibrant green.

Phoenix

Everything stops.
My heart.
My ability to breath.
The world.

I don't speak. I don't move. I don't think I could if I tried. All I can do is stare. Stare into the abyss of his eyes - deep pits of emeralds. *They are the right shade.* Nothing is different. Nothing is strange. For the first moment since I have woken up, I feel like everything is going to be OK. He continues to stare at me and I force my mouth into a tight smile. He doesn't return one. His eyes travel away from mine, ending on my fingers that are still wrapped around his arm.

I panic, his eyes shifting from soft to confused. I slowly lift one finger away at a time until our skin is no longer in contact. The electricity running through my body ripped abruptly away. I remain standing next to the bed, frozen in this space.

His eyes are now back on me because of my retreat. I wait for him to speak but it never comes. Every fiber of my body is in agony. Confusion. Desperation. He continues to stare at me, his direct line of sight burning a hole though my chest. The sound of an opening door fills the room.

"Braeden?" I hear a male voice say.

Braeden's eyes linger on me for a few more seconds before shifting.

"Dad?" he says through squinted eyes.

Dr. Harris comes around to the other side of the bed, pulling a small flashlight out of his doctor's coat.

"How are you feeling?" he asks as he checks him over. I can tell he is holding back his emotions, the doctor mode in him overtaking.

Braeden's full attention is on his father now. My body pounces into fight or flight, the latter taking over my body. I start to slink backwards, grabbing the curtain between my finger tips for support.

"Stay," I hear someone day, Neil looking up at me briefly as he continues to scan his son. *How I wish it was Braeden uttering those words.*

I stop where I am, needing and wanting to be here

but I can feel my anxiety starting to rise, my throat feeling as though it's rapidly closing. All I can do is watch the rise and fall of his chest. *Up. Down. Up. Down.* It's the most mesmerizing thing I have ever witnessed. I hear sounds, which I assume is them conversing. Both of their voices are low. The world around me becomes blurry and I can't make out much that they are saying, except for one sentence.

"Who is she?" his voice whispers and it's like being stabbed in the heart with thousands of arrows. In that instant my knee's buckle and I grip onto the curtain again for balance.

"Phoenix?" Neil says, noticing my almost fall.

"I'm fine, I'm fi..." I say, my world spinning. "I just need some fresh air."

With every ounce of energy I have left in my body I push myself around and out the door. I walk out into the busy hospital hallway, my head spinning. This can't be happening. Reaching over I pinch any exposed skin, my arms soon covered with large red spots.

"Wake up, dammit!" I cry out.

Everything was perfect. I was with Braeden. Braeden was with me. We were together. Happy. *He doesn't know who you are. You're a stranger to him. You don't exist to him.* How was I able to remember him? Pushing myself forward I roam the halls, numerous set of eyes watching me. I nervously walk up to a nurse's station.

"I need to go outside," I demand.

"Not without a nurse present," she tells me. "Let me get someone for you."

She gets up from her desk and disappears behind the counter. When she comes back there is someone behind her. My heart drops instantly.

"Howdy!" her voice says, her tone pleasant.

I think I laugh out loud a little. *Is this the fucking twilight zone?*

"I'm Chelsea," she says holding her hand out towards me. "You must be Phoenix. Let's go get you some fresh air." She smiles. "I'm sure you can use it."

I don't respond but follow her until she stops just a few feet down the hallway, grabbing something from one of the dark rooms.

"Get in." She smiles.

She unfolds the wheel chair before me. Climbing in, she starts off at a fast pace, the wind blowing my hair backwards. I think I even let out a laugh. She is exactly how I remember her. *But I don't really know her.* When we get outside I inhale the fresh crisp air. As I do so, I feel pain radiate through my ribs.

"Ouch," I mumble.

"Oh, yeah," she says while she stops pushing. "Your ribs are bruised and your throat may hurt. We had to put a tube down there to pump out all of the water you swallowed."

"Where do you wanna hang?" she asks.

I look around the courtyard, seeing a large tree way off.

"Over there," I point.

She pushes me further and the shade underneath its branches is breezy.

"I'll be back in a little bit to come get you." She smiles.

"Don't you have to keep an eye on me?"

"I have a feeling you're not going anywhere," she winks.

It was like she could read my mind. As long as Braeden was here, I couldn't go anywhere. Even if he doesn't remember me.

"Will you stay?"I ask quietly, suddenly feeling like being alone was the last thing I wanted.

"Of course." She grins.

She walks around my chair and places her body next to mine on a nearby bench. We don't speak for a while. I peer off into the city, things moving at their usual rapid pace.

"Do you believe in soul mates?" I blurt out.

Chelsea's eyes are now on mine.

"Absolutely." She smiles. "Why do you ask?"

"No reason," I huff.

She places a hand atop on mine.

"I know you're still young sweetie, but when you find yours, it will be indescribable. Your soul mate is the one who makes life come to life."

A chill runs down my spine.

"Can I ask you something else?"

"Of course."

"Are you and Dr. Harris dating?"

Her eyes widen.

"No," she says shyly.

"You like him though?"

She gnaws on her lower lip and slowly nods.

"You should ask him out."

"I can't," she starts. "I don't think he feels the same."

I almost laugh but hold in my emotions.

"Just ask him. I think you'll be pleasantly surprised."

I can see her eyes lost in thought and we both fall silent.

~

Chelsea has to eventually leave and I beg for her to let me stay. The night sky begins to darken and my arms and legs become numb from the changing wind. When it becomes too dark I wheel myself back, thinking how stupid I feel in this thing when no one is pushing me. Ditching the wheel chair in a vacant corner I walk the rest of the way back to my room.

Our room.

My hand hovers over the door handle. I press my palm to the cool metal and push open. It's dark except for the light that the machines emit. I remain standing.

Listening.

Waiting.

The sound of a soft snore reaches my ears and I can't tell if it comforts me or scares me. *This is real. He's real. I'm real. We are not real.*

Finding my way to my bed I crawl in, pulling the covers up and over my head.

Maybe I can hide from this world.

I try to sleep but it never comes.

~

After flipping myself over a million times, I stare up at the ceiling trying to count the dots on the ceiling from memory. I let my eyelids drift close. I inhale through my nose. I try to keep my mind off the boy on the other side of the curtain. The boy who still owns my heart.

"Fuck," I mutter to myself, my eyes flying back open.

My body jumps at the sight hanging over me.

"You scared me," I utter out loud, my eyes fixated on his.

Braeden's form is standing over my bed. He doesn't move, not even to blink.

Maybe it's just a vision.

I don't move. I watch his hand move out towards me and I inhale, waiting for it. Waiting for contact. He watches his fingers move closer to my skin, almost as though it's not really him doing it. My body pleads for his touch.

"Something seems so real. Familiar," he whispers,

his eyes back to their confused state.

"I am real," I answer, my voice shaky. "You know it. You have to remember."

He still hovers.

"Touch me," I implore.

The gaps between our bodies close as he drags the tip of his fingers across the skin on the back of my hand. My body is instantly in a state of calm, almost like a drug addict finally getting a fix. His eyes remain on our hands, watching his every movement. My eyes linger on his face. I watch as every emotion is displayed on his face. His jaw tightening then relaxing.

Please remember. I can't be crazy.

His fingers travel along my arm and across my throat, finding their way to my face. He touches it all over, much like a blind person would. I slide up and lean closer, pushing my face into his hands. I close my eyes, taking in everything, my heart beating so fast that I feel I might pass out. His touch is still light, just like I always remembered. His movements stop. I fly open my eyes and his face is mere inches from mine. I look deep into his eyes. He does the same to me. Something washes over me. Maybe it was courage. Fear. Desperation. I couldn't tell you.

Leaning forward, I place my lips gently on his, holding back the passion flowing through my body. He pulls back slightly. At first only my lips move against his, his hand delicately placed against my shoulder.

After a few seconds I feel his lips part ever so slightly, his hand traveling up to the side of my face, his palm resting on my cheek. Then I let all my inhibitions go, this kiss everything that I remember. Then everything stops. His body frozen. My body begins to shake, waiting for him to retreat. Runaway. But instead his other hand comes out from his side, it lying on my opposite cheek.

"Seraph?" he whispers.

And just like that, I can't hold back the tears any longer. All I can do is nod excessively, tears running down my cheeks. He reaches down and takes me in his arms, lifting my whole body off the bed and into his arms. We both don't speak for a long time, his arms around me saying enough. When we pull back I see tears streaming down his face.

"I thought I lost you," I say through the tears, placing small kisses on his face.

"I'm so sorry to have done that to you," he says softly.

"It doesn't matter now," I say into his chest.

I wait for inevitable questions. I wait for him to become confused. For him to ask me why we are here. But they never come.

~

We both lay in my bed together, my tiny form curled inside his arms. We don't take our eyes off each other. I feel warm. Safe. *What I always feel when I am with him.*

I watch him twirl a piece of my hair around his fingertips.

"I think I would miss you even if we never met," he whispers.

My heart slams against my ribcage.

"Let's get out of here," he says just above a whisper. I don't know how to respond. "Just you and me."

"What about your father? Your life here?"

"None of that matters. I can never be without you again. If you were the air I breathed, I would not exhale for fear of losing you."

He leans over and places a kiss on my lips.

"I know how to get out of here without being caught." He smiles. *The most beautiful of smiles.*

Still in our hospital robes we leave the room, our hands intertwined. No one stops us. When we reach the outdoors I inhale the crisp air, it almost stinging my lungs.

"Where to?" he asks. "North?"

He winks at me. *He remembers.*

Wherever you are is where I want to be," I say with a crooked smile.

Phoenix

I stand there. My heart is racing so fast that I fear it may burst through my chest at any moment. The high winds make me shiver and I wrap my arms around myself for warmth. I stare out in front of me, the lights of the city illuminating the night sky. It's beautiful. Breathtaking. Taking another step towards the edge I reach out for the cold hard railing, my finger gripping it tight. The frosty metal burns my skin.

Lifting myself up, I let the wind whip through my hair, the ever-moving fog rolling in over the hills to the south. Goosebumps break out all over my body, my eyes staring at the endless pit below me. Slowly, I spread my arms out to the side and close my eyes. I listen to the sounds around me. The sounds of love. The sounds of a life worth living. I inhale, happy to feel the cold air stinging my lungs.

Moments later I feel something wrap around my waist and a warmth flowing through every part of me. Reaching down, I run my fingers along his arm, a smile breaking across my face.

"I won't let you go, Seraph. Ever," he whispers into my ear.

With a tug, he pulls me from the railing and into his arms. His lips are planted against my neck and I am no longer cold. He slowly sets me down, my back remains against his chest, both of us facing outwards.

"It was here," I say softly. He squeezes me lightly.

I can't even begin to explain how much my life has changed since I stood at this very spot five years ago. I thought I had nothing to live for. No one to live for. But that has all changed now. He changed that.

Once we left the hospital we headed North, an eerie sense of mutual direction between us. We didn't talk too much about what happened between us. It was almost like I couldn't differentiate between what was real and what was fantasy. To us it was all reality, even though we were technically strangers to each other. Everything I felt for him during my time in the hospital was still there when I awoke. It was the same for him. I guess I would be lying if I said I wasn't nervous during our "first time."

Things in real life weren't as we expected. When we got to Oregon there was no house waiting for me. Our town had suffered a large fire a few summers back and my father's house had burned to the ground along with half the neighborhood. I was distraught. Braeden comforted me for as long as I needed it.

I can never explain what happened to us. Why fate chose us but I thank God for it each and every day.

But not every moment of our reality has been pleasant. I had to face my fears but it was much easier with Braeden by my side. It was only a matter of time before Elaina came looking for me. Well, more like she called the cops to do it herself. To be honest, I was surprised she even cared. Luckily, there wasn't much they could do considering I was an adult and free to do what I wished. Free to be with Braeden. And that was exactly what I planned on doing.

We continue to stare out at the city, holding onto each other. I smile into the crook of his elbow.

"I love you so much," he whispers into my ear.

I spin around so that I am now facing him, my face against his chest. It only takes a second before I feel his sweatshirt zipped around my torso.

"I can hear your heartbeat," I say softly. "It's so fast." I look up at him, a smile wide across his face.

"It's only like that when you are around. It beats for only you."

I put my head back on his chest. Listening. Listening

to my favorite sound in the world. However it's interrupted when I hear his phone chime. The screen illuminates his face in the darkness.

"Ready, Seraph?" he asks me. "Dinner is almost ready."

I nod into his chest and pull myself away. We walk the length of the bridge, heading back into the city. I don't look back. I walk forward, into the direction of my brand new ending.

a brand
new ending
a novel by S.A. ROLLS

I want to take this time to give a shout out to a very important organization offering support and knowledge on this tragic situation. "To Write Love on Her Arms is a non-profit movement dedicated to presenting hope and finding help for people struggling with depression, addiction, self-injury and suicide."

If you or anyone you know suffers from suicidal thoughts, please call 1-800-273-8255.

ABOUT THE AUTHOR

Stephanie Rolls is a native of the Bay Area, where she attended culinary school and obtained a degree in baking and pastry. When she is not baking, she spends her time reading and writing. Stephanie reads anything - from biographies of her favorite president to the most popular YA series. Inspired by her surroundings, she has written her first YA novel, based in San Francisco, her favorite city. She currently lives with her boyfriend and their five-year-old pug.

21917739R00283

Made in the USA
Lexington, KY
04 April 2013